Palgrave Studies in the Enlightenment, Romanticism and Cultures of Print

Palgrave Studies in the Enlightenment, Romanticism and Cultures of Print will feature work that does not fit comfortably within established boundaries–whether between periods or between disciplines. Uniquely, it will combine efforts to engage the power and materiality of print with explorations of gender, race, and class. By attending as well to intersections of literature with the visual arts, medicine, law, and science, the series will enable a large-scale rethinking of the origins of modernity.

Titles include:

Scott Black
OF ESSAYS AND READING IN EARLY MODERN BRITAI

Claire Brock
THE FEMINIZATION OF FAME, 1750–1830

Brycchan Carey
BRITISH ABOLITIONISM AND THE RHETORIC OF SEN
Writing, Sentiment, and Slavery, 1760–1807

E.J. Clery
THE FEMINIZATION DEBATE IN 18TH-CENTURY ENGLAND
Literature, Commerce and Luxury

Adriana Craciun
BRITISH WOMAN WRITERS AND THE FRENCH REVOLUTION
Citizens of the World

Ildiko Csengei
SYMPATHY, SENSIBILITY AND THE LITERATURE OF FEELING IN THE EIGHTEENTH CENTURY

Elizabeth Eger
BLUESTOCKINGS
Women of Reason from Enlightenment to Romanticism

Ina Ferris and Paul Keen (*editors*)
BOOKISH HISTORIES
Books, Literature, and Commercial Modernity, 1700–1900

John Gardner
POETRY AND POPULAR PROTEST
Peterloo, Cato Street and the Queen Caroline Controversy

George C. Grinnell
THE AGE OF HYPOCHONDRIA
Interpreting Romantic Health and Illness

Ian Haywood
BLOODY ROMANTICISM
Spectacular Violence and the Politics of Representation, 1776–1832

Anthony S. Jarrells
BRITAIN'S BLOODLESS REVOLUTIONS
1688 and the Romantic Reform of Literature

Jacqueline M. Labbe
WRITING ROMANTICISM
Charlotte Smith and William Wordsworth, 1784–1807

Michelle Levy
FAMILY AUTHORSHIP AND ROMANTIC PRINT CULTURE

April London
LITERARY HISTORY WRITING, 1770–1820

Robert Miles
ROMANTIC MISFITS

Tom Mole
BYRON'S ROMANTIC CELEBRITY
Industrial Culture and the Hermeneutic of Intimacy

Catherine Packham
EIGHTEENTH-CENTURY VITALISM
Bodies, Culture, Politics

Nicola Parsons
READING GOSSIP IN EARLY EIGHTEENTH-CENTURY ENGLAND

Jessica Richard
THE ROMANCE OF GAMBLING IN THE EIGHTEENTH-CENTURY BRITISH NOVEL

Andrew Rudd
SYMPATHY AND INDIA IN BRITISH LITERATURE, 1770–1830

Erik Simpson
LITERARY MINSTRELSY, 1770–1830
Minstrels and Improvisers in British, Irish and American Literature

Anne H. Stevens
BRITISH HISTORICAL FICTION BEFORE SCOTT

David Stewart
ROMANTIC MAGAZINES AND METROPOLITAN LITERARY CULTURE

Rebecca Tierney-Hynes
NOVEL MINDS
Philosophers and Romance Readers, 1680–1740

Mary Waters
BRITISH WOMEN WRITERS AND THE PROFESSION OF LITERARY CRITICISM, 1789–1832

P. Westover
NECROMANTICISM
Travelling to Meet the Dead, 1750–1860

Esther Wohlgemut
ROMANTIC COSMOPOLITANISM

David Worrall
THE POLITICS OF ROMANTIC THEATRICALITY, 1787–1832
The Road to the Stage

Palgrave Studies in the Enlightenment, Romanticism and Cultures of Print
Series Standing Order ISBN 978–1–4039–3408–6 hardback 978–1–4039–3409–3 paperback
(outside North America only)

You can receive future titles in this series as they are published by placing a standing order. Please contact your bookseller or, in case of difficulty, write to us at the address below with your name and address, the title of the series and the ISBN quoted above.

Customer Services Department, Macmillan Distribution Ltd, Houndmills, Basingstoke, Hampshire RG21 6XS, England

Romantic Misfits

Robert Miles

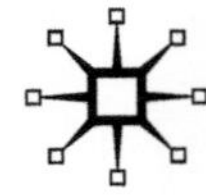

First published in hardback 2008
First published in paperback 2012 by
PALGRAVE MACMILLAN

Palgrave Macmillan in the UK is an imprint of Macmillan Publishers Limited, registered in England, company number 785998, of Houndmills, Basingstoke, Hampshire RG21 6XS.

Palgrave Macmillan in the US is a division of St Martin's Press LLC, 175 Fifth Avenue, New York, NY 10010.

Palgrave Macmillan is the global academic imprint of the above companies and has companies and representatives throughout the world.

ISBN 978–1–4039–8993–2 hardback
ISBN 978–1–137–01852–6 paperback

This book is printed on paper suitable for recycling and made from fully managed and sustained forest sources. Logging, pulping and manufacturing processes are expected to conform to the environmental regulations of the country of origin.

A catalogue record for this book is available from the British Library.

Library of Congress Cataloging-in-Publication Data
Miles, Robert, 1953–
Romantic misfits / Robert Miles.
p. cm. — (Palgrave studies in the Enlightenment, romanticism & cultures of print)
Inludes index.
ISBN 978–1–4039–8993–2 (cloth)
ISBN 978–1–137–01852–6 (pbk)
1. English literature—18th century—History and criticism. 2. English literature—19th century—History and criticism. 3. Romanticism—Great Britain. 4. Books and reading—Great Britain—History—18th century. 5. Books and reading—Great Britain—History—19th century. 6. Literature and society—Great Britain—History—18th century. 7. Literature and society—Great Britain—History—19th century. 8. Great Britain—Intellectual life. 9. Canon (literature) I. Title.
PR447.M45 2008
820.9'005—dc22 2008016318

10 9 8 7 6 5 4 3 2 1
21 20 19 18 17 16 15 14 13 12

Printed and bound in Great Britain by
CPI Antony Rowe, Chippenham and Eastbourne

In memory of Bruce Serafin, 1950–2007

'*Romantic Misfits* is a truly groundbreaking study of Romantic literature and its relationship to the institutions and media of the Enlightenment. More than a study of how the Romantic canon took shape, Miles's book is an inquiry into the nature of canonicity itself, that is, why highly unconventional discourses become the basis for conventional thinking. It has fundamentally changed the way I think about the Romantic period and the critical ethos that is its legacy.' – Alexander Dick, Assistant Professor, University of British Columbia, Canada

'This project creates the opportunity for a wide-ranging discussion on the vexed issue of the 'canon', and Miles's five chapters consider a comprehensive selection of writers.' – *English Studies*

'Robert Miles's wonderful new book, *Romantic Misfits*, examines the dialectic of inclusion and exclusion in the formation of the Romantic poetic canon... Miles's wide-ranging chapters – on W.H. Ireland's Shakespeare forgeries, Wordsworth's Gothic, Thomas Carlyle's and Coleridge's abjects, the Romantic novel's technologies, and Anna Laetitia Barbauld's feminism – are chock-full of magical and fresh material.' – *Studies in English Literature*, 49:4

'Professor Miles' striking Romantic Misfits is a very important – and newly informative – book for scholars of both British Romantic and English 'Gothic' writing. I believe that Gothicists and Romanticists at every level of serious study should and will be unpacking this intense, deeply theoretical, and most revealing book for many years to come.' – Jerrold E. Hogle, University Distinguished Professor, The University of Arizona, USA

Contents

Preface to the Paperback Edition

A great benefit of having a book go into paperback is that it provides an opportunity for reflecting on the work, perhaps making a little clearer the obscure object towards which it was tending. Critical works start their lives drawn forward, not by a clear end, but a vague sense of some inadequacy in current accounts. This was certainly true of *Romantic Misfits*, the germ of which announced itself at the first ever NASSR conference, in London Ontario, in 1993. I was then emerging from seven or so years of hard labour in the Gothic archives. The customary world of institutional Romanticism – dominated by the 'big six' – seemed, by comparison, strange. The feeling I had was of airlessness, of critical discourse in too close a dialogue with itself. If the initial motivation behind *Romantic Misfits* could be summed up in a word, it would be 'ventilation'. As I laboured toward that end, other works emerged that quickly moved the argument forward, rapidly changing the critical scenery, refreshing the air. I refer, largely, to that body of work we now retrospectively categorize as 'New Historical'. Even as the canon rapidly and radically changed, with old arguments swept away, and new ones put in their place, the vague – as yet unnamed – unease remained.

Paul Keen puts the matter well in his review of *Romantic Misfits*. 'The vast majority of the critical work of the past couple of decades', he writes, 'aimed at replacing' the 'Romantic image' of the neglected genius, or romantic misfit, 'with a more grounded vision of the age as a highly mediated and internally heterogeneous literary world animated by unstable and often fraught relations between writers, readers, and people in the trade across a range of uneasily related genres.' *Romantic Misfits* does not go in this direction, focusing, instead, on Romanticism's early genealogy, its first generation. The point, Keen continues, 'in returning to one of the founding Romantic images, is that we have not always been attentive enough to the ongoing influence of the processes of canon formation which it helped to legitimate.'[1] That we live within the past is one of the great clichés of Romanticism, whether one means Wordsworth's renovating 'spots of time', or the Gothic's dystopic version, where we don't so much live, as languish, within it. *Romantic Misfits* is dedicated to the proposition that the cliché is also true of our critical institutions. We work within contours of thought laid down long ago, in ways of which we are frequently unaware.

To recast Keen's point, much recent criticism of the Romantic period has been content with breaking up 'Romanticism' altogether, reducing the term to a placeholder for the diverse and contested forms of literary expression that flourished during the period 1789–1837; forms occluded by a preoccupation for the 'big six' that lasted nearly two hundred years. *Romantic Misfits*, to the contrary, sticks with Romanticism, arguing that the term designates a key period in the rise of modernity, and that the ideological and cultural dynamics put in play by the very process of winnowing that produced the Romantic canon are active still, churning deep in an unconscious, social imaginary. *Romantic Misfits* focuses on this 'winnowing' through a series of 'case histories' from Romanticism's first phase. I focus on representative moments of inclusion and exclusion, what I term 'misfitting', where some Romantic misfits came to fit, while others did not. The purpose of these case studies was to help change the ways in which we think about Romanticism.

As I explain in the Introduction, the key to this different way of thinking is understanding how, in the transition from Enlightenment to Romanticism, Enlightenments and their 'Counters' are dialectically related. *Romantic Misfits* deals with a series of conventional oppositions; for instance, between public and private, Gothic and Romantic, the material and the transcendental. As Romanticism became institutionalized, as a canon and a critical field, one side of this set of oppositions was prioritized over the other. *Romantic Misfits* argues that both sets of oppositions are present in the literature of the period, in ever-changing, historically determined, dialectical play. I can illustrate the upshot of this way of thinking about Romanticism by posing some of the questions the book answers. Why does talk of spectres and spectrality still haunt our contemporary critical discourse? Why do we persist in dividing the Gothic from the Romantic? Why do we carry on discussing Coleridge's theory of the transcendental imagination as if it were coherent on its own terms? Why do we privilege symbolism over allegory? In so far as these questions may be legitimately asked they are symptoms of our unexamined critical life.

The motivating unease, then, of *Romantic Misfits*, was the persistence of a certain kind of critical talk that felt more like a symptom than an act of self-reflexive knowledge. It was, of course, evident in my own critical practice, and consequently reassuring, as it pointed to the fact that I, too, was the product of a long process of Romantic formation. It was stepping outside into the Gothic that first alerted me to how deeply immured I was in Romantic spaces. If I was now half-Goth, I was still half-Romantic. It was while inhabiting the Romantic that I began to feel a critical claustrophobia as I heard my colleagues talk. To put it in the Gothic language of Edgar Allan Poe, as they marvelled at the transcendental power of the haunted mind, it seemed as if I could hear the faint click of another brick being slotted into place.

As already mentioned, Gothic was not the antidote to the Romantic ideology, just a recurring polarity in a series of dialectical gyrations. Thus, by way of example, for Godwin writing in the 1790's, 'Gothic' was a pejorative term for Burke's idealization of a mythic constitution that served only to lock the present ever more firmly in the past, figured as a kind of mental Bastille. This pejorative sense was common currency among Jacobins, such as John Thelwall and Thomas Christie.[2] 'Gothic' was a key term in their rhetorical arsenal as they sought to batter down Burke's regressive constitutional fantasies, securing the electoral franchise buried within, and so strengthening the public sphere. In the 1790's, 'Gothic' was a word Jacobins pinned on other, feudal-thinking people. But by 1818, when Thomas Love Peacock came to write *Nightmare Abbey*, the Gothic was now attached to Godwin himself, who was satirized in the novel through reference to the reclusive spaces of 'devil-man', Peacock's joke term for Godwin's *Mandeville*. Whereas for the Jacobins 'Gothic' was a politically charged word, for Peacock it was a mere byword for a kind of factitious inwardness, a fashionable gloominess, even a glamorous transcendentalism, that was the enemy of the 'public-sphering' Godwin had earlier championed. In the dialectical gyre, 'Gothic' had switched its valence. But in each case, for both writers, the perceived values under threat were those linked to the public sphere, with the threatening force conceived of as the glamour arising from a set of values antithetical to 'public-sphering', ones clustering around inwardness, interiority, and 'depth'.

James MacIntosh produces one of the earliest descriptions of what we now call Romanticism in his review of De Stael's *D'Allemagne*: 'We have successively cultivated a Gothic poetry from nature, a classical poetry from imitation, and a second Gothic from the study of our own ancient poets.'[3] That we refer to Romanticism when we talk about the literature of the period, rather than the 'Gothic Revival', as we do with architecture, is partly a historical accident, and partly not: as *Romantic Misfits* endeavours to show, the very existence of such a split in our critical vocabulary perpetuates the recurring pressure to raise the 'private', at the expense of the 'public', to esteem the Romantic grappling with the ever-receding noumenal, while throwing down the politically inflected work of Gothic critique. The recurrence of the Gothic in *Romantic Misfits* is partly a residue of my own intellectual formation – of my experience of coming to stand outside Romanticism – but it is also marks the points in the book where the argument returns to the makings of this unexamined cleavage in our critical discourse.

Since the publication of *Romantic Misfits*, I have, naturally enough, continued to worry away at these matters. The advantage of writing a belated preface is that, as I've mentioned, the benefits of hindsight are freely available. I now want to take advantage of them by reframing the argument of *Romantic Misfits* from the perspective of two recent developments that have expanded my thinking. The first may help explain the weight I have been placing on the word 'public'; the second goes to the issue of unexamined critical practice.

The first arises out of my involvement with the Re-Enlightenment Project, a group of academics, administrators, and curators who periodically meet to explore the legacies of Enlightenment.[4] The project is dedicated to the following propositions: Enlightenment was 'an event in the history of mediation';[5] recent developments in the technology of mediation have opened up new opportunities, which might be described as Re-Enlightenment; the first Enlightenment understood itself to be engaged in the production of knowledge that worked in the world, changing it in the process; from which it follows that Re-Enlightenment should also concern itself with the development of 'platforms', capable of producing new, effective (but not necessarily 'instrumental') knowledge.

While not exactly a duplication of a London coffee house, or a Paris salon, the Re-Enlightenment Project is, nevertheless, an instantiation of what, in the present, passes for the public sphere. Obvious differences naturally separate the eighteenth-century networks from contemporary ones. For a start, such networks were not composed of salaried academics, curators, or administrators, as is the case with the Re-Enlightenment Project. But then this is simply to note the history of how, post-Enlightenment, knowledge was institutionalized and disciplined. As the cliché now has it, we produce knowledge within our disciplinary silos. The Re-Enlightenment Project represents a determined effort to step outside of our little towers, engaging our peers, across, not just disciplines, but jobs (academic, curator, administrator), motivated, not by the protocols of our particular fields, narrow and deep, but by larger purposes, such as supporting, maintaining, and possibly building those of our civic institutions that have as their mission the production, or curating, of knowledge.

The project starts from its premises. The Enlightenment happened, not because the small knots of thinkers who came together in Edinburgh or Glasgow, or Warrington and Hackney, had high ambitions, but because similar networks of like-minded people were springing up elsewhere, forming a scaled-up web of communication. The last chapter of *Romantic Misfits* relates the story of how Coleridge visited the Lunar Men, intent on selling subscriptions of his paper, *The Watchman*, understood by him as a platform, a vehicle for knowledge that would work in the world. Unsurprisingly, the dissenting communities visited by Coleridge understood the possibilities of print technology much better than he did, and were able to access the 'web', more or less instantly securing Coleridge his needed subscriptions, one thousand strong (which the feckless poet just as quickly lost).

When Clifford Siskin and William Warner claim that Enlightenment was an event in the history of mediation, they mean the way the saturation point of print, reached during the latter half of the eighteenth-century, changed the nature of mediation, and with it, knowledge environments, and ultimately, knowledge itself.[6] The numerous nodal points or clusters of individuals spread out across much of Europe and parts of North America, formed a web, linked by correspondence, newspapers, and other forms of print organized by genres too numerous to mention. As Jürgen Habermas famously argued, this very complexity led to the structural transformation of the public sphere, undermining its original, motivating ideal (that the public sphere was a place where some men – and rather fewer educated women – could come together to discuss matters of public moment in a rational way). The technological environment has changed again, deepening in complexity, but here the complexity of the mediating technology promises to resurrect something that looks like the eighteenth-century public sphere, at least at first glance. The best example of this, and the most obvious, is the Arab Spring. As William Warner has argued, the corresponding societies of the American Revolution supported independence through the identity they built of free-born, entitled citizens, through innumerable acts of communication, a connectivity that helped secure the enfranchisement that was the ultimate object of these innumerable acts of correspondence.[7] The Arab Spring appears to follow a similar contour, only on fast forward, sped up by the connectivity of social media, including instant messaging.

If Enlightenment was an event in the history of mediation, so was Romanticism; and one way of situating Romanticism within that history was that it occurred as the public sphere was being structurally transformed, as change in the means of mediation intensified. What was Romanticism's contribution? More particularly, what has our institutional representation of Romanticism contributed to public-sphering? As I put it in the Introduction, Romanticism was built on the ruins of the public sphere, where by Romanticism I meant, not the diffuse, diverse, and complicated literary culture of the period, but the codified form we have come to call 'Romantic'. In our principles of selection, in the construction of the Romantic canon, we have unwittingly reinforced Romanticism's 'counter-Enlightenment' tendencies; and we have done so through systematic preference for withdrawal, from the public square to the Lake District, from revolution to personal reformation, from public form to private language, from the social protocols of knowing which fix facts as 'objective' to inner-generated valuations that invest objects with the nimbus of subjective glory. In short, it was a transition from the Georgic form of work and matters of public moment to lyric intensity.

This 'lyric turn from history' was the pivot on which much of 1990's New Historicism turned; my hard-to-articulate unease related to my sense that the language of revision somehow left matters as they had been found. To return to Paul Keen's phrase, *Romantic Misfits* argues that we have not 'been attentive enough to the ongoing influence of the processes of canon formation', especially to the ways in which our critical discourse reinforces the marginalization of the public sphere, even when it effects to do the reverse. Each case study endeavours to reveal a different aspect of this process.

Its deep normalization in our critical discourse takes me to my second, framing development, my recent encounter with Charles Taylor's notion of a 'social imaginary', by which he means common ways of regarding the world that are, as it were, too deep for thought. The social imaginary emerges out of a 'background'. Taylor's use of 'background' draws upon the philosophical work of Hubert L. Dreyfus and John Searle. He describes it like this:

> It is in fact that largely unstructured and inarticulate understanding of our whole situation, within which particular features of our world show up for us in the sense they have. It can never be adequately expressed in

> the form of explicit doctrines, because of its very unlimited and indefinite nature. That is another reason for speaking here of an 'imaginary' and not a theory.[8]

When Taylor refers to 'our' background understanding he does mean 'our': not the more specialized, often theoretical conceptualizations of the intelligentsia, but assumptions that permeate a culture, making the culture that particular culture, rather than some other (in Taylor's case, the culture we habitually designate 'the West'). As he maps out in his synoptic *Modern Social Imaginaries*, Taylor's project involves relating the story of how we have come to believe that three historically particular attitudes, peculiar to the West, are in fact truths universally acknowledged: that there is a self-regulating thing called an 'economy', where it is a good thing that it should be self-regulating, based as it is, on its own immanent order; that there is an extra-political dimension to social interaction we call a public sphere, in which the opinion of the mass of the people (the 'public') comes to be known; and that, finally, political legitimacy ultimately derives from this opinion, because the general will of the people is sovereign. Taylor argues that each of these related, mutually reinforcing 'mutations in the social imaginary' came into being during the Enlightenment, at that time assuming their modern shape.[9]

Taylor argues that these three mutations now seem natural to us, in part, because they are understood to be instrumental in delivering the two overriding goods of the modern, Western, world: prosperity and security. As Slavoj Zizek likes to joke, the market economy now seems so inevitable to us, that even if the world was destroyed, capitalism would somehow live on.[10] In Taylor's terms, this attitude is merely an expression of our social imaginary, where we literally cannot conceive an alternative to capitalism, as capitalism rests on the assumption that the economy expresses its own, self-regulating, immanent order, where any alternative to this unquestioned reality involves a material decline in both prosperity and security.

Throughout the history of Taylor's three cardinal mutations in the social imaginary, there is a constant, dialectical relation between the public and private, much as Habermas argued in *The Structural Transformation of the Public Sphere*. That is, the public sphere initially came into being in order to secure private goods cherished by the expanding, middling classes, while the articulation of these private goods in turn empowered the public sphere, which, in its turn, strengthened the public grip of these private goods. But as Western democracies – and capitalist economies – have matured, this dialectic has weakened, so much so that the public seems seriously under threat: hence the springing up of associations such as The Re-Enlightenment Project. While this dialectical relationship between public and private is constitutive of the literary culture of the Romantic period, our critical discourse habitually tends towards the 'private' end of a series of Romantic values. *Romantic Misfits* works to reveal the hidden contours of our current social – and critical – imaginary.

What is at stake in this labour? When writing the book I would have said something about reinvigorating studies in Romanticism by returning our attention to the messy vitality of Romantic-era writing, reuniting the split in our critical discourse typified by the Gothic/Romantic division. But with the benefit of hindsight I now want to urge resistance to the siren call of a modest formalism, from one side, and from the other shrill warnings against historicism as the mere fag end of the culture wars. Historicism has not finished its work, where its work is to formulate the arc that connects Romanticism with the present. We form this arc, not by excavating the ideological underpinnings of the works we study, fine though this labour is, but by establishing connections between the peculiar conditions of the Romantic period, and our own. These connections, I now want to suggest, are the conditions of both possibility and peril that typify the efforts to imagine a new Jerusalem (to use the words of a Romantic misfit otherwise conspicuous by his absence from the pages that follow), a Jerusalem, that is, of successful civic engagement, the ideal towards which public-sphering tends. In my reading of Romantic literary culture, imagining of community is central in either of its two chief modalities: success (shades of joy), or failure (Gothic horror). As my case histories show, in the earliest moments of Romanticism's foundation, 'Romanticism' was raised up as communal imagining was thrown down. *Romantic Misfits* invites the reader to consider the extent to which we recover our Romanticism by re-thinking these foundational moments.

Notes

1. Paul Keen, 'Landscaping: Rebuilding the Romantic Field', review of *Dreaming in Books: The Making of the Bibliographic Imagination in the Romantic Age*, by Andrew Piper, *Romantic Misfits*, by Robert Miles, and *Family Authorship and Romantic Print Culture*, by Michelle Levy, *European Romantic Review* 23: 1(2012), 58.
2. See the first section of Chapter 2, below, on Gothic and ideology.
3. James Mackintosh, review of *D'Allemagne*, by Madame de Staël, *Edinburgh Review*, xxiii (1813), 207.
4. For information on The Re-Enlightenment Project see http://www.reenlightenment.org/.
5. Clifford Siskin and William Warner, 'This is Enlightenment: An Invitation in the Form of an Argument', *This is Enlightenment* (Chicago: the University of Chicago Press, 2010), 1.
6. Siskin and Warner, 19–21.
7. William Warner, 'Transmitting Liberty: The Boston Committee of Correspondence's Revolutionary Experiments in Enlightenment Mediation', in *This is Enlightenment*, 102–19.

8. Charles Taylor, 'Afterward: Apologia pro Libro suo', in *Varieties of Secularism in a Secular Age*, ed. Michael Warner, Jonathan VanAntwerpen, and Cirag Calhoun (Cambridge, Mass. and London, England: Harvard University Press, 2010), 309.
9. Charles Taylor, *Modern Social Imaginaries* (Durham and London: Duke University Press, 2004). These points, and phrasing, recur throughout the book, but, for instance, see pp. 143, 152.
10. Slavoj Zizek, 'Attempts to Escape the Logic of Capitalism', review of John Keane, *Vaclav Havel: A Political Tragedy in Six Acts*, *LRB*, Vol. 21, No. 21 (28 October 1999). http://www.lrb.co.uk/v21/n21/zize01_.html.

Acknowledgements

Romantic Misfits was written with the generous assistance of the Arts and Humanities Research Council of Great Britain.

I owe a particular debt of gratitude to Alison Chapman whose support over many years – moral as well as intellectual – sustained this project. I would like to express my admiration for the two anonymous colleagues who performed the thankless task of providing reports for the press. Their commentaries were not only full, constructive and acute but also unfailingly accurate as to where work remained to be done. I thank them for helping me make this a better book. I owe a debt to the following, who either read parts of this work or provided salutary assistance: Kim Blank, Alison Chapman, Richard Cronin, Alex Dick, Michael Harris, Anthony Jarrells, Michael Gamer, Tom Mole, Murray Pearson, Bruce Serafin, Dale Townshend and Nicola Trott. I would also like to thank the series editors for their encouragement, Tony Power for his help in the Wordsworth special collections at Simon Fraser University, and Amy Collins, my research assistant, who helped with the final stages of preparation.

Abbreviations

BL Samuel Taylor Coleridge (1983), *Biographia Literaria, or Biographical Sketches of My Literary Life and Opinions*, ed. James Engell and W. Jackson Bate, *The Collected Works of Samuel Taylor Coleridge* (London and New Jersey: Routledge and Kegan Paul, and Princeton University Press): Vol. VII.

SP William Wordsworth (1988), *Selected Prose*, ed. John O. Haydon (Harmondsworth: Penguin).

Introduction

Although all Romantics are misfits some misfits did not fit. This simple sentence may be parsed in numerous ways. If all Romantics are misfits, 'Romantic misfits' is a tautology. The cliché obscures the pleonasm as it circulates through popular culture, perhaps advertising the merits of the central protagonists of the latest wacky romantic comedy, or describing the tortured life of an artist grievously ahead of his (seldom her) time. Apart from the novels of Jane Austen and the Gothic, the notion of the 'romantic misfit' is about all that now popularly survives of the literary culture of the Romantic period. Indeed, the phrase – together with its virtual synonym, 'neglected genius' – may be said to encompass the common understanding of what Romanticism is. Apart from Byron and Scott the writers who came to define 'Romantic' for nearly a hundred and fifty years – Blake, Coleridge, Wordsworth, Keats and Shelley – were conspicuous, initially, for their paltry sales and invisibility to all but the most dedicated habitués of the literary networks that dominated the publishing scene.[1] If these writers survived in the face of such adversity, it was owing, in part, to their firm sense that they wrote for a 'fit audience ... though few';[2] that real art was demanding, obscure and deviant; and that not fitting in with the mainstream was a sure sign that they were, artistically, on the right path, a conviction they were able to sustain, in almost all cases, because they were embedded in a coterie of likeminded souls. The tension between the ideal of the isolated artist and the reality of artistic communities – the fantasy of complete originality and the truth of the collaborative nature of art – typified the ideological circumstances of the writers of the Romantic period and, like all ideologies, was generated by a change in material circumstances.

Writing around the start of the period literary historians conventionally designate as 'Victorian', the Sheffield poet James Montgomery offers the following retrospective comments on the literary market.

> The unprecedented sale of the poetical works of Scott and Byron, with the moderate success of others, proves that a great change had taken place

> both in the character of authors and in the taste of readers, within forty years. About the beginning of the French Revolution scarcely any thing in rhyme, except the ludicrous eccentricities of Peter Pindar, would take with the public: a few years afterwards, booksellers ventured to speculate in quarto volumes of verse, at from five shillings to a guinea a line, and in various instances were abundantly recompensed for their liberality. There are fifty living poets (among whom it must not be forgotten, that not a few are of the better sex – I may single out four: Mrs. Joanna Baillie, Mrs. Hemans, Miss Mitford, and L.E.L.) whose labours have proved profitable to themselves in a pecuniary way, and fame in proportion has followed the more substantial reward. This may appear a degrading standard by which to measure the genius of writers and the intelligence of readers, but, in a commercial country at least, it is an equitable one . . .[3]

In the words of Stuart Curran, the Romantics were 'simply mad for poetry'.[4] Literary periodizations are notoriously arbitrary and inexact; the advantage of Montgomery's 'degrading standard' is that it provides an indisputable event to which one may tether Romanticism. According to Montgomery's 'equitable' measure, Romanticism was the forty-year period, starting from 1789, in which the literary marketplace boomed, creating an unprecedented sale for poetry, before the publishing business shifted once more (in poetry, to literary annuals, souvenirs and gift books). Surprisingly, technological innovation does not account for this shift in material circumstances. The invention of the steam press in 1812 transformed print technology and the publishing market, but the takeoff in print production preceded the technological change.[5] The significant difference was sociological. Three deflection points dominate the economic landscape of the eighteenth century: the 1740s, when the money supply takes a historic spike upward;[6] a period some forty years earlier, when the English population begins its modern rise; and then again around 1810, when it accelerates once more.[7] In short, the period we think of as Romantic coincided with the swelling in the ranks of the reading classes, and the literary genre to which they aspired, the one with greatest cultural capital, was poetry, the genre that had previously been associated with the social class – the aristocracy – who embodied the values after which the expanding middle class aspired. As Montgomery's comments also reveal, the central players in the rapidly expanding literary market were the publishers, who were themselves, in turn, highly conscious of another change to the material circumstances of print, the consequences of a House of Lords judicial decision, in 1774, to enforce the copyright laws of 1710, laws that had been honoured, previously, almost entirely in the breach. Publishers were able to re-impose restrictive practices in 1808 by lengthening copyright beyond the fourteen years, renewable, provided by the act of 1710; but in the 'brief copyright window' that intervened the price of the 'old canon' plummeted, because no longer protected, while the costs and copyright returns for new texts – that is, 'originals' – soared.[8] A general consequence was that a greater premium was placed on originality as a quality that distinguished the copyrightable as a commodity that sold. A final change to the complexion of the literary market was that it was becoming ever more nationalistic in tone. Both circumstances contributed to the durability of nationally inflected notions of 'original genius'.

The surge in demand for poetry, noted by Montgomery, was certainly a great boon for would-be poets, but the benefit was, at the very least, double-edged, for if there was a great increase in the number of people willing to lay out good money for poetry, there was a corresponding bulge in the number of poets vying for their attention. To use the critical term now associated with the French sociologist, Pierrre Bourdieu, both buyers and producers sought distinction, the one through the éclat associated with good taste, the other through the fame accorded to those whose works were considered to determine what that taste was.

For Bourdieu distinction belongs to the sociology of consumption. It is a product of capital growth and the institution of classes, of social divisions based on profession rather than on rank and status – on 'exo-socialization' rather than on birth and networks of kinship. Bourdieu begins by distinguishing middle- from working-class attitudes towards art. For the Bourgeoisie, art is autonomous – art for art's sake – while individual works are such by virtue of their relation to a tradition of representation (to their place in the history of form). Working-class attitudes are more 'utilitarian'. The 'popular aesthetic' of facile or vulgar involvement and enjoyment, in which art is valued for its representational qualities (a window on the world), is thus contrasted with the customary, bourgeois, meaning of 'aesthetic'. The working class adopt a moral posture towards art with works roughly divided between the pleasurable and the harmful, a posture that allows Bourdieu to contrast plebeian 'ethics' with patrician 'aesthetics':

> Although art obviously offers the greatest scope to the aesthetic disposition, there is no area of practice in which the aim of purifying, refining and sublimating primary needs and impulses cannot assert itself, no area in which the stylization of life, that is, the primacy of forms over function, manner over matter, does not produce the same effects. And nothing is more distinctive, more distinguished, than the capacity to confer aesthetic status on objects that are banal or even 'common' . . . or the ability to apply the principles of 'pure' aesthetic to the most every day choices of everyday life, e.g. cooking, clothing, or decoration, completely reversing the popular disposition which annexes aesthetics to ethics.[9]

For Bourdieu the aesthetic covers all aspects of contemporary life, not just art, and constitutes a dense semiology of class attitudes. Bourdieu's sociology of consumption (of luxury as opposed to need) thus breaks with the

Kantian distinction between 'the taste of sense' and the 'taste of reflection'.[10] Wordsworth endeavoured to create the taste by which he was to be relished by instilling in his readership a belief in the superiority of the 'taste of reflection' (active and difficult) over the 'taste of sense' (passive and stupefying), the one the true basis of the aesthetic, the other simply of consumption. In this respect, Wordsworth was Kantian. But, for Bourdieu, Kant's distinction is class politics by another means. Bourdieu describes the consumer of the emerging, Romantic aesthetic:

> In short, never perhaps has more been asked of the spectator, who is now required to 're-produce' the primary operation whereby the artist (with the complicity of his whole intellectual field) produced this new fetish [of 'art']. But never perhaps has he been given so much in return. The naive exhibitionism of 'conspicuous consumption', which seeks distinction in the crude display of ill-mastered luxury, is nothing compared to the unique capacity of the pure gaze, a quasi-creative power which sets the aesthete apart from the common herd by a radical difference which seems to be inscribed in 'persons'. One only has to read Ortega y Gasset to see that the reinforcement of the charismatic ideology derives from art, which is 'essentially unpopular, indeed anti-popular' and from the curious 'sociological effect' it produces by dividing the public into two 'antagonistic castes', those who understand and those who do not.[11]

The 'self-legitimating imagination of the "happy few" ' (31), as Bourdieu puts it, dates from the beginning of the Romantic period.

In Bourdieu's terms the modern cliché of the Romantic misfit begins its life as the mark of distinction that sets apart the true writer at a time in history in which the 'Bourgeoisie' was coming to dominate consumption. As it happens, Bourdieu's phrasing fits Wordsworth with uncanny accuracy. As critics have noted from as early as Thomas De Quincey, Wordsworth's coterie was electrified by the 'charismatic ideology' that surrounded the master, a difference grounded by Wordsworth in the ideal of a 'pure gaze' that was itself a 'quasi-creative power'. For Wordsworth, this 'radical difference' was indeed inscribed in 'persons', for the true poet, Wordsworth tells us in 'The Preface' to the *Lyrical Ballads*, differs from the rest of us 'being possessed of more than usual organic sensibility', a sensibility seated in the organism (*SP*: 283). Made differently, the poet is more perceptive, his gaze 'pure'. More prosaically, Marilyn Butler has noted how in the Romantic period writing was increasingly promoted on the basis of the writer's personality – on his or her 'depth' – as a means of establishing a saleable identity or brand in an expanding, increasingly anonymous, commercial market,[12] a point further elaborated by Clifford Siskin, who argues that the discipline of literature – the work of writing – constitutes an institutionalized form of exo-socialization in which writing ('Romantic discourse') produces and reinforces 'behaviours that configure the psychologized self'.[13]

'Romantic misfits' accordingly operates in two linked, yet antithetical, senses: as a description of all those figures who did not fit 'Romanticism' and as a description of those who did; of those who were not canonized and those who were; of those whose pretensions to depth, or individuality, were judged fraudulent and those who passed. Both groups, often, or typically, shared the same identity, as 'misfits'; accordingly a tension exists between the two groups. The first was excluded from literary history in order to secure the status of those writers who did 'fit' (the 'Romantics'), even as the Romantics themselves based their claim to high literary status on their status as misfits – on their success in transcending the literary marketplace to which other writers were represented as in thrall (because fitting too well). As we have seen, the Romantic period was one in which there was an unprecedented expansion in the number of books produced. That expansion inevitably encouraged a distinction to be made between a group of books distinguished by their quality, 'literature', and a group better understood as manufactured in obedience to the profit motive, 'trash'. The writers since canonized as the 'Romantics' are those who self-consciously claimed to produce 'literature', that is, to write independently of and in defiance of the demands of the marketplace. It follows that 'Romantic literature' was from the first defined by its exclusion of other kinds of writing, and hence is best understood in terms of the particular kinds of writing that it excluded.

In recent years critics have dissolved the old canon of the 'big six', bringing back the excluded, such as, especially, the women poets who achieved signal success during the period, as Montgomery notes, but also the novelists and dramatists – the writers of the popular genres of the day – who also played a significant role in Romantic-era literary culture. While this work of literary recuperation is not complete, by any means, it is certainly well advanced. But that is not my concern. My objective, rather, is to look closely at the original moment of canon formation – of Romantic misfitting – in order to understand the constitution of Romanticism more fully through an analysis of what was excluded in the process.

Given that all Romantics are misfits, in one sense or another, this study could easily have gone on, ad infinitum. Principles of selection were therefore imperative. I have concentrated on the 'first generation' Romantics, on those writers who span two literary cultures, the one we have come to call the 'Enlightenment' and then Romanticism itself. I have balanced the book between those who fit, and those who did not, on those who were foundational to institutionalized Romanticism – to Romanticism as a disciplinary field in the academic study of English literature – as well as those who were spectacular failures. I have sought to find representative figures or subjects. Finally, the process of selection itself has been filtered through the methodologies of print culture, of book history informed by sociological theory, principally Pierre Bourdieu and Jürgen Habermas. The first chapter focuses on the career of the Shakespeare forger W. H. Ireland as an example of the print culture forces that forged Romantic identity. The chapter moves back in time, to the late 1780s, when Ireland's identity was formed, and forward to his career as one of the most prolific, self-identified misfits of the Romantic era. Chapter 2 examines the early career of William Wordsworth. In the process it explores what was radical about his early style and how it was left behind in the process of Wordsworth's Victorian canonization. Count Cagliostro, Thomas Carlyle and S. T. Coleridge form the focus of Chapter 3, figures connected by a shared tension between the material and the transcendental, where the transcendental predominates as an essential criteria of canonization. The last two chapters turn to more representative subjects, the Romantic novel, or, as I call it here, the philosophical romance, and the rational Dissenters, who, as a group, may be considered the radical architects of a social transformation that was eventually to exclude them.

Although each essay is allowed to go its own way, there are recurring themes, such as the manner in which the 'structural transformation of the public sphere' during the Romantic era is itself an integral aspect of the story of how 'high' literature was constructed at the expense of the 'low' (where 'public engagement' becomes a defining feature of the 'low', and self-cultivation a quality of 'high'). Other themes include: the denigration of public, visual entertainment (increasingly stigmatized as 'spectacle'); an aesthetic prejudice against materiality, the body and allusive, corporeal language; the aesthetic transformation of Romance, from high to low; the exclusion of 'philosophy' from the novel, meaning the rise of the inductive method in the novel uncoupled from the synoptic systemizing that would constitute a properly critical dialectic; the glamorization of the deep self and marginalization of the more publicly directed Dissenters. In my terms, virtually all of the women writers of the period who enjoyed signal success in the literary marketplace are Romantic misfits, with Mary Robinson, Joanna Baillie and Charlotte Dacre among the most salient, early examples in poetry, drama and fiction (and 'L.E.L.' a conspicuous late one). However, gender is not one of my recurring themes other than as it relates to a signal consequence of the transformation of the bourgeois public sphere, which was the excision of the precarious place in the literary public sphere that had so emboldened, and enabled, women writers of the late Enlightenment, such as Catherine Macaulay and Ann Radcliffe. The domestic ideology that tightened its grip in the gathering conservatism of the late Romantic period fundamentally transformed the terms on which women writers were allowed to speak.[14] As a consequence there is a significant difference between an early writer such Anna Letitia Barbauld, and those noted by Montgomery from later in the period, such as L.E.L. and Felicia Hemans. Barbauld is the female misfit I concentrate on, in Chapter 5, but I treat her misfitting as exemplary of the fate of rational Dissent, rather than gender per se. Although

I do not explore the connection, it is perhaps worth stating here that I see the rise of domestic ideology as a structural support of institutionalized Romanticism.[15]

In its cumulative force *Romantic Misfits* seeks to offer a fundamental critique of institutionalized Romanticism by arguing that the cultural investments that were made in the original moment of Romantic misfitting are still, unconsciously, with us. By 'institutionalized Romanticism' I mean the hundred or so years (from the late Victorian period to the last decades of the last century) in which British Romanticism was routinely conceived of, and taught, as a period of cultural expression built on the nucleus of the 'big six', a singularity of gender and genre unique among the customary periodizations of literary history. Institutionalized Romanticism, in this sense, was built on Romantic misfitting, on the myth of the isolated genius (as male poet) at odds with a materialistic society. Francis Jeffrey may have insinuated that the 'Lake School' were a dangerous sect of Dissenters, but the real Dissenters found the Lake poets' withdrawal from society odd, and reprehensible, because also a drawing back from the necessary political struggle.[16] A recurring theme of *Romantic Misfits* is that the disintegration – the structural transformation – of the bourgeois public sphere was the precondition on which institutional Romanticism formulated itself. So when I say that the cultural investments made in the original moment of Romantic misfitting are still, unconsciously, with us, I mean the way in which criticism still thinks inside the historical accommodation that was made, in literary aesthetics, which took isolation and withdrawal as normative in the act of creation.

I realize that in phrasing it in this way readers will wonder how *Romantic Misfits* moves the argument on from the 1980s, when New Historicist critics made similar sounding claims. In particular, readers may wonder how *Romantic Misfits* differs from Jerome McGann's *The Romantic Ideology*, perhaps the most influential of the books making the New Historicist argument that institutionalized criticism tended to repeat, rather than critique, Romanticism. Romanticism was marked by the belief that poetry had the power to transcend the fragments of history and modernity; McGann argued that whereas the poetry understood the belief to be illusory, critics took the illusive hope at face value, thus perpetuating the false consciousness the poetry subverted. Perhaps the most obvious difference is that McGann left Romanticism where he found it, in the poetry of the big six. If a work did not share with other Romantic poems a transcendental illusion it felt compelled to critique it also did not share the 'ideological commitments' that defined Romanticism.[17] As McGann's characterization of these commitments were identical with those that had long dominated the field – a characterization Frank Kermode synthetically summed up as the always already troubled pursuit of the Romantic image[18] – nothing much was changed, and little produced, other than a goad to the critics to stop making a fetish of Romantic irony.

In contrast, *Romantic Misfits* aims to shift the way we think about the emergence of Romanticism. Richard Cronin nicely summarizes the central problem. He is characterizing Marilyn Butler's difficulties with it in *Romantics, Rebels, and Reactionaries*:

> In Butler's book 'Romanticism' vies as a period label with two other terms, 'Enlightenment' and 'Neoclassicism'. At times Butler writes as if she wishes to confine the term Romanticism to the central phase of a history in three parts, the period extending from about 1798 to about 1812, the period dominated by what she calls the literature of counter-revolution. Before 1798 she prefers her other terms, and after 1812, she argues, the second generation of Romantic poets made a brave effort to restore neoclassicist and enlightenment modes. Romanticism, in this narrow definition, is represented as distinctively reactionary, but is flanked by two brief periods in which literature allies itself, not exactly with rebellion, but at any rate with a set of progressive social and political values. Neoclassicism is essentially social, cheerful and outward-looking; Romanticism, on the contrary, is marked by a gloomy, egotistical inwardness.[19]

I won't repeat Cronin's deft summary of the 'obvious problems' of Butler's scheme.[20] Instead I want to produce my own solution to it, which is to suggest that Romanticism should not be thought of as a set of 'ideological commitments', a kind of poetic, hermeneutic struggle or as a flight from georgic to lyric, but as a period in the long history of modernity's emergence in which two formations first come to be set in dialectical opposition to each other: a radical Enlightenment and its reactionary counter.

Both the Enlightenment and Isaac Berlin's Counter-Enlightenment have been on the receiving end of a full-scale revision in recent years, and while it is not possible to offer even the beginnings of a proper survey, a number of trends are evident. It was not until the twentieth century that the Enlightenment was conceived of as a period; prior to that it was a process, was something you did.[21] For historians of ideas, returning to this usage has been salutary.[22] The old story of the Enlightenment 'process' as the enactment of secularization has also been thoroughly revised, to the extent that one may say that France has emerged as the exception that pitted Deistical Philosophes against religion; elsewhere, as in the case of the English Dissenters, a belief in revealed religion and doing Enlightenment go hand in hand.[23] This is not to say that the Enlightenment witnessed the entrenchment of religion as it was; rather there was a tendency to modernize it, to rid it of its anachronisms so that it was fit for modern purposes.[24] And then there has been the influence of Habermas's work on the bourgeois public sphere:

> The main effect of his work has been to accelerate the cultural and social historical turn in Enlightenment studies. Recent historical studies of the

> rise of polite culture have greatly enhanced our understanding of the workings of the eighteenth-century public sphere, yet they have shifted Habermas's original emphasis, away from rational outcome and towards questions of social process. The public sphere itself has come to seem intelligible not so much as the seedbed of civil society, more as a response to the growing demands of eighteenth-century consumer culture. Polite rules of social engagement, along with the media, institutions and social spaces to facilitate them, are seen to have been prerequisites for orderly commercial exchange. And so the critical Enlightenment of the Second World War and Cold War eras has been subsumed by discussions of the social practices of bourgeois civility and capitalism.[25]

According to Karen O'Brien, there is an emerging consensus that there was

> a process of intellectual change worth naming as the Enlightenment, that it started as early as the mid seventeenth century, with a key role for Spinoza and Spinozists, that theological ideas (Latitudinarianism, Arminianism, Socinianism) were central to the process, and that it is best understood as a trans-national phenomenon traceable through the history of social and print networks.[26]

If one recalls Coleridge's early flirtation with Unitarianism and Shelley's later commitment to a Spinozaon spirit of mutability (the singular material principle driving continuity and change), one can see how both represent the survival of a radical Enlightenment, bracketing an intervening period of conservatism, in line with Butler's schema.

Berlin's Counter-Enlightenment has had an even rougher ride.[27] The shortcomings of his thesis are easily identified: his characterization of the Enlightenment as a fantasy of reason is itself a highly partial representation of the French Philosophes. As Pocock and others have shown, the French Enlightenment was exceptional in pitting philosophy against religion, reason against the supernatural, and, as a consequence, Berlin dangerously blurs the division between religious progressives and reactionaries.[28] His grouping of Vico, Herder, Hamann, Rousseau and De Maistre is highly problematic, with each appearing, in different lights, as a theory breaking exception. And while there were salons, coffeehouses, reading groups, essay writing competitions and grand schemes like encyclopaedias to bind together those who might conceivably be categorized as members of a common project, Berlin's Counter-Enlightenment is, in comparison, reactive, scattered and disparate, to such an extent that, for many, his category breaks under the strain. Despite the scepticism, the Counter-Enlightenment has also made a resurgence of late, largely because it is, I believe, indispensable.[29] However, I also think it true to say that Berlin's Counter-Enlightenment will never succeed as a chapter in the history of ideas, as his different figures, at a conceptual level, do not really cohere. Much better to think of the Counter-Enlightenment in line with Darrin McMahon's suggestion that it should be considered as analogous with – indeed, as a continuation of – the Counter-Reformation, which is precisely how the enemies of the French Revolution regarded matters.[30] Individuals, groups, cultures do not simply discard one set of ideas for another, especially when of revolutionary import; such ideas are embedded in loyalties, identities, mentalities, and out of these deep-seated instincts a great many diverse behaviours flow. Drawing on Berlin, one can identify a range of Counter-Enlightenment positions, such as the primacy of the local, singular and particular over the general and systematic; the national over the cosmopolitan; a hostility to theory and universal principles; a deep unhappiness with the 'growth economy' and the boosterism of political economists; a hostility to any smack of dirigisme; a belief in a cultural 'organicism' that entailed, as a matter of course, a respect for custom, including prejudice; the sacredness of hierarchy, subordination and the manners that cemented and smoothed local accommodations; the umbilical connections of church and state, nation and family, king and father; opposition to materialism in all its forms; and, finally, a belief that the prosletizers of economic modernism were sufficiently driven by selfish motives to resort as a matter of course to conspiracy and violence.[31] Despite the cohesiveness of this set of attitudes, none, on their own, may safely be identified as Counter-Enlightenment unless coupled with a revulsion that self-consciously understands itself as flowing from instinctual opposition to modernity.

Moreover, Enlightenment and its counter must be understood as in dialectical relation to each other. As Darrin McMahon argues, Counter-Enlightenment 'ideologies' were themselves produced by Enlightenment and revolution. Such ideologies were radical, and new.[32] In the French context, their proselytizers (and they were many) did not naively call for a turning back of the clock and the restitution of the old supremacy of church and state; they developed their arguments in the light shed by what they considered a world-changing breach wrought by the Philosophes and the Jacobins who were their natural consequence; hence, for example, the fetish made of nature as a site of organic change, instinctual submission and the sui generis (so that singularity of the organicism defeated 'theory'). One might say that such argument merely recast 'Legitimacy', as Hazlitt might put it, from exploded Divine Right to something else that served; but that is the dialectical and ideological point.

In other words, as much as their adversaries, even the most virulent advocates of Counter-Enlightenment, such as Joseph de Maistre, understood, explicitly and polemically, that history had struck a deflection point that was also a tangent. From now on humanity was in territory that was new and unrepeatable. Richard Maxwell has argued that a third sense of history comes to the fore during the Romantic period, as a challenge to Scots stadialism and Burkean organicism, one we might call global synchronicity.[33] Scots

Stadialism was a theory of differential development: thus American Indians and Scottish Highlanders might find themselves in each other, just as Chinese traders might see eye to eye with their London equivalents. Organicism focused on how the past – thankfully – repeats itself in the present. In contrast to both, global synchronicity suggested that there was a process of commercial and technological change afoot that spanned the globe, and was leaving the past behind, for good.

The narrow focus of *Romantic Misfits* is the process of inclusion, and exclusion, that was influential in the final shaping of institutional Romanticism. But the broader context engages with the marked ideological shifts of the Romantic period, of the kind gestured towards in Butler's scheme. With the above terms in place, I can now articulate my difference from both Butler and McGann. As I see the literary culture of the period, there is a dialectical play between the radical Enlightenment and its counter. But instead of seeing the period Balkanized into three generations, with the first and last favouring 'enlightenment modes' and the middle settling into 'reaction' (or 'Counter-Enlightenment'), I detect a constant dialectical play between these two poles that were subjectivities as much as they were political positions and, as a consequence, also stubbornly resistant to rational argument. This dialectical play is driven less by reaction to the French Revolution and more by the historical rupture it was seen to constitute. As E. J. Hobsbawm comments, between 1789 and 1815 few long-established regimes 'had not been transformed ... Such traditional guarantors of loyalty as dynastic legitimacy, divine ordination, historic right and continuity of rule, or religious cohesion, were severely weakened ... all these traditional legitimations of state authority were, since 1789, under permanent challenge'.[34] The sense of crisis induced by the first intimation of 'global synchronicity', linked to the yawning question of what now did legitimate state authority, profoundly marks the literary production of the Romantic-era. The Enlightenment modes that survive in the 1790s differ substantially from those that reappear ten and fifteen years later, and they differ dialectically.

Romantic Misfits focuses on the first dialectical shift from the radical enlightenment of the 1790s to (in Butler's terms) a 'literature of counter-revolution', one 'marked by gloomy, egotistical inwardness' – marks of distinction that mark the Romantic misfit. As Gillian Russell and Clara Tuite have recently argued, the Romantics were every bit as sociable as the clubbable writers of the eighteenth century. As they also note, this sociability is distinctly lacking in the critical literature.[35] It is lacking, because the tradition of Romantic criticism that begins in the Victorian period has taken Romanticism's self-representation of gloomy egotistical inwardness at face value. The tendency of McGann's argument was further to entrench the ideological commitments of Romanticism as its defining features. In *Romantic Misfits* I aim to put large question marks around them by exploring the following contention: the Victorian reception of Romanticism tended to privilege those values that cluster around the Counter-Enlightenment pole of the dialectic between Enlightenment and its counter, values that inhered, especially, within the myth of the Romantic misfit, values that have had a long, and stubborn, survival. *Romantic Misfits* focuses on the first swing to Counter-Enlightenment, because it was here that the terms were set for Romanticism's Victorian reception.

As mentioned earlier, McGann's test for whether one work is more Romantic than an other is whether the work or writer is attached, in a deep way, to, variously, Romanticism's 'ideological commitments' or simply 'ideologies'. As others have analysed the contradictions and problems of McGann's old Marxist use of ideology I won't go into them here, other than to say that the main difficulty with his approach is that it is parti pris: it hinges on a notion of false consciousness, where answers to the begged question of 'what's the true?' are thoroughly political, and therefore dependent upon the ideological commitments of the viewer.[36] Such an approach, historically speaking, will get us nowhere. Instead I want to invoke John Schwarzmantel's purely analytical approach to the term. For Schwarzmantel, a constellation of beliefs qualifies as an ideology if it meets three necessary and sufficient conditions, which he terms critique (from Kant's 'What is Enlightenment?'), goal and agency.[37] For Schwarzmantel no ideology is any more true, or any less false, than any other; rather it is the nature of the modern world that ideologies are to be found in a constant state of contest with each other. In this respect an ideology begins with the realization that we are not bound by traditional authority, such as, for instance, the individual's unqualified subjection to a church and state girded by the Divine Right of Kings. We think ideologically when we subsequently ask, what is the good life? And how is to be achieved? Schwarzmantel's approach is also historical in that he argues that a major consequence of the Enlightenment was that it inaugurated ideological thinking on a mass scale for the first time in (at least Western) history.

Schwartmantel is not necessarily in opposition to the broad tradition of Marxist thinking on the subject. That is to say, it is conceivable that one could hold firm Althusserian views and still find Schwarzmantel's analysis useful for distinguishing one ideological position from another. It is as an analytical tool that I use Schwarzmantel's scheme, which is far more subtle, and useful, in practice, than it sounds. I invoke it in most of the chapters, in particular, to detect shifts in the attitude to critique, for it is here in particular that one can map the dialectical shifts from Enlightenment to Counter-Enlightenment. I must emphasize that my use of ideology as a concept (as defined by Schwartzmantel) is not political, nor is it about politics – at least, not in the ordinary meaning of the phrase. Rather it is a necessary means for asking the questions posed by *Romantic Misfits*. To be sure, the answers the argument prompts may take a political turn, but that is different from the work of clarifying how the initial consequences of Romantic misfitting continue, unconsciously, to infiltrate our critical language.

Several other key terms recur throughout *Romantic Misfits*, one of which is 'Gothic'. When James MacKintosh essayed an early definition of Romanticism, in the *Edinburgh Review*, the term he used for the contemporary resurgence in native traditions of writing, traditions that first flowered under Elizabeth, was 'Gothic'.[38] In the Victorian invention of Romanticism, Gothic retained its cultural capital as a descriptor of architecture, but lost it altogether when coupled with literature, having become a virtual synonym for the trash of the circulating library. One might say that 'Gothic' was a linguistic romantic misfit. 'Gothic' recurs throughout the book, as it is a common fault line in the diverse acts of inclusion and exclusion I analyse. Abjection also recurs, albeit shorn of its psychoanalytic accretions. While the reader is free to retain them, I have kept my focus steady on acts of raising up, and throwing down, and in this context 'abject' is simply descriptive.[39] 'Ideal presence' is also a key term in several chapters, for reasons I first explain in Chapter 2.

How I use Habermas's public sphere is the final matter that requires introduction. Habermas's phrase has achieved the kind of notoriety where it is known as much by repute as by reading, and as a consequence is frequently misunderstood. I end with a brief introduction of Habermas's theory as it relates to *Romantic Misfits*. The matter is especially pertinent, given the larger claim I make that institutional Romanticism was built out of the ruins of the public sphere.

1. Public-sphering

Since its translation into English, in 1990, Jürgen Habermas's *The Structural Transformation of the Public Sphere* has had a deep impact on how we think about the activity and reception of writing during the Romantic-era. Despite its great complexity the broad scheme of Habermas's thesis can be simply put. Habermas argues that the bourgeois public sphere came into being over the course of two hundred or so years, from the time of the late early modern period to the moment of the French Revolution, as a result of the newly emerging middle classes contesting aristocratic power. The public sphere was an extension of the private. Every bourgeoisie's home may have been his castle, but its borders had to be defended against the encroachments of the state, which is to say, against monarchical and/or aristocratic power. The public sphere arose as a means of defending gains made within the private. The animating idea of the public sphere was that there should be, in the normal course of political life, a communal space in which individuals might come together, across the divides of rank, to exchange ideas rationally about matters of public consequence. The ideal was gradually realized through a series of sporadic, but linked, institutions and practices: the intellectual exchange of international correspondence; Masonic lodges, where burger and feudal lord freely intermingled, in pursuit of free-thinking Deism; French Salons;

English coffeehouses; parliamentary reporting; newspapers, magazines and journals; and secularized institutes of learning, such as the Warrington or Hackney academies.[40] The practices that constituted the public sphere were not exclusively political. They were also literary in nature, hence Habermas's division of the bourgeois public sphere into the political and literary. Although those entering the imaginary spaces of the bourgeois public sphere might not have the vote, or any political representation to speak of, literary discourse served as a means of exploring and circulating ideas that might eventually materialize as political action.

In Habermas's account, the classical bourgeois public sphere had a set life span. After the French Revolution it began to unravel, fraying into the ideologically contested, the state sponsored or the commercially driven. Critics, such as Jon Klancher, Kevin Gilmartin and Paul Keen have tended to confirm Habermas's broad historical reading of the Romantic period, even as they have amended it. Thus, while they anatomized the manner in which the public sphere was 'structurally transformed' during the 1790s and after, they have also, in various ways, called into question aspects of Habermas's theory, which have been generally challenged. These challenges revolve around four basic objections: that Habermas's theory of the public sphere is ideal or utopian; that it excludes women; that there was not a single bourgeois public sphere, but many 'spheres', often plebeian in character; and, finally, that 'sphere' is a misnomer, as it suggests that rational discussion of politics only occurred in defined spaces.

All four objections turn on a single point of interpretation, which Habermas has sought to clarify, first, through his later theory of communicative action and, second, through references to J. L. Austin's speech act theory. Habermas's theory of the Enlightened Bourgeois public sphere certainly sounds ideal, if not utopian: that is, of men congregating from across the social ranks to discourse rationally on politics. At first glance this happy image appears to be a simple representation of civic humanist ideology, one taking the period at its own, flattering, self-estimation. Sensing the danger, Habermas tried to signal that this was not what he meant by indicating that the bourgeois public sphere ought to be understood as an ideological belief, that is, as an act of false consciousness. However, Habermas was already en route from a naive Marxist position in which 'false consciousness' would serve as an adequate gloss for ideology, and as a consequence he favoured 'normative ideal', a more nuanced locution.[41] One might interpret 'normative ideal' as the happy state in which an ideal had become the norm; Habermas meant, rather, that an 'ideal' (which might or might not be a thing good in-itself) had become a commonplace of social discourse within particular classes.

One might characterize Habermas's distinction as subtle, or just slippery. For the sceptical reader, it provided an opportunity for accusing Habermas of fatal naiveté. In response to this objection Habermas recast the expression as a 'performative' speech act. J. L. Austin developed his theory of 'performativity' as a way of dealing with the semantic status of locutions that did not make claims about the world, which could not be deemed 'true' or 'false', but which were, nevertheless, meaningful. His first case was the act of 'promising'.[42] One would not say of the expression 'I promise to marry you' that it was true or false; but neither could one say that it was meaningless, even though the phrase makes no truth claims. The solution to the puzzle, according to Austin, is that the phrase performs its own meaning: in the act of uttering a promise, we bind ourselves to various things. In order for an expression successfully to perform a meaning, certain conditions must adhere. In the case of promising, there must be a promiser, a promisee, and either the intentionality of the utterance must be manifest, or the context must be such that the intentionality of the utterance is unmistakable. Thus, if you were to say to your cat, 'I promise to marry you', no one would say that you were bound to be married; in any event, no one would seriously accuse you of breach of promise if you failed to do so. Similarly, one would not be bound, the meaning would not have been performed, if the words were whispered when your beloved was temporarily deafened by a passing train and facing the wrong way; or if the words were uttered loudly, in clear earshot of the addressed beloved, but under the influence of a travelling hypnotist. Austin calls such moments, when the conditions for a successful performative do not adhere, 'misfires'. Just so the public sphere. For Habermas, an act of 'public-sphering' may be said to take place when the necessary and sufficient conditions requisite for it have been met; when, for instance, two or more people meet and where they believe themselves entitled to converse upon matters of public or political moment – irrespective of class or political enfranchisement – and where they further believe that such discourse ought to be rational. For Habermas what is significant is not the truth content of this public-sphering (whether their discourse really is rational or disinterested or even ideal in character) but the fact that the conditions obtain for making the performative utterance possible. The meeting of a bourgeoisie and an aristocrat to discuss rationally the fundamental soundness of Burke's *Reflections on the Revolution in France*, in all its regressive detail, would be an instance of a successful performative, would be the bourgeois public sphere in action, whereas the conversation between the same bourgeoisie and a member of the London Corresponding Society, recently acquitted of treason, with no faith whatsoever in the possibility of rational, discursive, political intervention, would be a misfire, even if the London Corresponding Society member opined favourably on Burke's analysis, in an apparently rational manner, if he was doing so in order to save his skin. The point becomes clearer when we think of another performative: swearing. If a Methodist, say, were to find himself in the company of a band of ruffians who blasphemed freely, perhaps also indicating several dire things they would like to do to canting Methodists, should they catch one, and should this Methodist swear, in order to pass, one would say it was not true swearing (it would be a misfire in Austin's terms) insofar as it lacked intentionality (much as if one had promised to marry prodded by a shotgun). The material point becomes evident once one imagines the ruffians suddenly converted by Wesley: not only would the Methodist's swearing desist, but so would that of the ruffians. In such a manner the public sphere might also wither, should the intentionality material to it decline. In the 1790s there was just such a collapse, not least because one's favourite coffeehouses were infested with Government spies waiting to entrap the naive through carefully baited expressions of Jacobinism.

Austin's notion of performativity allowed Habermas to sidestep neatly two of the recurring objections to his theory. To the accusation that it was hopelessly utopian Habermas could reply that he was referring to the social dissemination of attitudes requisite for a successful act of public-sphering (attitudes which may have been, in themselves, politically regressive); and to the charge of spatial literalism he could say that the public sphere came into being whenever and wherever two or more people came together to talk about politics in a rational manner, be it the Charing Cross Coffeehouse or adjacent to Godwin's outdoor privy.[43]

The other two objections are not so easily dealt with. The feminist case has been most notably advocated by Nancy Fraser and Anne Mellor.[44] The objection here is that regardless of how one regards Habermas's theory, whether as normative ideal or as a performative, it belies the historical facts of the case, while reinforcing a partial, Enlightenment bias. In Habermas's theory women play an important role in the private and in the literary public spheres; both spheres, meanwhile, are part of the public (as different halves of two dyads: the private/public; and the literary and political public sphere). However, given that women lacked political enfranchisement, and given that most men who constituted the political public sphere subscribed to this disenfranchisement, it followed that women were debarred from direct participation in the full, bourgeois public sphere. In some respects Habermas's performative refinement simply compounded the problem, as it suggested that, as there was no widespread belief in the possibility of rational political intervention by women, no such performative activity was possible. Lacking the social grounds for intentional action female 'public-sphering' would be as strange, as much a misfire, as a Methodist swearing under duress or your cat accepting your marriage proposal with a nod of its head. Of course, for many contemporary commentators, such as the Reverend Powhele, such was indeed the case. For a woman to adopt the language of the political public sphere was as unnatural, as much of a misfired locution, as your cat talking. In other words, Habermas's 'normative ideal' threatened to substitute a common prejudice for historical fact. As both Fraser and Mellor have forcefully argued, women were indeed full participants in the public sphere, in ways that must be said to constitute public-sphering, if the phrase has any historical meaning at all. Catherine Macaulay, Mary Wollstonecraft and Hannah More (to name but three) all manifestly believed that they were entitled to discourse rationally on matters of public moment; they also believed, with differing degrees of confidence or polemical fervour, that there was a public that recognized that right, thus ratifying their intentions.

Habermas has freely acknowledged the validity of the feminist case while maintaining that a gendered exclusion was nevertheless a structuring principle of the bourgeois public sphere.[45] In any event, it is open to Habermas to argue that his theory originally envisaged the participation of women in the literary public sphere, and that there was not a single, monolithic, normative ideal, but many, different, contested versions of it held by diverse 'publics' or constituencies. As such the feminist case overlaps with the objection that there was not a single, bourgeois public sphere, but many such 'spheres'.[46] As Geoff Eley puts it, 'the public sphere makes more sense as the structured setting where cultural and ideological contest or negotiation among a variety of publics takes place, rather than as the spontaneous or class-specific achievement of the bourgeoisie in some sufficient sense'.[47] Terry Eagleton specifies what some of these publics might be: 'the Corresponding Societies, the radical press, Owenism, Cobbett's *Political Register* and Paine's *Rights of Man*, feminism and the dissenting churches . . . '[48] Geoff Eley's own general statement about the rise of the public sphere is, I think, correct: 'Historically, its growth occurred in the late eighteenth century with the widening of political participation and the crystallizing of citizenship ideals.'[49] The endless constitutional debates in a revolutionary era sharpened notions of political inclusion and exclusion, notions defended through 'rational' interventions in print, one of the principal characteristics of Habermas's public sphere. Many, if not most, of these interventions came from 'below', from the politically disenfranchised. A key question is therefore whether we should regard such opposition as emanating from '*alternative* public spheres and *counterpublics*',[50] that is to say, as conflict inherent within the bourgeois public sphere, or whether dissent on such a massive scale discredits the whole theory altogether.

Habermas's performative refinement once again clarifies the point. Imagine that the acquitted members of the London Corresponding Society, and other suspect characters have so lost their faith in the possibility of rational intervention that they cease to engage their political opponents in good faith, but turn instead to satire, to pornography, to prints discrediting the established church, perhaps featuring an 'arsebishop' fond of sodomizing guardsmen, and other proscribed acts of publication designed to bring the establishment's authority into disrepute. One might describe this 'radical underworld' as an alternative public sphere; alternatively, one might argue that in it the conditions for 'public-sphering' no longer obtain, and such communicative acts are not constitutive of a 'counter-public sphere' at all, but predicate its dissolution.[51]

My argument follows on from Jon Klancher's. That is to say, I do not see that the 'counter-publics' anatomized by Kevin Gilmartin, Iain McCalman and David Worrall (among others) constitute a fatal challenge to Habermas's theory. I see them, rather, as evidence of the break-up (or 'structural transformation') of the eighteenth-century public sphere theorized by Habermas, owing, above all, to increased social complexity. Part of that break-up was the waning of the 'normative ideal' Habermas understands to be crucial to the performative meaning of the public sphere. The normative ideal itself recapitulated the driving premise of the 'republic of letters', that all were permitted to speak who obeyed the republic's codes of polite discourse.[52] In the literary realm, no topic was deemed more central to an Englishman's entitlement to speak than Shakespeare, the national bard. As a consequence, no event tested the republic of letters as severely as the forgery of his works, an event that was to influence the formation of English Romanticism.

1

The Original Misfit: The Shakespeare Forgeries, Herbert Croft's *Love and Madness*, and W. H. Ireland's Romantic Career

1. W. H. Ireland and print culture

W. H. Ireland was the last of the great eighteenth-century literary forgers. To use the period's own sense of this genealogy, the line includes William Lauder, Psalmanazar, James MacPherson and Thomas Chatterton, and culminates in the forgery of the Shakespeare manuscripts, which from 1795 to 2 April 1796 enthralled the capital, before the forgeries were put to the test of public opinion through the performance of *Vortigern and Rowena* at Drury Lane, where they spectacularly failed.[1]

In forging Shakespeare, Ireland constructed a Romantic identity. If identity is, as some critics have argued, performative, then Ireland's self-fashioning constitutes what J. L. Austin would have termed a 'misfire'. Ireland is the historical 'infelicity' that stands in articulate contrast to Wordsworth's accomplished utterance. Whereas Wordsworth harnessed his love of distinction, so that it pulled him through a dignified literary career, Ireland's skipped the traces, running roughshod over the literary proprieties. To shift the metaphor, Ireland mimicked and mocked common literary attitudes, in a tragic-comic burlesque of a Romantic career. He was an echt-Romantic in his mimicry of Chatterton, and, in his misfiring, beyond the pale. He was the original Romantic misfit.

Ireland's Romantic identity has its primal scene. In his *Confessions*, published in 1805 to restore his damaged 'literary character', William Henry Ireland recounts how his father, Samuel, was in the habit of reading aloud to the family after dinner.[2] The text was often Shakespeare, a 'God among men' in the Ireland household,[3] but on another momentous occasion it was the Chatterton sections from Herbert Croft's *Love and Madness* (1780), a work that was instrumental in shaping the legend of the marvellous boy. William Henry Ireland has a reason for telling us this: it explains how he first heard of the genius Chatterton whose example proved so calamitously irresistible. But there are other reasons of equal moment that William does not explain. *Love and*

Madness is itself the forged love letters of the tragic celebrities James Hackman and Martha Ray. Hackman was a respectable clergyman, Ray, the long-term mistress of the Earl of Sandwich. Both entered the limelight when a rejected and jealous Hackman stalked Ray to the Covent Garden Theatre, blowing her brains out with a pistol. What William Henry Ireland does not mention is that his mother, 'Mrs. Freeman', was herself a former mistress of the Earl of Sandwich before becoming Samuel's.[4] According to Bernard Grebanier, Mrs. Freeman's real name was Anna Maria de Burgh Coppinger and she was herself a published poet (the author of *The Doctor Dissected*). She, not William's father, Samuel, was the real literary artist of the household. What information we have about Mrs. Freeman comes from Joseph Farington's diary:

> Mrs Freeman who lives with Samuel Ireland, and is the Mother of the Children, had it is said a fortune of £1200, and is of a good family. Her brother is now living in London in great circumstances, but disowns Her... Ireland behaves very ill to her. The children for many years bore the name of Irwin; and it was at the birthday of one of them, when many persons were invited, & Westall was one off the party, that it was signified by Mrs Freeman that the young people were to be addressed by the name of Ireland. They had passed as her nieces.[5]

Samuel Ireland may have had progressive ideas with regards to animal rights and politics, but in his sexual mores he was old fashioned and drew the line at marrying the ex-mistress of an aristocrat, even if she was the mother of his children. As Sandwich's déclassé cast-off Coppinger required a name that was neither her maiden one nor Ireland's. 'Mrs. Freeman' replaced 'Irwin', possibly as a private joke derived from *Love and Madness*, where 'Mrs. Freeman' serves as the pseudonym of an incognito, lesbian aristocrat.[6]

In the fraught aftermath of the Shakespeare scandal, William Ireland for a time changed his name to Freeman, reminding his father that Samuel had long intimated that there was a mystery attached to his birth:

> I have said if you are my parent being at a loss to account for the expressions so often used to Mrs. Freeman & which she has repeatedly told me of 'that you did not think I was your son' besides after slight altercations with Mrs F you have frequently said that when of age you had a story to tell me which would astonish and (if I mistake not) much shock me.[7]

Almost all of Ireland's biographers conclude that he believed, or chose to believe, that he was not his father's son (Grebanier speculates that William thought he was Sandwich's). William Henry felt himself doubly a bastard: in blood terms, a counterfeit of a counterfeit. William Henry's primal scene was thus shadowed forth in *Love and Madness*, through Ray as a figuration of his mother (both were Sandwich's mistresses); through

Hackman/Sandwich/Croft as the paternal imago; and through Chatterton – and his literary progenitor Richard Savage – as himself. If one were using Althusserian terms one would say that Ireland was interpellated into eighteenth-century print culture in the role of the bastard, the illegitimate forger-trickster who rises, self-propelled, through the force of his own genius.

If the Ireland story is, as I contend, a weirdly eloquent instance of the print culture forces that were shortly to shape Romanticism, Croft's *Love and Madness* is a crucial part of it, partly because of the multiple affiliations it bears to Ireland's life story and family circumstances – so that we may easily imagine his reading of it as an especially strong form of internalization – and partly because *Love and Madness* is significant in its own right. As John Brewer has shown, the case of Hackman and Rae was the most sensational murder of the eighteenth century – an event that saturated contemporary media – while *Love and Madness* was 'a huge success and one of the truly important works of fiction written during the twenty years following ... *Humphrey Clinker*'.[8] Croft may be obscure now but he was a celebrity when *Love and Madness* first cast its spell over Ireland; while the work itself contains, as we shall see, a surprisingly cogent reflection on the very print culture forces that propelled the Ireland story.

Mobility and interiority (depth or psychology) are integral facets of what I mean by Romantic subjectivity.[9] The issue has two principle sides: the rise of celebrity culture and what Roland Barthes might call the birth of the Author. As the cliché has it, the Romantic Author is a man of genius with depths measureless to man, like Kubla Khan's. Out of these depths the media generates a dangerous, vampiric charisma.[10] Which brings me to the final two reasons why I shall be looking closely at *Love and Madness*: it reinforces the argument that if Romantic subjectivity is primarily viewed as an effect of print culture the novel plays a more central role in its formation than has generally been allowed; and as a 'faction' it highlights the crucial border between celebrity (as a function of media) and genius.

Jürgen Habermas provides our way into the connections between the novel, interiority and the public sphere. For Habermas the novel was a key agent in the formation of Enlightenment privacy: 'The relations between author, work, and public changed. They became intimate mutual relationships between privatized individuals who were psychologically interested in what was "human," in self-knowledge, and in empathy.'[11] The psychological novel was the site where these 'intimate mutual relationships' were most intense. Moreover, 'the psychological novel fashioned for the first time the kind of realism that allowed anyone to enter into the literary action as a substitute for his own, to use the relationships between the figures, between the author, the characters and the reader as substitute relationships for reality'.[12] For Habermas, the bourgeois private and public spheres form a single, mutually reinforcing, dyad. The development of interiority creates a demand for privacy that needs to be defended through an expanded public sphere, which in turns creates more space for 'privacy'. The novel has an especially important place in this cultural dynamic because it offers a means by which interiority, or depth, may be performed, a cultural practice it extends to its readership through its promise of vicarious enjoyment. The standard complaint lodged against the novel – that it induces ideas above the reader's station while loosening her grip on reality – is, in Habermas's terms, precisely the point: bribed by realism novel readers practised 'interiority' (the 'human', self-knowledge, empathy), thus reinforcing the demand for 'privacy' and, in consequence, a stronger public sphere. *Love and Madness* is central to our story, then, in part because of its role in what I have called Ireland's primal scene, but also because it both exemplifies and reflects upon Habermas's theory of the novel, as a sensational 'faction' dwelling on what was, at the time, the most celebrated instance of the human puzzle.

2. The Ireland story

As one might expect the dominant factor in William Henry Ireland's family environment was his father, Samuel, whose entrepreneurial career in late eighteenth-century print culture fits Pierre Bourdieu's theory of cultural capital, like a hand to a glove. Although not mentioned by John Brewer in his *Pleasures of the Imagination*, Samuel Ireland is at one with the many others Brewer documents, who assiduously laid up their store of cultural capital, in order to raise their social status, in the eventual hope of material gain.[13] He rose from a middling-low position in life to a middling-high one, where, at his apogee, he could expect to be entertained by royalty and to mix with the leading literary men of his day. This rise was not lost on the public. As the contemporary accounts never tired of saying, Samuel Ireland began his career as a weaver, in 'Spitalfields, but soon made his way to the West-end, where he found an ample field for his talents in the compilation of Illustrated Tour Books to which he added the more profitable calling of a speculator in rare books, prints, and drawings'.[14] Apparently an autodidact, Ireland made a number of shrewd investments in artistic commodities – in Hogarth and Shakespeare – whose values were about to rocket. Ireland became a noted authority on Hogarth, compiling a large private collection that formed the basis of his deluxe edition of the artist's works. Ireland next cashed in on the fashion for the picturesque travel book, publishing four lavishly illustrated works between 1790 and 1795. His *A Picturesque Tour Through Holland, Brabant and Part of France: Made in the Autumn of 1789* is a typical production. Ireland represents himself as the soul of clubability, conducting his readers round the picturesque sights of the countryside and, in Amsterdam, when not waxing lyrical over paintings, slyly taking the reader along with him on a purely investigative tour of a brothel. He is à la mode in his overt support for the French Revolution; and, as the subtitle informs us, his book is commercially as well as artistically up-to-date: *Illustrated with Copper Plates in Aqua Tinta From Drawings Made on the Spot by Samuel Ireland*. The key is 'acqua tinta'. According to the *Gentleman's Magazine* British exports of prints produce a surplus of £60,000 per annum, partly owing to the success of Boydell's Shakespeare, and partly owing to the revolution of costs produced by the new technique: 'The new method... Mr. Sandby and six or seven English artists have brought to a degree of perfection which no foreigner has yet been able to equal ...'[15] Samuel Ireland (a student of Sandby's) was at the vanguard of this patriotic, cultural commerce.[16]

It is unclear whether Samuel Ireland made his move from the artisanal environment of Spitalfields to the upmarket address of Norfolk Street, in the West End, entirely under his own steam. Bernard Grebanier speculates that Samuel Ireland derived an income from the Earl of Sandwich for taking 'Mrs. Freeman' off his hands;[17] alternatively, it may have been Anna Maria de Burgh Coppinger's £1200, mentioned by Farington. William Henry had three siblings: an older brother, Samuel, who died as an infant, and two younger sisters. William later claimed he was born in 1777, rather than 1775, in order to exaggerate his precocity.[18] Samuel completed the transition from weaver to respectable bourgeois, by apprenticing William to the law, in the chambers of William Bingley of New Inn, sometime in the early 1790s.

Samuel's road to ruin began with his bardolatry. In 1793 he took his son with him on the field trip that was to produce, in 1795, *Picturesque Views on the Upper, or Warwickshire Avon*. Visiting Stratford they scoured the countryside for relics. Frequently hearing his father say that nothing would please him better than to possess an authentic Shakespearian document, William set to work in his solicitor's chambers where he was underemployed and unsupervized. Armed with a piece of old parchment, black ink, and soot, he produced one: a title deed. This first deception led to ever more elaborate entanglements, with William Henry feeding his father's insatiable appetite for discoveries with a stream of bogus documents, including: a profession of faith (establishing the poet's Protestant credentials); a thank you letter from Elizabeth; a love letter to 'Anne Hatherrwaye'; annotated books from Shakespeare's libraries; a manuscript draft of *Lear* (with the play's 'vulgarisms' excised); a portrait of Shakespeare as Shylock; a deed of gift from Shakespeare to W. H. Ireland (an alleged ancestor), signing over to him the possession of his papers as a reward for having saved Shakespeare from drowning; and, finally, the lost Shakespeare plays, *Vortigern and Rowena* and *Henry II*. As Edmond Malone was later to argue, in these matters, provenance is all.[19] But to Samuel's urgings to disclose where he procured his treasures, William would only respond, from a wealthy gentleman to whom the value of the relics meant nothing, and who wished to remain anonymous. The literary world – indeed, one is tempted to say, the entire literary public sphere of London – was agog at the news, with many streaming to Norfolk Street to view the relics, including, famously, Boswell, who after a stiff shot of brandy, fell on his knees in veneration, thanking God that he had lived long enough to see them. Samuel Parr and Joseph Warton publicly pronounced on the transcendent genius of the profession of faith, much to their later embarrassment. Samuel Ireland was not slow to profit from his cultural windfall. On Christmas Eve, 1795, he published a magnificent facsimile edition of the manuscripts, minus the plays, still being hurriedly written by William, priced four guineas, with a list of 118 prominent 'believers'.[20]

In the first excited flush of the discoveries, Sheridan contracted to stage *Vortigern*, a decision he apparently soon regretted, possibly as a result of the sceptical reception of the manuscripts, possibly as a result of conversations with his friend, Malone, who made no secret of his contempt for the forgeries, nor of his intention of exposing them. Indeed, *Vortigern* was put on, just after April Fools' day, 1796, under the impending shadow of Malone's demolition. There is some uncertainty over whether the play failed because the audience, smelling a rat, spontaneously rioted, or whether its failure was owing to subversion by the actors, especially Kemble. Whatever the cause, the play ended in uproar. Although the controversy rumbled on, the Shakespeare bubble had burst, with the decisive prick delivered by Malone's *Inquiry*; nearly four hundred pages of lifelong Shakespearian scholarship, it appeared an irrefutable demolition of the Irelands' claims.

Samuel Ireland's 'credit', and character, were ruined; his art and travel books no longer possessed cultural currency, and sales plummeted. In a letter to Talbot, 5 July 1796, his son's confidant and ex-colleague, Samuel Ireland makes clear the brutally direct connection there was between cultural and literal capital: he and his family face financial ruin, owing to the 'odium thrown on my character, & the pecuniary injury I sustain from the total stop of the sale of my literary productions'.[21] James Gillray caricatured Samuel Ireland's self-portrait under the strap line 'Notorious Characters'. Gillray's single lethal alteration was to change Samuel's lips from a smile to a smirk, while William Mason appended lines suggesting Samuel was merely the latest in a line of forgers, stretching from Laud, through Chatterton and Macpherson, to Sam. Claiming that he wished to spare these unwarranted assaults on his father's reputation, William Henry published his *Authentic Account* (1796), confessing his fabrication, but to no avail, in part because the pamphlet was so clumsily written that it undermined his claims,[22] a conclusion also drawn by his father, who thought William too dull-witted to have done such a thing. The public disagreement of the two over the papers' authorship merely inclined the sceptical to see the father and son as a pair of scoundrels falling out as a result of their exposure. Samuel's ruin was complete.

3. *The Confessions*

William Henry Ireland three times sought to justify himself before the public: first, with the *Authentic Account*; next, the more developed *Confessions*

(1805); and finally, and at the close of his life, in a new preface to *Vortigern* (1832).[23] In all three, he maintained that he had embarked upon his forgeries with no premeditated plans for authorship, but was helplessly drawn into the tangled web that enveloped him, with no other motivation than the desire to please his father. Such an account is implicitly contradicted by the *Confessions*, where William's construction of himself bears close examination. At the beginning of his narrative, under the rubric 'first impressions', William tells us that he 'gradually' imbibed his father's 'fondness and veneration for every thing that bore a reference' to the divine Shakespeare. In the next, he tells us he contracted his father's 'predilection for old books': his father's antiquarian enthusiasm 'naturally impressed itself on my mind' (7). William's 'fondness for ancient books' led him to 'peruse their contents'; as a consequence he became enamoured, first with Chaucer, then with 'various old romances and tales of knights-errant ... to such a degree that I have often sighed to be the inmate of some gloomy castle; or that having lost my way upon a dreary heath, I might, like Sir Bertram, have been conducted to some enchanted mansion' (8). According to this implicit, dis-inculpating narrative, W. H. Ireland is indeed a 'Sir Bertram', lost in the ruined castle of Gothic art, led astray by the factitious glamour of print culture, with its enchanting promises of fame.[24] He then relates how Walpole's *Otranto* and Percy's *Reliques*, inspired his childhood reveries. This reconstruction of the inner life of the child ends with a section entitled 'Love and Madness'. In the succeeding parts Ireland relates the pilgrimage he made to Bristol, in the wake of his disgrace, where he pays homage to 'the unfortunate and neglected Chatterton; whose talents I revere, and whose fate I commiserate with unfeigned tears of sympathy...' (17).

Ireland's representation of his childhood trajectory is not as innocent as it may appear. The key to understanding it is lightly buried in the short 'Love and Madness' section. 'I cannot call to mind on what occasion Mr. Samuel Ireland read aloud some of the letters in Mr. Herbert Croft's very entertaining work ... ' Inspired by its references to Chatterton, William read the whole, 'when the fate of Chatterton so strongly interested me, that I used frequently to envy his fate, and desire nothing so ardently as the termination of my existence in a similar cause' (11). Croft's *Love and Madness* – with its story of Chatterton – was part of the furniture of Ireland's childhood mind; more than that, it structured his subjectivity. Far from being a spur-of-the-moment 'frolic', Ireland's Chattertonian forgeries had very deep roots indeed.

Interiority is a key aspect of Ireland's self-construction, which is best read backwards, inferentially, from his representation of Chatterton. 'From the contiguity of their residence to Redcliff church, [Mrs. Newton] also told me, he continually frequented the interior of that Gothic structure, where he would sit for hours, reading, beside the tomb of Canning...' (1805 [1969]: 15). This passage sounds two recurring motifs in Ireland's version of Chatterton: the precocious youth's inwardness (his delight in reading) and his veneration of the Gothic. Ireland asks if Chatterton ever did '"betray any extraordinary symptoms when young?"' (14), in the process making genius both a pathology and a fetish. Mrs. Newton says there was none, apart from a refusal to take his reading lessons 'from any book of modern type', but only 'black letter'. In another anecdote we are told that Chatterton was reserved and 'fond of seclusion' (13), and that, after a long absence, he was chastised, whereupon he complained that it was *'hard indeed to be whipped for reading'* (14). In another, the young Chatterton flies into a passion after his sister had turned his old parchments to domestic use, saying she had destroyed 'what would have been to the family a fortune for ever' (15).

Ireland's sketch of Chatterton is simultaneously autobiography. He, too, has a fondness for Gothic antiquity – for olde English things – and is inward and dreamy, a bookworm whose spirit of 'emulation' (7) promises to enhance the family fortune forever. Via Chatterton, Ireland imagines himself internalized in a Gothic – which is to say, a patriotic – structure. Chatterton reads beside the tomb of 'Canning', Rowley's supposed and Chatterton's imagined patron, Maecenus and surrogate father. The sentence is constructed like a Chinese doll, as the syntax relays three different versions of interiority, one within the other: Chatterton immured within the Gothic church built by Canning, his spiritual father; Chatterton inwardly revolved, reading Gothic matter; and, next to him, Canning interred within his tomb. Read as Ireland's secret autobiography this becomes Ireland enamoured by a Gothic taste, which prompts his own interiority – his reading and, by extension, writing – in turn linked to a homage to an imaginary father, either his own invented Canning (the mysterious Mr. H) or an idealized version of his true father, possibly Samuel Ireland, but now transformed into an appreciative paternal imago.

In both the 1805 *Confessions* and the 1832 preface to *Vortigern* the Gothic is a central reference, its meaning following the term's changing significance. The key, disinculpating trope of the later text is borrowed from 'a German amalgamator of the horrific'. Ireland believed a single forged document would satisfy his father's passion for Shakspeariana: 'Your German writer of the marvelous would exclaim: "No, no! it was then too late: you had fallen into the demon's snare – was spell-bound – within the vortex of his machinations . . .:" be this as it may, I was not permitted to continue passive'. Insofar as Ireland is active in the forgery, it is owing to his 'evil genius'.[25] In *The Confessions* the Gothic represents both a patriotic taste in English antiquities and a series of examples that license his fabrications. We pass from the authentic Gothic of Chaucer to a series of respectable imitations and creative editorial practices that constitute a self-validating genealogy: the Aikins, Walpole, Percy, Chatterton, Ireland. The Gothic was an architectural style and a literary fashion but, in both cases, pastiche. At the beginning of his career Ireland represents the two as reasonably distinct but by the end the irresistible glamour of the literary fad, with its promise of celebrity, has been internalized, pathologized and troped, as a Gothic 'evil genius', as if Ireland's will had been paralysed by the printer's devil. However, the meaning of his forgery is embedded less in his seduction by the Gothic and more in the example of yet another fabrication: Croft's *Love and Madness*.

4. *Love and Madness*

Herbert Croft's *Love and Madness* (1780) purported to be the letters of two real-life characters, James Hackman and Martha Ray, the central actors in one of the most sensational stories of the late eighteenth century. Hackman was a young clergyman of respectable family who contracted a hopeless passion for Ray. Eleven years older than Hackman,[26] Ray was the long-term mistress of John Montagu, the fourth Earl of Sandwich. Plucked from obscurity as a Clerkenwell mantua-maker at the age of sixteen, Ray bore Montagu five surviving children, including Wordsworth's friend, Basil. On first meeting Hackman in 1775, she was just thirty. The young cavalry officer was smitten by her beauty and accomplishments. Surrendering his commission to be near her, and taking orders as a profession more propitious for marriage, he fruitlessly pressed his suit. Under the impression that Ray had a new lover, and mad with jealously, Hackman lay in wait for her outside the Haymarket Theatre in Covent Garden, armed with two pistols, with the intention of putting an end to his miserable existence in the presence of his beloved. As Ray left the theatre with her companion and singing instructor, Signora Galli, John Macnamara, a young Irish attorney, offered his assistance in securing a passage to their waiting coach.[27] According to his own account, Hackman mistook Macnamara for a rival. At the sight of Ray's new escort, Hackman's mind spontaneously 'convulsed', with the result that he put a pistol to Ray's head and shot her dead. Hackman then turned the pistol on himself, but missed. He was apprehended by passers-by, attempting to finish the business by beating his head with the pistol butt. The fact that Hackman was armed with two pistols was held to be a clear contradiction of his plea that he had no premeditated plan to kill Ray, and he was hanged at Tyburn two weeks later.

The status of the characters involved ensured that the story was received as one of extreme sensibility and sensation. As the *Gentleman's Magazine* reported, its narration 'struck every feeling heart with horror'.[28] The germ for Croft's project appears to be this report of Hackman's hanging, also from the *Gentleman's Magazine*: 'A Particular account of a man who could perpetrate such a murder will no doubt be expected; and when any authentic materials appear, our readers shall be gratified.' 'Authentic materials' duly appeared, fabricated by Croft, who was seizing an opportunity already well formed. Shortly after the murder, there appeared *The Case and Memoirs of the Late Rev. Mr. James Hackman, and his Acquaintance with the Late Miss Martha Ray: with a commentary on his Conviction, distinguishing between his crime in particular, and that of others who have been condemned for murder* (Dawes 1779). This was an unauthorized account, published by G. Kearsly, who appears to have cultivated a line in scandalous and/or sentimental material. Anonymously written by Hackman's lawyer, Mannaseh Dawes, in his client's support, it sought to make the case that violence produced by the madness of love, in persons of otherwise good standing, ought not to be categorized as murder.[29] Dawes embedded Hackman's story in a sentimental narrative of excessive love, a moment's irrationality, and sincere and noble repentance. Hackman's speech to the Jury at Newgate was commended by the judge for its 'manliness', in that it was frank, honest and lachrymose. His speech was the 'transcript of his heart': 'A very brilliant and crowded auditory was softened into tears by it... ' Hackman went to his death like a gentleman – 'not with the horrors attendant on a savage assassin when about to receive the due of his deserts, but with the composure and anxiety of a man who had survived every thing near and dear to him'.[30] The defenders of Ray responded with a pamphlet of their own, *The Case and Memoirs of Miss Martha Reay, to which are added Remarks, by way of refutation, on the case and memoirs of the Rev. Mr. Hackman.* This work differed primarily in attributing Ray's seduction by the Earl of Sandwich to the connivance of her own father and a notorious bawd (in the pro-Hackman pamphlet she is picked up in a park) and in denying the earlier pamphlet's claim that they cuckolded the Earl under his own roof (a detail retained in Croft's version). Kearsly published the pro-Hackman pamphlet, Fourdinier the pro-Ray; but within the year Kearsly published them both, together. Engravings of the two protagonists were quickly produced, Ray's based on a painting by N. Dance, R.A., from 1777, and Hackman's, on a likeness taken by 'Mr. Dighton' on the morning of his execution, and etched by Isaac Taylor, in which Hackman is portrayed as an extremely youthful clergyman, bowed in contrition, head bruised from his self-administered pistol-whipping. There also appeared a poem, written by Hackman on the morning of his execution, in which he again protests that Ray was dearer to him than life itself. The poem appears to have initiated its own mini-genre, in that thereafter several poetic effusions appeared, affecting to be either Hackman's last poetic words or the poetic consequences of Hackman's moving death.

In several respects the affair was seen as being absolutely of the moment, and therefore original and unprecedented. Or rather, it was constructed in such a way as to play up its supposedly novel features. The affair was seen almost entirely from Hackman's perspective. Observers were especially struck by the 'fact' that Hackman was motivated by love. For the believers, his courtroom speech was gospel: 'I protest with that regard to truth, which becomes my situation, that the wish to destroy her, who was ever dearer to me than life, was never mine until a momentary phrenzy overcame me, and induced me to commit the deed I now deplore.'[31] Observers also commented on another unprecedented aspect of the case: he did not love her and leave. On the contrary, Hackman's love increased, rather than diminished, with sexual gratification. In the pro-Hackman version (echoed by Croft), the clergyman himself puts an end to their physical intimacy, swearing he will not enjoy his mistress under any other circumstances than wedlock. As Hackman's personality increasingly adapted itself to the tenets of sensibility, in the course of the affair, so his apparent rationality rose. His representation was intentionally moulded to fit the psychology of the fashionable norm in order to make the contrast with his momentary phrenzy all the more pointed. As Novak comments, Hackman was, or appeared to be, or was construed as, 'that ideal of the age – a man of exquisite feeling, who had seemingly sacrificed all for love'.[32] Celebrity, argues Peter Briggs, is a 'sort of dance' or collaboration between celebrity behaviour and audience expectations.[33] Hackman was famous because he performed his half of the dance to perfection. As an example of an infelicitous performance, one might cite the contrasting case of John Vincent who was 'convicted of feloniously killing and slaying Mary Dollard', his long-time lover, 'by shooting and wounding her in the Back and Shoulder' (or 'hinder parts', as another report has it) 'with a Gun loaded with Powder and Shot, of which Wound she languished some time, and then died, in the Parish of Fulham'. Vincent was convicted of manslaughter and given the standard punishment: he 'was immediately burnt in the Hand, and discharged'. Happening at the same time as Hackman's trial, the case was virtually ignored, even by Croft, who otherwise assiduously collected analogues of Hackman's crime. The story might well have made the subject of a final, concentrated reflection. But neither Vincent nor his crime tallied with the expectations of Croft's readership.[34] A gentleman experiencing a sentimental convulsion was one thing, a ruffian blasting the 'hinder parts' of his doxy, quite another.

As subsequent newspaper reports reveal, another novel aspect of the case, much feared, was contagion: for some time after, the press reported various copycat incidences from around the country. There was another, implicit aspect to this. As most observers up-to-date in their reading would have known, Hackman's actions eerily echoed those imagined by Goethe, in the *Sorrows of Young Werther* (1774), 'the seemingly dominant text for the way [Hackman] conceives of the world'.[35] Hackman's assertion that his actions were the work of a momentary phrenzy seemed a sinister duplication of *Werther*, as it suggested that the contagion of example was unconscious. As Croft was to put it, in the guise of Hackman, glamorous crimes of the Werthean sort possessed an 'indisputable magnetism' (Croft 295). The construction of Hackman as a sentimental hero (including Hackman's self-construction) was one aspect of his perceived modernity. The dangerous glamour of the press was another, as was the press's expressions of alarm at the very thing it perpetuated, for profit. Dawes's claim that he wrote not 'to catch the penny of the curious', is fittingly supplemented by the information that the pamphlet in fact costs a shilling.[36]

Croft's genius was to understand the issues arising out of the glamour of fame produced by print culture, with utter thoroughness. In exploiting the

Hackman-mania Croft was aided and abetted by Kearsly who published *Love and Madness* and nearly everything else produced by the affair. By publishing the work as the actual correspondence of Hackman and Ray (although mostly Hackman's), Croft and Kearsly could expect the forgery to produce maximum returns. The *Gentleman's Magazine* seized the point: 'In this age of literary fraud we are not surprised that a tale so bloody should give rise to a suppositious correspondence.' Hackman and Ray, 'it is needless to add, never penned a line of these 65 letters, except the 57th, which was printed in the sessions-paper'. The reviewer approaches the matter with a fair mind: 'Yet, granting the imposition, and considering only their contents, they have some intrinsic merits . . . ' He singles out Letter 49 as an example in which Hackman, ostensibly to satisfy his mistress's curiosity, relates the history of Chatterton, strongly arguing for the marvellous boy as the author of the entire Rowley oeuvre, while including much new, valuable material on the subject (eight unpublished Chatterton letters and a 'life'). The reviewer then praises 'our author' for his shrewd riposte to Walpole's famously 'harsh' censure on Chatterton, that 'all of the house of forgery are relations' (with the backhanded compliment to Chatterton that he did not, given his poverty, and facile hand, turn to forging bank notes). 'Hackman' rejoins that Walpole's *Otranto* and *Richard III* were both, themselves, forgeries, and the objects of Chatterton's emulation. The reviewer next commends Croft's clever self-reflexivity: 'with some amusing anecdotes this writer has interwoven so many horrid catastrophes (similar to [Hackman's]) of murders, execution, &c. . . .'[37]

5. Interiority and the novel

In reading Ireland's *Confessions*, we are confronted by wheels within wheels. In justifying his own fabrications, Ireland cites the work of Croft, a respectable forger, and associate of his father's. In reconstructing his childhood influences, Ireland singles out two other alleged inmates of the house of forgery, Percy and Walpole, whose example Croft has already mobilized, in advance, in defence of his own dubious practice. Ireland's highly mediated rhetoric may appear to be aimed at withdrawing the sting from the accusation of forgery, through the marshalling of sanctified precedents – Percy, Walpole, Chatterton, Croft – but its significance is even more far reaching, as becomes apparent once we situate it within Habermas's *mise en scène* of the conjugal family rehearsing the 'interiority' intimately linked to entrance into the literary public sphere. In so doing, two fundamental questions confront us: what is the nature of this new subjectivity and what relationship does it bear to the erasure of the boundary between illusion and reality, truth and fiction?

The answers take us to the uncanny literalization of Habermas's theoretical scenario. In the private space of the Ireland family Samuel reads aloud *Love and Madness*, a work that in itself comprised the two halves of Habermas's argument about the novel. Through Hackman it focusses on 'what was "human"', the possibility of 'self-knowledge' and 'empathy', and through the Chatterton material it provides a real-life example of the vicarious experience of rising in the social scale, of sharing the psychological glamour and gains of genius. 'Interiority', as Habermas speaks of it, acts as a form of power. In Bourdieu's terms, interiority conveys distinction, and with it cultural capital, transferable in a social marketplace. Samuel Ireland's response to the rising value of interiority (by which one rises) is to accumulate its external manifestations: the relics – the books and pictures – of past instances of genius, which is to say, of transformative interiority. But in endeavouring to nurture interiority within his son – the primal scene of reading aloud *Love and Madness* in the family circle, with its multiple affiliations to the Irelands – the son internalizes what is external in the father: interiority becomes more than the marks of distinction which procure entrance to an exclusive club, but an identity. William Henry lives out the life of Chatterton, thus reversing the trajectory of *Love and Madness*, from 'life to fiction' to 'from fiction to life'. The key opportunity the novel exploits is that in the eighteenth century there is now a permeable zone between fiction (where interiority and power are nurtured) and fact, where they might be realized. Part of the uncanniness of this literalization of Habermas's theory is that *Love and Madness* explicitly plays with that zone of permeability.

Love and Madness is a text in which the relationship between the real and the illusory, the authentic and the fabricated, the true and the forged, is both the occasion and the meaning of the work. Just as Horace Walpole had done with his 'found' *Otranto*, Croft's seeks to reinvigorate the shock of the real through his imposition. Unlike Chatterton or Macpherson, Croft does not forge the work of a supposed artist, but fabricates the letters of real people, so dissolving the boundary between the epistolary novel and 'fact'. In an early letter, Croft, writing as Hackman, introduces the theory of his 'true life novel' with reference to Defoe's *Robinson Crusoe*.

> That fertile genius improved upon his materials, and composed the celebrated story of Robinson Crusoe. The consequence was that Selkirk, who soon after made his appearance in print, was considered as a bastard of Crusoe, with which spurious offspring the press often teems. In De Foe, undoubtedly, this was not honest . . . I can easily conceive a writer making his own use of a known fact, and filling up the outlines which have been sketched by the bold and hasty hand of fate. A moral may be added, by such means, to a particular incident; characters may be placed in their just and proper lights; mankind may be amused (and amusements sometimes prevent crimes), or, if the story be criminal, mankind may be bettered, through the channel of their curiosity. But I would not be dishonest, like De Foe, nor would I pain the breast of a single individual connected with the story. (Croft 32–3)

The passage is ironically self-referential. It not only plays with the issue of legitimacy and the literary public sphere (in Selkirk becoming his own textual bastard) but also undercuts the very theory it advances, for Croft sets out to do what Hackman criticizes in Defoe: to so improve upon his sketchy real-life material as to produce an artefact capable of overturning the order of the real. Like Defoe, Croft 'dishonestly' makes his story more real than the truth, by turning his 'fertile genius upon it'. Moreover, Croft neither spares the numerous relatives of the victims, by rushing his sensationalized story into print nor does he provide a useful moral.

Or rather, he provides one, only to undercut it. Hackman advances a theory in which 'factions' are defended on the grounds that the writer should construct a cautionary tale, supplying the 'proper lights' omitted by the 'bold and hasty' hand of fate. In this way, 'amusements may prevent crimes'. Hackman then expatiates on what he means by a useful, '*criminal*' story: 'Faldini and Theresa might have been prevented from making any proselytes, *if they ever have made any*, by working up their most affecting story so as to take the edge off the dangerous example' (33 [my italics]). And of course they have, as the reader well knows: Hackman himself. Hackman's knowledge of the fatal couple comes from Jermingham's poem, based on the true story of Faldini and Theresa Meunier, who committed suicide with pistols to the head, in a direct prolepsis of Hackman's fate, in Lyons in the summer of 1770 (according to Voltaire, an act in turn based on the example of Auria and Paetus). Hackman's moral stands doubly confuted. Even as he 'works up' the Meuniers' 'affecting story', the reader knows that Hackman will become their most celebrated 'proselyte', as if contemplation and contamination were the same thing. Moreover, Hackman knows of the couple through an artful amusement, Jermingham's poem, which ought to have blunted the story's 'dangerous edge'. The irony is multi-layered: in real life the Meuniers copy a fiction, before they, in turn, are transformed into text, thus serving as an unconscious model for another real-life couple, Hackman and Ray, whose story has been fictionalized and thus rendered dangerous. Croft drives the lesson home by cramming the book with real-life variations of what Hackman was himself to suffer. In his letters, Hackman continuously arranges the raw material of daily tragedies – of doomed love affairs and suicides – into useful narratives, thus taking the 'edge' off their danger. If such stories truly had a prophylactic effect, their filter, the letter-writing Hackman, above all, should be safe. Instead he stands as living proof of the contagious glamour of 'true stories', no matter how swaddled with moral glosses, or how artfully arranged, a glamour cynically exploited by Croft, in his bid to sell books and establish his fame.

At this juncture it helps to recur back to what Habermas has to say about the novel: 'The relations between author, work, and public changed. They became intimate mutual relationships between privatized individuals who were psychologically interested in what was "human," in self-knowledge, and in empathy'. In line with what Habermas has to say about these relations, *Love and Madness* sets out to erase the boundaries of the illusory and the real – through the pretence of being the letters of real people, by actually including real letters by real people, by continually referring to real events, and by begging the question of the relationship between truth and fiction—in order, above all else, to evoke empathy (terror and pity) in the reader. Hackman's references to morality in fiction is not Croft providing himself with self-justifying camouflage, but an integral part of the larger project. At one point the scoffing Hackman asks whether he should 'pistol myself', just because he has read *Werther* (Croft 74). The point of this grimly ironic prolepsis is that fiction is more real than our commonsense apprehensions of the probable. The moral aligned with this point – if moral it be – is best summed up by the *Gentleman's Magazine*'s initial report of the catastrophe: 'This murder affords a melancholy proof that there is no act so contrary to reason that reasonable men will not commit when under the domination of their passions.'[38] The self-knowledge *Love and Madness* offers to the reader is that no insight into the self is capable of deflecting the fatal course of the passions. The reason Hackman's and Ray's case struck the readers of the *Gentleman's Magazine* with peculiar horror was because Hackman was one of them: by all accounts, a reasonable man of status, of place and education – in other words, the embodiment of the rational or, as Habermas might say, 'the human'. Even so, the numerous cautionary tales Hackman himself relates to his mistress – real-life stories couched in a moral light – proved useless: the self that drove Hackman on was, finally, unknowable, even to Hackman. Hackman's death is the final source of pathos for the story as it is only in his final moments, when all is lost and the end irrevocable, that Hackman abandons his prevarication, taking sufficient control of himself to die with discipline, that is to say, like a gentleman. Indeed, nothing became Hackman's life as much as his manner of leaving it. He travelled by cart to Tyburn; deported himself in a manly fashion; owned his guilt; prayed for fifteen minutes, before standing and dropping a handkerchief as a sign that he was ready for the drop, the hangman drawing the ire of many by deliberately botching the signal, as if wishing to catch Hackman unawares, when he was no longer composed and no longer the gentleman.

The extensive Chatterton section in *Love and Madness* has often been seen as extraneous to the whole. For instance, the only connection the *Gentleman's Magazine* can find is one of shared guilt. 'We are not surprised that the forger of these letters should endeavour to extenuate the forgeries of Chatterton.'[39] In fact, the link to Chatterton is fundamental. Croft locates the origin for his title in a poem of Dryden's, which identifies love with madness; but as the 'novel' unfolds, it is clear that madness is also a synonym for genius. Croft does not advance the view that all madness is genius, but he does suggest something like the converse. *Love and Madness* is in fact an important text in the genealogy of Romantic genius, partly because it was a significant intervention in the promotion of Chatterton as its modern archetype – precocious, reclusive, driven, misunderstood and prone to excess – and partly because it is one of the few texts that steps outside the discursive formulations of the aesthetic mainstream, of, for instance, William Duff and Alexander Gerard.[40] Rather than the theory of genius, Croft gives us genius 'novelized' and, as such, the inflections of the figure are different from either Duff's or Gerard's. Croft's Chatterton is actually closer to Edward Young's notions of the original genius, in not only being firmly allied against classical learning and art, as a genius child of nature, but in being open to his daemon, to – as Young puts it – the 'stranger' within.[41] As Croft's alter ego, Hackman is split between madness as genius and madness as love. In comparison with the letters of Ray – few and perfunctory – Hackman's are a cascade of self-invention and self-fabulation, as he indefatigably gathers together, and expatiates on, prolepses of his own fate. Hackman in the end is a genius manqué, for a reason Croft discloses through his version of Chatterton, who he presents not as licentious but as chaste, whereas Hackman squanders his madness on sexual love. What Croft offers the reader is the view that genius, like sexual passion, is a fatality.

Inflecting what Habermas has to say about the private sphere with Bordieu's concept of cultural capital will help us understand why this view was so appealing to Croft's readership. As we saw, for Habermas, the Bourgeois private sphere bears a close, dynamic relationship to the public; and one way of understanding this is that the subjectivity the bourgeoisie endlessly rehearsed – through the medium of letters – was a means of raising cultural capital. Habermas's 'empathy' was thus a zone of crisis. Empathy promised the magic assimilation of the cultural value inhering within the subjectivity represented before the reader. Attending to the representation of genius, to, say, the life of Chatterton, promised cultural profit, but at the price of 'fatality', of opening one's door to the stranger within. The risk one ran was that one's inner self – the self unknowable – was, like Hackman's, flawed. 'Genius' may be the means of rising in the literary public sphere, as in Chatterton's rapid, posthumus assent, but the implicit crossing of social boundaries mobilized intense anxieties. Croft's erasure of the boundaries between the fictive and the real attested to the contagious power of the 'fictive', where by fictive I mean stories (regardless of provenance) transformed into print. Croft attempts to contain its threat by bringing Hackman back within his proper sphere, by having him end as he begins, a Christian gentleman. But as with Hackman's life of Chatterton, this was not enough to contain the dangerous glamour of example. In one of the British Library's editions of *Love and Madness* someone has pasted in newspaper clippings of would-be Hackmans following his desperate expedient in their bids for fame, by shooting their lovers and themselves.

What, then, is the nature of this new subjectivity of the mid-eighteenth-century novel? According to the narrow evidence of Croft's 'faction', and

William Henry Ireland's internalization of it, it is the self-validating nature of genius. Genius dissolves customary boundaries, as between the real and the fictive (the example of Croft); the authentic and the forged (Chatterton as well as Croft); the ordinary and the extreme (Hackman and Chatterton). By the same token, it dissolves the boundaries circumscribing an identity built on rank, in favour of another, built on 'literary character'. If assiduous reading, as a means of raising cultural capital, is the equivalent of dripping savings into a bank account, genius is the equivalent of the lottery. Once won, everything changes, and old rules no longer apply.

Through the persona of Hackman Croft wonders over the story of the servant's love affair which finds its way into the pages of *The Spectator*; of how, through sheer happenstance, two very ordinary people – a footman and his below-stairs sweetheart – have been transmogrified into famous individuals (Croft 77). Croft worries over a new fact of modern print culture: one can become famous for nothing. Inured as we are to daily examples of this we can easily overlook the modern feel of the phenomenon during the eighteenth century. Another aspect of this expanding print culture was that identity had become a commodity. If it was printable, it was marketable. When Habermas considers the relationship between the novel and the private/public sphere, he imagines a situation in which the reader rehearses and strengthens his interiority via psychologically complex characters made identifiable-with through new, literary techniques of realism. But what, we might ask, is this 'interiority'? At its simplest, it is a mark of difference between the bourgeoisie and the aristocracy, a token of the privacy the former defend through an emergent public sphere. At its most complex, it is an ideological structure that conditions the personality of individuals. From Bourdieu's point of view, it is a mark of distinction translatable into cultural capital. From a print culture perspective, it is a marketable identity, a narrative. Croft confers genius upon his construction of Hackman because it is the highest status mark of interiority, one conforming to the bourgeois ideology of the private subject. At the same time Croft shrouds Hackman with the glamour of print, of life transformed into 'fiction', as a promise/threat to the reader that she, too, is potentially newsworthy, or famous. One could say that Habermas's own scenario of the empathetic reader developing her interiority through novelistic projection is itself caught up within the bourgeois ideology of the subject. Regarded more dispassionately, one might characterize the reading process as a desire for the glamour – the distinction and value – of the identity a novel celebrates; and, for this process, a facsimile of depth does just as well as the real thing.[42] What Croft may be said to have supplied to his readers was just such a facsimile, albeit a strangely self-reflexive one.

I earlier asked two questions: what was the nature of the new subjectivity to which Habermas refers and what relationship does it bear to the erasure of the boundary between the real and the fictive? My answer was that this subjectivity is linked to the emerging cult of original genius, which we might characterize, in Bourdieu's terms, as a sign for the radical fluidity of cultural capital (Moretti's 'mobility').[43] Habermas dwells upon the slow accumulation of cultural capital, the disciplined cultivation of interiority gained through the reading of fiction; but Croft exploits the radical fluidity of cultural capital when exemplified through the marketable real, which is to say, of fame as a print culture commodity.

6. Ireland's Romantic identity

Judging from his confessions, and from what we know of his life, William Henry Ireland internalized fully the subjectivity represented in Croft's *Love and Madness*. When he tells us that on his visit to Bristol, in the aftermath of his exposure, he wept unfeigned tears of sympathy for Chatterton, we can believe him, for Chatterton (or, rather, the cultural construction of Chatterton) is Ireland's own self-image. So strong was this identification that, once freed from his father's house, he began to live out the emerging myth of Romantic – Chattertonian – genius, taking up with unrespectable women, growing his hair long, and rambling about the country in unconventional clothes. Ireland constructs himself as a Chattertonian genius retrospectively, in his 1805 *Confessions*; but that this was indeed how he saw himself, in the middle of his forgeries, is attested to by this letter from 1796, written from near Bristol, to Byng, one of his father's intermediaries:

> At length my Dear Sir I think I have a situation which is at once perfectly retired as well as Romantick – I am within a mile of the finest spot in the kingdom which overlooks all the Bristol channel the sea and the welsh mountains. It is within 6 miles of the ferry which crosses the river Severn to Chepstow... I went to Chatterton's sister and made enquiries about that unhappy young man I learned but little more than I had already heard and read in Love and Madness I also saw the chests in which he is said to have found the parchments I firmly believe he did find some papers containing in prose & verse stories which he afterwards embellished & work'd up into poetry Be it as it may he was a wonderful young man.[44]

In many other respects, Ireland's identity was, indeed, 'Romantick'. For example, consider the following statement with its seamless intertwining of fashion and politics (Ireland writes to his father Samuel in the guise of the gentleman owner of the manuscripts):

> Feb 23 1795: I saw my young friend yesterday morning we spoke on the subject of the new [taxes]. I was surprised by what he said to find you a friend to [Ministry] when by what he has always told me I thought you of the Minority. You must allow that all who contribute their guineas for powder give money for the support of the war as I have never been a friend

> to it in any one instance neither will I in this and I do no [?] on my Honour my hair is now combed to its real colour and will remain hanging loosely on my shoulders 'that ladys may now perfume it with their balmy kisses'. Besides you cannot be an enemy to the manner in which our Willy wore his hair let me I beseech you see your son with flowing locks it is not only Manly but showing yourself averse to blood shed I should not even regret to see you yourself out of powder. But however your son I should lay a stress on as he also seems to wish it.[45]

Long, 'natural' hair was both a fashion statement and a protest against Pitt's tax on hair powder, considered by many as a war measures bill.

In this note written by his mother we glimpse William's self-fashioning as a Romantic genius:

> to quiet (as he may think) the public mind, he has invented some story that will involve the mystery still deeper, & my opinion is strengthened by a determined resolution he has formed to quit the kingdom immediately, though he says that of late he has been inspired with all the furor of a Divine Poet. Such is the pitiable situation in which we are likely to be left, nor does he seem to feel a grain of remorse in the occasion, but has deserted his office (for a genius, like his, he says cannot condescend to sit at a Desk) and does nothing but lounge about the streets and drive about either on Horseback, or in a curracle with a groom after him like a man of the first fashion. The curracle & horses he told us, about 3 weeks since, cost 100 guineas and were given him by the Gent. But we find they are to cost 70, *50* of which has been paid by him, no other gent. having had any thing to do in the business.[46]

However, it is through the letters William writes to his father posing as the mysterious gentleman, that we gain our deepest insights into Ireland's self-fashioned Romantic character, the longest of which is worth considering in detail:

> July 25 1795
>
> Dear Sir,
> For some time back it has been my wish to give you a letter unknown to your son. In doing this I assure you I break my promise & therefore must beg nay insist on the strictest secrecy from you and as his father I think it but right that you should know/by what he often tells me is general thought of him. The contents I am conscious of this letter will not a little astonish you & I myself must equally confess myself lost in wonder. He tells me he is in general look'd upon as a young man that scarce knows how to write a good letter. You yourself shall be the judge by what follows –

In the very act of imposing upon his father Ireland vindicates himself as someone capable of writing a good letter – good enough, at least, to fool Samuel.

> I have now before me part of a Play written by your son which for stile and greatness of thought is equal to any one of Shakespeare's let me intreat you Dear Sir not to smile for on my honour it is most true. He has chosen the subject of Wm the Conqueror & tells me he intends writing a series of Plays to make up with — Shakespeare's a complete history of the kings of England. He wishes it to remain unknown therefore I again rely on your honour in this affair

In informing Samuel that he was in the process of writing a Shakespearean history cycle William could hardly have contrived a stronger hint that he was himself the author of the manuscripts, especially *Vortigern* and *Henry II*. The 'gentleman' then explains himself, riddling in a fashion that would have been easy to catch, had Samuel the least faith in the abilities of his dim-witted son:

> It must appear strange why I should have taken so particular a liking to him His extraordinary talents would make any one partial – I often talk with him never before found one even of triple his age that knows as much of human nature & [I?] not think this flattery for again vouch to the truth of my assertion No Man but your Son ever wrote like Shakespeare. This is bold I confess but it is true he often says he knows learning will not make a Poet neither will he look to any author he often has told me his blood boils a little when he is held a silly young man but still he is determined to remain a secret.

Ireland revenges himself upon his negligent father by boldly confessing his forgeries, his underlining making the riddling obvious. Ireland's motivation nevertheless extends beyond mere paternal ridicule: it also reveals the extent to which he has identified himself with Romantic genius. He represents himself as precocious (outdoing those triple his age), a deep student of human nature, and as a poet born rather than made. He is a product of nature, not learning (a view of genius most notably argued by Edward Young). In complete contradiction of the facts of the case (as Ireland afterwards admitted, *Vortigern* was an open-book pastiche of the Bard's works) Ireland reports himself as not looking to any authors when he composes: but then, at this point in his letter, he relates the inner facts of his mythic identification with Chatterton, that he can ape Shakespeare, thus strengthening, not undermining, his belief in his genius (and therefore originality). That his transcendent qualities are patronizingly dismissed boils his blood as his thoughts move from his inner identity to his family treatment. To convince the disbelieving father, the 'Gentleman' encloses a sample of William's writing, in secret:

> I assure you but you may judge of the stile and grandeur of thought then see if it is not close on the heels of Shakespeare. It was originally composed in my room & in the writing it he made but three blurs. He wished to make alterations but I begged to have it from the rough copy which is just as you find it. He never comes in to me but instantly notes down every thing that has struck him in his walk I have asked frequently where he can get such thoughts all the answer he makes is this 'I borrow them from nature'. I also enquire why he wished to be secret to which he says 'I desire to be thought by the world but little'. Let me beg you to examine him closely you will find what I advance is but the truth.

The passage is extraordinary in that it does not actually refer to the virtues of the actual writing but with great compression bundles together the major symptoms of Romantic genius: William's writing was spontaneous, with 'but three blurs', the rough copy being perfectly finished (a feat to rival the later Keats); he is preternaturally observant, an attribute Ireland may have internalized from Johnson's *Life of Savage*, which makes the same claim; he 'borrows from nature' (wild, rather than 'methodiz'd'); and, like Wordsworth's true disciple, he values poetry for its own sake, rather than for the distinction it brings (the burden of the *Letter to Mathetes* [*SP*: 115]) wishing the world to think of him 'but little' (an outrageous fib).

> He likewise very often says his mind loaths the confined dingdong study of the law & yet says he will remain quiet till a proper opportunity. He has a large ledger in which as I may say he chronicles every thing that strikes him from thence he forms his speeches. He told me he took the inclosed from walking alone in Westminster Abbey – Mr. I – upon my honour & soul I would not scruple giving £2000 a year to have a son with such extraordinary faculties. If at 20 he can write so what will he do hereafter. The more I see him the more I am amazed – if your son is not a second Shakespeare I am not a man. Keep this to yourself do not even mention it to any soul living only [?] what I have told you I shall not give you the Inventory now as it would very strange to him but will make him the bearer as usual.
>
> I remain dear sir, yours most sincerely & truly WH
>
> Put a seal upon your lips to all that has past but remember these words: Your son is brother in genius to Shakspeare [obscured by seal] is the only man that ever walked with him hand in hand.[47]

The letter quibbles outrageously to the very end. '[I]f your son is not a second Shakespeare I am not a man': which is indeed true, the mysterious gentleman being first fictitious and, second, as William, not yet twenty-one. The '20' is decisive proof that William Henry was born in 1775, not 1777 as he afterwards claimed, as he could hardly expect to fool his own father by lying about his age: but the quibble nevertheless reveals how hard he clung to his sense of Chattertonian precocity. The letter also has clever touches, such as William's double voicing, so that as the Gentleman he produces his own free indirect speech ('dingdong study of the law'). It seems astonishing that Samuel did not cotton on to his son's games, especially when the mysterious gentleman's initials happened to be his son's (WH): but then William was extremely clever at playing upon his father's weaknesses. Thus, he closes with a reference to the Gentleman's inventory of remaining Shakespeare treasures, the mere mention of which seems to have frozen Samuel's critical faculties with greed. In much the same manner Ireland provides an inflated estimate of his value as a genius: £2000 per year.

Ireland's fair-minded critics have always granted that the forgeries showed great ingenuity. Still, Samuel's gullibility has frequently posed a problem. Jeffrey Kahan (1998) has argued that Samuel Ireland knew full well what was going on, but cynically connived in his son's activities, for fame and profit. Kahan's argument turns on interpretation rather than new evidence. Reviewing the same body of material Schoenbaum concluded that Samuel did indeed have his suspicions, especially after the affair of John Heminges's signature, when William, not knowing Heminges's signature was extant, produced a specimen only to have it controverted by Albany Wallis, who happened to have recently acquired a document with Heminges's autograph. With great expedition William scurried back to his chambers, on the pretext of visiting the Gentleman, and produced a new document and signature having memorized the authentic one in Wallis's possession. The Gentleman's explanation for the confusion was that there were actually two John Heminges at the time (known as 'Tall' and 'Short' Heminges), hence the disparity. The similarity of the new signature to Wallis's and the speed of its procurement stifled doubts, although Schoenbaum speculates that Samuel may well have glimpsed the truth, but preferred not to know.[48]

Samuel Ireland did commit doubts to paper, including his panic over the Heminges signature.[49] But that is also the problem the case poses for sceptics. Samuel Ireland appears to have documented the affair from its very beginning, systematically cataloguing information relative to it under three main heads, documents now in the possession of the British Library: letters, thoughts and speculations by, of, from or to himself, William and Mrs. Freeman; all transactions relative to the negotiations with Sheridan for the production of *Vortigern*; and press reports either of the papers or the production of *Vortigern*. As regards William's authorship of the papers the first volume minutely records the bewilderment and disbelief of both Samuel Ireland and Mrs. Freeman. If Samuel did know, he was playing a very deep game in which he, too, was fabricating letters full of synthetic grief, fury and befuddlement in order to bamboozle futurity.

However, the role of William's sisters is not so clear cut – at any rate, is more shadowy – and there is 'A Prologue penned by my Mother for my Play of Vortigern'. There are at least two extant versions, one in the Huntingdon Library and the other in Firstone Library at Princeton. The first ends at an ambiguous moment where it is unclear whether the new work that Mrs. Freeman celebrates is the Bard's or the work of a 'youth' that will do him credit. The Princeton version adds several verses, where the ambiguity appears to be resolved, in that Mrs. Freeman asks the audience to nurture a new talent (implicitly, William Henry):

> In early Spring, the blossom fair to sight,
> If kindly shelter'd from a nipping blight,
> Will in due season, fruit spontanous yield,
> And a rich harvest crown the plent'ous field.
> But if no fost'ring hand, with tender care,
> 'Gainst the rude blast, a Covert safe prepare,
> The blossom fades, the plant untimely dies,
> Nor to maturity will ever rise.

Did Mrs. Freeman know? Is she the 'fost'ring hand'?[50] It is impossible to say. While complicity in the secret seems the readiest solution to Mrs. Freeman's prologue, it leaves one with the problem of her letters, which express (if a lie) a very accomplished and extensive sense of bewilderment. What one can conclude is that W. H. Ireland imbibed his bardolatry from both parents, not just one, and that he was thoroughly steeped in the belief in the transcendent, creative powers of natural genius, and that, if he drew his antiquarian tastes from his father, his mother provided his pattern for poetic identity. While Samuel stood for the cash nexus underlying the rising trade in books – new and old – Mrs. Freeman represented the creative impulse that defied, not just pedantic rules, but social decorum (in her own case, as an Aristocratic mistress and female poet, who, presumably, lost all for love).[51]

When I earlier said that W. H. Ireland's identity was Romantic, in a precise sense, I meant that his self-fashioning typified a certain strain within 1790s' youth culture. To use Jerome McGann's influential terms, Ireland embodied the Romantic ideology. For Karl Marx, ideology acted like a camera obscura, in that it projected an image of the world in which the relationship between abstract explanation and material reality were turned upside down. The cult of original genius was central to the Romantic ideology, for it advanced an illusion (the spontaneous creation of an ideal art by the isolated poet) that inverted the facts of art (that it is in reality the product of collaborative labour). W. H. Ireland's great talent was his ability to live out, and so literalize, the ideological contradictions inhering within the age of personality. In terms of the 'dance' of celebrity, articulated by Briggs, Ireland blundered, for the dance requires that contradictions should be glossed not exposed.

7. Ireland's later career

In forging Rowley, Chatterton hurt no one: in passing as Shakespeare, Ireland grievously wounded all those with an ideological investment in bardolatry. As a consequence W. H. Ireland was never forgiven for his forgeries. Years later, James Boaden, himself badly caught out by them, explained why: 'You must be aware, sir, of the enormous crime you committed against the divinity of Shakespeare. Why, the act, sir, was nothing short of sacrilege; it was precisely the same thing as taking the holy chalice from the altar; and *******therein!'.[52] Through his forgeries, Ireland parodied the divinity of genius, on which the Romantic ideology rested, and in so doing he brought the porous boundary that separates the real from the fake in an age of mechanical print production uncomfortably close to the surface. A literary character was not sustainable on such a basis.

It required an oppositional figure, like Cobbett, to cut through the cant. In his obituary of Ireland, Cobbett comments on the consequences of the publication of the *Authentic Account*:

> Instantly the base wretches, from every quarter, poured in upon him; instead of admiring his ingenuity, and apologising, as well as they could, for their own folly, in having been Shakespeare-mad, they pitched upon him, like tigers, called him a forger, called him an impostor, and almost hunted him from the face of the earth.

Samuel Ireland joined the pack, disowned his son, cancelled William Henry's articles with the attorney, and drove him from his house to a mean hovel in Swallow Street, where he lived for ten days on five pounds of potatoes. Cobbett's analysis is sharply political:

> With regard to Mr. Ireland, let these facts be borne in mind; that he was no forger, no impostor, according to the usual meaning of those words; that he had a perfect right to put forth the publications he put forth; that there was nothing illegal and nothing immoral in any of his proceedings as to this matter; that Doctors Warton and Parr were deemed the two most learned men in the Kingdom; that they declared and certified that it was their conviction that no human being could write those manuscripts but Shakespeare; that when Mr Ireland was discovered to be the real author, the whole band of literary ruffians fell upon him, and

> would have destroyed him, if they had been able, with as little remorse as men destroy a mad dog . . .

Ireland's subsequent literary career was blighted, with Ireland and his family sentenced to a life of poverty. Writing like a radicalized Bourdieu, Cobbett calls for a public collection to support Ireland's widow and children. Such a collection

> will serve the purpose of marking our indignation at the conduct of the literary ruffians who were his oppressors, and who are real impostors, living in luxury, generally on taxes raised from the sweat of the people; sometimes off the fruit of the delusions which they practice on that credulity, which ascribes learning, and piety, and fitness to guide, to all those who have the impudence to put forward pretensions, and to so assume the style of "learned men".[53]

It is hard to imagine a more direct puncturing of the Romantic 'aesthetic' (in Bourdieu's sense) or ideology (in McGann's).

As a result of the *Authentic Account* Ireland found himself in an anomalous position. As his father presciently warned, 'let your talent be what it may – who do you think will ever sanction you, or associate with you after shewing an ability for such gross and deliberate impositions on the public through the medium of your own father?'[54] Having married Alice Crudge on 4 June 1796, in Clerkenwell Church[55] (apparently as unprepossessing a bride as her name suggests) and living off what little dowry she had, Ireland found himself in dire straits. Having quit the 'dingdong' of the law, either voluntarily or cut off by his father, he had little choice but to continue his career as a literary genius. With his 'character' now notorious he had no option but to write – usually anonymously – which he did with extraordinary industry for the next thirty-five years.

Ireland's position was marginal in every sense of the word. Writing anonymously he was unable to build a career or establish a name: he was always in the shadows, starting anew. Ireland's most revelatory comments usually occur in the persona of someone else, such as the mysterious gentleman writing to Samuel, as we earlier saw, or as the pseudonymous authors of his own works, which at some point or other find an opportunity of reviewing, sympathetically, the Ireland affair. In one such anonymous note, he writes of himself, that in

> respect to the merits of this writer, whose works are very numerous, it would be unfair to have recourse to the reviewers; the stigma of having deceived the public uniformly follows his career, and, be his efforts what they may, the lash of severest criticism at all times pursues him. It is said, however, that many productions from his pen have appeared without

> any signature, which have been much commended: it is therefore to be regretted that this gentleman does not avow to the world all he has written, that they may be fully enabled to appreciate the extent of his literary acquirements. (Ireland, *Scribbleomania* 1815: 122)

Caught between no-name and notoriety, he starved. His surviving letters are filled with schemes and impositions for money, or dodges for escaping his creditors. He was not always successful as the poems written from York gaol testify – yet another instance of Ireland attempting to translate the hardships of life into profitable art. But there was also a silver lining, of a sort: as an anonymous author, with no centred, public identity, he could shift styles and genres at will. With a hungry nose cocked to the shifting winds of fashion he became the great chameleon author of the age, changing his spots as opportunity dictated.[56]

Ireland's circumstances led to a splitting between his public and private selves. The public self was paradoxically private. With the ability to appear in print under his own name limited, his public face was restricted to non-print media, such as letters. His private self was in turn public, insofar as it was the material for his anonymous publications. Ireland had a name for each of these personae: the 'gentleman' and the 'bastard'.

It seems that Ireland's notoriety provided him with a raffish cachet, one savoured by the aristocracy. One of the bizarre aspects of reading his now scattered literary remains is that one passes from letters in which Ireland is doing his best to beg, borrow or wheedle relatively small sums of money from friends, acquaintances and strangers, to evidence of impressive hobnobbing, from the Duke of Devonshire up to, and including, the Royal family. For example, the Huntingdon library has a copy of *Frogmore Fete*, a masque written to commemorate a garden party held by George III in 1802. The work was commissioned by Princess Elizabeth and finished around 1805, although the Huntingdon's text is a copy made by Ireland (the internal evidence suggests 1815 or later), the original having gone missing after being lent to some Whig grandees, careless, as ever. Ireland was helped to the commission by Sir Lumley St. George Skeffington, for whose play, *The World of Honour*, Ireland had written the prologue and epilogue, the latter containing the following heartfelt lines of sublime bathos: 'Why was I Poet born? Why Author, Actor?/ Why was I not created a Cornfactor?'.[57]

The manuscript contains Ireland's account of the affair. If he was a gentleman in public, he was a bastard in private, for the account is full of Ireland's spleen at the 'Brunswicks', for their low, broad taste. He characterizes the 'Quelphs' as German buffoons, never missing the opportunity of using a dismissive, Teutonic, patronymic. He glances aside at a 'Royal toad eater' and recounts how he returned his measly fee of £5 for *Frogmore Fete* to the richest oafs in the kingdom, standing on his pride as a gentleman, though starving.

In another letter to a noble lord Ireland adopts a more submissive attitude, as he supplicates for 'the procurement of any situation which would ensure myself my wife and child the certainty of existence':

> My lord
> An introduction to your lordships notice which took place some years since when my name created a degree of interest in the literary world would not have entitled me to intrude on your time in the present instance but a full reliance on your lordships urbanity coupled with the statement I shall make.

Ireland than rehearses his excuses: he was young, the fabrications were not premeditated, 'popular praise' inspired his vanity, turning the head of 'one so youthful'. He now 'bitterly' repents the 'criminality' of his actions. He suffers the world's 'odium' and 'frequent distress', hardships his 'youthful education' left him unprepared for:

> From the age of 19 I became an alien to my father's house and it was only upon a death-bed that we became friends, in short my Lord for the last ten years of my existence my own indefatigable labours have alone supported me and though frequently destroyed indeed; I have never I trust in conduct on external appearances belied the gentleman.

As a further recommendation he says that he has heard from friends that the Prince of Wales 'has frequently spoken of me in terms which I but little merit'. Ireland does not ask for much: 'my desires are humble for my spirit is broken . . . ' In seeking patronage, Ireland dusts down the language of supplication to which Dr. Johnson had been so averse. That Ireland is not entirely sincere in his professions as a 'gentleman' is evident from the '19', which is written over a blotted-out '21': even in extremis, Ireland holds to the fib of his precocity.[58]

If Ireland adopted the persona of the gentleman, to secure patronage, internally he was still the *Wunderkind* lauded as a second Shakespeare. In 1812 he produced one of his most heartfelt poems: *Neglected Genius: A Poem, Ilustrating the Untimely and Unfortunate Fate of Many British Poets; from the Period of Henry the Eighth to the Aera of the Unfortunate Chatterton. Containing Imitations of Their Different Styles, &C, &C.*. Published under his own name, he keeps within gentlemanly proprieties as he laments the hard lot of Britain's neglected geniuses, paying homage to them through a series of imitations in their own styles, while upbraiding patrons for not doing better. He thus begins with a dedication to his own patron, the Most Noble William Spencer Cavendish, Duke of Devonshire, Marquis of Hartington, as an exception to the skinflints that follow. Ireland moderates his sycophancy by complimenting his patron's father, rather than the son, in a 'Monody' upon his death. The late Duke is praised for his 'innate worth' rather than nobility, his Whig principles, his defence of freedom and patriotism, and his support for neglected genius: at which point, with honour satisfied, Ireland extols the present Duke as just such another.

Ireland's subject is the 'shameful neglect which the Sons of Genius have experienced, not only in England, but in distant climes' which 'has been the disgrace of every age and country' (1812: xvii). He writes his homage so 'that the tear of pity should flow, and a sentiment of indignation animate the reader's breast', thus honouring 'the departed children of Genius', while affording 'a pleasing though melancholy recompense for the labours of a sorrowing bard' (xxiv). Ireland can only ask for sentiment because he spends the first part of his preface lambasting the mean-minded materialism of the age (centred in the pelf-mad Bristol that oppressed Chatterton) while drawing a distinction between money-grubbing merchants and a distracted populace, on one side, and unworldly poets, on the other, who care about wealth solely as a means to their art: so he can hardly ask for money, directly. Apart from the 'narrow principles' of the majority, the 'children of Fancy' suffer 'the malign impulse of envy, that rankles in the souls of *would-be wits*, on beholding another being endowed with intellectual properties, never to be attained by themselves' (xxii). Ireland guns for the rich, titled and/or learned, who 'cannot brook the lofty independence of Genius': 'the enlightened spirit' is thus left 'an isolated wanderer on the turbulent ocean of this world, with genius and fancy its sole inheritance' (xxii).

Beneath his sycophancy, Ireland's, like Wordsworth's, is a levelling muse, in which genius trumps rank, and bastards gentlemen. Ireland's list of neglected geniuses includes Spenser, Milton, Otway, Butler, Dryden, Hammond, Goldsmith, Savage, Chatterton. It is the last two who really concern him, as they shadow his identity. The collection begins with a series in 'imitation of the Rowleian style of poetry' produced by 'the youth divine', which Ireland then 'translates' into the 'modern style of versification'. He follows that with 'The Poet's Entry into Bristol', a record of Ireland's homage to Chatterton's departed shade, apparently based on his trip of 1796, following the *Vortigern* disaster. 'Elegiac Stanzas to the Memory of Thomas Chatterton' are conventional in language and form but Keatsian in subject matter, featuring melancholy, urns, nightingales, groves and untimely death.

But it is in the next, untitled poem, in which the shades of 'bastard Savage' and Chatterton hail the poet that we discover a deeper clue as to Ireland's hidden subjectivity. Ireland knows of Savage, partly through *Love and Madness* but mainly through Johnson's *Life*. Savage was the illegitimate son of Lady Macclesfield. Estranged from her husband, Lady Macclesfield had a clandestine affair with Richard Savage, the fourth Earl Rivers, bearing him two children, before securing a divorce from her husband, in 1698, whereupon she married a Colonel Henry Brett. Although Earl Rivers's natural son, Savage would still have inherited the Macclesfield name and fortune. His mother's divorce – a stroke of a pen – thus rendered him doubly a bastard, as he was fond of saying.

Or so he said. Lady Macclesfield had put both children out to nurse, where, she told Colonel Brett, they died. Savage claimed, on the contrary, that he lived. Whether he did, or whether he was a child of one of the wet nurses, or someone else mixed up in the affair, is still an open question.[59] What does seem clear is that Savage passionately believed that he was – passionate enough, at least, to convince Johnson – while Mrs. Brett, with equal conviction, believed he was not. From her perspective, he was a blackmailing stalker, arising from who knows where, who heartlessly played upon her secret shame, publicizing it the length and breadth of the kingdom, by taking the name of her lover and writing about it. She did everything in her power to silence him, from selling him off to America as an indentured servant to claiming he had entered her house bent on murder (whereas Savage protested he was only seeking to throw himself into the arms of his dear 'Mama', having discovered her door was open in his nightly ramble past her window). With even more address, Savage stymied her every move, placing her in check with an escalating press campaign in which he dramatized her unnaturalness as a mother, a campaign reaching a peak with 'The Bastard', Savage's signature poem. Mrs. Brett's appeal to the Queen not to pardon her 'son' when he was convicted of the murder of James Sinclair in a tavern brawl, and set to swing, was her last move in an endgame comprehensively won by Savage.

With 'The Bastard' and his pardon Savage had become a celebrity, in the precise terms articulated by Briggs: he lived out the contradictions of an emerging print culture in the form of a precarious social dance with his audience, documented through his poetry, the most fashionable, potent and appropriate medium of the day. On the one side he was doubly a gentleman, missing a fortune and a title through an untimely stroke of the pen while being the natural son of yet another aristocrat; on the other, he was a bastard – in fact, 'The Bastard' – with no money, no lineage, no status, other than what he gained through his pen, which he used, obsessively, to promote himself and his life story. He claimed a double prerogative: to act like a gentleman (no more so than when he ran his man through as a roistering 'blood', as his 'father', Earl Rivers, had himself done) and as a licensed poet, a genius bound by different rules and a different clock.

One could be a gentleman and a genius, but vice versa posed problems. Savage maintained the balance, until a misstep threw him off the high wire. Slaying Sinclair made rather than undid Savage as he played the part of the gentleman to perfection. Savage could have taken refuge behind the one companion who had started the brawl, or the other, who, it seems, had broken his sword, and was in immanent danger of being skewered by Sinclair, and who, therefore, in law, could be defended in the manner Savage adopted, of skewering Sinclair first. Savage did not play the poltroon, but stepped forward as the ranking brawler to lead the case, acting as his own counsel, pleading self-defence in a speech of an hour's duration, which won the admiration of all present – including the quality crowding the court room – except for the notoriously irascible Judge Page, presiding, who was simply irritated by Savage's gentlemanly airs: 'Gentlemen of the Jury, you are to consider, that Mr. Savage is a very great man, a much greater Man than you or I, Gentlemen of the Jury . . .'. Savage has finer clothes and more money; 'but , Gentlemen of the Jury, it is not a very hard Case . . . that Mr. Savage should therefore *kill* you or me, Gentlemen of the Jury'. As Richard Holmes argues, 'shorn of its sly repetitions' the speech goes to the heart of the case and the basis of Savage's defence: 'social privilege'.[60] The jury straight away convicted.

Savage may have had a fool for a client, in the courtroom, but in the larger game he won by establishing his bona fides as a gentleman. He thus made himself pardonable, once Lady's Macclesfield's influence was countered, and pardoned he was. With Savage's celebrity at its zenith, and now adopting 'rougher measures'[61] with his 'mother' – meaning a step up in his press campaign – Lord Tyrconnel, Mrs. Brett's nephew, capitulated, offering Savage a substantial pension of £200 per annum, whether on the basis of extortion, Savage's genius, or kinship, it is hard, exactly, to say. But such ambiguity is the material point. Soon after securing his pension Savage offered Tyrconnel a fulsome tribute, as his patron, in the dedication to his masterpiece, the weirdly introspective *The Wanderer*. As Johnson explains,

> This was the Golden Part of Mr. Savage's Life; and for some Time he had no Reason to complain of Fortune; his Appearance was splendid, his Expences large, and his Acquaintance extensive . . . To admire Mr Savage was a Proof of Discernment, and to be acquainted with him was a title to poetical Reputation. His presence was sufficient to make any Place of Publick Entertainment popular; and his Approbation and Example constituted the Fashion.[62]

Buoyed by his status as a celebrity poet, Savage turned on his patron, assuming outrageous licence. He treated Tyrconnel's domestic establishment as his own, bringing his motley entourage home from the tavern, whenever he pleased, ordering up Tyrconnel's best wine, while his companions, including, it seems, prostitutes, performed 'lewd frolics'. But it was the public biting of the hand that fed him – through various printed insults – that brought about his downfall, with an exasperated Tyrconnel terminating his pension.

Penniless, and now ragged, Savage was no longer the gentleman writer, just a poet: his smart acquaintance dropped him, his new companions being, like the young Johnson, other social desperadoes intent on scraping together enough cultural capital to set them on their feet, as viable hacks. It was from the experience of this period that Johnson drew the iconic picture of the two cash-strapped, threadbare poets haunting the newly fashionable

West-end squares, in their rambles by night, outsiders looking in, wanting. If Savage was formerly the Bastard, he was now the Wanderer, himself becoming the subject of his strangely introspective, visionary poem, vouchsafing canons of morality and virtue the rich were too heedless to acknowledge, thus becoming – in the process of Johnson's *Life* – 'an archetype of the Romantic outsider'.[63]

For Ireland, Johnson's portrayal of Savage formed the very type of the 'neglected genius'. It

> has but too frequently become manifest, that, owing to some momentary and unrestrained expression of contempt, the poet has been precipitated from the sumptuous mansion of an affluent patron, to the miserable garret of penury and neglect: still the inherent fire of genius has enabled the sufferer not only to support this transition, but also inspired him with energies to struggle against the tide of adverse fortune... (1812: xx–xxi)

In the process the poet forms truths too capacious for 'the narrow principles of the community at large' (1812: xxi). Ireland does not mention Savage by name. Any struggling genius would get the reference.

If Savage was confused about whether he deserved a pension, or patronage, because of his birth or his abilities, Ireland and the Romantics were not. He deserved it because he was a genius. The 'bastard', in this respect, is an individual stripped of all family ties, all vestiges of rank and status, save those created through the virtue of his genius. In *Rhapsodies*, of 1803, Ireland sets out the Bastard's dialectic in a series of three poems.

'The Bastard', the first in the series, states the thesis, echoing Edmund's lines from *Lear*. The speaker extols the bastard's greater vigour because begot in heat rather than conceived betwixt 'nod and waking', like his legitimate sibling: 'Thou bold imagination doubly hot, / Because in passion's two-fold blaze begot' ('The Bastard', ll. 15–16). It is also a reworking of Savage's 'The Bastard': 'No sickly fruit of a faint compliance he; / He stampt in nature's mint of extasy!' (Savage, 'The Bastard', ll. 5–6). Ireland also echoes Savage's theme of energetic self-creation:

> More proud to own thyself a Bastard free,
> Than heir begot of lineal progeny,
> O! may thy tale, conceiv'd in freedom's mind,
> Protection in each free-born bosom find!
> May Bastards, tho' bereft of friend and name,
> Feel in their breast eternal thirst of fame!
> May they with glorious emulation burn!
> And may the wreath in death adorn their urn!
> May they thro' life astound weak mortals gaze!
> May they fell after-ages with amaze!
> And may their memories wear the lasting bays! (Ireland 1803: 62, ll. 21–31)

'The Bastard's Complaint' forms the antithesis. Here the speaker feels sorry for himself and longs for death. Self-pitying, and pulling himself back into his gentlemanly cocoon, he thinks of himself as bereft of all family, haunted by spectres of woe in the visionary manner of the depressed Wanderer. The synthesis is then advanced in 'Reply to the Bastard's Complaint'.

> Why should the Bastard rail his hapless fate?
> The proud in suff'ring are supremely great:
> 'Tis when oppression would the mind control,
> That genius rends the fetters from the soul,
> Burst thro' the barrier of opposing ill,
> And proves itself the agent of free-will.
> Thou know'st no father's love, no mother's sigh,
> No kindred but the fost'ring power on high;
> By one neglected, and the other's shame,
> Thy sole inheritance the Bastard's name.
> Be such thy lot, and with it rest content;
> 'Tis Heav'n decrees it – God Omnipotent.
> Thou hast no fetter to enchain the soul
> 'Tis godlike will each action must control;
> 'Tis to be more than mortal, more refin'd,
> To be in form the man, the God in mind.
> Arouse the dormant feelings of thy breast,
> In every action stand thyself confess'd;
> Mar not the will supreme, but lustrous shine,
> Prove thyself foster'd by a God Divine. (Ireland 1803: 64)

Although written in Savage's heroic couplets, Ireland takes an uncanny tour through his contemporaries' favourite tropes, from Wordsworth's 'fostring power on high' to Blake's 'mind-forg'd manacles', or mind-controlling fetters.

It is as the chameleon bastard that Ireland most enjoys a Romantic life, cannily copying, or weirdly anticipating, the work of his canonical contemporaries. In the preface to *Ballads in Imitation of the Antient* (1801) Ireland aims to disarm the 'severe lash of criticism' (i), by citing Percy's *Reliques*: 'From the earliest dawning of reason to the present period of my life, I have constantly experienced the most pleasurable sensations on the perusal of those early specimens of poetic production for the preservation of which we are so much indebted to Doctor Percy.' In so doing, he anticipates Wordsworth by fourteen years, who in the 'Essay Supplementary to the Preface' (1815) extols Percy's example over McPherson's and Chatterton's, by arguing that the poetry of 'our own country . . . has been absolutely redeemed by it' (*SP*: 281). As recent criticism has pointed out, Percy's importance was commonly acknowledged in the 1790s; yet the position still seemed novel enough for Wordsworth to make a point of it, years later. Ireland then echoes

Wordsworth's Preface of the previous year. Ireland expects that some will censure his taste 'and be deemed puerile by others' (Ireland 1801: ii). It's as if Ireland knew the controversy over Wordsworth's diction was coming, even before Jeffrey's review set it off: 'Instead of the cultivated garden of the Muses I now range amid the wild plains of unadorned Nature. No radiant effusions of fancy, no studied phraseology, will here be found; all is simplicity for the mere imitation of a *Chevy Chace*, and the feats of *Robin Hood*, are what I have aspired to ...' (Ireland 1801: ii). Ireland's adjective ('studied') was not as provocative as Wordsworth's 'inane', but there was no difference in substance in their declared hostility to conventional 'phraseology'.

Rhapsodies, of 1803, as we have seen, contained Ireland's 'Bastard' poems. As always Ireland includes something on Chatterton (in this case 'Elegiac Lines' to his memory); the rest of the poems are self-conscious fragments and modish ballads: poems of melancholy, sensibility, mad people, paupers, peasants, the supernatural; poems on genius, a boy of feeling, and Wordsworth's favourite topic, the jilted lover:

> Poor Polly, the Mad Girl (deserted by her lover).
>
> Poor Polly was mad, and she sigh'd all alone,
> Her bed the damp turf, and her pillow a stone,
> A poor tatter'd blanket envelop'd her form,
> But her bosom was bar'd to the pitiless storm;
> For, alas! in that breast reign'd love's ardent desire,
> And she thought the bleak winds might perhaps cool the fire.
>
> Her hair was dishevelled, and straw bound her head,
> And lovely her face, though its roses were fled;
> Her notes, though untutor'd by musical art,
> Were plaintively wild, and sunk deep in the heart:
> And the strain that unceasingly flow'd from her breast,
> Was, 'the vulture has plunder'd the nightingale's nest'.
>
> Quite frantic I saw her, and pitied her fate;
> I wept, and my bosom was swelling with hate;
> My curses, perfidious despoiler! were thine;
> My sorrow was offer'd at sympathy's shrine;
> For remorseless though fledst her, and scoff's at her pain;
> Thou alone art the vulture that prey'st on her brain.

'Anacreontic' reads like a conventional, preparatory sketch for the second stanza of Keats's 'Ode to a Nightingale':

> I lov'd a maid, she prov'd unkind,
> And laugh'd my vows to scorn;

My plaints I wafted to the wind,
  With grief my heart was torn.

But, as the brimful cup I seiz'd,
  Love spreads his pinions wide;
I quaff'd, and felt my bosom eas'd –
  'Twas Bacchus by my side.

No more than willow spray I'll twine,
  Farewell, deceitful fair;
Weave me a chaplet of the vine;
  Avaunt, corroding care!

Fill me a bowl, a brimmer fill!
  'Tis thus I cure love's smart;
No wound but sparkling wine will kill,
  Though rankling in the heart. (Ireland 1801: 22)

Ireland includes a couple of Gothic ballads: 'The Little Red Woman, a Legendary Tale, From the Romance of the Abbot of Oraonza', and 'The White Lady; or, The Nun of Strasburg's Tale'. 'Song – Poor Jane' is strangely Blakean, and reads like a 'Song of Innocence'. The ballad features a brother and sister, Ben and Jane, who are inseparable. Ben ails, but says nothing, not wanting to alarm Jane; when he dies, she follows not long after, through grief. While more sentimental than Blake, it is Blakean in its uneditorialized naiveté.

The Angler, a Didactic Poem appeared the previous year (1804) but was little more than a dry run for Ireland's proudest accomplishments, *The Fisher Boy: A Poem. Comprising His Several Avocations, During the Seasons of the Year* (1808). The preface picks up the themes of nature and simplicity from Ireland's introduction to the *Ballads* of 1801, but now as a settled, public preference: 'As the taste for literary labours, simple in their construction, and founded on facts, has of late years been highly cherished by the public, I sincerely hope that the ensuing pages may find sanction with the admirers of such species of compositions.' He distances himself from those 'sublime versifiers' who veer 'into the rhapsodical heaven of heavens' – such as, for instance, the writer of *Rhapsodies* – taking refuge from the 'vindictive lash' of 'pedantic critics' in simple truth: 'For as truth is invincible, I have the most implicit reliance on her irradiating influence, which certainly emanates from every line of my little poem.'

The poem is Thomsonesque, following the fisher boy through the seasons. The poem begins in a Wordsworthian fashion in telling the story of 'maniac Jane', seduced and left on the road. Like *The Thorn*'s 'Martha Ray', Jane was engaged to be married and 'yields all to her betrayer', who leaves her to seek his true love, money. His venture fails, he turns to robbery, and is hanged in an act of poetic justice. The liaison nevertheless produces a child, the illegitimate Ned, the fisher boy of the poem. As the poet's pastoral altar ego Ned breaks into a ballad, singing Ireland's familiar tune:

> Nor should this ditty less allure
> The children of the cot
> By love are levell'd rich and poor
> Distinction quite forgot. (Ireland 1808: 61–4)

Ned is the staff on which his mother leans. The poem follows him through his several vocations as the seasons change. The narrator names the fishes, plus the various occupations of the fisherman, with explanatory notes. The poem is part travelogue and part narrative, the main story concerning smugglers, tragedy at sea, Ned's instinctive heroism in trying to help, with the whole ending with a patriotic hymn to the Royal Navy. That Ireland should include a section on 'nutting' is not too startling, given Wordsworth's 'Nutting' had appeared in 1800. His depiction of samphire picking, with Ned suspended down a cliff shouldering the blast, clinging to a precarious ledge, is more surprising, in that it echoes Wordsworth's description of his cragging egg-plundering which was not to be published for another forty years (Ireland 1808: 197–242). But then, Ireland was always something of a preternatural magpie.

According to Benjamin Fisher, Ireland turned to satire to vent his frustrations at his lack of success as a mainstream poet. In the manner of Butler's *Hudibras*, and eventually influenced by Byron's *English Bards and Scotch Reviewers*, Ireland produced *Stultifera Navis; or, the Modern Ship of Fools* (1807), *Chalcographimania* (1814) and *Scribbleomania* (1815). In all of these anonymous publications he dishes the dirt, where he can, getting even wherever possible with his antagonists in the Shakespeare scandal.

But Ireland was not just a failed poet: he was also a jobbing writer. He wrote Gothic novels, including the Lewis-influenced *The Abbess* (1799), his first publication in his own name after the *Authentic Account*, and *Gondez, the Monk* (1805) (written under a pseudonym). Late in life he produced a four-volume biography of Napoleon (1828), in which he argues that Bonaparte's true greatness as a military figure, leader and man can be recognized, now that passions have cooled. With his usual nose for changing fashion, he cashed in on the rising interest in the local, with *A New and Complete History of the County of Kent* (1828–30). One might say that he was reviving the genre of his father's illustrated picturesque travel books, except that it was also true that he plundered much of it straight from Edward Hastings's *A History and Topographical Survey of the County of Kent*, also four volumes (1788–99). According to John W. Brown, Ireland's history was reviewed as a miserable work, but was nevertheless influential, given that it met a new and rising demand. Ireland's last work was *Rizzio; or, Scenes in Europe During the 16th Century, by the Late Mr. Ireland*, which was found among his posthumous papers, and then edited and published by G. P. R. James (1849). Or rather, the last to be published: shortly before his death he had written a biography of Mrs. Jordan, the actress, and long-term mistress of the Duke of Clarence, soon to ascend the throne as William IV. Mrs. Jordan had acted the part of Flavia in *Vortigern*, and unlike John Kemble and Dignum, had striven to play it well.[64] She had also complimented and soothed the fretful William backstage, as he waited for the verdict of the crowd. It seems that Ireland had kept up his acquaintance with the actress; at any rate, he knew her secrets, and planned to publish them – indeed, apparently wrote the text – until a consideration was forthcoming, cancelling the need.[65] It seems that even late in life Ireland was ready – like Savage – to play the bastard.

Deprived of the possibility of a professional identity, and subsequent to his exposure, always a problematic gentleman, Ireland took recourse in the only available alternative, the figure of the 'bastard' or 'neglected genius', who rises solely on personal merit, on the qualities of personality. Divorced from a context in which a name might be built – in the manner achieved by Wordsworth, slowly, but successfully, over an entire career – his identity remained chameleon-like, but therefore also unknown, apart, that is, from his notoriety, his negative celebrity, which always worked against him, until, through the curious workings of the market, his forgeries achieved rarity value, rising in price at the end of his career, when he no longer possessed them, and when he could not afford to buy them back. Undeterred, he forged his own forgeries, selling multiple copies of the 'originals'. With a mind to the provision of his family, he planned an autobiography in which he aimed to turn his infamy, and hoarded gossip, to account. Without a centre of gravity – a public identity on which he could build – his works were essentially flighty and parodic. In them we encounter Romanticism in form, but without substance. The great architect of Romantic substance, in the decades immediately following his death, was Wordsworth, who succeeded in transforming the giddy figure of the 'bastard', or genius, by weighing it down with gravitas and 'depth'. W. H. Ireland's career nevertheless serves to remind us that what we think of as Romantic subjectivity (the genius as self-creating individual) first of all begins as parody, as the lived-out consequences of eighteenth-century print culture, before being rescued, and ennobled, by the canonical Romantics.

8. Conclusion

With the reputation of the national Bard at stake, the reception of Ireland's Shakespeare was always going to mobilize intense passions. The affair roused all those with an interest in literary matters – the entire republic of letters. While it would be a gross exaggeration to say that the affair broke, or even transformed, the Republic, it did make visible the changes that were rapidly occurring within it, changes set in train by events in France. These changes would help set the cultural framework for the emergence of Romanticism.

As we saw, the one and only performance of *Vortigern* ended in fiasco. According to William Henry Ireland, the play was sabotaged by Kemble's satiric delivery of the line 'And when this solemn mockery is over'. To make matters worse, Kemble quieted the crowd with a solemn pretence of fair play, but instead of moving on, repeated the line in the same sepulchral tone, with masterly, comic timing. Ireland speculated that it was a 'preconcerted signal' for Kemble's faction to riot.[66] The uncritical repetition of this story in the critical literature is presumably owing to the vividness, and comedy, of the anecdote: it sounds too good not to be true. The evidence to support Ireland's version of events is in fact contradictory.

The first reviews provide the best evidence of what happened.[67] All reports agree that the audience was unusually large and that it acted with candour and impartiality. The play was heard respectfully until the end of Act 3, when the audience grew restive, prompting Kemble to intervene to request a fair hearing for the play. It is here where the reports begin to differ. Those papers hostile to the Irelands, such as the *Oracle* or the *Telegraph*, attribute the riotous laughter to the play's risible language. The *Morning Post*, which affected a studied neutrality, and the *True Briton*, which was friendly, both attribute some of the blame to Dignum's atrocious acting (according to Ireland, he employed his notoriously squeaky voice to risible effect in delivering the line 'Let the trumpets bellow on'). None of these cite Kemble, except to mention his intervention for fair play. To this extent, the reports are consistent with Boaden's recollections, from late in life, which attribute the subversion, not to Kemble himself, but to the male actors around him, who knowing his opinion, did his dirty work for him.[68] *The Times* of 4 April was the only paper to mention Kemble's 'solemn mockery' speech, but attributes Kemble's repetition of it to the crowd's unruliness over the play being a 'palpable forgery'. In so far as it refers to acting, *The Times* claims that the 'Performers were well and perfect ...' However, the same issue also carries a short note alluding to the 'unhandsome' behaviour of a 'principal actor', who acted as one of the play's leading 'critics', a view also supported by the *Star*, of 4 April:

> We hesitate not in declaring that much of the ridicule and censure thrown upon the piece, ought to have fallen to the lot of Mr. Kemble himself for his most execrable acting. He is monotonous at all times, but on Saturday night he was studiously so; or if at any time he altered his modulation, it appeared to be evidently for the sole purpose of giving a ludicrous emphasis to some expression, to destroy its natural weight in the sentence, and thereby to give to the whole an arbitrary meaning of his own ... Mr. Kemble was absolutely desired from the boxes to go through his part without grinning. Actors should know their duty to the Public better than to take upon them by either look or gesture to dictate an opinion to the audience.

The *True Briton*, the Irelands' most loyal supporter, subsequently promulgated the view that Kemble assumed the 'the double character of the actor and the critic' (25 April 1796). From that point on, Kemble's intervention became a central feature of the story.

Kemble may indeed have acted the part of the 'critic' but, if so, it seems odd that he had no recollection of doing so when recalling events late in life. It was obviously not a personal matter as Kemble and W. H. Ireland were shortly after exchanging friendly correspondence.[69] Nevertheless such contradictions are material to the story, as the main point that arises from the reporting was that it had become hopelessly politicized. For example, take this notice from the *Telegraph* of 7 April:

> After a fair trial and a clear conviction, it is not indecent to talk of the guilt of the prisoner. Mr. Ireland has put himself upon the country. An immense amphitheatre of Jurors was empanelled. They were indisputably prejudiced in favour of the dramatic action ... Neither the sound of drums and trumpets, the beautiful scenery, the splendid processions, the love of spectacles so natural to the weak mind of Englishmen, no, nor yet a conjoined talent of Barrymore, Kemble, and Mrs. Jordan, could save the devoted victim. The piece was heard throughout with more than apostolic patience; propped up by sweet music and good acting, and yet was universally condemned. It was surely, a glorious sight to behold a vast assemblage unanimously pronouncing a verdict in direct opposition to their prejudices...

The report is obviously not compatible with the tale of farcical misadventure and sordid double-dealing best and most colourfully told by Bernard Grebanier. The clue is in the date. A week after the event, the *Telegraph* was already settling into its preferred version: a triumphant vindication of the republic of letters, in general, and Apollo's court, in particular. However, the item seems motivated less by a desire to report accurately than it is by a wish to squash the claims of Samuel Ireland's supporters that the fatal sentence was the work of Malone's faction.

The reporting was politicized, because the matter was, indeed, political: 'We understand from good authority, that the Lord Chamberlain has refused to licence the plays of the *new* Shakespeare, upon three distinct grounds of objection – that it is *immoral, indecent,* and *Jacobinical*'. So reported Boaden's *Oracle*, on 18 February. The *Monthly Mirror* of the month before went further, rhetorically asking why, if the gagging acts allow us to destroy books of a politically incendiary nature, should we not burn Ireland's Shakespeare, as it 'aims at the disgrace of the noblest poet of British genius...?' (January 1796: 177). The republic of letters may have been the newspapers' preferred trope for the fair hearing given the play (at least, for those hostile to it), but the political passions were such that a rational consideration was virtually the last thing the audience could deliver. The tensions at work in the reporting of the play are perfectly exemplified in a handbill collected by Samuel, referring to a last-ditch attempt to resolve the matter through a proper mustering of the republic of letters:

> Brewer Street, Jan 9, 1797. Vortigern and Rowenna. "Do the Shakespearean Manuscripts, the Play of Vortigern and Rowenna, and the Apology of Mr. Ireland Junior exhibit stronger proofs of Authenticity, flagrant imposition, or the credulity of persons of genius?" In the Westminster Forum, held at the Assembly rooms, Brewer street, Golden-Square, the above question is (by particular desire) appointed for public debate on Jan. 9. The Many strange circumstances attendant on the production of the Shakespeare ms. have induced several literary gentlemen to solicit a discussion of the subject in the Westminster forum; where, by publicly convening all parties, the truth will more probably be discovered, than in an controversy issuing from the press – under this impression the managers thus publicly announce, that the attendances of the Mess. Irelands, Dr. Parr, Mr John Kemble (if convenient) and all the various literary gentlemen who have seen or written concerning these supposed remains of our immortal Bard will be esteemed a favour. From such assistance, joined to the talents which at present adorn this literary institution, we augur a discussion the most interesting that has been for many years submitted to the Public. As there is every reason to expect that some of the many female writers, who have distinguished themselves in the various walks of erudition, may be anxious to address the chair on this occasion, the managers respectfully apprise them, that it will not be contrary to the etiquette of the evening: they would hold themselves unpardonable, if by their rigid adherence to punctilio, an Inchbald, a Cowley, a Smith, or Robinson, were prevented developing the mystery which encircles this subject.

The bill recommends early attendance ('price six pence') but adds: 'no political remarks permitted'. The Westminster Forum appears to be a perfect instance of what Habermas would call the literary public sphere, down to the ambiguous position of erudite 'female writers', who are, and are not, allowed in by the conventions defining it. The writers of the advertisement politely call into question the ability of the press to carry out its function of rationally pursuing issues of public moment, such as the Shakespeare controversy; but with their self-imposed injunction against politics, the forum was clearly doomed to failure. It was at once an evisceration of the normative ideal that had previously constituted the public sphere, and a hopeless appeal, given that politics and the Shakespeare papers were now inseparable.

In the late 1790s, then, the shock of the Shakespeare forgeries reverberated throughout the republic of letters for the reasons I earlier noted: it concerned the national poet at a key juncture in his nationalization; it raised awkward questions of the discipline that was to emerge, ultimately, as 'literary criticism'; and it drew upon the dangerously blurred distinction between literary fabrication and forgery. The event reverberated so loudly because it was in tune with general anxieties about the permeability of the public sphere in politicized times. At a period when literature and government overlapped, talk of insurgency and despotism in the republic of letters naturally conveyed alarmist overtones.[70]

However, the most significant contribution the Shakespeare controversy has to make lies elsewhere, in the issues of disciplinarity and nationalism. 'And so, whoever has the legislative or supreme power of any commonwealth, is bound to govern by established standing laws, promulgated and known to the people, and not by extemporary decrees...' Habermas quotes Montesquieu in order to make the point that the polemical claim for legal rationality was a key feature in the development of the public sphere.[71] The reception of W. H. Ireland's fabrications quickly turned to considerations of 'lawful' behaviour within the literary 'republic'. Countering Malone's 'extemporary decrees', the believers sought to establish 'standing laws' of critical behaviour.[72] It is not just that the proto-discipline of belles letters interpenetrates with legal discourse; it is that legal discourse also interfuses with the language of 'political science' – with debates about the constitution. This triple fusion comes together most vividly in the exchanges on libel between T. J. Mathias and the chief apologist for the believers, the Scottish antiquarian, George Chalmers.[73] As Michael Scrivener points out, the indiscriminate invocation of both blasphemous and seditious libel was a principal weapon in Pitt's suppression of dissent. In 1792–93, prosecutions rocketed.[74] Mathias and Chalmers both begin as if talking about personal libel, but their language quickly segues into charges of sedition. This exchange does not so much herald the eventual separation of the various disciplines embryonically mixed in the combatants' discourse as it signifies a watershed in the practice of the public sphere in the course of the 1790s. Whereas at the start of the controversy, Samuel Ireland could confidently appeal to the courts of the republic of letters for standards of rational arbitration, by the time the dust had settled such belletristic discourse had become hopelessly politicized. The republic of letters was now indeed in trouble, and 'trouble' was shorthand for Jacobinism. As Mathias complained in his anonymous retort to Chalmers, Jacobin 'in the present acceptation of the term, comprehends every thing which is an object of aversion and horror in a civilized nation'.[75] Where all opposition is promiscuously smeared as Jacobin, the practice of rational discourse ceased to be a possibility. The Shakespeare controversy was, naturally enough, not the cause of the precipitous decline in the quality of the national debate, but it did register it.

Finally, the lingering question of nationalism, which Habermas self-confessedly left dangling, is here simply unignorable. 'Forging' the national poet was not only to pollute the sacred, as Boaden's anecdote of the fouled chalice vividly demonstrates; it was also to call up fears of miscegenation, as we see from Edmond Malone's use of metaphor, as he settles down, in his *Inquiry*, to destroy the Irelands' claims:

> It has been said, and I believe truly, that every individual of this country, whose mind has been at all cultivated, feels a pride in being able to boast of our great dramatick poet, Shakespeare, as his countryman: and proportionate to our respect and veneration for that extraordinary man ought to be our care of his fame, and of those valuable writings that he has left us; and our solicitude to preserve them pure and unpolluted by any modern sophistication or foreign admixture whatsoever.[76]

Acting as a metonym for the nation the national poet is menaced by 'foreign admixture' (where the overdetermination of Malone's metaphorical vehicles – blood, currency, the sacred – enacts the previous point about the overlap of disciplinary references). And here we begin to gain a clear sense of difference. Those engaged in the political project of forging English nationalism, such as Malone and Mathias, do not appeal to the courts of the republic of letters. Rather they narrow their claims to national authorities, such as Blackstone and Gilbert, whereas the purely literary nationalists, such as Samuel Ireland and Chalmers, do employ the figure 'the republic of letters' with its concomitant internationalism. At the same time, there is an obvious class inflection at work.[77]

These conclusions are born out with startling clarity in an anonymous letter received by Samuel Ireland, in his darkest hour, after *Vortigern*'s catastrophic debut. Evidently written by a young admirer, the letter seeks to offer succour to the stricken Samuel at extraordinary length (close to thirty hand-written pages):

> Perhaps Sir you will be surprised that an anonymous youngling should presume to inveigh against a person of Mr. Malone's rank and dignity – I will however convince you Sir, that a system far different from that of aristocracy: a system of glorious equality obtains in the republic of letters...[78]

The 'anonymous youngling' fights a rearguard action against the re-imposition of aristocracy in the arts by appealing to threatened Enlightenment values, such as the 'glorious equality' of the literary republic. The force of reaction is centred on Malone:

> In the midst of my pleasing reverie, and anticipation of the raptures with which the public would receive the play of *Vortigerne*; the thundering mandates of Mr. Malone, issued in a pamphlet of 400 pages, made their appearance – the learned overawed by the bulky edict, bowed obedience

> at the shrine of this dictatorial colossus of criticism – the giddy multitude, unaccustomed to [reflect], danc'd round the dancing bear, charmed with the tunes of approbation fiddled by his brother critics. (1)

In representing Malone as an aristocratic apologist the letter draws upon the full arsenal of Enlightenment tropes. Malone is a papal figure issuing edicts ecstatically received by an ignorant multitude; a pagan dictator-cum-god, worshipped by the superstitious; and the embodiment of medieval sport (a dancing bear). The spread of learning is linked positively to historical progress, internationalism and theory ('political jargon'):

> Does [Malone] imagine that we are a nation of *Chinese*, when he advices us to cut off all communications with our brethren on the continent? Ever since the first dawn of philosophy, national prejudice has gradually declined. The character of a Newton is naturalised in every civilised soil; he is alike the Brother of the English, and the French philosopher. – Political jargon has never yet injured the character of a Montesquieu in the estimation of a British seminary. The learned are the brothers of the learned in every country. (22–3)

The letter ends with a Volneyian peroration on the triumph of history over superstition and Enlightenment, and not just over ignorance but nations.

Though young, the letter writer is already an anachronism. Malone and his literary dictatorship, rather than the republic of letters, will prevail, a victory that was to have significant consequences, not only for the literary 'movement' that was to become Romanticism but also for the discipline that constituted it. Whereas Samuel and the believers insisted on the right of the general public to participate in literary debate, trading opinions on questions of style, Malone hemmed in discussion, to include only those few connoisseurs in a position to judge, or to those schooled in law and questions of provenance, who formed the true body of literary scholars. The upshot of Malone's influence was the consideration of literature, not as experiments in style, in which all might judge of formal felicity, or its failure, but as the quintessence of genius, to be guarded as a sacred trust by the discerning, professional few, in which legal knowledge, not stylistic acumen, predominated as the supreme virtue. It was as the keeper of the sacred, national flame – the true spirit of Shakespeare – that Malone made common cause with Burke.

Wordsworth and Coleridge both complained that the problem with modern poetry was that it was too easy to write. The production of competent verse was a matter of mere mechanical proficiency, as if a by-product of recent technological progress, with the result that England suffered, not from a scarcity of good poetry, but from a commercial glut. True poetry, poetry that was sui generis, original and rare – and therefore 'authentic' – was either, as Wordsworth argued, the product of deep study of the best of the local tradition (Spenser, Shakespeare, Milton) or the result of an affinity with the true animating genius of the English language, a product of its capacity for particularity (or 'desynonomy' as Coleridge called it). Both solutions stood in ideological opposition to the kind of democratic internationalism favoured by Samuel Ireland's 'anonymous youngling'. To appreciate poetry, as Malone,[79] Wordsworth or Coleridge imagined it, was not a matter of the free exchange of rational opinions upon literary issues which were the vestibule to political ones; on the contrary, it was more a matter of isolated worship, in which the spirit of genius might be sensed, cherished and reproduced, either through extraordinary feats of sympathetic imagination (the role of the modern poet) or through the dedicated study of authentic English originals. As both Wordsworth and Coleridge insisted, such was the best way to defeat the scourge of the modern 'counterfeit'.

2
Gothic Wordsworth

1. Gothic and ideology

If Wordsworth has not come down to us as one of the great Gothic writers of the 1790s – the heyday of the 'genre' – it was not for the want of trying. Prior to 1798, and the appearance of *Lyrical Ballads*, Wordsworth's main publications were *An Evening Walk* and *Descriptive Sketches*, poems which include 'social Gothic', as David Simpson puts it.[1] But he also strove hard to bring out *Adventures on Salisbury Plain* and *The Borderers*, works fundamentally conditioned by the conventions of terror writing.[2] *Lyrical Ballads* embraced the Gothic, although partitioned, with Coleridge producing the supernatural poems whereas Wordsworth's 'subjects were to be chosen from everyday life' (*BL*: II, 7). By the time of the second edition of 1800, the Gothic, like Coleridge, had become exiguous. The quotidian predominated, presided over by the lofty strain of 'Tintern Abbey'. Critics have conventionally seen Wordsworth's abandonment of the Gothic as the natural consequence of his maturation, the letting go of a mode Wordsworth himself identified as belonging to his 'juvenalia'.[3] If this perception has dimmed to the degree that *Adventures on Salisbury Plain* and *The Borderers* have been reassessed as significant productions of the poet's decade of genius, it has yet to be fully rectified by a recognition that these are, indeed, deeply Gothic works. Wordsworth himself was complicit in this great forgetting when, in the Preface to the *Lyrical Ballads* he further consolidated his inward turn towards the lyric mode with a full frontal assault on the Gothic as popular works – mass entertainments – calculated to rot the reader's mind. The second edition of the *Lyrical Ballads* may be a cornerstone of English Romanticism, but it was set amid Gothic ruins.[4]

As a young writer looking to make his mark, Wordsworth would have been aware that, in the book trade, terror was the order of the day.[5] From the perspective of 1793–95 (the years in which he was first composing versions of *Salisbury Plain*) and 1795–97 (*The Borderers*), the terror-writing scene would have appeared fast-moving and ubiquitous.[6] The key to this ubiquitous yet diverse and inchoate school of writing was not generic, but ideological, and at the centre of it stood Edmund Burke. His *Reflections on the Revolution in France* is not usually thought of as a Gothic work, and yet no text did more to inform the ideological content of 1790s 'Gothic'. In general terms it laid the ground for the mood of paranoia, conspiracy and terror that gripped the public later in the decade.[7] More particularly, it shaped the Gothic's ideological meaning, in three principle ways. Burke rehabilitated 'chivalry' (otherwise done-in by Cervantes's satiric shafts) as the glory of European civilization, including the French ancien régime. An uplifting spirit of fealty (one compact with an instinctive, protective respect for women), Burke's chivalry was a quicksilver element that formed our manners, enlivened our customs and ensured good government by oiling and smoothing all our daily interactions, from small to large, including the comfortable rule of kings, who, assured by its emollient presence, extended liberty to their subjects secure in the knowledge that they would not be murdered in their beds by bare-footed assassins, or, if the attempt were made, a thousand scabbard-leaping swords would defend them. Second, and related to the first, Burke extolled 'proud submission' to one's country, to things as they are, to King and constitution, as the public sphere's noblest virtue.[8] And third, he defended primogeniture.

All three positions enraged the Jacobins. Wollstonecraft and Paine railed against the evils of primogeniture, such as the sentencing of younger sons to professions for which they were unfitted and the prostitution of daughters to mercenary marriages or 'family alliances'. 'Proud submission' was dwelt upon as an especially contumacious phrase, one summing up an abject politics of abasement and surrender (with Burke frequently represented pulling his forelock before a prostitute Queen, Marie Antoinette or Catherine the Great) while chivalry was recast as 'Gothic', meaning the feudal and backward. For the Jacobins, 'Gothic' (now signifying Burke's idealized chivalry with its self-serving genealogy of the constitution) summed up the obscurantism and hocus pocus used to mesmerize the superstitious mob while safeguarding the privileges of a corrupt elite. It was a key term in what Karl Marx would not hesitate to call the 'false consciousness' of intellectual subalterns, such as Burke. If Marx's phrase was unknown to English Jacobins, its substance certainly was not. A single example, from the Scottish Jacobin, Thomas Christie, will serve to make the point. Here Christie attacks Burke's use of eloquence, which, detached from truth, has become a 'wandering prostitute':

> As the apologist of ancient prejudice, he is without a rival: in that bad eminence he has attained the first rank. But what avails his tuneful periods, that only cheat us into error and deception? What avail his brilliant colours, that only varnish the deformity of folly and oppression? With majestic grace, worthy of a nobler office, he conducts us to the Temple of Superstition, and the magic of his language soothes our hearts into holy reverence and sacred awe. But when we enter to the consecrated portal,

> and behold a miserable deformed Gothic idol in the corner of the temple, set up as a god of our adoration – in place of prostrating ourselves before it, we spurn with indignation at the delusion: the gaudy ornaments of the place serve but to render it more shocking; we turn with disgust from the false splendour of the mansion of Idolatry, and hasten with cheerful steps to the humble abode of unadorned Truth ... [9]

In the Advertisement to the *Lyrical Ballads* Wordsworth refers to the 'gaudy and inane phraseology' of the fashionable verse he sought to explode through his poetic 'experiments'.[10] Wordsworth does not deliberately echo Christie, although there is every reason to suppose Wordsworth knew the pamphlet.[11] The point rather is that for the Jacobins 'gaudy' was the stock phrase that linked the trappings of aristocracy with the meretricious. For Jacobins, the connection was embodied by Marie Antoinette, the royal whore. While English Jacobins did not follow their French counterparts' pornographic assault upon the Queen, they did frequently play upon the equation of meretricious, female royalty and Gothicism, reworking the language of Protestant anti-Catholicism in the process.[12] Thus Coleridge who writes, in *A Letter from Liberty to Famine* (1795), that instead of finding Religion in the palace he encounters 'a painted patched-up old Harlot. She was arrayed in purple and Scarlet colours ... and upon her forehead was written "Mystery" '.[13] Christie's attack on Burke's rhetorical defence of a 'deformed Gothic idol' (that is, chivalry) is a clear echo of the standard, Jacobinical charge that Burke offers mercenary protection to a prostitute Queen, a 'gaudy idol', whether the French monarch or the whore of Babylon (the Pope).

Burke's *Reflections* thus served to clarify and make available a radical idiom in which chivalry, ruined castles, priestcraft, superstition, mystery, sexual perversion, the ills of primogeniture and endemic social violence were the readily understood terms of Jacobinical attacks on monarchy's repressive, outdated order.[14] As used by Jacobins, 'Gothic' was not a genre but another word for an exploded feudalism.[15] Or, as Tom Paulin puts it, Burke was 'associated with the dark murderous power of the gothic: bloody castles, churches, organized religion, murderous statecraft, a kind of heritage modernity'.[16]

All these elements of a radicalized, Jacobinical Gothic pervade and condition Wordsworth's writing, before 1798. We see it in the desolate landscape lowering in the background of Sarum's ruined castle, from *Salisbury Plain*, the locus of a socially endemic violence iconographically linked to the human sacrifice of its ancient inhabitants. Like the Druids, monstrous old corruption eats up its own, such as the 'female vagrant' broken by imperial adventure in America. It informs Wordsworth's appeal, at the end of the poem, to eradicate 'error' until 'till not a trace / Be left on earth of Superstition's reign'.[17] It is there in the phantasmal haunting suffered by the Sailor in *Adventures on Salisbury Plain*, as he imagines submitting to a brutal, backward power, epitomized by the twisting gibbet. It explains the climatic scene of *The Borderers*, in which Mortimer, led astray by Rivers, loses his moral compass among the ruins of the Gothic castle, and it pervades both works, with their shared settings of feudal ruin as chivalry's loathsome underbelly, as if Wordsworth were unmasking Burke's 'deformed Gothic idol', as the morality of the leprous Lord Clifford.

Critics have long been fascinated with Wordsworth's progress towards 'apostasy', his conversion from Jacobin to Tory. The matter is made complex by its unconscious nature. Like Coleridge, Wordsworth might assert that, over his career, he stood absolutely still, while the rest of the world turned around him.[18] In his self-understanding Wordsworth's core position remained steady, even if shorn of youthful enthusiasm. Wordsworth's conversion, then, is not to be found in self-conscious statements of political intention but in shifting attitudes buried deep in the poetry. James Chandler has argued that if Wordsworth had not yet experienced a Tory conversion by the time of the 1805 *Prelude*, a number of subtle adjustments had already occurred in his political outlook as to make formal revelation redundant. In the 1805 *Prelude*, Wordsworth reproves Burke the politician even as he internalizes Burke's elision between nature and nation. For the later Wordsworth, to humble oneself before nature was to accept the nation as it is, or as it was, as an organic, all-shaping ideal. I believe Chandler is essentially right, the only rider I would add being that the decisive shift in Wordsworth's ideological outlook occurred with his abandonment of the Gothic, as this was the key moment in his withdrawal from the public sphere. There are a number of factors that make this withdrawal a complex – and therefore difficult to read – affair, not least of which is Wordsworth's abiding interest in 'others'.

2. Moving spectacles

In the Preface to the *Lyrical Ballads*, Wordsworth might seem to be concerned with defamiliarizing the world and making it strange (throwing over 'ordinary things' a 'certain colouring of the imagination' so that they appear to the mind 'in an unusual aspect' [*SP*: 281]). Put simply – and this is the burden of *The Prelude* – Wordsworth does not wish us to see *things* differently so much as he wishes us to see *others* differently, so that we *feel* differently. If the egotistical sublime is one common view of Wordsworth's typical subject matter, another is Wordsworth encountering a taxing other, whether an idiot boy, a girl with a stubborn sense of numbers, the ghostly figure of a war veteran, peddlers, leech gatherers, drowned corpses, desperate mothers, highland reapers, gypsies, Cumberland beggars, sturdy peasants and a host of other others. Wordsworth's encounters with others has frequently been a source of unease among his readers, and for a variety of reasons, from Francis Jeffrey's intuitive sense that Wordsworth's demotic representation of his motley crew of the low and middling was Jacobinical, to more recent expressions of discomfort at Wordsworth's strange way with others, veering between a disturbing patronage and an equally off-putting disinterest arising from his ability, as the *Quarterly* put it, to 'penetrate further in the passive properties of living beings – their properties not only as agents but as objects'.[19] As David Bromwich points out, we are comfortable with others as agents, but not as objects, and it is as objects that Wordsworth frequently treats others.[20] By otherness I partly mean that others possess, as George Eliot reports through Dorothea Brooke's free indirect speech, an 'equivalent center of self, whence the lights and shadows must always fall with a certain difference'.[21] But more particularly I mean the recognition that this 'equivalence' poses intractable moral and ethical problems. For Eliot, the realization of otherness was the beginning of the moral sense. This is a decidedly post-Enlightenment view, and although it profoundly influenced Eliot's outlook, it was, in historical terms, relatively recent. In a society in which identity is determined by birth, rank and status, otherness, while an issue, is not especially vexed; in a post-Enlightenment society, it is. It is not simply that identity becomes fluid and free floating once unpegged from traditional social categories: there is the problematic question of strangers and their needs. Are such needs to be determined by the Bible or by some other received code? Or have strangers natural rights (and by extension, have we obligations)? If the former, we all know our duty as good Samaritans. If the latter, what are the social and political consequences of these rights and obligations, and how far do they extend?

In an extremely percipient review of Wordsworth's poems of 1807, the distinguished Dissenting critic, Lucy Aikin, comments on Wordsworth's notion of the poet as described in the Preface to the *Lyrical Ballads*: 'It is only that of a person of strong sympathies, who possesses in an unusual degree the power of imagining and describing the feelings of other human beings. A good novel writer must be all this – a descriptive or lyric poet, though perfect in his kind, need not.'[22] One might speculate that the eighteenth-century novel partly came into being in order to negotiate the complexities of otherness that arose as the consequence of urban growth that shifted moral enquiry from traditional patterns of social responsibility (based on the family and parish) to those attendant upon needs of suddenly visible, and unaccommodated, others. Regardless, otherness, and empathy for others, had not yet been naturalized as a poetic theme, hence the puzzled reaction of Wordsworth's first readers at his prosaic subjects. Charles Burney is a case in point: 'When we confess that our author has had the art of pleasing and interesting in no common way by his natural delineation of human passions, human characters, and human incidents, we must add that these effects were not produced by the *poetry*: – we have been as much affected by pictures of misery and unmerited distress, in *prose*.'[23]

Wordsworth's strange way with others is the natural consequence of his approach to poetic agency, that is to say, it follows from his answer to the question of how it is that poetry affects readers' sympathies, enlarging and improving their view of the world into an outlook that might lead to the realization of the good life as Wordsworth conceives it. It is in his early Gothic work – but especially the *Salisbury Plain* poems – that Wordsworth first develops a poetic praxis turning on the otherness of others (thus venturing onto the territory of the novel, as Aikin notes). His poetic system was revolutionary, in both senses. Consuming truly imaginative works, 'the understanding of the Reader must necessarily be in some degree enlightened, and his affection strengthened and purified' (*SP*: 283). According to John Hayden this passage from the Preface to the *Lyrical Ballads* is the 'first instance in the history of literary theory in which the morality of literature is clearly said to work indirectly, not directly by precept and example' (*SP*: 493). One might interpret Hayden as meaning indirectness of form versus obvious content; the point, rather, is that Wordsworth's originality lay in his efforts to embroil his readers in a more complicated engagement with otherness than was afforded through simple depictions of unmerited distress. His system was novel, but it was also revolutionary in its political intent, as is evident from the following rhetorical question posed by the 'Essay, Supplementary to the Preface' (1815):

> And where lies the real difficulty of creating that taste by which a truly original poet is to be relished? ... Finally, does it lie in establishing the dominion over the spirits of readers by which they are to be humbled and humanised, in order that they may be purified and exalted? (*SP*: 408)

The answer is a defiant 'yes'. As Hazlitt argued, Wordsworth's is a militantly levelling muse, reducing the high and mighty (sneering, cosmopolitan reviewers, such as Jeffrey) below the level of the meanest peddler, in order that they might, eventually, for their own sakes, be raised.

Moving spectacles of others, and otherness, was thus at the very centre of Wordsworth's revolutionary theory of poetic agency. What was moving about these spectacles had nothing to do with that calculus of self-interest of moral economists, such as Adam Smith, where pity and kudos are part of a single system of exchange,[24] and everything with the writer's power to throw the reader into a quandary in which the needs of strangers remain stubbornly ineluctable; nothing to do, that is, with fashionable sensibility, and everything with the reader seeing, and feeling, differently. Wordsworth's clearest expression of his revolutionary aesthetic occurs in *The Ruined Cottage*, written around the time it was coming to full fruition (1797–99).[25] The narrator reports how the poem's central character, Armytage, has related the tale of the absent protagonist, Margaret, the owner of the now-ruined cottage:

> He had rehearsed
> Her homely tale with such familiar power,
> With such an active countenance, an eye
> So busy, that the things of which he spake

Seemed present, and, attention now relaxed,
There was a heartfelt chillness in my veins.[26]

The ability to make the absent spectrally present for the unselfconscious auditor constitutes the conventional half of Wordsworth's aesthetic. The more revolutionary aspect is described next. Armytage continues:

It were a wantonness and would demand
Severe reproof, if we were men whose hearts
Could hold vain dalliance with the misery
Even of the dead, contented thence to draw
A momentary pleasure never marked
By reason, barren of all future good.
But we have known that there is often found
In mournful thoughts, and always might be found,
A power to virtue friendly; were't not so
I am a dreamer among men, indeed
An idle dreamer. Tis a common tale
By moving accidents uncharactered,
A tale of silent suffering, hardly clothed
In bodily form, & to the grosser sense
But ill adapted, scarcely palpable
To him who does not think.[27]

The meaning of the common tale 'by moving accidents uncharactered' only discloses itself through thoughtful feeling, or feeling thought, as the auditor is moved to troubled introspection, spurred by the tale 'hardly clothed'. Othello employs 'moving accidents' (*Othello*, I, iii, 135) to signify the tales of adventure that enraptured the listening Desdemona. Armytage's 'uncharactered' signals a more subtle kind of story, one not suited to the 'greedy ear' (*Othello*, I, iii, 149). By 1800, in Part Two of 'Hart-Leap Well', Wordsworth essays another version of the oxymoron he's after: the 'thinking heart', a quality he associates with his own 'simple song', as opposed to the 'moving accidents' of the literary 'trade' in terror.[28] Wordsworth's aesthetic was revolutionary, because it sought to 'humble' and 'humanise' the perplexed reader. Still, it contained an area of inherent difficulty: what was the difference between a moving spectacle of otherness 'hardly clothed' and a simple spectacle; between complex matter for the 'thinking heart' and a debasing 'moving accident'; between true art and a commercial, even self-regarding, product, with its 'vain dalliance' and 'momentary pleasures'?

In *The Prelude* Wordsworth is frank about the quarter in which the danger lies. He refers to a period when he, too, wrote 'popular verse', such as 'An Evening Walk' and 'Descriptive Sketches', poems of a vitiated taste in which the 'action and situation' determine the feeling:

The state to which I now allude was one
In which the eye was master of the heart,

> When that which is in every stage of life
> The most despotic of our senses gained
> Such strength in me as often held my mind
> In absolute dominion.[29]

Wordsworth is conflicted as regards sight. Wordsworth drinks in nature's visionary forms through his eyes, while his verse is vivid, pictorial and given to prospects both picturesque and sublime. At the same time, from 'Tintern Abbey' through *The Prelude* to his late poems, Wordsworth insists upon the sensual despotism of the eye as a dominion the poet must free himself from if he is to become 'a sensitive, and a creative soul' (*Prelude*, XI, 257). The dual nature of sight is registered as the difference between the bodily or carnal eye and inner vision or 'inward eye', a doubleness expressed in *The Prelude* through the calculated slipperiness of the frequently used 'spectacle'.

Wordsworth's reliance upon, but antipathy towards, the visual ties him into common notions of Romanticism. Lockean empiricism firmly entrenched the visual as the dominant field of knowledge within the eighteenth century, largely through the equation of sense data (the perceptions inscribed on the mind's receptive tablet) with 'ideas' or images.[30] According to Locke's usage, we are invited to think of the mind's contents as arising, in the first, or primary instance, from the ghostly impressions left on the mind, from things. The Romantic reaction, the story used to go, was the insertion of an active, shaping imagination, in contradistinction to the passive materialism and rationalism of Locke's legacy: the lamp over the mirror. Wordsworth's hostility to the visual can certainly be put in these terms, but it is part of a larger picture, covering a longer time frame.[31]

In *The Shock of the Real* Gillen D'Arcy Wood provides a fresh perspective on Romantic antipathy to visual culture or, rather, to its 'low' forms. Wood argues that the 'Romantic ideology was constructed not in opposition to the enlightenment rationalism of the eighteenth century, but as a reaction to the visual culture of modernity being born'. The opposition was not 'between M. H. Abrams's mirror and the lamp, but between the lamp and the magic lantern: between Romantic, expressive theories of artistic production emphasizing original genius and the idealizing imagination, and a new visual-cultural industry of mass reproduction, spectacle, and simulation'.[32] The Romantics baulked, not at the 'visual', per se, but at panoramas, giant billboards and raree shows (just to name the debasing spectacles Wordsworth recalls in 'Residence in London', Book VII of *The Prelude*), to which we may add phantasmagorias, dioramas, stereoscopes, a theatre based on celebrities and stunning stage effects, together with a welter of popular and commercial entertainments.[33] Wood focusses on 'shows' which featured, as a major selling-point, a simulation of the real and thus a usurpation of the viewer's interpretative and imaginative powers ('those mimic sights that ape / The absolute presence of reality' [*Prelude*, VII, 248–9]). Stunned by the reality effect, there is nothing left for the consumer, but 'savage torpor'.[34]

As Wordsworth developed a revolutionary aesthetic built around the complicated spectacle of otherness, the world rapidly changed. He may have been preoccupied with his compromised dabbling in the pictorial 'despotism' of fashionable verse – with its inadequate response to revolutionary pressure – but as time passed a new enemy became increasingly present: the stupefying 'reality' effects of low literature and commercial culture.[35] Although revolutionary, Wordsworth's aesthetic naturally emerged out of an older model of aesthetic response, which, for the purposes of the argument, can be largely equated with Lord Kames's thoroughly Lockean theory of 'ideal presence'.

Ideal presence is a simple concept to grasp, at least superficially. Kames imagines a perceptual axis, with real presence at one end, and reflection at the other. Real presence is perception itself, the act of seeing. Reflection is when we introspect about the process of perception. Ideal presence occurs somewhere in between these two poles. An act of memory, when we are lost in a reverie of the past, and seem to relive old events with an eidetic vividness, would be an example of ideal presence, as would the inward turn taken when viewing a painting, where we find ourselves mentally living in the imaginative world it depicts. Ideal presence is also operative in the appreciation of novels and poems. Indeed, it is ideal presence that accounts for the 'reading trance', in which the world depicted by the book appears to unfold before our eyes. To lose oneself in a book is to find oneself in ideal presence. When we introspect about our memories, or focus on the words on the page, or otherwise interrupt our willing suspension of disbelief, the spell breaks, and real presence once more intrudes.[36]

As can be seen from this short description, ideal presence was ocularcentric. Although hallucinatory experiences of taste, smell, touch or hearing are all compatible with ideal presence, Kames imagines the condition almost entirely in terms of sight. One could say that it was bound to, given its origins in Lockean empiricism. If perception is the process of receiving sense data, ideal presence is their unselfconscious recollection and reproduction: and what we reproduce most are images. Although Kames was not an overt associationist, associationism was nevertheless an intrinsic aspect of the aesthetic Kames built around his theory of ideal presence, not the least of which was the moral and ethical mission he conceived for it. A firm Hutchesonian, Kames subscribed to a belief in an innate moral sense. We were fitted by providence to respond with disgust, when presented with a spectacle of vice, and with warm approval when witnessing visions of virtue. To put the matter in this way is immediately to remind ourselves that Kames was not an innovator but a codifier; and what he codified was the moral-aesthetic mechanism of 'sensibility'. To put it at its simplest, Kames's 'ideal presence' was a theory for why 'virtue in distress' was an improving aesthetic subject: through ideal presence, novels, dramas and poems set loose among the reading public a repertoire of scenes and images which were bound, by the nature of things, to exercise our moral sense in beneficial ways, as feelings of revulsion towards vice and approval towards virtue were variously flexed by a parade of moving spectacles.

The 'ideal' in 'ideal presence' thus carried a double meaning. The mental phenomenon pointed to by Kames was ideal in the sense of being the visionary experience of recollected sense data (and thus opposed to real time sense perceptions); but it was also 'ideal' in the sense of implicating an idealizing process whereby, in the act of revisioning a picture, a landscape (real or depicted), a memory, or a novel, we reorder our sense impressions aesthetically and morally. In ideal presence we idealize the ideal. We earlier saw how Wordsworth condemned London's commercial art as 'mimic sights that ape / The absolute presence of reality' (*Prelude*, VII, 248–9). The unspoken opposite of 'absolute presence' is 'ideal presence', meaning a non-mimetic space where the mind is free to idealize the art it reflects upon (unlike modern simulations of the real, where the mind is held in thrall, stupefied by the trick).

It would be difficult to overstate how influential and pervasive the Kamesian aesthetic was towards the end of the eighteenth century. It was, so to speak, second nature.[37] As we shall see, it pervades Wordsworth's early verse in an unselfconscious way – it is, in fact, part of what makes his early poetry conventional. But beginning with the *Salisbury Plain* poems, and coming to a peak in *Lyrical Ballads*, Wordsworth developed an aesthetic practice which broke with the 'ideal presence' model. In Kames's terms one might say that Wordsworth deliberately dispelled ideal presence by encouraging reflection; in Lucy Aikin's, that Wordsworth introduces the techniques of the novel into poetry whereby sympathy for others is both encouraged and complicated by the narrative. I earlier quoted John Hayden's assertion that Wordsworth's Preface 'was the first instance in literary theory in which the morality of literature is clearly said to work indirectly, not directly by precept' (p. 67). Although Kames never explicitly advanced a literary theory of moral indirection, the implication is clear. Kames recommends novels, not because they are good at delivering precepts or examples, but because they have proved an effective technology for the production of ideal presence in which consumers will respond warmly to scenes of good or evil, kindling with sympathetic benevolence towards virtue and firing with indignation at vice. It was an affective, rather than semantic, theory of literary meaning. In this respect Wordsworth remained a Kamesian, but he so complicated the nature of the indirect moral responses invited by his works as to cease being recognizable as such.[38]

3. Gothic visions

Between *An Evening Walk*, *Descriptive Sketches* and *Salisbury Plain*, there is a clear progression towards the *Lyrical Ballads*, as regards a more revolutionary representation of the spectacle of others. The literary diction, personifications, antitheses, transferred epithets and zeugmas of *An Evening Walk* – its marked 'pre-Romantic' style – will prove material to the issue of representing others, primarily because such language makes it impossible to sustain the illusion that we, the reader, are encountering a 'man speaking to men', in the sense of a recognizable social actor speaking to (and of) other social actors. What we are presented with, rather, are a series of verbal sketches in a conspicuously aestheticized language geared towards an already ritualized consumption (the picturesque). There are, indeed, others present in these poems, but they are either distantly offstage, as in peasants glimpsed on the brow of far-off cliffs, or heard only, as the faint booming of quarry blasting and boat hammering. Alternatively, the human interest is figured anthropomorphically through 'sweetly ferocious' cocks and tragically maternal swans. 'The pomp is fled, and mute the wondrous strains, / No wrack of all the pageant scene remains . . .'[39] The reference to *The Tempest* is more than the self-conscious allusiveness of earnest adolescence; it redundantly reminds the readers that a visual train of associations – a visionary pageant – has been unfolding before their inward eye in proper Kamesian fashion.

> Stay! Pensive, sadly-pleasing visions, stay!
> Ah no! as fades the vale, they fade away:
> Yet still the tender, vacant gloom remains:
> Still the cold cheek its shuddering tear retains.[40]

As the objects productive of the sense data that form real presence fade away, ideal presence lingers on, a visionary state stimulating the appropriate moral-aesthetic response in the poet (the 'shuddering tear') and, by implication, in the reader.

If the politics of *Descriptive Sketches* were revolutionary, its poetic practice was not. In terms of method, the *Salisbury Plain* poems were a great advance, and not simply because Wordsworth has rid his style of the hackneyed language of the earlier poems, finding, in the frequently enjambed, alternatively rhyming lines of the Spenserian stanza, a less obtrusive, more moving, voice. The *Salisbury Plain* poems were also narrative. The previous poems were locked into the gentlemanly connoisseurship of the loco-descriptive tradition in which the artificiality of the language served as a virtual window on the world, with transparency a function of meeting readerly expectations. *Adventures on Salisbury Plain* disturbs such distanced consumption by introducing marked voices, most obviously, the voice of the sailor's widow, who narrates her story in a style deviant from the 'gaudy' norm of polite verse.

The narratives of the sailor and the sailor's widow he meets are twin stories of war, press gangs, fraud, poverty and desperation, and therefore have a clear, Jacobinical valence (to oppose Pitt's war in 1794 and 1795 was to be on the pro-French side, was to pitch one's lot in with the masses congregating across the country in protest against the war). The widow's depictions of family misery are more vivid than the sentimental figurations of freezing birds, in *An Evening Walk*, partly because they are overheard, rather than heard directly, and partly because narrated in a homely voice in which the needs of strangers can be distinctly heard. The narrator's voice, though, is more puzzling. Is this a Jacobin masquerading as an Elizabethan – a literary sans culotte in olde-English clothing? If so, why the conventional, pietistic ending, in which the repentant sailor hangs, twisting, a Christian lesson to all? Or is the very cruelty of the sentence a satire upon it? The reader is left to wonder, and as the reader wonders, disturbing images infiltrate the mind, of Salisbury plain encrusted with the imposing relics of ancient, oppressive powers, of Gothic castles, gibbets, Stonehenge and a quondam hospital, now a 'dead house', as if mercy had utterly deserted the land.

The poem's themes follow a narrative order generated by a grammar abstracted by Wordsworth from the terror-school of novel writing. The poem proceeds through images of human ruin, despair, isolation, violence, punishment and the phantasmal. The next item in this dystopic sequence follows the emerging logic:

> But all was chearless to the horizon's bound;
> His weary eye – which, whereso'er it strays
> Marks nothing but the red sun setting round,
> Or on the earth strange lines, in former days
> Left by gigantic arms – at length surveys
> What seems an antique castle spreading wide;
> Hoary and naked are its walls and raise
> Their brow sublime: in shelter there to bide
> He ran; the pouring rain smoked thick as on he hied.[41]

For any attentive reader of 1790s Gothic, privation will lead to an 'antique Castle', and from there to live burial, the master trope of Gothic conventions.[42]

Live burial may be described as the principle of the perverse barrier. Thus, in *The Mysteries of Udolpho*, the doors Emily St. Aubert wants to open remain locked, while the ones she wants to lock stay stubbornly open. Figuratively the trope plays on the deep human need to make contact with others. Live burial thus extends from the literal expression of imprisonment (often in a coffin-like cell) to finding oneself isolated; or, if accompanied, speechless; or, if furnished with speech, incapable of being understood (while in the reverse mode it turns on fears of invasion, bodily or psychic).

In conventional Gothic live burial almost always occurs in a castle shadowed by the Bastille's stock representation as the 'cemetery of the living'.[43] In Jacobin Gothic entrapment happens within the feudal system, or 'things as they are', in either the literal Bastille or its metaphorical equivalents.[44] *Salisbury Plain* was written in 1793; *Adventures on Salisbury Plain*, after 1795.

Although there is no direct evidence that Wordsworth deepened and complicated the narrative method of the later poem as a result of reading Godwin's *Caleb Williams* (1794), it seems a reasonable speculation that he had and that the systematic nature of Government violence in *Adventures on Salisbury Plain* is owing, if only subliminally, to Godwin's fictional analysis of how the tyrannical spirit of Government pervades (and corrupts) everyday life. The narrative logic of isolation, violence and live burial thus inevitably leads to 'what seems an antique castle spreading wide'. This 'castle', we soon learn, is Stonehenge. The point is not that it is Stonehenge rather than a castle. It is both, each deepening the other's negative meaning:

> Thou hoary Pile! Thou child of darkness deep
> And unknown days, thou livest to stand and hear
> The desert sounding to the whirlwind's sweep,
> Inmate of lonesome Nature's endless year;
> Even since thou sawest the giant Wicker rear
> Its dismal chambers hung with living men,
> Before thy face did ever wretch appear,
> Who in his heart had groan'd with deadlier pain
> Than he who travels now along thy bleak dominion.[45]

Wordsworth's apostrophe, and personification, complicates the 'hoary Pile' in a Godwinian fashion. The cant phrase 'child of darkness' stigmatizes the pile as Satanic, as Thomas Christie might very well do, when attacking Burke's 'gothic idol'. But as the line develops an alternative Godwinian meaning emerges: just as Godwin refuses to blame the murderer, because his act was the product of a thousand unseen, institutional, causes, so Wordsworth permits us to regard the pile as the 'child', or product, of prior darkness, so that it is set apart and against the Wicker, as a silent witness. Stonehenge stands not only as an image of isolation, privation and violence but also as a sign of the inscrutable etiology of evil. The giant Wicker, with the Druids' sacrificial victims buried alive within its 'dismal chambers', unambiguously doubles the gibbet, a modern totem of barbaric, 'Gothic' violence. Just as 'the living men' are the victims of the Wicker (or Bastille), so the sailor is the victim of a gibbet serving as an obvious metonym for institutional state violence. Unable to conceive his own death, the sailor imagines himself a living man, strung from the gibbet. His groan signals not only his guilt but also his status as victim. As Blake would put it, the sailor's feudal fetters are in his mind.

To his mastery of Gothic and Jacobin conventions Wordsworth adds peculiar fears that enrich his theme. Although the abstract logic of the perverse barrier operates in Wordsworth's poetry he invests it with emotional depth by transforming its operation into privation and exposure, mediated by touch, figurative and literal. In his preface to the 'Immortality Ode' Wordsworth recalls how a boyhood refusal to acknowledge the fact of death led to a solipsistic tendency to see the world as an extension of his own mind: 'Many times while going to school have I grasped at a wall or tree to recall myself from this abyss of idealism to the reality.'[46] The 'Immortality Ode' explores the reverse condition, where nature has become a barrier, a blank surface denuded of metaphysical promise. If childhood 'idealism' is one of metaphysical plenitude it is also a state of privation, an 'abyss', because lacking in human touch. Perversely, too much 'touch' (the mother's, or mother nature's) manufactures the 'prison-house' of adult experience, a simultaneous state of exposure (to the alienating human) and privation (from nature's 'presence').

In Wordsworth, then, the Gothic trope of the perverse barrier is transformed into the emotionally rich logic of privation, as the loss of either human touch (idealism) or its converse (exposure), meaning too much 'touch', in the sense of artificial or man-made environments (a Bastille, the Wicker, London, the 'prison-house'). In his post-Gothic career Wordsworth rescues privation by subliming it: thus blank nature is sublimed through an intangible presence just as empty cityscapes are sublimed by nature (as in 'Westminster Bridge'). But in his early career the sublime function is provided by human touch, which becomes tragic, when absent.

Embedding is the principle syntactic device of the Gothic grammar governing the poem's narrative structure. The 'spital', rather than the 'antique castle' or 'hoary pile', stands at the literal and figurative centre of the poem, for although the tenor of the poem is tragic, it hinges on hope. The spital is an obvious image of live burial. The protagonists find themselves imprisoned – by weather and circumstances – within the 'dead house of the Plain', which in turn contains within its stones a newly buried corpse, latterly, or so the widow fears, a ghost. As the sailor wakes the stranger he meets there, so she wakes him; as he reaches out to touch her, she touches him, through her story (just as the reader, in turn, is touched). Although thrown back into themselves through the institutional violence that has scarred them both, the magnetism of human sympathy revives them, each ministering to the other's needs, turning a night of privation into a transcendent, or sublime, moment.

Such ministering brings life to each, but only within the limited context of the 'dead house', for these are dead men walking. In conventional Gothic the narrative moves from a place of pastoral safety (where the heroine is usually nurtured by her father, a lone parent) to a Gothic castle, into which she is abducted or seduced and threatened with violation, before eventual release and a pastoral return. Instead of using the pastoral to frame the narrative Wordsworth embeds it within the widow's narrative, from which there is no egress, no happy return. In structural, narrative terms, the pastoral is buried alive.

The widow's story explains much. The fact that it serves as a double of the sailor's (of forced service in a war that ultimately leaves their families fragmented and destroyed) is not the result of Wordsworth trying to please the 'vulgar' by tying the story's pieces into a 'palpable knot', as is often assumed. Rather it is an act of Gothic repetition, where doubling testifies to a deeper malaise.[47] The widow's embedded tale embeds the meaning of the poem. For instance her 'heart is touched that men like these, / The rude earth's tenants, were my first relief'. The gypsies provide her succour, after disembarking, widowed and indigent in England, meaning that it is those outside the system who retain the primordial instinct of human sympathy – or those forced outside who regain it, such as the widow and the sailor. Moreover, the system denatures men by turning them against themselves ('But, what afflicts my peace with keenest ruth / Is, that I have my inner self abused'). The first cause of this tale of woe is not a medieval baron out of romance but a very present, avaricious aristocrat bent on engrossing the surrounding land. Deprived of the family's 'hereditary nook' they soon lose their independence and are fed into the monster's maw.

The embedded tale may disclose the meaning of the poem, but that is a different thing from understanding. Both the widow and the sailor are locked within a form of false consciousness whereby the meaning of their lives escapes them, which is where Wordsworth's use of the supernatural comes in.

> Now dim and dreary was the Plain around;
> The ghosts were up on nightly roam intent;
> And many a gleam of grey light swept the ground
> Where high and low those ghostly wanderers went,
> And whereso'er their rustling course they bent
> The startled earth-worms to their holes did slink,
> The whilst the crimson moon, her lustre spent,
> With orb-half visible, was seen to sink
> Leading the storm's remains along the horizon brink.[48]

The Gothic generally divides into the explained and unexplained supernatural. Wordsworth's is explained, in the Radcliffe manner, although his explanations are psychic rather than quotidian.[49] The supernatural in the poem is an emanation of the characters' wounded psyches. As we saw earlier, for Jacobins superstition was a form of obscurantism, whether the mystic jargon of priests (Coleridge's 'mystery') or the slavish rhetoric of 'apologists', such as Burke. This intellectual point is made concrete in the narrative as the supernatural fears suffered by its protagonists, where fear is the measure of the psychic damage done to them. Within the Gothic system we are, as it were (and the bathos is telling) mere worms frightened into isolated burrows by ghosts of our own making.

Ghosts, then, are traumatic disturbances in the poem, emanations of the psychic violence done to the victims of a Gothic – feudal – society. They are, literally, Gothic visions. One such vision assails the widow in the 'dead house' when wakened by the sailor, until human sympathy lays it to rest (she fears she sees the wraith of a recent murder victim). The point, though, is most explicit in the case of the sailor. He has just encountered the gibbet, a premonition of his own end:

> It was a spectacle which none might view
> In spot so savage but with a shuddering pain
> Nor only did for him at once renew
> All he had feared from man, but rouzed a train
> Of the mind's phantoms, horrible as vain.
> The stones, as if to sweep him from the day,
> Roll'd at his back along the living plain;
> He fell and without sense or motion lay,
> And when the trance was gone, feebly pursued his way.[50]

The 'dire phantasma'[51] that assail him are indeed (from a Jacobin's perspective) Gothic visions: a trance produced by the violence endemic within the ancien regime. One might characterize these visions, 'a train / Of the mind's phantoms', as ideal presence in a Gothic key.

In *Devices of Wonder*, Barbara Stafford and Frances Terpak offer the following speculation on the possible therapeutic meaning of Gothic visions:

> The intense yearning, expressed on both sides of the English channel, to bring back the butchered innocents and vandalized monuments destroyed by the Terror reached hallucinatory proportions in the Gothic-Romantic museum displays of Alexandre Lenoir, the ghoulish wax replicas of Madame Tussaud, and, above all, the trancelike phantasmagoria where the dead miraculously rose again. This "therapeutic theatre" ... was intended to relieve the trauma of unbearable loss.[52]

The 'phantasmagoria' was the commercial brainchild of Etienne Gaspard Robertson. Starting in 1797 Robertson transformed the Gothic setting of a 'defunct cloister of the Capuchins in Paris into a theatre of the macabre' through his 'fantascope', a large sliding magic lantern, in which images of the recently departed were projected onto a screen through a haze of sulphurous smoke. Through these means, the dead would live again. The 'fantasmagorie' (Robertson's coinage) was the technological transformation of ideal into real presence. The term quickly took on a life of its own as a byword for the irreality of post-Revolutionary life, in which the boundary between the real and the phantasmal (no longer indelibly etched by old certainties) constantly blurred.[53]

Although Robertson did not begin his spectral demonstrations until 1797, phantasmagorias were staged as early as 1793, at London's Lyceum Theatre, where they competed with the other shows 'aping' real presence noted by

Wordsworth in Book V of *The Prelude*. We cannot know for sure if Wordsworth took in any phantasmagorias during his London days. Nevertheless, he seems to share Stafford's and Terpak's views on the therapeutic effects of the phantasmagoria in dealing with the trauma of Revolutionary violence. Thus the meaning of the September massacres escapes Wordsworth as he crosses the square of the Carrousel, where the tortures and eviscerations had so lately happened (a 'volume' whose 'contents' remain 'locked up' [*Prelude*, X, 50–1]), but which later form into 'substantial dread' as he conjures the horror from 'tragic fictions', some read, others heard, as he lies dreaming on his attic bed, assailed by Gothic visions (*Prelude*, X, 65–6). Part of that meaning was his equivocal participation in these events as a Girondin. *Adventures on Salisbury Plain* represents pre-Revolutionary violence, but for committed Revolutionaries, as Wordsworth was during the poem's composition, the Revolutionary violence of the September massacres was a belated product of the ancien régime and the feudal Allies' bellicosity. The phantasmal violence of the poem is thus psychically overdetermined.

They left him hung on high in iron case,
And dissolute men, unthinking and untaught,
Planted their festive booths beneath his face;
And to that spot, which idle thousands sought,
Women and children were by fathers brought;
Now some kindred sufferer driven, perchance,
That way when into storm the sky is wrought,
Upon his swinging corpse his eye may glance
And drop, as he once dropp'd, in miserable trance.[54]

The lines describe the sailor's execution that terminates the poem. The obvious reference of this passage is the kind of festive hanging common to British penal practices prior to the war with France, a period when Britain led Europe in public executions.[55] But for the reader of 1795 images of the French Terror would come readily to mind, possibly reinforced by the subliminal reference in the third line to the Jacobin exhortation to 'plant the tree of liberty'.

For Wordsworth, such violence has become phantasmagorical. Is the poet himself a 'kindred soul', who, at the sight of the sailor swinging from his gibbet, falls into a 'trance' of 'dire phantasma' (troubled by the 'substantial presence' of the massacred)? According to most critics Wordsworth softened his vision when he revised the poem, late in life, as *Guilt and Sorrow*, with the last stanza now becoming:

His fate was pitied. Him in iron case
(Reader, forgive the intolerable thought)
They hung not: – no one on *his* form or face
Could gaze, as on a show by idlers sought;

> No kindred sufferer, to his death-place brought
> By lawless curiosity or chance,
> When into storm the evening sky is wrought,
> Upon his swinging corse an eye can glance,
> And drop, as once he dropped, in miserable trance.[56]

One might argue that in *Guilt and Sorrow* a disjunction opens up between the earlier vision of state violence as a merciless, Druidical power, with its equation of modern gibbet and ancient wicker, and this more merciful version.[57] But equally one can say that the changes deepen the visual theme. The 'Reader' can only forgive the intolerable thought if he or she first of all has it: as such the reader is placed on a par with the idlers who curiously gaze upon, or, when reading, idly entertain the thought of, the sailor hanging from his gibbet. If the sailor was previously hung up in chains, he is now (in the revised version) hung up in sentences. The significance of the last line also changes as the meaning of the punning 'drop' opens up.[58] In the 1795 version the obvious sense is that the guilty viewer might drop into a miserable trance at the sight of the gibbet, just as the sailor himself had previously done. In *Guilt and Sorrow* the implication of the reader brings out the other meaning of drop, so that we envisage the sailor in the act of being hanged, down to the detail of his eyes dropping, as he drops.

Later in life Wordsworth campaigned to make public hangings private. Instead of degrading public spectacles, observed by the hardened and curious, the meaning of capital punishment was to be internalized as the public privately contemplated the application of the ultimate sanction. So, too, in *Guilt and Sorrow* where the public display of the criminal's body has been rendered internal, a product of the reading trance. The later version is more explicit in its disciplinary function as we are warned against treating the sailor's death as an idle spectacle, a 'moving accident' fit for the curious, 'a vain dalliance with the misery / Even of the dead'. The theme of moving spectacles is nevertheless clearly present in *Adventures on Salisbury Plain*, as it narrates its embedded stories of strangers responding humanely to scenes of others in distress (the sailor first to the soldier and then to the sailor's widow; the gypsies to the widow; the widow to the sailor's wife), a subject matter further complicated as we witness the sailor's own distress as his previous violence becomes phantasmagorical.

In *Adventures on Salisbury Plain*, then, Wordsworth's use of 'ideal presence' has become vastly more complicated. It is no longer a device in which a writer instills a predictable morality in the reader through a moving spectacle, but one in which spectacles find themselves problematically framed, prompting the reader's troubled introspection. It is unclear whether the visionary trance induced in the sailor by the sight of a previous malefactor hung up in chains does him any good (there is no link between this observed moment of ideal presence and the one in which he reaches out to the widow in the 'dead house', no evidence that it is part of a moral softening); while the transference of the gibbet from its literal site in the text, where it is observed by the sailor, to its figurative position at the end, where the sailor, hung up in verse, is observed by the reader, complicates matters, by implicating us (insofar as we are surprised to find ourselves reading as the idle curious). By embedding his 'moving spectacles' in the complexities of narrative Wordsworth has shifted the moral work, from the writer, who composes scenic lessons, to the reader, who is left to tease out an ethical position from his or her own compromised engagement. In this self-conscious teasing the illusion of ideal presence is firmly broken as readers find themselves involved in the political project of sounding the needs of strangers in revolutionary times rather than responding, piously, to stock images of distress. In spurring the reader's 'thinking heart' Wordsworth effectively anticipated Brecht's epic theatre, for his poetry draws us in, through the sharply pictorial delineation of character, his 'objects' of sympathy, only to alienate us by redirecting the reader to language, to the medium of expression in which the spectacle is 'charactered' or 'hardly clothed', as in the arresting puns on thinking 'hart' or 'drop'. The techniques Wordsworth developed in the *Salisbury Plain* poems provided the foundation for the revolutionary practice of the *Lyrical Ballads*.

4. 'The Thorn': *Lyrical Ballads'* revolutionary praxis

As Don Bialotosvky has pointed out, it is the presence of multiple points of view that make the lyrical ballads ballads. They are narratives, not just because they tell a story, but because they are dialogic; and it is in his dialogism that Wordsworth moves towards a revolutionary poetic praxis, one turning on the otherness of others and the 'democratic' challenge otherness poses to his readers.[59] 'The Thorn' is an obvious example to take, given that Wordsworth cites it as an instance of throwing his voice into another's – a garrulous old sailor's.[60] 'The poem of the Thorn is not supposed to be spoken in the author's own person' (*SP*: 276). The narrator is 'loquacious', a gossip, and, naturally, unreliable. 'Wordsworth's poetry ... charts its way through a complex middle ground in which the speaker's own good faith is as frequently challenged as is the integrity or honesty of those he encounters'.[61] As we shall see, the speaker's 'good faith' is material.

The key to the poem is meant to be obvious, even if it has puzzled subsequent readers distant from the events it refers to. The key is Martha Ray, the poem's protagonist. As we saw in Chapter 1, Ray was the victim of one of the most celebrated society scandals of the late eighteenth century; she was also the mother of Wordsworth's friend, Basil Montagu. Wordsworth specifies the timeframe to scotch doubt that he means *the* Martha Ray: 'Tis now some two and twenty years'.[62] If the telling of the story is contemporaneous with the poem's composition or publication (both 1798), Martha Ray's seduction would map onto the historical Martha Ray's moment of tragic misfortune. Despite their differences the two Marthas have much in common. Unwed mothers abused by faithless men, both are innocent butts of cruel gossip. As we earlier saw, the real Martha Ray was represented by the gutter press as a young milliner (a byword for prostitution), bartered to the Earl of Sandwich by a bawd with her father's consent; and while Hackman was portrayed as being motivated by romantic love, Ray figured as a faithless, sexual predator. The popular press transformed Ray's story from a moving spectacle to a commercial one, in which 'vain dalliance' with another's death was the precise, remunerative point.

Descriptive Sketches turned its subject matter of a lone gypsy mother into an affective spectacle, a picture of maternal nature in distress; 'The Thorn' takes the same subject matter, but within a far more complicated frame:

> There is a Thorn; it looks so old,
> In truth you'd find it hard to say
> How it could ever have been young,
> It looks so old and grey.
> Not higher than a two year's child
> It stands erect, this aged Thorn;
> No leaves it has, no thorny points;
> It is a mass of knotted joints,
> As a wretched thing forlorn.
> It stands erect, and like a stone
> With lichens is it overgrown.
>
> Like rock or stone, it is o'ergrown,
> With lichens to the very top,
> And hung with heavy tufts of moss,
> A melancholy crop:
> Up from the earth these mosses creep,
> And this poor thorn they clasp it round
> So close, you'd say that they were bent
> With plain and manifest intent,
> To drag it to the ground;
> And all had joined in one endeavour
> To bury this poor thorn forever.[63]

The unstated in the poem is transparent to the reader. The thorn is Martha Ray and the mossy hillock next to it the grave of her child. The mystery is how the child died. There may have been a crime; or the child may have died naturally. We are left to speculate, where speculation, or gossip, is the focus of the poem: the mosses and parasitical lichens dragging the thorn down are the village gossips, including the poem's loquacious narrator. The anthropomorphized intent of the malevolent mosses poses the real puzzle.

Why don't the village gossips recognize themselves in the mosses, as the cruel and destructive agents of Martha's tragic fate? More particularly, why doesn't the loquacious narrator know that, in so gossiping, he too is an agent of her misery (figuratively, at one with the destructive mosses)? The issue of poetic figuration is central to the theme of otherness articulated by the poem. In *An Evening Walk*, Wordsworth figured a swan as a nursing mother, a sentimental move unkind to both swans and mothers. 'The Thorn' frames such acts of poetic figuration by placing them within a particular point of view, where the central question is the failure of recognition of the consciousness coining them (the narrator as gossip). Readers might congratulate themselves on their greater perspicuity (where the effectiveness of the identification between Martha and thorn gains from being unforced, or ironically expressed), but we are not thereby let off the hook, which is where the allusion to Martha Ray comes in. For while most metropolitan readers will not have village gossips filling their ears with news (and it is hard to conceive who the intended readers of the experimental *Lyrical Ballads* were, if not metropolitan) they will have newspapers and other print versions of gossip. As we find ourselves cornered, by irony, into thinking better of Martha Ray than the malevolent village gossips do (indeed, moved in her defence by the poetic identifications we ourselves make), so will we begin to question and rethink the story of the real Martha Ray, whose reputation was dragged to the ground, and her family injured, by unthinking or mercenary sensation mongers.[64] Failure to reassess the lesson of the original Ray, after all, places the reader in the same position as the loquacious narrator, who reproduces, without understanding, tropes; who remains locked within a violent literalism. To read literally is also to read Gothically, as Martha Ray is transformed into a shrunken, smothered shrub beneath the public's Medusa-like gaze; or, to shift the reference, into a Gothic Daphnae turned gray by a god of night – by the press, as a kind of anti-Apollo. If the narrator unknowingly Gothicizes Martha, burying her alive in gossip, the reader certainly ought not to. To read the poem well is thus to enlarge one's views on the question of otherness, including the perplexing needs of others, while remaining alert to the complexities of language and power.

Though a liberal, Jeffrey, as a Whig, detested the levelling impulse of Jacobins; and he detected Jacobinism in poems such as 'The Thorn' because they implicitly endorsed a 'democratic subject', by which I mean a striving towards the representation of the full otherness of others, which naturally begged the question of the social and political entitlements of others. The production of otherness in the *Lyrical Ballads* was a matter of new techniques (of which narrative and management of point of view were crucial) and it constituted the thematic unity of the work. 'The Rime of the Ancient Mariner' was thus entirely integral to the collection's scheme, as it, too, turned on a moment of otherness, of failed recognition (regarding the Albatross) followed by a compromised one (the sea snakes). Among other things, producing a complicated otherness meant moving beyond the sentimental paradigm embedded within ideal presence, along the lines I have suggested.

5. Border Gothic

Wordsworth's revolutionary poetic agency resided in his ability to produce narratives in which the reader was placed in a compromising position that could not be satisfied by the neat moral equations of conventional sensibility. Wordsworth drew upon 'ideal presence' to conjure moving spectacles, but so complicated by a new narrative method – drawing us in while pulling us out – as to undermine old pieties. The reader's only egress was through an investigation of his or her own role as social agent. The otherness of others – and the moral consequences of recognizing the otherness of others – followed naturally from Enlightenment critique: but critique itself raised a problem. Wordsworth's revolutionary aesthetic required us to feel differently, but feeling was not enough. You could not feel your way out of the moral quandary raised by, say, 'The Thorn'. Readers had to think their way out. But if readers were unbound (untied, that is, from conventional moral responses, as postulated by Kant), what limits were there? If old forms of authority no longer bind us – the church, monarchies, or divine right – what does? 'Reason', was Godwin's answer, but reason – through reason's resources – often proved another name for self. In *The Convention of Cintra* (1809) Wordsworth uses the issue as proof of his own intellectual and political consistency. If he opposed England's war against France, in 1793, but supports it now, it is because 'the spirit of selfish tyranny and lawless ambition' (*Convention of Cintra, SP*: 172) was then embodied in Pitt's regime while it is now incarnate in Napoleon's France.

The anatomy of Rivers from *The Borderers* is Wordsworth's single most sustained analysis of 'the spirit of selfish tyranny and lawless ambition'. In developing a poetic practice that would realize his ideas about agency – the revolutionary praxis of moving accidents 'hardly-clothed' – Wordsworth naturally adopted the Jacobins' critical, Gothic idiom, given that it was the perpetuation of the feudal system that turned man against man and man against himself. *The Borderers* invokes critique, but in a spirit different from the one motivating his earlier work. Whereas the *Salisbury Plain* poems encouraged critique, the striking off of mind-forg'd fetters, *The Borderers* investigated the limits of freedom, and for this enterprise the obvious model was Schiller's *The Robbers*.

Like the *Salisbury Plain* poems, *The Borderers* is an extremely astute intervention in the developing 'Gothic' mode. For a start it is set in the middle of the period conventionally known as Gothic, that is, the thirteenth century, during the early reign of Henry III. As Robert Mighall has argued, Gothic is a matter not just of time, but geography.[65] Gothic begins as pastiche, as a recreation of the feudal past. A contrast between the past and modernity is therefore one of its defining features. In *The Borderers* this contrast is geographical. Mortimer and his band reign in the borderlands between an emerging state power, to the South, and continuing tribal conflict, to the North. In this interregnum between past and future, like Karl Moor and his banditti, they seek, in a self-created way, to impose order and justice. The 'tumultuous age'[66] of the play's setting obviously echoed the contemporary scene in which the issue of justice created *ex nihilo*, etched on a blank slate, was then in the process of being put to the test across the Channel.

The Borderers is both a continuation of *Adventures on Salisbury Plain* and its obverse. As with the poem live burial is the play's key trope, perhaps most obviously expressed in the central image of the sea captain abandoned on his desert island by his mutinous crew, an island so denuded of vegetation or any means of support as to be little more than an open-air coffin:

> 'Twas a spot –
> Methinks I see it now – how in the sun
> Its stony surface glittered like a shield:
> It swarmed with shapes of life scarce visible;
> And in that miserable place we left him –
> A giant body mid a world of beings
> Not one of which could give him any aid,
> Living or dead. (1982: 230, IV, ii, 38–44)

The image is a brilliant combination of privation and exposure. Nature has been so denuded of the nurturing principle as to take on the characteristics of the artificial (it shines 'like a shield'), while the human touch is utterly absent, manifestly so from Rivers's cold, sadistic phrasing.

Adventures on Salisbury Plain balanced live burial with regeneration, with moments when empathy for others and the raw recognition of their needs melted barriers, or bridged privation, whereas the play focusses almost exclusively on the breakdown of communication and community, on the hardening rather than melting of borders. The crew are indeed moved by the spectacle of the captain in extremis ('The groans he uttered might have stopped the boat / That bore us through the water') (Wordsworth 1982: 232, IV, ii, 49–50) but only to scoffing. Elsewhere characters lament that they are unable to speak or curse and thus give vent to feelings that destroy them from the inside.

The central action of the play is the perpetuation of the cycle of violence emanating from the abused Rivers. Rivers repays Mortimer's kindness in saving his life with hatred, which becomes, through the curious logic of sadomasochism, the desire to turn Mortimer into a version of himself, someone raised above the petty moral trammels of a superstitious society blinded by its adherence to what Rivers would have no difficulty in describing as a 'deformed Gothic idol' – the customary values of a feudal society. Rivers is tutored in 'critique' by brigands when they use him in a conspiracy against the captain of the ship in which they sail, a primal act of violence that frees Rivers's mind, enlarging its capacity. Rivers has in fact been divested of one of his deepest human needs: the need and capacity for human fellowship. The point is made through an antithesis that structures the play, between the blind Herbert who reaches out to everyone and the all-seeing Rivers, locked within himself, blind to others.

Although Iago-like, Rivers's malignancy is not motiveless. But the motive the play gives us – that Rivers perpetuates a cycle of violence in which he, too, is caught – does not get us far. Why are the brigands so merciless and why do they conspire to suborn Rivers's better nature in such a capricious fashion (given they could mutiny without him)? Unlike *The Robbers, The Borderers* does not locate a ready answer in the system from which the banditti flee, but in 'the very constitution of [Rivers's] character',[67] in his pride and perverted reason, all of which stem from the sailors' original act of violence against him. In this respect the motiveless malignancy is simply transferred, from Rivers to the sailors. Nevertheless, there are some clues. Mortimer echoes Rivers's crime against the captain in abandoning the famished Herbert on a blasted heath without accommodating his needs, an act repeated by the shepherd, Robert, who fails to play the good Samaritan through fear. His wife, Margaret, makes dark references to the rack and other instruments of torture, suggesting that institutional violence may be a factor in the poor betraying their better natures. Similarly, Mortimer's darkest and most Gothic moment (a scene built on 'The Fragment of a Gothic Tale') occurs within the crypts of Lord Clifford's castle where he finds himself caught between two forms of libertinage: Clifford as sexual libertine and Rivers as free thinker. It is certainly possible to read this scene Jacobinically, as a swipe at aristocratic corruption, but only up to a point, as Rivers's form of libertinage was typically associated, negatively, with 'empirics' and revolutionists. If it is a Jacobinical point, it appears divided against itself.

Within the castle Rivers bends Mortimer's mind, perverting him in the process. As subtle as Rivers is, his plot does not fully explain why Mortimer remains impervious to Herbert's needs on the heath, when, shy of a new-born babe crying for its mother, or vice versa, a blind old man calling for his daughter is the single most affective spectacle of human need contrivable by a playwright. Mortimer falters in carrying out Rivers's plan to murder Herbert, but only to ensure a more perfect repetition of Rivers's ur-crime of abandoning another to fatal privation. For further clues we are driven into Mortimer's psyche. Apparent jealousy of Herbert? A too credulous belief in the sexual frailty of womankind, given his ready acceptance of Matilda's willingness to consort with Clifford? A basic masochism that impels him to associate, self-destructively, with Rivers, despite an evil palpable to his companions?

The questions are unanswerable. Better to say that the work is a dark anatomy of the psychological chaos that reigns in a 'tumultuous' (that is, revolutionary) age. Nevertheless the play and its preface contain clues as to the direction in which Wordsworth's thought was tending. Wordsworth explains the peculiar relevance to the play of superstition:

> Having shaken off the obligations of religion and morality in a dark and tempestuous age, it is probable that such a character will be infected with a tinge of superstition. The period in which he lives teems with great events which he feels he cannot controul. That influence which his pride makes him unwilling to allow to his fellow-men he has no reluctance to ascribe to invisible agents: his pride impels him to superstition and shapes out the nature of his belief: his creed is his own: it is made and not adopted.[68]

Wordsworth begins with his version of Kant's definition of Enlightenment ('critique' as the shaking off of obligations), but then veers back to superstition. Rivers's 'superstition' is that he believes his creed has a special status, because self-fashioned, and based on his own interpretations. David Hume famously divided superstition into two kinds: the sort found in Catholic countries, when individuals surrender themselves, abjectly, to the authority of priests, and 'enthusiasm', the vice of Protestantism, where individuals, believing themselves the particular favourite of the Deity, set themselves above secular law. Although living in pre-Reformation times, Rivers is, in Hume's terms, a Protestant 'enthusiast'.[69]

Rivers discloses the origins of his enthusiasm. He describes his passage of soul making, in which, wandering 'Into deep chasms troubled by roaring streams', he contemplates the meaning of his actions:

> In these my lonely wanderings I perceived
> What mighty objects do impress their forms
> To build up this our intellectual being,
> And felt if aught on earth deserved a curse,
> 'Twas that worst principle of ill that dooms
> A thing so great to perish self-consumed.
> – So much for my remorse.[70]

For the unbound intellect, nature does not chasten and subdue, but uplifts the self, building an ungrateful, atheistic megalomania (the crux of Rivers's superstition).[71] For readers familiar with the later Wordsworth, the passage is bound to puzzle, given the tendency, of *The Prelude* especially, to celebrate such moments of transcendental 'impression'. The explanation is to be found in the ambiguity of the word 'intellectual'.

6. *The Prelude* and the flight from critique

In the *Salisbury Plain* poems Wordsworth accepts as given the need to free oneself from traditional authority, which he envisages, in his Jacobin phase, as a kind of gibbet, or wicker, that otherwise buries us alive, immured in a constitution that has become, not Blackstone's comfortable renovated mansion, but Christie's monstrous Gothic idol. But in *The Borderers*, to be unbound – free – is to be both Satanic and deluded. *The Prelude* narrates Wordsworth's own gradual acceptance of the need for discipline, of finding oneself bound:

> It might be told (but wherefore speak of things
> Common to all) that, seeing, I essayed
> To give relief, began to deem myself
> A moral agent – judging between good
> And evil, not as for the mind's delight
> But for her safety – one who was to *act*,
> As sometimes, to the best of my weak means,
> I did, by human sympathy impelled:
> And, through dislike and most offensive pain,
> Was to the truth conducted; of this faith
> Never forsaken, that by acting well,
> And understanding, I should learn to love
> The end of life, and every thing we know. (*Prelude*, VIII, 665–77)

Thus 'Retrospect', Book VIII of the 1805 *Prelude*. Whereas Rivers intellectually preens himself for being beyond good and evil, judging selfishly for 'the mind's delight', Wordsworth submits himself to hard truths, by sympathy impelled, a moral trajectory embedded in his developing aesthetic where Wordsworth's embrace of moral agency is to be recapitulated in the experience of reading Wordsworth. Just prior to this passage Wordsworth recounts the moment of illumination that led him to it:

> Then rose
> Man, inwardly contemplated, and present
> In my own being, to a loftier height;
> As, of all visible natures, crown; and first
> In capability of feeling what
> Was to be felt; in being rapt away
> By the divine effect of power and love;
> As, more than anything we know, instinct
> With godhead, and, by reason and by will,
> Acknowledging dependency sublime. (*Prelude*, VIII, 631–40)

In the 1805 *Prelude* Wordsworth dismisses Burke's rhetorical flights as 'grave follies'; in the 1850 *Prelude* Wordsworth begs the 'Genius of Burke' for forgiveness, while praising Burke for his denunciation of 'theory' and of all 'systems built on abstract rights' (1850, VII, 525). As *The Prelude* itself narrates,

Wordsworth had held to 'critique', to the view that we are not bound by traditionary authority; the subsequent inclusion of a hymn to Burke's proclamation of the 'majesty' 'Of Institutes and Laws, hallowed by time' thus represents a volte face. However, as James Chandler has argued, the turn towards Burke is already evident in the 1805 *Prelude*, which echoes one of Burke's most controversial slogans from *Reflections*: 'proud submission'.[72] Burke urged his readers to submit proudly to their country, as it was, to things as they are, and to present authority. Radical commentators replying to Burke picked up on the phrase – as much as they did the 'age of chivalry is dead' – as the expression of a shameful capitulation to corrupt authority and as an abdication of personal political responsibility.[73] It was not a phrase Wordsworth could be unfamiliar with. The 1850 *Prelude* substitutes the nation for nature as the object we submit to; and as such it is a more sharply nationalistic poem.[74] The 1805 *Prelude* nevertheless moves in this direction through its elevation of nature to the object before which we acknowledge our 'sublime dependency', or, as Burke would put it, our 'proud submission'. The stately cadence of the lines

> As, more than anything we know, instinct
> With godhead, and, by reason and by will,
> Acknowledging dependency sublime. (*Prelude*, VIII, 638–40)

surely echoes Milton's, in Book II of *Paradise Lost* (ll. 557–61), where the devils lose themselves in a syntactic maze as they puzzle, badly, on fate and free will – echoes it, that is, by way of contrast with the sublime dependency of Wordsworth's unvexed lines.

Wordsworth characterizes the overarching narrative of *The Prelude* as 'the growth of the poet's mind'. One could as easily characterize it as 'power regained'. *The Prelude* begins *in media res*, with the narrator 'enfranchised and at large' after his sojourn in the city. Nature's 'vital breeze', a recognized 'power' (*Prelude*, I, 9) vexes the narrator in the moment of his liberation, because he does not know what road to take. It augurs 'prowess in an honourable field' (*Prelude*, I, 52). But which field? The rest of the poem solves the riddle. The mind of the young Wordsworth had been fed by nature in his Lakeland home, albeit in a curiously superficial way. Although it nurtured his soul, Wordsworth fed upon nature as if it were an appetite or a passion: he drank it in through his eyes. Although this nurturing fed the future poet, it left the boy with an easily vexed double consciousness, fed by a power both familiar and inscrutable. The poem takes us through the past, as if a labyrinth through which the narrator found his way, or had his way found for him, and which ends with his regaining the power he first experienced as a youth, only one he now understands. And part of that understanding is that the true purpose of this power is poetry and that reason and politics are false turnings.

If the 1805 *Prelude* is the main narrative of Wordsworth's life up to that date, *The Borderers* is its intriguing subplot. Rivers, like Wordsworth, was a young man 'fired by a love of distinction'[75] who sets out to make his mark in revolutionary times. It is highly unlikely that Rivers represents Wordsworth as he was although one might plausibly argue that he represents Wordsworth as he feared he might be, or might become. Whereas Rivers is atheistically indignant at the 'mighty objects' that 'impress their forms / To build up this our intellectual being' (*Borderers*, I, ii, 136), as prefatory to our snuffing-out, Wordsworth acknowledges 'dependency sublime' (*Prelude*, VIII, 640), a proud submission key to his final succession to poetic power.

The 'spots of time' passages from Book XI narrate this moment of empowering humility, hence their pivotal position in the poem. Wordsworth's two examples of renovating memories are built around chastisement and discipline, but also, paradoxically, power. The spots of time are constituted by feelings of omnipotence (dubbed 'superstitious' in the context of Rivers's megalomania):

> This efficacious spirit chiefly lurks
> Among those passages of life in which
> We have had deepest feelings that the mind
> Is lord and master, and that outward sense
> Is but the obedient servant of her will. (*Prelude*, XI, 269–73)

Such power is swiftly qualified by the assertion of a greater, chastening force in which Wordsworth's poetic vocation is obscurely figured. The first example has two parts: the 'monumental writing was engraven' (*Prelude*, XI, 295) in the grassless spot where a murderer had mouldered on a gibbet and, nearby, a young woman with a pitcher on her head straining into a strong wind: together the scene constituted a 'visionary dreariness' (*Prelude*, XI, 311). The preternaturally legible writing in the earth recalls Wordsworth's anxieties in Book V, that poetry is perishable. The 'monumental' writing thus figures poetry itself, writing that endures. With this in mind a number of questions arise concerning the young girl with the pitcher. Is she Wordsworth's muse? More particularly, is she a figure of (or for) his sister or his wife, both of whom are central to Wordsworth's original scene of writing, as emblems of uncorrupted nature? The scene holds law, inspiration and writing in an ambiguous equipoise.

If inspiration and correction, malefactor and muse, are simply juxtaposed in the first example, they are causally linked in the second, in which Wordsworth lies sheltered in the hills straining to see a plain below, through the mists. Not long afterwards his father dies. To the young Wordsworth this seemed a 'chastisement' (*Prelude*, XI, 370), as if the 'anxiety of hope' (*Prelude*, XI, 372) with which he peered through the mists was a guilty pleasure and penetrative sight a sin: 'yet in the deepest passion, I bowed low / To God,

Who thus corrected my desires' (*Prelude*, XI, 375–6). As a consequence, the recollected scene, in which he peered through the mists, is reconstituted as a reusable memory (an ideal presence, Kames would call it):

> The single sheep, and the one blasted tree,
> And the bleak music of that old stone wall,
> The noise of wood and water, and the mist
> Which on the line of each of those two roads
> Advanced in such disputable shapes;
> All these were spectacles and sounds to which
> I would often repair, and thence would drink,
> As at a fountain ... (*Prelude*, XI, 378–85)

The movement from 'spectacle' to other senses ('sounds', 'drink') recapitulates the poet's own journey, his 'growth', as he calls it, from the visual to other forms of sensory apprehension. The movement is made even more explicit elsewhere in *The Prelude*:

> ... for I would walk alone,
> In storm and tempest, or in starlight nights
> Beneath the quiet heavens, and at that time
> Have felt whate'er there is of power in sound
> To breathe an elevated mood, by form
> Or image unprofaned; and I would stand,
> Beneath some rock, listening to sounds that are
> The ghostly language of the ancient earth,
> Or make their dim abode in distant winds.
> Thence did I drink the visionary power. (*Prelude*, II, 321–30)

Sound is elevated over sight in a bizarre synaesthesia in which the visual (now visionary) is drunk in through his ears.

The derogation of the faculty of sight (where images profane) and the emancipation from the despotism of the eye thus become a pivotal moment in Wordsworth's autobiographical arc. Hence his reference, as we saw earlier, to the time when the eye was the 'master' of his 'heart', holding his 'mind' in 'absolute dominion'. How he comes to break this sensual dominion, achieving poetic agency in the process, is left a mystery:

> Gladly here
> Entering upon abstruser argument,
> Would I endeavour to unfold the means
> Which Nature studiously employs to thwart
> This tyranny, summons all the senses each
> To counteract the other, and themselves,

> And makes them all, and the objects with which all
> Are conversant, subservient in their turn
> To the great ends of Liberty and Power. (*Prelude*, XI, 176–84)

Following on from the French Revolutionary books it appears that the meaning of liberty and power has shifted from a political register to a personal one, but in fact the meaning has simply reverted to what these terms meant at the start of the poem: tokens of the poet as the epitome of the sovereign subject. Even as 'Liberty' is emptied of its political content it accesses a nationalist one, as a linguistic sign for the quality that sets apart the liberty loving Briton. The poet achieves sovereignty only after his emancipation from despotic powers, foremost, the eye's. The abstruse means by which nature assists such emancipation, however, is 'matter from another song' (*Prelude*, XI, 185). Still, Wordsworth provides some clues:

> Here only let me add that my delights
> (Such as they were) were sought insatiably,
> Though 'twas a transport of the outward sense,
> Not of the mind, vivid but profound:
> Yet was I often greedy in the chase,
> And roamed from hill to hill, from rock to rock,
> Still craving combinations of new forms,
> New pleasures, wider empire for the sight,
> Proud of its own endowments, and rejoiced
> To lay the inner faculties asleep. (*Prelude*, XI, 186–95)

The proud, imperial eye, greedy for outward sense, finally learns 'dependency sublime' (thus awakening the inner faculties) through example:

> And yet I knew a maid
> Who, young as I was then, conversed with things
> In higher style; from appetites like these
> She, gentle visitant, as well she might,
> Was wholly free ... (*Prelude*, XI, 199–203)

The maid is Mary Hutcheson, Wordsworth's future wife. As with Dorothy in 'Tintern Abbey' Mary serves as a figure of purity and innocence who vouchsafes the possibility after which the poet aspires; so that the poet is led upward by devotion to her, as Dante is by Beatrice, Milton by the Holy Ghost, and the hero of *The Prelude* by the girl with the jug.

Wordsworth's denigration of visuality, of that which appeals to the eye, pervades both the1805 and 1850 *Preludes*, is, in fact, an aspect of Wordsworth's revision: thus, repeatedly, the 1805 'eye' is qualified, pejoratively, as the 'bodily eye', and on numerous occasions the text is changed to raise inner over outer vision. Thus, too, the tendency to esteem other senses, but especially hearing, as the prime inlet of 'presence'. One might say that in Wordsworth's revisions one catches the lyric turn in process, for the humbling of the empire of the eye is also an aspect of Wordsworth's switching liberty and power from a political to a visionary register. In the spots of time passages, critique is abandoned as a Rivers-like enthusiasm – a selfishness linked to the pagan pleasures of sight. Critique (meaning freedom from traditionary authority) is exchanged for being creatively bound by nature/nation: only then is Wordsworth empowered.

7. The institutionalization of the Wordsworthian reader

Of course Wordsworth did not stop writing complicated poetry after 1800 nor did he even cease to write what David Simpson calls poems of encounter (after Frederick Garber) in which suspect narrators engage with distressed or distressing others in ways bound to perplex and disturb the wary reader.[76] However, a complex interaction began to take place that was fundamental both to Wordsworth's reception and to the formation of what was to become Romanticism. Wordsworth did begin to create the 'taste' by which he was to be relished (remembering the complex disciplinary meanings this term had for Wordsworth). But his readers – including and perhaps especially his disciples – in turn instructed Wordsworth in the taste by which he was to become successful. His readers wanted fewer lyrical ballads, and more of the uplifting strain of blank verse found in 'Tintern Abbey', which of course they got, in spades, with *The Excursion.* In the end Wordsworth's baffling metaphysics proved less of an obstacle to understanding and appreciation than his awkward others and perplexing dialogisms. So, too, the controversy over his poetic 'system', with its low diction – as with the metaphysical question, this faded away as an issue. Just as readers accepted the need to modernize language so they also learned to regard the metaphysics as a non-specific, non-denominational and finally uplifting expression of the religious impulse. What was once considered as possibly Jacobinical pantheism, and certainly as Unitarian and Dissenting Deism, was now viewed as the sanative, purifying verse Wordsworth always insisted it was, in the very terms in which Wordsworth so insisted.[77]

The broad contours of Wordsworth's reception are well known. Contrary to common belief, the *Lyrical Ballads* were positively received, as Byron claimed. However, in Jeffrey's famous, 1802 review of Southey's *Thalaba*, the first shots were fired in what became an onslaught on Wordsworth, as the head of the Lakers, following the publication of the poems of 1807, after which it was fashionable to sneer at Wordsworth until around 1815, when John North's review in the *Champion* began to turn the tide.[78] By the 1820s Wordsworth was esteemed the greatest of all English philosophical poets and the third, overall, after Shakespeare and Milton. By 1834 the *Quarterly* was extolling his 'purifying, fertilizing, exalted influence', thus striking the key notes of his Victorian reception (*QR* LII [1834]: 321).

The facts of Wordsworth's reception altered the eighteenth-century myth of neglected genius, giving it its modern form. Wordsworth had been shunned, not just by the arrogant rich, or 'witty worldlings', but by obtuse critics (*QR*, LII [1834]: 355). Hence the now familiar ideas about genius that were novel to Wordsworth's contemporaries and which were worked out by them, in the act of puzzling over the Wordsworth phenomenon. The writer, as genius, was ahead of his time; by the same token, the true reader was a disciple, a member of a select, highly educated and attuned cult. The genius was marked by a peculiar inwardness and by strange depths, which challenged the uninitiated. Whereas Johnson had simply referred to Savage's perceptiveness, the Wordsworthian poet was marked out, physically, through his more developed organic powers.[79] Paradoxically, the true poet understood the many through isolation and withdrawal, sounding the wider world through nature.[80] Alert to the present and, indeed, to the future, the poet developed new, strange ways of writing, and new forms – hence the historicity of writing. Finally, the poet's art and his life became one, an erasure of the boundaries between public and private central to a new cult of personality.

As a number of recent critics have pointed out, the formulation of this myth was foundational to the English canon, to Romanticism and to literature itself as a discipline.[81] Or rather, there were several developments, each tending towards the same end. The glamour of depth generated by the poet-as-genius demanded a canon of the anointed; the anointed in turn recapitulated the nation; in its turn the nation was recast, following Burke, as the customs of the country in which immemorial rights and manners were embodied in the landscape that nurtured the yeomen who were its age-old and authentic product, on whose behalf the poet spoke, authorized (a phenomenon Kate Trumpener calls 'Bardic Nationalism'). The rise of the cult of personality may have prompted the lyric turn from history, but it was accompanied by the rise in the prestige of the pastoral and georgic .[82] Thus, whereas in 1798, the celebration of the peasantry carried the whiff of insurrection, by 1816 the *Quarterly* was praising Wordsworth for rightly estimating the patriotism, submission, and conservatism of the landed poor, in contrast to the insurrectionary nature of urban plebeians.[83]

From a political scientist's point of view, all of this is part-and-parcel of the rise of nationalist ideologies that accompanied the bourgeois revolution, where power was consolidated in the hands of a wider few, on new, secular terms.[84] From a sociologist's, it is part of the evolution of those disciplines that helped consolidate the power of the middle class. Henry Reed in a biographical note to his Wordsworth edition of 1852 makes the relevant point:

> The more the whole course of Wordsworth's life shall become known, the more will it be seen that it was a life devoted, in a deep and abiding

> sense of duty, to the cultivation of a poet's endowments and art, for their noblest and lasting uses – a self-dedication as complete as the world has ever seen.[85]

Wordsworth was devoted, not just to his art, but to his job. He was, in this respect, the first professional poet.[86]

If the rigours of the profession of letters became more stringent, as the bourgeois revolution progressed, so were the demands placed upon the reader. In the Introduction I cited Pierre Bourdieu's argument on this point. How arduous the demands were is evident from one of the important early reviews that helped shift opinion towards the 'Lakers'. The review is in fact of Coleridge's *Remorse*, from the *Quarterly*, and is by J. T. Coleridge, the poet's nephew, but its assessment of the 'lake poets' is focussed almost entirely through Wordsworth. The lake poets are not understood, says Coleridge, because no manifesto of their poetic principles has yet been issued, a deficiency he sets out to repair in his review, albeit judiciously, praising them where they are strong, but also correcting them where they go astray:

> To a profound admiration of Shakespeare, Milton, and our earlier poets, the authors of the system, on which we are remarking appear to have united much of metaphysical habit, and metaphysical learning. This admiration was not of the kind which displays itself in the conventional language of criticism; it was real, practical and from the heart; it led to ceaseless study, to imitation of its objects. Analysing by metaphysical aids the principles on which these great men exercised such imperial sway over the human heart, they found that it was not so much by operating on the reason as on the imagination of the reader. We mean that it was not so much by argument, or description, which the reason acknowledged to be true, as by touching some chord of association in the mind, which woke the imagination and set in instantly on a creation of its own. (Hayden 1971: 178)

Coleridge offers a virtual gloss of the claim that Wordsworth was doing something novel in poetry, by appealing, not to meaning, but association. He locates the claim, philosophically, by citing 'Mr. Alison's beautiful Essay upon taste', a work that sets out 'the true theory of poetic delight' (179). One of Kames's most influential pupils, Archibald Alison, updated Kames's theory of ideal presence by recasting it in the language of semiology, of natural or material 'signs'.[87] There were two main components of Alison's theory: the notion of an uncorrupted viewer and the tendency of natural images to act as signifiers. Recollecting nature's spectral traces in the bewitching introspective reverie that is ideal presence, a youth's mind will naturally move from images of decaying leaves, say, to thoughts of mortality and its associated emotions, or conversely will shift from the bright, uplifting colours of spring, such as those embodied in daffodils, to thoughts and feelings of rebirth.[88] Alison greatly assisted Wordsworth's reception by helping to transform the issue of Wordsworth's nature imagery from a question of pantheism to one of art, so that Wordsworth's metaphysics became less a sly form of Unitarianism (the usual objection) and more a case of an obscure manner of articulating an acceptable aesthetic, one that turned on a universal iconography of art, drawn from nature, and based on the figure of uncorrupted youth (the key lines being the ones quoted by the *Quarterly* in its canonizing review of 1834: 'If thou be one whose heart the holy forms / Of Young imagination have kept pure–').[89] Thus, when Wordsworth spoke of a flower being haloed in a nimbus of light he could be understood to mean, not that God inhered in the plant, but that to young, pure hearts the flower was an archetype of healthy religious emotion.

J. T. Coleridge argues that the lake poets have so far 'sacrificed the chance of general popularity for the devoted admiration of a few' by dwelling too much on the metaphysics of their art and not enough on its practice. Coleridge's praise is carefully judicious:

> Another source of peculiarities in the poets under consideration is the particular warmth and energy of their feeling in the contemplation of rural scenery. They are not the tasteful admirers of nature, nor the philosophic calculators on the extent of her riches, and the wisdom of her plans; they are her humble worshippers. In her silent solitudes, on the bosom of her lakes, in the dim twilight of her forest, they are surrendered up passively to the scenery around them, they seem to feel a power, an influence invisible and indescribable, which at once burthens and delights, exalts and purifies the soul. All the features and appearances of nature in their poetical creeds possess a sentient and intellectual being, and exert an influence for good upon the hearts of her worshippers. Nothing can be more poetical than this feeling, but it is the misfortune of this school that their very excellences are carried to an excess. Hence they constantly attribute not merely physical, but moral animation to nature. (181)

The passage is typical of Wordsworth's positive reception. The last two lines indicate that it was still a work in progress (with objections to the 'pathetic fallacy', eventually to be so termed by Ruskin, not being fully overcome until later in the century). It uses Wordsworth's own language to explain him, drawing especially heavily on 'Tintern Abbey' ('burthens and delights'); it focusses on what was conventional in Wordsworth's use of ideal presence, eliminating, almost entirely, what was radical; and it swaddles him in aestheticized religion. More to the point, as one disciple, possibly to another, Coleridge's essay instructs the reader in how to join the 'happy few'. The ideal Wordsworthian reader must recreate the poet's own encounter with nature as the shifting ground of the fleeting noumenal, by revolving inward, and idealizing the ideal (glimpsing the 'presence' that inheres, fleetingly, in nature's images). The imagined scene of instruction is not, say, the socially inflected one of 'The Thorn', or that of any other poem of social encounter, but an isolated engagement with scenery. In the aesthetically orthodox terms set out by Alison it amounts to the reader re-imagining the connection between natural signifiers and the signifieds arrived at by 'Young imagination', so that the ideal presence the reader surrenders to, in a reverie of artistic response – a fit of wise passiveness – becomes a test of the reader's associative mettle, especially its purity. In the philosophical terms then coming into fashion, and fast gaining respectability, the scene of instruction amounts to a transcendental engagement in which nature, as the thing-in-itself, promises to disclose itself as 'a sentient and intellectual being', before veiling itself in the moment of apprehension. In effect, the Wordsworthian reader submits to the discipline Wordsworth imagines for himself in the spots of time episodes of Book XI, from *The Prelude*, in which the vivid, visual and sensory (with the lurking failed desynonymy, sensual) is sublimated, and disciplined, as the visionary.

'In short, never perhaps has more been asked of the spectator, who is now required to "re-produce" the primary operation whereby the artist (with the complicity of his whole intellectual field) produced this new fetish' (Bourdieu: 31). One can describe this fetish, as it relates to Wordsworth, in numerous ways: as the birth of the Author; as the rise of the Author-as-personality; the art work as sanative and purifying; as something aglow with noumenal insight. The reader seeking to join Wordsworth's disciples – who through ideal presence recapitulate the work as the spectator's own inner, visionary (re)creation – not only internalizes the spectral encounters of 'Tintern Abbey', but reproduces the 'intellectual field' that lends it meaning. One might call this field 'Literature', or just 'Romanticism'. One might characterize it, with Clifford Siskin, as the disciplinary means by which the 'psychologized self' reproduces itself, as that through which we create inwardness and enjoy 'depth'. Alternatively, one might refer to it as the institutionalization of the Wordsworthian reader.

Insofar as academic Romanticism amounted to such an institutionalization, it institutionalized Wordsworth's counter-revolutionary turn (Rieder). In recent years this has been understood in various ways: as a rejection of the public sphere in favour of an atomized, private consumer (Gilmartin; Klancher); as the lyric turn from history (Siskin; Liu; Levinson); as a recapitulation of Burkean nationalism in which the individual surrenders political freedom in favour of a nationally inflected 'second nature', rebinding the subject within the customs of the country (Chandler; Deane). But in many respects it was put first, and best, by J. Russell Lowell. As an American steeped in the political afterglow of his own country's revolutionary moment Lowell had an instinctive feel for ideology.

> Wordsworth had been convinced, perhaps against his will, that a great part of human suffering has its root in the nature of man, and not in that of his institutions. Where was the remedy to be found, if remedy indeed there was? It was to be sought at least only in an improvement wrought by those moral influences that build up and buttress the personal character. Goethe taught the self-culture that results in self-possession, in breadth and impartiality of view, and in equipoise of mind; Wordsworth inculcated that self-development through intercourse with men and nature which leads to self-sufficingness, self sustainment, and equilibrium of character.[90]

Wordsworth abandoned critique for internalized self-discipline ('institutions' for the 'nature of man'), an internalization institutionalized within an academic Romanticism which understood its task as the pursuit of the Romantic image, as a reproducing of the hermeneutic moment in which signifier and signified, nature and meaning, either transcendentally met or (and here one can choose one's school of deconstruction) unravelled. The measure of how central this tradition has been is the virtual invisibility in Wordsworth criticism of the Gothic modalities explored by Wordsworth in his early development of critique before his flight into nature, nationalism and the isolated individual, and the slow recovery of Wordsworth's poetry of encounter.

3
The Romantic Abject: Cagliostro, Carlyle, Coleridge

> Now the Philosophic reflection we were to indulge in, was no other than this, most germane to our subject: the portentous extent of Quackery, the multitudinous variety of Quacks that, along with our Beppo, and under him each in his degree, overran all Europe during that same period, the latter half of the last century. It was the very age of impostors, cut-purses, swindlers, double-goers, enthusiasts, ambiguous persons; quacks simple, quacks compound; crack-brained, or with deceit prepense; quacks and quackeries of all colours and kinds. How many mesmerists, Magicians, Cabalists, Swedenborgians, Illuminati, Crucified Nuns, and Devils of Loudun! To which the Inquisition-biographer adds Vampires, Sylphs, Rosicrucians, Freemasons, and an *Etcetera*. Consider your Schropfers, Cagliostros, Casanovas, Saint-Germans, Dr. Grahams; the Chevalier D'Eon, Psalmanazar, Abbé Paris and the Ghost of Cock Lane! As if Bedlam had broken loose; as if, rather, in that 'spiritual Twelfth-hour of the night', the everlasting Pit had opened itself, and from *its* still blacker bosom had issued Madness and all manner of shapeless Misbirths, to masquerade and chatter there.[1]

> In London in the 1780s – and, indeed, in Western Europe very generally – there was something like an explosion of anti-rationalism, taking the form of Illuminism, Masonic rituals, animal magnetism, millenarian speculation, astrology (and even a small revival in alchemy), and of mystic and Swedenborgian circles. (Thompson 1993: xix)

In 1833 Thomas Carlyle published a long essay on Count Cagliostro in *Fraser's Magazine*. It may seem an odd choice of subject – a Sicilian mountebank from the previous century, the source of whose lasting notoriety was a bit part in the Diamond Necklace Affair that rocked pre-Revolutionary France, and whose most enduring work was the confession extracted by the Roman Inquisition, a tome published in 1792, three years previous to Cagliostro's demise in an Inquisitional cell. An obscure story, perhaps, but for Carlyle history's unfoldings always concealed fruitful matter: not only heroes, but their shadows – not just true coin, but counterfeits – signified. Carlyle's essay thus holds a great deal of interest for us, for in the act of identifying what was false about Cagliostro, Carlyle essays a version of the 'true', a separating of the wheat from the chaff that leaves us with Carlyle's historical kernel. In the middle of this winnowing, the cultural and institutional formation we call 'Romanticism' begins to assume a shape. Viewing the process of Romanticism's self-becoming it helps to focus on those moments where the Romantic encounters – throws down and expels – its necessary other. Carlyle's essay on Count Cagliostro is just such an illuminating instance. The essay was written on the verge of the Victorian period (1833) about a figure whose career terminated in the 1790s. The essay is by a late-Romantic, about a pre-Romantic; by a member of the belated, Romantic generation (born in 1795, the same year as Keats) about one of the most sensational members of the earliest possible Romantic generation. As such, I believe it tells us something about how Romanticism was generated.

Carlyle on Cagliostro keys us into Carlyle on Samuel Taylor Coleridge, another counterfeit Carlyle feels impelled to dwell upon and expose. For any historian of Romanticism as an institutional practice, few relationships hold as much interest as that between Carlyle and Coleridge. Wordsworth's poetry may have been a decisive, practical factor in the formation of a Romantic style, but the two weightiest voices responsible for the importation and embedding of German Transcendentalism – the Kantian legacy – into the Anglo-American tradition of Romantic studies were undoubtedly Coleridge and Carlyle. That Carlyle should feel Coleridge's impostor status, viscerally, may seem counter-intuitive, especially given Carlyle's self-avowed vocation of identifying the heroes whose mission it is to disclose the winding ways of the 'Divine Idea' to the uncomprehending masses. And who, in the province of criticism, had done more than Coleridge to prepare the ground for an enlightened transcendentalism? We have a range of easy answers: jealousy, envy, rancour at being pre-empted. Carlyle's response to Coleridge was, indeed, personal – but for Carlyle the personal and the critical were not separable. Carlyle on Cagliostro and Coleridge echo each other because both figures embodied the same transcendental quackery Carlyle felt necessary to distance from his own, more disciplined concern.[2] The real surprise is that Carlyle on Coleridge anticipates Coleridge on himself.

In this chapter the motive force I trace is not the power of an idea, such as, for instance, the imagination's transcendental capacities, but the power of an emotion: disgust or, as Julia Kristeva styles it, abjection.[3] As disgust is manifestly cultural, abjection is susceptible to historical analysis.[4] In the present case I aim to trace a significant theme among the first generation Romantics: revulsion, indeed horror, at materialism in general, but the body in particular. I glanced at this in the previous chapter through references to Wordsworth's mounting animus towards the 'bodily' eye, an anti-materialism I shall now trace across a series of borders: between quackery and transcendental philosophy, the phenomenal and noumenal, the counterfeit and the authentic; and, stylistically, between pun and image, simile and metaphor. As we shall see, this line of tracing terminates with Coleridge's celebrated distinction between the imagination and fancy, in his *Biographia Literaria,* the hook on which so many Transcendental Romanticisms have been hung. My purpose is not to arraign the early Romantics for Puritanism but to analyse how one of the founding texts of English Romanticism – Coleridge's *Biographia* – internalized and codified an anti-material reflex where the trace of the physical became the ruination of the ideal, with profound consequences for the kinds of writing that were deemed to fit, or not fit, Romanticism. I begin with Carlyle on Cagliostro, in part because it starts our anti-material hare, and partly because his essay makes clear how our conventional, Romantic periodization was already in place at the very time it was supposed to have terminated (1833), a periodization constructed out of the anti-materialism in question.

1. Carlyle on Cagliostro

One of the overriding purposes of Carlyle's essay on Count Cagliostro is to sustain the high reputation of the 'Romantics', as they would come to be called, against the incursions of precursors, such as Cagliostro. Continental Romanticism – in the shape of Goethe, Schiller and Mozart – found Cagliostro an intriguing, if ambiguous, person.[5] Cagliostro was a self-inventing questor on the margins of the great European courts. He was a restless traveller, an Orientalist (a cultivator of Egyptian mysteries), and finally an Illuminati and a revolutionary.[6] This does not make Cagliostro a Romantic, as he was not an artist, unless one includes con-artistry. My point, rather, is that the boundary between Cagliostro and 'Romanticism' is not so impermeable as Carlyle insists.

But first, who was Cagliostro? A mystery wrapped in an enigma, or to quote the even more colourful Carlyle: 'In such enigmatic duskiness, and thrice-folded involution, after all inquiries, does the matter yet hang' (Carlyle 1869: V, 73). The received story is that Cagliostro began life as Joseph Balsamo in Palermo, from a family of artisans fallen on hard times. After numerous scrapes, petty swindles and counterfeitings Balsamo absconded to Rome where he seduced, then married, the luscious fifteen-year-old Lorenza Feliciana. Finding a life producing bogus pencil etchings too tedious for his liking, Balsamo and Feliciana went upon the road, first as erstwhile pilgrims journeying to Santiago, and then more comfortably among the retinue of various wealthy marks infatuated by Feliciana's beauty. In the general view, Balsamo pimped his wife for a living across the Iberian peninsula until they found, arriving in London in 1771, a Quaker willing to pay considerable sums to keep his name out of the papers, having been caught in flagrante with Feliciana.

It was in 1776 that Balsamo re-emerged as Count Cagliostro accompanied by the Countess Serafina (as Feliciana now styled herself), once more in London. During the intervening continental wanderings Cagliostro assembled his identity as an Eastern magus, master of the Egyptian mysteries, crystal ball gazer, devotee of the Grand Architect, and friend of mankind. Decamping to the continent the Cagliostros passed through Nuremberg, Berlin, Leipzig and Konigsberg on their way to St Petersburg where Cagliostro drew the special attention of Catherine the Great. Hunted out of St Petersburg Cagliostro made his way to Strasbourg, the scene of his greatest triumphs, along the way passing back through Germany – some say Leipzig, others say Ingolstadt – where he took time off to be initiated into Adam Weishaupt's Illuminati, a revolutionary, Masonic offshoot dedicated to overthrowing the last remnants of the European feudal order.[7] In Strasbourg Cagliostro's greatest supporter was the Cardinal Rohan, who was shortly to find himself a leading figure in the Diamond Necklace Affair at Versailles. Looking to deflect attention from her part in the confidence trick, Jean de La Motte identified Cagliostro as the mastermind of the swindle. Cagliostro was able to prove, conclusively, that he could have had no part in the matter, and was released, but not before spending time in the Bastille, thus increasing his standing as a Masonic martyr. Thrown out of France Cagliostro returned to London in 1786 where his decline began, slow at first, then meteoric. Supplied by French intelligence, the London-based *Courier de l'Europe* ran stories disclosing Cagliostro's earlier career in dishonesty as Joseph Balsamo of Palermo. His reputation in tatters, and with Feliciana feeling homesick, the Cagliostros resumed the peregrinations that fatefully took them to Rome in 1789, where Cagliostro fell into the snares of the Inquisition. Having been put to the question, a full confession appeared in 1792. Cagliostro was detained at the Vatican's pleasure in a dungeon in the Apennines where he died in 1795.[8]

Caught between the Inquisitorial confession and Masonic counter-blasts, the truth of Cagliostro's story remains elusive.[9] 'In such enigmatic duskiness, and thrice-folded involution, after all inquiries, does the matter yet hang' (Carlyle 1869: V, 73). And that, precisely, is the point. For it is in his shape-shifting, self-invention, and boundary crossing that Cagliostro enjoyed a Romantic life. It is not hard to pick out Romantic affinities from Cagliostro's narrative, for instance the Swedenborgian strain in which, like Blake, Cagliostro claimed he conversed with Angels, while the rumours of his Illuminati past, involving subterranean caves near Frankfurt, were, for the young Shelley writing *Zastrozzi* and *St. Irvyne*, the very acme of all that was exciting and revolutionary in his present age. Again, before Byron, we have the invention of the moody but philanthropic Aristocrat endlessly traversing the continent, trailing clouds of eastern glory, in himself a persistent satire on 'things as they are'. And if that is pushing it, it is hard to see where the renewed interest in alchemy, as a metaphor for transcendental striving, came from, if not from Cagliostro and the European-wide notoriety of his Egyptian mysteries.

But more than any of these the real Romantic lesson of Cagliostro lay in his self-invention, his flair for counterfeiting, not theatre tickets, but an identity. In the age of self-validating genius, you were whatever your genius prompted you to be. Cagliostro was in himself a sign of modernity, of porous boundaries, interchangeable costumes, the ever-permeable drama of being, where initiation and transformation were one and the same thing. To complain of mystery was to commit oneself to origins, genealogy, history, the order of the past: irrelevant baggage summarily jettisoned by Cagliostro. In the Masonic lodges of Europe, the Count's final extirpation at the hands of the Inquisition was received as the authentic stamp of his status as a true friend of mankind.

For Carlyle, the lives of famous men are always worth attending to, even if only distinguished by exploits as dubious as Cagliostro's; for such lives tell the tale of their time, however obscurely. Carlyle draws out the lesson of Cagliostro's life history as the 'most perfect scoundrel' (1869: V, 67): 'Old feudal Europe, while Beppo flies forth into the whole Earth, has just finished the last of her "tavern-brawls", or wars, and lain down to doze ... for the brawl had been a long one, *Seven Years* long ...' But she does not sleep in order to renew herself:

> old Feudal Europe has fallen a-dozing to die! Her next awakening will be with no tavern-brawl, at the *King's Head,* or *Prime Minister* tavern; but with the stern Avatar of DEMOCRACY, hymning its world-thrilling birth- and battle-song in the distant West; – there from to go out conquering and to conquer, till it has made a circuit of all the Earth, and old dead Feudal Europe is born again (after infinite pangs!) into a new Industrial one. (V, 82)

Cagliostro's moment is an interregnum, a lacuna between epochs, a stagnant gap in history:

> In that stertorous last fever-sleep of our European world, must not Phantasms enough, born of the Pit ... flit past, in ghastly masquerading and chattering? A low scarce-audible moan (in Parliamentary Petitions, Meal-mobs, Popish Riots, Treatises on Atheism) struggles from the moribund sleeper: frees him not from his hellish guests and saturnalia: Phantasms these of 'a dying brain'. (V, 83)

The scene spread before Balsamo is Europe gripped by nightmare – his phantasmal life as Cagliostro being a choice symptom.

For Carlyle, the Seven Years War was the last gasp of the Feudal Age before the advent of a new, industrial one. Europe was to go through three distinct stages. The first stage of social decay – of national dishonesty and universal Quackery – came to an end with the Revolutionary seizures that gripped Europe, convulsions that were no more than a peristalsis afflicting the body politic, the unavoidable symptoms of ineluctable historical change: the 'birth pangs' of the industrial age. This period of upheaval is Carlyle's second stage; his third, implicitly, is his industrial present. Carlyle's analysis contains several assumptions that will migrate into Romanticism. First, he dates it from after 1789: before, and we are in the phantasmal world of the *Le siècle des lumières*, the 'swindler-century', as he elsewhere terms it,[10] with its rampant quackery. Second, although wracked by symptoms of epochal transition, Romanticism was distinguished by a will to truth, by the antithesis of eighteenth-century sophism. Third, Romanticism falls on the modern side of the historical divide signified by the French Revolution. And, finally, Romanticism has been placed in jeopardy by the new industrial hegemony, with its armies of placemen, its 'Undeclared Quacks', as Carlyle calls them.

Carlyle has a vested interest in imposing a clear boundary between the pre-Romantic and the Romantic. For Carlyle, 1789 is that clear boundary. Carlyle has a similar need to reinstate Cagliostro south of the line. The thrilling call to truth which for a moment awoke old, cultural Europe from its slumbers has subsided into Carlyle's meretricious, industrial present, a time made phantasmal by the unrealized lies and counterfeiting of a mundane, commercial society. For Carlyle, materialism has made the present spectral, a point Carlyle underlines in an essay that forms a companion piece to the present one, on the Diamond Necklace Affair, where Carlyle borrows Gaspard-Etienne Roberstson's 'phantasmagoria' to describe the spectralization of modern, everyday life.[11] By contrast, Cagliostro has the merit of being a 'decided liar', hence his queasy attraction to Carlyle. Modernity has assumed the condition of moral greyness and confusing unreality; in that limited respect it compares unfavourably with the stark clarities of eighteenth-century Quackery where the simple principle of inversion will see one right.

What was invested in the need for this historical and moral diorama? The language Carlyle lavishes upon Cagliostro offers us clues. At birth, Balsamo was 'A fat, red, globular kind of fellow, not under nine pounds avoirdupois . . .' (V, 74). Adolescence gives us 'a fat thickset Beppo ... ' filching sausages (V, 75). Balsamo's 'leading capability seemed only the Power to Eat' (V, 76). For Carlyle, Cagliostro is no more than an anthropomorphosed gastropod: the 'voracious' Beppo 'sumptuously supported, for a long course, the wants and digestion of one of the greediest bodies, and one of the greediest minds ... ' (V, 70). Later Carlyle waxes lyrical on Cagliostro's portrait:

> Fittest of visages; worthy to be worn by the Quack of Quacks! A most portentous face of scoundrelism: a fat, snub, abominable face; dew-lapped,

> flat-nosed, greasy, full of greediness, sensuality, oxlike obstinacy; a forehead impudent, refusing to be ashamed; and then two eyes turned up seraphically languishing, as in divine contemplation and adoration ... (V, 110)

What is clear is that, for Carlyle, being comfortably built is not a sign of ruddy health, nor even of excessive appetite. It is the mark of corruption: 'Putrescence is not more naturally the scene of unclean creatures, in the world physical, than Social Decay is of quacks in the world moral' (V, 83). Moral decadence finds its complement in physical putrescence: Cagliostro swells, not with rude, healthy flesh but with a peculiar moral / physical, putrid viscosity. Cagliostro is 'stupid, pudding faced ... there is a vulpine astucity in him; and then a wholeness, a heartiness, a kind of blubbery impetuosity, an oiliness so plausible-looking ... ' (V, 80). The oily putrescence of Cagliostro's physical uncleanness is sharpened, is made more disgusting by, the monumental energy of Cagliostro's hunger, together with its vulpine cunning. Cagliostro is the abject antithesis of transcendental striving, a spiritual hunger that has become all body, a travesty caught in the contrast between Cagliostro's sagging flesh and his fey, upward gaze. Carlyle's rhetoric revolves around a symmetry: the voracious Beppo of the early part of the essay is mirrored by the sociological analysis of the later part where we hear how dishonesty was the 'raw-material' of pre-Revolutionary Quackery, hunger its 'plastic energy' (an analeptic reference to Coleridge's famous 'esemplastic power' of the imagination, one hinting at Carlyle's equation of Cagliostro with Coleridgean flummery). For Carlyle, Cagliostro (but also, as we shall see, Coleridge) is this 'raw material', this 'plastic energy', incarnate.

At its baldest Carlyle's historiography amounts to the simple sequence: putrescence, catharsis, decline; late Enlightenment decay, Romantic cleansing, industrial and commercial muddying. Carlyle's deepest need is to maintain the possibility of there having been a hygienic moment – in which phantasmal corruptions and counterfeitings were for a time sloughed off – by which to measure and damn his mediocre present. The corruptions of the Romantic body therefore had to be cast off – 'abjected' – the dead skin liquefying around the oleaginous Beppo, while a purer being stepped forth across the flames of 1789. One could say, more prosaically, that Carlyle preferred a lean, fit Romanticism, kept trim through obsessive pedestrianism among the lakes and dales. What we see in Carlyle's essay is a deep, and doubtless unconscious, need to purify the esemplastic power of the Romantic imagination by purging it of the plastic power of bodily hunger, separating the Romantic imagination from material realities of all kinds. Such a purification is not simply effected through the adoption of genres in which the personal prevails over the social and historical but is also constituted at the level of personality formation.[12] For Carlyle, Romanticism and materialism did not fit. Compared to Carlyle on Coleridge, the encounter was mere shadow-boxing.

2. Carlyle on Coleridge

In his *Life of John Sterling*, published in 1851, Carlyle appears to provide a balanced, picturesque and appreciative view of the elderly Coleridge, the celebrity sage of Highgate, a figure Carlyle represents as – to quote J. Russell Lowell on Edgar Allan Poe – 'two fifths pure genius, three fifths pure fudge':

> Coleridge sat on the brow of Highgate Hill, in those years looking down on London and its smoke-tumult, like a sage escaped from the inanity of life's battle; attracting towards him the thoughts of innumerable brave souls still engaged there. His express contributions to poetry, philosophy, or any specific province of human literature or enlightenment, had been small and sadly intermittent; but he had, especially among young inquiring men, a higher than literary, a kind of prophetic or magician character. He was thought to hold, he alone in England, the key of German and other Transcendentalisms; knew the sublime secret of believing by 'the reason' what 'the understanding' had been obliged to fling out as incredible; and could still, after Hume and Voltaire had done their best and worst with him, profess himself an orthodox Christian, and say and print to the Church of England, with its singular old rubrics, and surplices at Allhallowtide, *Esto perpetua*. A sublime man; who, alone in those dark days, had saved his crown of spiritual manhood; escaping from the black materialisms, and revolutionary deluges, with 'God, Freedom, Immortality' still his: a king of men. The practical intellects of the world did not much heed him, or carelessly reckoned him, a metaphysical dreamer: but to the rising spirits of the young generation he had this dusky sublime character; and sat-there as a kind of *Magus*, girt in mystery and enigma; his Dodona oak-grove (Mr Gilman's house at Highgate) whispering strange things, uncertain whether oracles or jargon.[13]

As the portrait develops the poison concealed within this genial appreciation of the newly canonized figure leeches to the surface. As with Cagliostro, Carlyle narrows in on Coleridge's body, his material characteristics:

> Brow and head were round, and of massive weight, but the face was flabby and irresolute ... The whole figure and air, good and amiable otherwise, might be called flabby and irresolute ... He hung loosely on his limbs, with knees bent, and stooping attitude; in walking, he rather shuffled than decisively stept ... His voice, naturally soft and good, had contracted itself into a plaintive snuffle and singsong; he spoke as if preaching ... earnestly

> and also hopelessly the weightiest things. I still recollect his 'object' and 'subject,' terms of continual recurrence in the Kantean province; and how he sang and snuffled them into 'om-m-mject' and 'sum-m-mject' with a kind of solemn shake or quaver, as he rolled along.[14]

The spirit may be willing, but the flesh is evidently weak, with the repeated 'flabby' the measure of Coleridge's spiritual irresolution, as if fat were the outward manifestation of his decayed will. Even Coleridge's greatest quality, his gift for words, is materialized: 'Nothing could be more copious than his talk ... it was talk not flowing any whither like a river, but spreading everywhither in currents and regurgitations like a lake or sea'. Without aim or 'logical intelligibility' the listener felt 'swamped near to drowning in this tide of ingenious vocables'. Carlyle ends by acerbically noting that 'To sit as a passive bucket and be pumped into, whether you consent or not, can in the long-run be exhilarating to no creature.'[15] The run of suggestion, from incontinent flow to 'regurgitation', leaves it open to the reader's imagination to decide on the bodily effluent with which Coleridge's talk ought best be compared, for which the listener is the unwilling recipient.

Carlyle's Coleridge doubles Cagliostro, another counterfeit 'magus' swaddled in transcendentalisms and excess flesh. Carlyle's acquaintance with John Sterling, a disciple of Coleridge's, dates from 1835. Although that is the occasion of the recollection, Carlyle's meeting with Coleridge dates from 1824, nine years previous to the essay on Cagliostro. Of this first meeting, in his letters and notebooks, Carlyle's assessment of Coleridge is, in comparison, unbuttoned. On 20 December 1824, Carlyle writes to his wife that 'Coleridge is sunk inextricably in the depths of putrescent indolence'; while to his brother he observes, a month later, that 'Coleridge is a mass of richest spices, putrified into a dunghill ...'[16] Coleridge not only shares Cagliostro's putrescence but also his disgusting viscosity: 'A round fat oily impatient little man, his mind seems totally beyond his control.' He also displays the Sicilian's undisciplined appetites: 'When all was said, Coleridge was a poor greedy, sensual creature.'[17] Alimentary metaphors are also resorted to. If Coleridge suffered from intellectual diarrhoea in the portrait from the *Life*, in Carlyle's late *Reminiscences*, on the occasion of their first meeting in June 1824, he is afflicted by something like the opposite:

> Coleridge, a puffy, anxious, obstructed-looking, fattish old man, hobbled about with us, talking with a kind of solemn emphasis on matters which were of no interest ... I had him to myself once or twice, in *narrow* parts of the garden-walks; and tried hard to get something about *Kant* and Co. from him, about 'Reason' *versus* 'Understanding,' and the like; but in vain ...[18]

It is as if Carlyle has gently urged the costive sage into a private space, in order to help him deliver himself of his Kantean profundity, hopelessly compacted within the great man.

In a letter to his brother, dated 24 June 1824, Carlyle introduces another aspect of Coleridge's abject condition. After introducing him as 'the Kantean metaphysician and quondam Lake poet', he observes:

> Figure a fat flabby incurvated personage, at once short, rotund and relaxed, with a watery mouth, a snuffy nose, a pair of strange brown timid yet earnest looking eyes, a high tapering brow, and a great bush of grey hair... He is a kind, good soul, full of religion and affection, and poetry and animal magnetism. His cardinal sin is that he wants will; he has no resolution, he shrinks from pain or labour in any of its shapes... He is also always busied to keep by strong and frequent inhalations the water of his mouth from overflowing; and his eyes have a look of anxious impotence; he would do with all his heart, but he knows he dare not.[19]

The 'animal magnetism', inserted after the run of qualities Coleridge himself might have embraced, as his fondest self-characterization, lethally deflates the poet, from magus to quack. After again making the point about the copious, a-methodical nature of Coleridge's talk (echoing the physical imagery of an unpleasant, boundary effacing facial deliquescence), Carlyle concludes by noting that he reckoned Coleridge 'a man of great and useless genius – a strange not at all a great man'.[20] 'Useless genius' points to Coleridge's impotence, the very centre of Carlyle's queasy fascination. In a letter to Thomas Murray, Coleridge is characterized as 'a steam-engine of a hundred horse power – with the boiler burst'.[21] In a letter to Jane Carlyle, Coleridge has become unmanned: 'Poor Coleridge is like the hulk of a huge ship; his mast and sails and rudders have rotted away'.[22] This was, it seems, a favourite metaphor, for it is re-run in a letter to Mrs Basil Montague (18 July 1825): 'A seventy-four-gun ship, but water-logged, dismasted, cannot set a thread of sail.'[23] In a journal entry from 26 May 1835, the impotence nearly takes a bizarre, literal turn: 'I do *not* honour the man; I pity him (with the *opposite* of contempt); see in him one glorious up-struggling ray (as it were), which perished, all but ineffectual, in a lax, languid, impotent character ... '[24] It's as if Coleridge's transcendental brio has detumesced into bathetic quackery. The major encomium granted in the *Life of John Sterling* – that Coleridge had escaped from the deserts of materialism with his 'crown of spiritual manhood' intact – is privately withdrawn. Or rather, once alerted by his personal opinions, one sees that Carlyle's positive assessment was only ever held in the suppositions of free indirect speech, as Carlyle represents a common view he quietly deflates.

Why this hostility? And why this disgust? The phrase 'useless genius' provides an initial clue. According to the transcendental lights Carlyle and

Coleridge share, 'useless genius' is a contradiction in terms. By definition, the genius is prepotent, not by dint of physical prowess, to be sure, but by virtue of being connected – deeply, perhaps intuitively, but finally, manifestly – with the noumenal reality (the Divine I AM) from which true power ultimately derives. The glorious ray of genius is forever 'up-struggling'. Coleridge's physical attributes, his outward, spiritual clothes, are in tatters, betraying his impotence and also – for Carlyle, much the same thing – his fraudulence. If Coleridge is not a counterfeit genius, the alternative is too terrible to bear, for this shambolic figure, with his endless, pointless talk and his lubbery body must be the real thing. The fact that for John Sterling, and for others of a rising, younger generation, Coleridge was a Magus, incarnate, whispering 'oracles', lent urgency to Carlyle's delicate task of expressing, without undue prejudice, his visceral sense that Coleridge's Delphic utterances were mystic 'jargon'.

However, to unmask Coleridge – to demote the newly canonized Romantic saint – was to put at risk the periodization Carlyle is at pains to establish in his essay on Cagliostro. Carlyle wants to argue that the immediate post-Revolutionary period witnessed a spiritual advance his materialistic present presently needs. Denouncing Coleridge as a fraud would seem to undermine the narrative Carlyle wants to establish, effacing alike the boundaries between Cagliostro's flummery and Coleridge's oracles, and between late Enlightenment quackery and the German transcendental project. Charles Sanders' observations are to the point:

> the ideas of Coleridge and Carlyle, both great readers of German literature and philosophy, have much in common. But because personality meant much to Carlyle, even more than ideas, he could rarely apprehend Coleridge's ideas except as they filtered to him through his intervening impression of Coleridge's personality and through the very powerful emotions associated in him with that impression. Accordingly, he more than once failed to recognize in Coleridge some reflections of himself.[25]

Or, conversely, because he did not fail. Coleridge was Carlyle's abject, a version of himself he feared, deep down, he might be. And not just of himself, for Coleridge was also a living parody and negation of the project they shared. Both wanted to allot to genius an oracular position in modern culture, hence the issue of Coleridge's 'personality', which was unlike anything Carlyle wanted to envisage when it came to heroes and hero-worship. The figure of the genius was also part of a larger project pertaining to the institutionalization of a new school of criticism. If at an intellectual level Carlyle 'filtered' Coleridge's ideas 'through his intervening impression of Coleridge's personality', at a deeper, psychic level he filtered them through his impressions of Coleridge's body, the abject embodiment of the materiality Coleridge ought to have transcended.

The broad outlines of Carlyle's project are evident in his essay, 'The State of German Literature', first published in *Frazer's Magazine* in 1827. Carlyle's thesis in the essay is that German 'Romanticism' inaugurated a new science of criticism, which 'England' would do well to emulate. To pave the way for the reception of the 'New School' of criticism Carlyle feels he needs to slay the two main prejudices which frighten inquisitive English readers: that the culturally primitive Germans evince chronic bad taste; and that they are prone to mysticism.

In tackling the subject of Teutonic tastelessness, Carlyle touches upon many of the topics on which the received views of Romanticism have recently been challenged. Carlyle begins by characterizing the popular view of German literature:

> If one were to judge from Heinse, Miller, Veit Weber the Younger or Kotzebue, one might establish many things. Black Forests, and the glories of Lubberland; sensuality and horror, the spectre nun, and the charmed moonshine, shall not be wanting. Boisterous outlaws also, with huge whiskers and the most cat-o'-mountain aspect; tear-stained sentimentalists, the grimmest manhaters, ghosts and the like suspicious characters.

But then Carlyle asks, 'what should we think of a German critic that selected his specimens of British Literature from the Castle Spectre, Mr. Lewis's Monk, or the Mysteries of Udolpho, and Frankenstein or the Modern Prometheus?' (I, 32). Carlyle, we should recall, is here referring to the most successful playwright of his day, as well as a novel-writing *Wunderkind*; the period's leading romance writer, whose recent death had occasioned expressions of the highest critical esteem; and, currently, the period's single most canonical work. In other words, Carlyle takes as read one of the main consequences of the cultural formation we now know as 'Romanticism': the division of high and low literature, with its implicit relegation of women writers (and, it must be said, a token homosexual) to a second division.

Carlyle's next target is Germany's alleged lack of a public sphere. The view that German society was so bereft – caught between a backward aristocracy and an unenlightened peasantry – was a late eighteenth-century commonplace.[26] According to English prejudices, German writers were isolated hacks deprived of civilized society who necessarily wrote for money (I, 33), a lack Carlyle turns into an advantage. He concedes that German booksellers cannot pay as English ones do; and that the German writer has nothing like an Englishman's chance of attaining a sinecure given the proliferation of literary institutions, of 'universities, libraries, collections of art, museums, and other literary and scientific institutions of a public or private nature ...' For Carlyle, this is, however, of questionable benefit to the good taste of the English writer, as 'it tempts him daily and hourly to sink from an artist into a manufacturer . . .' (I, 37). Carlyle endorses the Romantic withdrawal from the public sphere by taking the lack of one as a benefit: untroubled by commerce, German writers are able to keep their gaze fixed on higher aims.

The German writer's commitment to weightier artistic goals is reinforced by the intellectual culture of the German nation, which is far ahead of all others in 'the practice or science of Criticism' where it 'proceeds on other principles, and proposes to itself a higher aim'. Carlyle accurately summarizes the criticism of a 'half-century ago' – the school of rhetoric and belles-lettres based in the Scottish universities – as 'concerning the qualities of diction, the coherence of metaphors, the fitness of sentiments, the general logical truth, in a work of art'.[27] For modern reviewers, the question is now 'mainly of a psychological sort, to be answered by discovering and delineating the peculiar nature of the poet from his poetry' (I, 43). German criticism concerns itself with both these things, but it also tackles a far more difficult and important question about 'the essence and peculiar life of the poetry itself': namely,

> by what far finer and more mysterious mechanism Shakespeare organised his dramas, and gave life and individuality to his Ariel and his Hamlet. Wherein lies that life; how have they attained that shape and individuality? Whence comes that empyrean fire, which irradiates their whole being, and pierces, at least in starry gleams, like a diviner thing, into all hearts? Are these dramas of his not verisimilar only, but true; nay, truer than reality itself, since the essence of unmixed reality is bodied forth in them under more expressive symbols? What is this unity of theirs; and can our deeper inspection discern it to be indivisible, and existing by necessity, because each work springs, as it were, from the general elements of all Thought, and grows up therefrom, into form and *expansion* by its own growth? Not only who was the poet, and how did he compose; but what and how was the poem, and why was it a poem and not rhymed eloquence, creation and not figured passion? (I, 43–4)

There is much Coleridgean matter here, as would have been familiar to Carlyle via Coleridge's *Biographia Literaria*, published a decade earlier, or *The Friend*. There is the distinction between verse and poetry, between Pope and Milton, or between Wordsworth and the rest of his contemporaries; implicitly, the distinction between allegory and symbol; 'organicism'; the creative unity of the primary and secondary imagination (the general elements of all Thought); and, underlying all, a pervasive transcendentalism. If these similarities speak to Carlyle's self-conscious mission, others reveal his unconscious one, such as the automatic equation of poetry with literature (at the implicit expense of unpoetic drama – staged drama – or prose), or the equally automatic acceptance of Shakespeare's late eighteenth-century apotheosis.

Despite the manifest similarities in their views, and in their shared commitment to the institutionalization of the New School of higher criticism, Carlyle never mentions Coleridge in the essay. Coleridge's absence seems even stranger when it comes to Carlyle's characterization of the source of poetic beauty, as here Carlyle is less directly concerned with German transcendentalism (where one might say Carlyle was simply bypassing Coleridge's representation of it) and more directly trespasses on ground Coleridge marked as his own.

> Poetic beauty, in its pure essence, is not, by this theory, as by all our theories, from Hume's to Alison's, derived from anything external, or of merely intellectual origin; not from association, or any reflex or reminiscence of mere sensations; nor from natural love, either of imitation, of similarity in dissimilarity, of excitement by contrast, or of seeing difficulties overcome. On the contrary, it is assumed as underived; not borrowing its existence from such sources, but as lending to most of these their significance and principal charm for the mind. It dwells and is born in the inmost Spirit of Man, united to all love of Virtue, to all true belief in God; or rather, it is one with this love and this belief, another phase of the same highest principle in the mysterious infinitude of the human Soul. To apprehend this beauty of poetry, in its full and purest brightness, is not easy, but difficult ... to apprehend it clearly and wholly, to acquire and maintain a sense and heart that sees and worships it, is the last perfection of all humane culture ... Sensation, even of the finest and most rapturous sort, is not the end, but the means. (I, 47–8)

It is not simply that Carlyle ends with an echo of Coleridge's discussion of pleasure and the ends and means of poetry (*BL*: II, 12–13). More profoundly, Carlyle structures his thought directly on the pattern of the *Biographia Literaria*: like Coleridge, Carlyle distances himself from associationism and its material empiricism in order to establish a deeper analysis of poetic effect, which like Coleridge he grounds in the active, creative powers of the imagination. Finally, the passage's insistence on the creative synergy of spiritual unity strongly echoes Coleridge's famous championing of the 'one life'.

But the oddest aspect of Coleridge's omission is that if anyone had a reputation for introducing the new school of German criticism into England, and therefore a right to be acknowledged, it was Coleridge. Why this silence? A glancing allusion to the sage of Highgate suggests an answer. The German school of criticism is no easy matter: it is conducted through 'rigorous scientific inquiry' based on sound philosophical principles 'deduced patiently, and by long investigation'. It is not to be accomplished through 'a vague declamation clothed in gorgeous mystic phraseology' or by 'vehement tumultuous anthems to the poet and his poetry; by epithets and laudatory similitudes drawn from Tartarus and Elysium, and all intermediate terrors and glories'

(I, 44). Among these Cagliostros of criticism, with their 'gorgeous mystic phraseology', Carlyle appears to intend Coleridge.

The problem is not simply that Coleridge evinces an unfortunate tendency towards mysticism, to 'jargon'. Carlyle cites Fichte's characterization of the Transcendental project.

> According to Fichte, there is a 'Divine Idea' pervading the visible Universe; which visible universe is indeed but its symbol and sensible manifestation, having in itself no meaning, or even true existence independent of it. To the mass of men this Divine Idea of the world lies hidden: yet to discern it, to seize it, and live wholly in it, is the condition of all genuine virtue, knowledge, freedom; and the end, therefore, of all spiritual effort in every age. Literary Men are the appointed interpreters of this Divine Idea . . . (I, 49)

'Literary men' is a significant equivocation as it covers both 'creative writers' (assumed to be poets) and 'critics'. Carlyle is at pains to establish that the practitioners of the new criticism are strenuous philosophers who conduct their enquiries on sound, albeit abstruse principles, pursued in a spirit of great moral earnestness. He is also anxious to remove the stain of mysticism that had seeped into the reputation of Kant and his followers, hence the last half of the essay, which devotes itself to the task of establishing the intellectual probity of Kant, Fichte and Schelling. For Carlyle, the present age was marked less by an upsurge in poetry, and more by the inception of a beautiful system of criticism, first invented in the cafes of Weimar. Indeed, so significant does Carlyle feel this new criticism to be that he compares its advent to the Reformation. The task of this criticism was to interpret poetry as the prime literary medium of the Divine Idea. But throughout the essay Carlyle's stress falls, not on the creation of poetry, but on its appreciation, on the role of the philosopher-critic who redeems society by interpreting the Divine Idea, poetically expressed, which the mass of mankind are unable, themselves, to know. For this new critical project to work – for it to secure the cultural dominance Carlyle wishes it to have – the idealism it propagates must not be contaminated by untoward associations with 'magi', mysticism, intellectual flabbiness or impenetrable cant. Simply put, in Carlyle's estimation of their shared, transcendental project, Coleridge did not fit.

3. Coleridge on himself – *Biographia Literaria*

The real measure of the oddness of Carlyle's exclusion of Coleridge from the transcendental project is that, up until Carlyle's essay on the state of German literature, Coleridge was its chief architect. Coleridge was banished from his own building.

The similarities between Carlyle's essay on German literature, and Coleridge's *Biographia Literaria* are worth dwelling on, as are their differences. Fundamental points of agreement include the necessity of placing criticism on a sound, philosophical, Kantian footing, an ambition Coleridge characterizes as the adoption of 'fixed canons of criticism, previously established and deduced from the nature of man ... ' (*BL*: I, 62). As we have seen, they are also alike in sharing a developed sense of 'high and low' literature; in associating literature with poetry, as a matter of reflex; and in adopting Shakespeare as the gold standard for 'genius'. They are equally suspicious of 'counterfeits' (*BL*: I, 42). Here Coleridge supplies a 'Carlylean' assessment of the problem:

> In the days of Chaucer and Gower our language might ... be compared to a wilderness of vocal reeds, from which the favourites only of Pan or Apollo could construct even the rude Syrinx; and from this the *constructors* alone could elicit strains of music. But now, partly by the labours of successive poets, and in part by the more artificial state of society and social intercourse, language, mechanized as it were into a barrel-organ, supplies at once both instrument and tune. Thus even the deaf may play, so as to delight the many ... Hence of all trades, literature at present demands the least talent or information; and, of all modes of literature, the manufacturing of poems. The difference indeed between these and the works of genius, is not less than between an egg and an egg-shell; yet at a distance they both look alike. (*BL*: I, 38–9)

Coleridge concurs with Carlyle's anxiety that literature is being hollowed-out through commercialization and mechanical production – but there is also a distinctly Coleridgean inflection. In a *Notebook* entry from 1799, Coleridge comments: '*Of* the harm that bad poets do in stealing & making *unnovel* beautiful images' (*Notebooks* I, 470). '[S]tealing & making' embodies a conundrum that haunted Coleridge the poet: wherein lies originality, when each locution (barring outright plagiarism) is distinct? To recast an image is also to 'make' it. In this grey area, how do you draw the line between making new and stealing? The strong, 'Romantic' sense in which Coleridge understood genius compounded the problem, as it placed an impossible premium on originality. In the above passage, Coleridge partially reveals his historicist answer to the problem, what he elsewhere refers to as 'desynonymy', or the philosophical obligation to separate near synonyms, revealing their essential differences (such as, most famously of all, 'fancy' and 'imagination').[28] At the start of *Biographia Literaria* Coleridge asserts that if a word is translatable into another it is 'vicious' (*BL*: I, 88). Coleridge's critical philosophy is in this respect deeply historicist. Words and images – poems – must be distinct and new. Hence the damage done by those creative artists who recast beautiful, yet 'unnovel', images.

Coleridge's sense of originality is slippery, because mystical and quasi-Kantian. In the *Biographia*, Coleridge anxiously explains that his metaphysical system is not 'incompatible with religion, natural or revealed', and this includes what it is he has taken from Kant. Reacting against the 'lawless debauchery and priest-ridden superstition' of the Prussian court, Kant's bold, Christian metaphysics might be mistaken for atheism, as was the case with his disciple, Fichte:

> In spite therefore of his own declarations, I could never believe it was possible for him to have meant no more by his Noumenon, or Thing in Itself, than his mere words express; or that in his own conception he confined the whole *plastic* power to the forms of the intellect, leaving for the external cause, for the *materiale* of our sensations, a matter without form, which is doubtless inconceivable. (*BL*: I, 155)

If Kant was hesitant to ascribe no more meaning to the noumenal than the 'Thing in Itself', Coleridge was not so cautious.[29] For Coleridge, the noumenal and Wordsworth's 'correspondent breeze' were much the same thing. The intellectual history of Coleridge's quasi-Kantian understanding of the Noumenon is not hard to reconstruct. The figure of the spiritual breeze that rolls through all things, setting the poet's imagination, his Aeolian harp, in motion, was fatally compromised by the materialism of the Hartleyian system of association on which it was initially based. Coleridge's break with Hartley, begun as early as 1794, and apparently completed by 1801, when he claimed to have 'overthrown the doctrine of Association' (Letter to Poole, 16 March 1801), is too well known to require yet another rehearsal.[30] Suffice to say that Coleridge came to identify the Hartleyian system with four main, related shortcomings: first, it left no place for volition, and therefore the 'subject' in the creative act; second, as a materialist theory, it transformed the subject into a mere machine, or 'automaton'; third, as a 'necessitarian' philosophy it was without the philosophical wherewithal to address the question of creativity; and, finally, it had become indelibly associated with Jacobinical politics of Dissenting philosophers, such as Joseph Priestley, Hartley's editor and popularizer, or with Godwinian utopianists. At the same time as Coleridge was breaking with Hartley, he was discovering Kant, who apparently offered a way out of the Hartleyian impasse through a series of unities: of the phenomenal with the noumenal; the subject and the object; the active and passive; the plastic power of the 'forms of the intellect' with the 'materiale' of our sensations; willing and feeling; words and things; symbols and referents. In endeavouring to explain the mysterious, organic unity of thought, Coleridge was pushed to one of his most famous metaphors:

> Most of my readers will have observed a small water-insect on the surface of rivulets, which throws a cinque-spoted shadow fringed with prismatic

colours on the sunny bottom of the brook; and will have noticed, how the little animal *wins* its way up against the stream, by alternative pulses of active and passive motion, now resisting the current, and now yielding to it in order to gather strength and a momentary *fulcrum* for a further propulsion. This is no unapt emblem of the mind's self-experience in the act of thinking. There are evidently two powers at work, which relatively to each other are active and passive; and this is not possible without an intermediate faculty, which is at once both active and passive. (In philosophical language, we must denominate this intermediate faculty in all its degrees and determinations, the Imagination). (*BL*: I, 124–5)

The analogy appears to shadow forth the symbiotic mysteries of the imagination, but its ground is theology. Coleridge was at ease with neither revealed nor natural religion or, as the tension was theologically registered, neither the Trinitarian beliefs of the Established Church nor the Unitarianism of rational Dissent, as one led to idolatry and the other to pantheism. Revealed religion risked literalism (severing the letter from the spirit), whereas Natural religion inculcated the atheistic belief that God was not only in everything but also was everything (including evil).[31] Kant's noumenon, or rather, Coleridge's revision of it, bridged the gap. Thus nature was essentially dead without the perceiving subject; and yet the perceiving subject elicits from the object its divine intentionality – the noumenal and immanent – without the risk of pantheism, an act of perceptual synergy (a marriage of the active and passive principles) which, while common, is best expressed by the unifying faculty Coleridge denominates as 'imagination'.

Unity is the leitmotif that ties together the *Biographia Literaria* (just as division provides the drama). Coleridge begins his intellectual history by dwelling on the stylistic lesson his revered school master beat into him: that ornament is vicious, because otiose. An expression is proper, when there is a seamless, un-redundant unity between words and thoughts. The rest of Coleridge's intellectual history (as portrayed in the *Biographia Literaria*) is a voyage of discovery to the language – to the philosophical and critical principles – capable of explaining Coleridge's school-master's advice in its deepest and most philosophical light. Thus, too, the overthrow of Hartley's system, which he comes to understand, as not just a mechanical but as a fragmented and fragmenting philosophy: 'Again, from this results inevitably, that the will, the reason, the judgement, and the understanding, instead of being the determining causes of association, must needs be represented as its *creatures*, and among its mechanical *effects*' (*BL*: I, 110). Associationism transforms the faculties into mere disparate effects. The upshot of such materialism is that it 'removes all reality and immediateness of perception, and places us in a dream-world of phantoms and spectres, the inexplicable swarm and equivocal generation of motions in our own brain' (*BL*: I, 137). Without a transcendental principle, the material world is surreal, a counter-intuitive version of experience Carlyle will help cement in the public imagination by borrowing's Robertson's coinage ('phantasmagoria') as his tag phrase for the spectral effects of modern materialism.[32]

In contradistinction to Hartley, first through Kant and then through Schlegel, Coleridge fashioned a philosophy in which he was able to attribute to a deep or unified self the originating source or energy that impelled the plastic, creative breeze. 'The existence of an infinite spirit, of an intelligent and holy will, must on [Hartley's] system be merely articulated motions of the air' (*BL*: I, 120). This 'infinite spirit' was the something more that Kant meant, but could not quite say, by 'noumenon'. But if Coleridge was transcendental when it came to the subject, he remained largely empirical when it came to objects. What Coleridge broke with was not the vocabulary of associated sense data – of ideas marshalled through similarity, contrast or contiguity – but with the 'non-sense of vibrations' (*Letters* I, 626), with senseless concatenations of cause and effect among the inscribed residues of the mind's tabula rasa, set going by 'motions of air'. In the place of vibrations, Coleridge inserted a perceiving, willing, creative 'absolute' self, which commanded the associative field. Subject and object formed a dynamic, seamless ying and yang: hence our free will, 'our only absolute *self*, is co-extensive and co-present' in the 'living chain' of association (*BL*: I, 114), while its function is 'to controul, determine, and modify the phantasmal chaos of association' (*BL*: I, 116).

'The postulate of philosophy, and at the same time the test of philosophic capacity, is no other than the heaven-descended *Know thyself*' (*BL*: I, 252). This inward turn is an inevitable aspect of Coleridge's transcendental philosophy, as it is through the 'subject' that the noumenal finds expression. In the ten theses that precede his explication of the imagination, Coleridge sets out his fundamental philosophical premises. The foundation of all other knowledge is 'a truth self-grounded, unconditional and known by its own light' (*BL*: I, 268).

> This principle, and so characterized manifests itself in the SUM or I AM, which I shall hereafter indiscriminately express by the words spirit, self and self-consciousness. In this, and in this alone, object and subject, being and knowing, are identical, each involving and supposing the other. (*BL*: I, 272–3)

Coleridge truncates Descartes's cogito, as the 'I think' is redundant. 'SUM', self-consciousness, is the irreducible ground of all else. Human self-consciousness echoes the divine: 'We begin with the I KNOW MYSELF, in order to end with the absolute I AM. We proceed from the SELF, in order to lose and find all self in God' (*BL*: I, 283). It follows that the truest 'spirit', 'self' or 'self-consciousness' is the one that is most closely attuned to the divine I AM, which it in some sense duplicates. Just as self-consciousness is the irrefragable ground of human ontology, so it is for the Divine Being. Here, in particular, 'object and subject, being and knowing' are indivisible. Hence Coleridge's famous definition: 'The primary *imagination* I hold to be the living Power and prime Agent of all human perception, and as a repetition in the finite mind of the eternal act of creation in the infinite I Am' (*BL*: I, 304). Creative perception, as the seamless intertwining of subject and object, is at its most intense in the repetition within the subject of the Divine I AM. What Coleridge says about the secondary imagination does not imply that it is a lesser faculty than the primary; on the contrary, the inflections denote the powers of genius to reproduce the seamless, creative perception of the divine I Am, powers distinguished by the capacity of the 'absolute self' to modify, consciously, the streamy nature of association:

> The secondary I consider as an echo of the former, co-existing with the conscious will, yet still as identical with the primary in the *kind* of its agency, and differing only in *degree*, and in the *mode* of its operation. It dissolves, diffuses, dissipates, in order to re-create; or where this process is rendered impossible, yet still, at all events, it struggles to idealize and to unify. It is essentially *vital*, even as all objects (*as* objects) are essentially fixed and dead. (*BL*: I, 304)

It was common during the pre-Romantic period to refer to the 'plastic power of the imagination';[33] Coleridge's innovation was to prefix the phrase with 'esem', meaning, as he earlier explains, to 'unify' (*BL*: I, 168). For the Transcendental Coleridge, the noumenal inheres within the phenomenal: to perceive this presence in disparate things is thus to unify, in the sense of bringing together what otherwise seems chaotically scattered. Instinct with the noumenal, the imagination is, by definition, 'vital', just as the phenomenal, stripped of the noumenal, is 'fixed and dead' (*BL*: I, 304). Fancy, by contrast, is the secondary imagination disconnected from the deep, productive self. Thus creative volition has become 'choice'; and instead of transcending the laws of association (the tracks of identification which our sense data have worn themselves into) fancy merely obeys them. By implication, in fancy, the self is prone to the phantasmal chaos of association, which 'thinking' otherwise (in the special, creative sense Coleridge allots to it) 'curbs and rudders' (*Notebooks* I, 1770).

For Coleridge language is the medium of creative perception; his theory is therefore historicist and linguistic. The roots of Coleridge's thought reach deep into the poet's early life. He touches upon the germane, linguistic issues in a letter to William Godwin from 1800:

> I wish you to write a book on the power of words, and the processes by which human feelings form affinities with them – in short, I wish you to *philosophize* Horn Tooke's System, and to solve the great

> Questions – whether there be reason to hold, that an action bearing All the *semblance* of pre-designing Consciousness may yet be simply organic, & whether a *series* of such actions are possible – and close on the heels of this question would follow the old 'Is Logic the *Essence* of Thinking?' in other words – Is *thinking* impossible without arbitrary signs? & – how far is the word 'arbitrary' a misnomer? Are not words &c parts & germinations of the Plant? And what is the Law of their Growth? – In something of this order I would endeavour to destroy the old antithesis of *Words & Things*, elevating, as it were, words into Things, & living Things too. All the nonsense of vibrations etc you would of course dismiss. (*Letters* I, 625–6)

Horne Tooke's philology was based on the premise that words have their origins in natural analogies. Rather than purely arbitrary signifiers, words imitate, or enact, their objects, a series of connections lost over time. The philological act, for Tooke, is the chasing down of the original connection between word and thing obscured through subsequent linguistic change.[34] In urging Godwin to philosophize Tooke, Coleridge hints at his own transcendental project. Reading back from the *Biographia Literaria*, we can see that the language of organic vitalism stems from Coleridge's belief that true creativity derives from the seamless unity of subject and object in the imaginative act of perception, a perceptual unity that also characterizes the invention of language (the product of primitive genius). If this invention is a product of the transcendental moment, it follows that its connections will not be arbitrary, but the product of organic growth. Given the indivisibility of the moment of creation, or linguistic coinage, it would also follow that words and things are themselves indivisible, having, indeed, the same unity as subject and object in the creative moment of perception.

A shifting field of language and poetry confronts the genius. He cannot pretend to be a Chaucer or Gower faced by a 'wilderness of vocal reeds'. Such false naiveté would be historically retrograde; worse, by not confronting the contemporary challenges of language and poetry, the poet risks masquerading as a primitive, adopting vicious ornaments, or producing not a poem but a damaging simulacrum (a shell and not an egg). His task, rather, as Coleridge makes clear in his discussion of Wordsworth, is to defamiliarize the world, to dissolve the film of customary perception by reconnecting words and things (*BL*: I, 81). But as poetry, society and language have all changed, are indeed changing, so will the poet's task alter; and not an inconsiderable aspect of this change is the progress German metaphysics, especially, has wrought. For Coleridge, Christianity was not being secularized; it was being placed on intelligible philosophical principles. Coleridge was a linguistic progressivist; hence his stress on desynonomy, his restless search for *le mot juste*, and his numerous coinages. The important principle was the vital capacity of language, linked to transcendental perception. It was this principle, and this principle alone, which could save poetry in the 'present artificial state of society' (*BL*: I, 38), with its mechanical trade in poems.

But if Coleridge's theory of the imagination, as adduced in the *Biographia Literaria*, was historicist, it was also cut adrift from a larger public, and therefore from direct social engagement. Like Carlyle, Coleridge bemoaned the debasement of the public sphere:

> Poets and philosophers ... addressed themselves to '*learned* readers'; then ... 'the *candid* reader'; till ... THE TOWN! And now finally, all men being supposed able to read, and all readers able to judge, the multitudinous PUBLIC, shaped into personal unity by the magic of abstraction, sits nominal despot on the throne of criticism. But, alas! as in other despotisms, it but echoes the decision of its invisible ministers, whose intellectual claims to the guardianship of the Muses seem, for the greater part, analogous to the physical qualifications which adapt their oriental brethren for the superintendence of the harem. (*BL*: I, 59)

Coleridge's views are reminiscent of debates from the 1790s, when the public sphere came under intense pressure. Suffice to say, that for the most part Coleridge sides with those who view the extension of the public sphere – the growth of a literate, discriminating, multitudinous public – with great alarm. Like many others critical of the public sphere, Coleridge's critique was both nationalist, and, by the same token, explicitly anti-internationalist:

> The youthful enthusiasts who, flattered by the morning rainbow of the French revolution, had made a boast of expatriating their hopes and fears, now disciplined by the succeeding storms, and sobered by the increase of years, had been taught to prize and honour the spirit of nationality as the best safeguard of national independence, and this again as the absolute pre-requisite and necessary basis of popular rights. (*BL*: I, 190)

Nicholas Roe has shown just how deeply implicated Coleridge was in such 'youthful enthusiasm': clearly, Coleridge is referring to himself, winking to let us know that he knows that we know.[35] Coleridge prepares the ground for his apostasy through his earlier references to his involvement with *The Watchman*, his organ of jejune political enthusiasm. In order to elude Pitt's stamp tax, Coleridge published *The Watchman* every eight days (*BL*: I, 179). What Coleridge does not spell out, but which any member of the opposition would have understood, was that Pitt's tax was designed, explicitly, to curb the circulation of information within the artisan and Dissenting classes, so preventing the formation of a 'counter-public sphere'. In the 1790s, Coleridge played a vigorous role in trying to create such a counter-public sphere, through lectures, newspapers and cross-country tours. Nearly twenty years later, he recounts his involvement in such a way as to welcome his own failure. His shift is registered in a simple alteration of prepositions: the task of the poet / philosopher is to plead 'for', rather than 'to', the 'poor and uneducated' (*BL*: I, 185).[36] Stripped of his audience (corrupted high and low by commerce and politics) the poet must needs turn transcendental, must fix his sights on 'higher aims', as Carlyle was to put it (I, 43). Such an inward turning, however, serves nationalist ends:

> If then unanimity grounded on moral feelings has been among the least equivocal sources of our national glory, that man deserves the esteem of his countrymen, even as patriots, who devotes his life and the utmost efforts of his intellect to the preservation and continuance of that unanimity by the disclosure and establishment of *principles*. For by these all *opinions* must be ultimately tried; and (as the feelings of men are worthy of regard only as far as they are the representatives of their fixed opinions) on the knowledge of these all unanimity, not accidental and fleeting, must be grounded. (*BL*: I, 190)

The glorious unanimity Coleridge refers to is the drawing together of the English nation against France and Jacobinism. As the discoverer, and communicator, of the philosophic principles that alike underwrite poetry, canons of criticism, and ethics, Coleridge reveals himself as a patriot soldier working in the interests of English 'glory'. As his notebooks attest, earlier in his career Coleridge was worried by charges that his metaphysics were ungrounded and dangerous.[37] By the time Coleridge came to write his intellectual life history, he had found that context: nationalism and national regeneration. In doing so, he was falling into line with *The Anti-Jacobin Review and Magazine,* which in its first number, in 1798, editorialized that the 'innate rooted attachment to sound principles, religious and political, which only requires to be called forth, in order to shine with transcendent lustre' needs urgently to be fostered, for to it we must turn 'for the preservation of our national establishments amidst the shocks of contending factions, the wreck of surrounding governments, and the general desolation of the civilized world'.[38] By the time of the *Biographia Literaria,* Coleridge understood himself to be deploying metaphysics in order to foster 'innate attachments' in a nationalist cause, in order that they should, in poetry, 'shine with transcendent lustre'. It was an anti-Lockean, anti-empirical, counter-Enlightenment aspiration.

4. His own misfit

Although published in 1816, *Biographia Literaria* has its roots deep in the 1790s, Coleridge's formative decade. However, Coleridge's literary biography does more than take us back to the beginning of his intellectual story: it represents the outcome of the profound poetic and philosophical conflicts that distinguished this portion of his intellectual career. It tends, therefore, to gloss and to obscure Coleridge's own losing arguments, the positions he adopted, or was interested in, but which he subsequently abandoned, renounced or suppressed. Coleridge was addressing a public substantially different in its political temper from the one he had felt the presence of twenty years earlier, and to the later public he sought to justify the ways of the younger man, often by misrepresenting him. We know this, partly from the historical record of Coleridge's political activities in the 1790s and also from Coleridge's notebooks and letters, which provide an alternative, contemporaneous *biographia literaria* of the significant decade. This material has to be read with some caution, as the letters and notebooks are not simple windows on what Coleridge then was; they are also interested self-representations staged before diverse audiences. Thus, the very Coleridge who announces to various paternal figures, such as his older brother George, or the father of Charles Lloyd, that he has broken his 'squeaking baby-trumpet of sedition' (he repeats the phrase), is the very same Coleridge on cordial and fraternal terms with John Thelwall and William Godwin, two of the decade's most notorious Jacobins. This caveat apart, the notebooks and letters do provide us with a sense of Coleridge's losing positions, of what it was he left behind, in constructing his mature views about the imagination, which is to say, about 'genius', the dominant concept in his poetical and philosophical self-identity. In a nutshell, during this period – from the mid-1790s to the early years of the new decade – Coleridge abandoned his self-identity as a poet for that of the metaphysical critic, whose mission it was to explain what the poet's achievement might have been, indeed, should have been. In his identity as metaphysical critic, Coleridge laid down much of the philosophical foundation for what was to become English 'Romanticism'. If this ensured his status as a canonical figure, it also came at a cost: his vocation as poet. The creative expectations Coleridge attached to genius, to the esemplastic power, were not ones that suited his talents, as he came to understand them. He was, or rather became, his own misfit.

Coleridge's anxieties about his vocation as poet intensified in the course of his gentleman's agreement with Wordsworth that on the whole it would be best if Coleridge occupied an even more exiguous position in the second edition of *Lyrical Ballads*, owing partly to the slow pace of Coleridge's creativity, and partly to its character: that is to say, besides being unfinished, 'Christabel's' praeternatural subject matter jarred with Wordsworth's sublunary themes (*BL*: II, 8). Understandably the rejection ate away at Coleridge's self-confidence. He tells Thelwall, in December 1800, that 'As to Poetry, I have altogether abandoned it, being convinced that I never had the essentials of poetic Genius, & and that I mistook a strong desire for original power' (*Letters* I, 656). The character of these 'essentials' would clarify by the time of the *Biographia Literaria*, but for now the matter was in the balance. Buoyed up by the composition, in April 1802, of the letter to Sara

Hutchinson containing a draft of the 'Dejection' ode, Coleridge asserts to William Sotheby that 'by nature I have more of the Poet in me', and to prove it provides a sample of 'Dejection' (*Letters* II, 814). Unfortunately, circumstance had forced him into '*downright metaphysics*', from whose snares he finds it difficult to escape (*Letters* II, 814). On 29 July 1802, Coleridge presents a much grimmer picture to Southey. After complimenting Southey's poetic prowess, Coleridge laments, 'As to myself, all my poetic Genius, if ever I really possessed any *Genius*, & it was not rather a mere general *aptitude* of Talent, & quickness in Imitation / is gone – and I have been fool enough to suffer deeply in my mind, regretting the loss'. Coleridge attributes his decline to several sources: 'Ill-health', 'private afflictions', and to his 'long & exceedingly severe Metaphysical Investigations' (*Letters* II, 831). However, Coleridge immediately follows this with another excerpt from 'Dejection', thus belying his self-deprecations. 'Dejection', of course, itself tells the story of Coleridge's failing 'genial powers', the suspension of 'what Nature gave me at my Birth, / My shaping Spirit of Imagination'.[39] So even allowing for the stratagems one poet might adopt before another, in the delicate task of poetic self-assertion, Coleridge undoubtedly felt himself in poetic crisis, to the extent that it had become his proudest poetic subject.

In his notebooks and letters he presents himself as a case history of 'genius gone wrong'. Throughout, Coleridge employs a medical register to describe his failure. To Poole, Coleridge freely discloses his symptoms without fear of poetic rivalry. On 6 December 1800, he describes his body as 'a very crazy machine' (*Letters* I, 650); a few months later (17 May 1801) 'the machine was crazed' (*Letters* II, 730). In the same letter, Coleridge indicates that his illness was complicated by opium. His habit undoubtedly compounded his problems; but it is not the source of Coleridge's poetic difficulties, nor does it account for the language he employs to describe his symptoms.[40] Coleridge's 'case history' is embedded in a quasi-medical, quasi-philosophical language, and it is through this web of discourse that we derive our deepest insights into Coleridge's creative crises. Thus, it is important to note that in this instance Coleridge's self-characterizations anticipate his attack on materialism in the *Biographia Literaria*, where the materialist conception of imaginative activity is described, we recall, as removing 'all reality and immediateness of perception and places us in a dream-world of phantoms and spectres, the inexplicable swarm and equivocal generation of motions in our own brain' (*BL*: I, 137). Without the ghost in the machine – without the something more Coleridge means by 'noumenal' – the mind becomes a spectre-crazed automaton.

Coleridge's 'subject and object' were designed to remedy the shortcomings of sceptical empiricism, from both ends. The problem with empiricism was twofold: first, it argued that there was no necessary connection between our sense data and the real-world objects that generated them; and second, in the empirical 'system' mind 'is always passive – a lazy Looker-on on an external World'.[41] Coleridge's philosophy sought to establish vital connections between an active observer and an immanent world through language as a non-arbitrary medium. Coleridge greatly suspected daydreams and reveries as mental states in which representational connections were severed: indeed, they seemed to replicate the materialist theory of the mind, as a 'lazy Looker-on' of swarming 'spectres'. At the same time, Coleridge was an inveterate daydreamer, addicted to its intense pleasures. Coleridge refers to daydreams (and, indeed, dreams) with ambivalence, or downright disapproval, from early on in his career, before his acknowledged addiction to opium. As early as November 1794 Coleridge exclaims to Mary Evans (the object of an early, hopeless love affair), referring to daydreams: 'But these are the poisoned Luxuries of a diseased Fancy!' (*Letters* I, 130).

During his period of poetic crisis, Coleridge characterizes his imagination as degrading, through disease, into 'materialism', meaning, in Coleridge's specialized, negative sense of the term, a propensity to the phantasmagoric. Thus Coleridge tells Humphry Davy (2 December 1800), a propos of his illness and the writing of poetry, that 'my voluntary ideas were every minute passing, more or less transformed into vivid spectra' (*Letters* I, 649). On 22 January 1802, he writes to Godwin that 'an unhealthy and reverie-like vividness of *Thoughts*, & ... a diminished Impressibility from *Things* ... ' accompanies the undoing of his will (*Letters* II, 782). It is a condition in which words and things disastrously come apart: 'all but dear & lovely Things seemed to be known to my Imagination only as Words' (*Letters* II, 737). Coleridge refers to a double disjunction: the quotidian is known to his imagination as words without referents, while 'dear & lovely Things' have become wordless, visual phenomena, or 'spectres'. Coleridge immediately adds a qualification ('even the Forms which struck terror into me in my fever-dreams were still forms of Beauty'), and then says:

> Before my last seizure I bent down to pick something from the Ground, & when I raised my head, I said to Miss Wordsworth – I am sure, Rotha! that I am going to be ill: for as I bent my head, there came a distinct & vivid spectrum upon my Eyes – it was one little picture – a Rock with Birches & Ferns on it, a Cottage backed by it, & a small stream. – Were I a Painter I would give an outward existence to this – but I think it will always live in my memory. (To William Godwin, 23 June 1801: *Letters* II, 737)

At this point in his development, and crisis, Coleridge registers ambivalence with regard to this 'spectralizing' of experience, in so far as he regards such images as potentially creative. The image that swims before his eye, is not only Romantically picturesque but highly reminiscent of the topography of 'My Lime-Tree Bower', and vivid enough to produce, if not a poem, then a painting.

However, the moment of crisis is indeed a turning point in Coleridge's career. On 7 August 1802, Coleridge writes to Southey thus:

> I am afraid, lest I should infect you with my fears rather than furnish you with any new arguments – give you impulses rather than motives – and prick you with *spurs*, that had been dipt in the vaccine matter of my own cowardliness –. While I wrote that last sentence, I had a vivid recollection – indeed an ocular Spectrum – of our room in College Street– / a curious instance of association / you remember how incessantly in that room I used to be compounding these half-verbal, half-visual metaphors. It argues, I am persuaded, a particular state of general feeling – & I hold, that association depends in a much greater degree on the recurrence of resembling states of Feeling, than on Trains of Idea ... I almost think, that Ideas never recall Ideas, as far as they are Ideas – any more than Leaves in a forest create each other's motion – The Breeze it is that runs thro' them / it is the Soul, the state of Feeling—. If I had said, no one Idea ever recalls another, I am confident that I could support the assertion. (*Letters* II, 961)

The passage is extremely rich. It begins with Coleridge's habitual association of his creative paralysis with disease, which has become, itself, aesthetized, through the quick run of inventive, quickly modulating, metaphors. This small creative act reminds Coleridge, vividly, of an earlier period in which his imagination was active, and, implicitly, un-diseased, a state of imaginative life he characterizes as 'compounding ... half-verbal, half-visual metaphors'. It is hard to know exactly what Coleridge means by this phrase, although there are a number of observations one can make. The shift towards the topic of association suggests that he has in mind how verbal ideas often invoke associated images, or vice versa: presumably, the run of thought from the notion of contagion to the physical act of inoculation is itself a case in point. One can also add that throughout his notebooks and letters Coleridge evinces great pleasure in word play, in puns and 'bulls'. Coleridge has a flair for overdetermination, for linguistic 'images' crowded and complicated by displacements and condensations. At this point I am not suggesting that Coleridge's creative process ought to be likened to Freudian dreamwork: I am saying that this appears to be how Coleridge himself understands the way his imagination works. As he tells Southey, years earlier, in 1794, 'I cannot write without a *body* of *thought* – hence my *Poetry* is crowded and sweats beneath a heavy burthen of Ideas and Imagery!' (*Letters* I, 137). 'Body of thought' is itself, I think, an example of what Coleridge means by a half-visual, half-verbal, metaphor. Ostensibly Coleridge is complaining that he loads his poems down with too much intellectual freight, but 'body' here does not simply invoke mass: it also veers in the direction of corporal physicality, of 'sweating'. The verbal idea (mass) simultaneously follows a visual track (the body). To put it another way, abstraction and materiality collide.

However, there is yet another aspect to Coleridge's poetic 'crowding'. In the same letter to Southey in which he refers to being unable to write without a 'body of thought', Coleridge appends the following sonnet to Bowles:

> My heart has thank'd thee, Bowles! for those soft Strains
> That on the still air floating tremblingly
> Woke in me Fancy, Love & Sympathy.
> For hence not callous to a Brother's pains
> Thro' Youth's gay prime and thornless Paths I went
> And when the *darker* Day of Life began
> And I did roam, a thought-bewilder'd Man!
> Thy kindred Lays an healing Solace lent,
> Each lonely Pang with dreamy Joys combin'd
> And stole from vain Regret her Scorpion stings;
> While shadowy Pleasure with mysterious wings
> Brooded the wavy and tumultuous Mind,
> Like that great Spirit, who with plastic Sweep
> Mov'd on the darkness of the formless Deep!
>
> (*Letters* I, 136)

A number of things co-exist here which Coleridge will later desynonomize, disentangle, or refine. 'Fancy' will become 'imagination', while the Divine spirit that plastically sweeps will lose its Deistic overtones, becoming instead the esemplastic power of the imagination, which creates not 'like', but as a repetition of, the infinite 'I am'. The 'shadowy Pleasure' that innocently 'births' the creative process will disappear altogether. Later in the same letter Coleridge begins his break with Hartley by characterising him, mockingly, as subscribing to a belief in the 'corporeality of *thought*' (*Letters* I, 137). What Coleridge was essentially to do, in *Biographia Literaria*, was 'decorporealize' the imagination, to rid it of its associations with pleasure and physicality, placing it, instead, in a transcendental key. The corporealized, material imagination, in contrast, has been relegated to the 'fancy', to empirical 'spectres' compounded through choice.

If one were to put the argument at its strongest, or perhaps crudest, one would say that Coleridge's 'fancy' best describes his own creative process, and product, with its puns and bulls, its crowded, sweating imagery, half-verbal, half-visual, irresolute, over-determined and pleasurable. But that is to simplify too much. For a start, in his conversational poems, especially, Coleridge himself achieves the kind of marriage of sound and sense, of streamlined diction concretely embodying the thought it conveys, unfurling through a muscular, vernacular, poetic line, that Coleridge identifies as the imagination in action (principally through the example of Wordsworth). I would argue, instead, that Coleridge's creative process lies somewhere in between Coleridge's definitions of fancy and imagination as we find them in the *Biographia Literaria*. I would also argue that these definitions are the consummation of a process begun twenty years earlier, in which the 'imagination' was increasingly conceptually cleansed of pleasure, physicality and arbitrary signification (of meaning beyond authorial intention).

Thus, if we return to the letter to Southey of 7 August 1802, we can see that Coleridge sets his flair for half-verbal, half-visual metaphors against Hartley and materialism, evincing association, not as a chain of colliding billiard balls but as the creative affinities of self-generated feelings, a transcendental 'breeze' eventually refined as the 'esemplastic power'. However, this empowering, positive self-identification was not to last, under pressure from the conclusions Coleridge was drawing from his observations of his own diseased currents of association.

Perhaps the single best example of Coleridge's gift for half-visual, half-verbal metaphors is this, from December 1803, written while Coleridge's unrequited love for Sara Hutchinson preys upon him:

> When in a state of pleasurable & balmy Quietness I feel my Cheek and Temple on the nicely made up Pillow in Caelibe Toro meo, the fire-gleam on my dear Books, that fill up one whole side from ceiling to floor of my Tall Study – & winds, perhaps are driving the rain, or whistling in frost, at my blessed Window, whence I see Borrodale, the Lake, Newlands – wood, water, mountains, omniform Beauty – O then as I first sink on the pillow, as if Sleep had indeed a material realm, as if when I sank on my pillow, I was entering that region & realized Faery Land of Sleep – O then what visions have I had, what dreams – the Bark, the Sea, all the shapes & sounds & adventures made up of the Stuff of Sleep & Dreams, & yet my Reason at the Rudder / O what Visions, (μαστοι) as if my Cheek & Temple were lying on me gale o' mast on – Seele meines Lebens! – & I sink down the waters, thro' Seas & Seas – yet warm, yet a Spirit– / (οι)
> Pillow = mast high
> (*Notebooks* I, 718)

The visual images of 'wood, water, mountains' segue (through paronomasia) from bark to barque, from water to sea, from mountains to pillow, and through a Greek pun (obligingly spelt out by Coleridge in a footnote) to 'breast', which through the pun ('mast high' is an English transcription of the Greek for breast) returns us back to the sailing bark (through the synecdoche 'mast'). The 'omniform Beauty' suggests Freud's 'oceanic feeling' of polymorphic pleasure, although one hardly needs Freud to conclude that Coleridge is describing an erotic reverie in which he pleasurably dissolves into sleep, and 'oneness' with his 'pillow' (Sara's breast). Equally crucial, however, is that this inward dissolution into polymorphous pleasure is curbed by 'Reason' at the rudder. The image recalls Coleridge's portrayal of the imagination in the *Biographia Literaria* as association guided by the will as conscious pilot.

A year earlier, in a letter to Sara Hutchinson, Coleridge hints at the horrors that ensue, should the reason abandon its station, or the pilot his rudder:

> I lay in a state of almost prophetic Trance & Delight – & blessed God aloud, for the powers of Reason & the Will, which remaining no Danger can overpower us! O God, I exclaimed aloud – how calm, how blessed am I now / I know not how to proceed, how to return / but I am calm & fearless & confident / if this Reality were a Dream, if I were asleep, what agonies had I suffered! what screams! – When the Reason & the Will are away, what remain to us but Darkness & Dimness & a bewildering Shame, and Pain that is utterly Lord over us, or fantastic Pleasure, that draws the Soul along swimming through the air in many shapes, even as a Flight of Starlings in a Wind. (*Letters* II, 842)

This is typical of Coleridge at his poetic best, in that the very thing he derogates (the fantastic pleasure of unconstrained reverie) spurs his strongest writing, as in the concluding, brilliant simile of the starlings (where Coleridge equally derogates the simile, as against metaphor). In the same month as he records his erotic reverie, Coleridge explores why the abdication of the reason and the will should be regarded in such grave terms:

> I will at least make the attempt to explain to myself the Origin of moral Evil from the streamy Nature of Association, which Thinking = Reason, curbs & rudders / how this comes to be so difficult / Do not the bad Passions in Dreams throw light & shew of proof upon this Hypothesis? – Explain those bad Passions: & I shall gain Light, I am sure – (*Notebooks* I, 1770)

In his search for a clue out of this moral maze, Coleridge first hits upon a false start: 'But take in the blessedness of Innocent Children, the blessedness of sweet Sleep, &c &c &c: are these or are they not contradictions to the evil from streamy association? – I hope not . . . ' If a child's streamy association is innocent of moral evil, it would follow that moral evil was environmental in origin, the product of experience, a Godwinian, Jacobinical position. Balked, Coleridge tries again:

> but what is the height, & ideal of mere association, – Delirium. – But how far is this state produced by Pain & Denaturalization? And what are these? – In short, as far as I can see any thing in this Total Mist, Vice is imperfect yet existing Volition, giving diseased Currents of association, because it yields on all sides & *yet* is – So think of Madness: – O if I live! (*Notebooks* I, 1770)

Rather than corrupted by the vicissitudes of life, association is providentially ordered with a countervailing reason and will ('rudder') which children and adults possess, regardless of experience. But in some adults volition may become diseased through 'pain and denaturalization', the terminus of which is unhindered association, delirium or madness.

On one side we have Coleridge's account of a swarming, half-visual, half verbal 'imagination', driven by pleasure, corporeal in nature, and characterized by complex verbal play; on the other, a guilt-ridden account of how this 'daydreaming' may tip into madness, disease and evil. As we earlier saw, Coleridge's talent for 'half-visual, half-verbal' metaphor was held in equipoise with his emerging definition of the imagination as an immaterial (rather than Hartleyian) 'breeze'. Increasingly, however, Coleridge comes to stigmatize this streamy, fecund, pleasurable, associative flow as a diseased, morally suspect faculty. In response, Coleridge does two things: he comes to envisage the imaginative act as a manifestation of subjective unity, in which reason and will are of a piece with creative intuition (both streamy association and the rudder; both creativity and self-consciousness); and he conceives of himself as being stricken by diseased, phantasmal currents of association. In contradistinction to Kant, Coleridge understands morality, not as one of the 'forms of the intellect' (*BL*: I, 155), as a product of reason, but as an expression of will and understanding emerging from the deepest recesses of our identity. So understood, the moral appetite is part of the 'one life', or subjective unity, that characterizes the genius.

Throughout the decade, Coleridge increasingly turns towards a moral vision of transcendental creativity. His older brother George naturally elicits Coleridge's guilty, defensive feelings. In the same letter (10 March 1798) that he announces the snapping of his 'squeaking baby-trumpet of Sedition' he says 'I devote myself to such works as encroach not on antisocial passions – in poetry, to elevate the imagination & set the affections in a right tune by the beauty of the inanimate impregnated, as with a living soul, by the presence of Life ... ' (*Letters* I, 397). By 'anti-social' Coleridge also means 'political'; thus, at the same time as Coleridge insinuates his withdrawal from the public sphere, he essays an early version of his moral, creative transcendentalism, one leading to the love of nature with 'almost a visionary fondness' (where the almost is inserted to signify a healthy distance from Deism). Coleridge's project has nearly assumed its finished shape, of imagination contra fancy, four years later in a letter to William Sotheby (10 September 1802):

> Nature has her proper interest; & he will know what it is, who believes & feels, that every Thing has a Life of it's own, & that we are all *one Life*. A Poet's *Heart & Intellect* should be *combined, intimately* combined & *unified*, with the great appearances in Nature – & not merely held in solution & loose mixture with them, in the shape of formal Similies. I do not mean

> to *exclude* these formal Similes – there are moods of mind, in which they are natural-pleasing moods of mind, & such as a Poet will often have, & sometimes express; but they are not his highest, & most appropriate moods. (*Letters* II, 864)

Metaphors knit together subject and object, as does the imagination, whereas similes (as Coleridge will say at the beginning of *Biographia Literaria*) are ornamental. As the letter continues, Coleridge develops his theme by contrasting the Greek habit of populating nature with mythological figures with the genuine spirituality of Hebrew monotheism. The former is 'As poor in genuine Imagination, as it is mean in Intellect – / At best, it is but Fancy, or the aggregating Faculty of the mind . . .' (*Letters* II, 865).

As he constructs his transcendental image of the poet, Coleridge is increasingly unable to recognize himself in it. On 1 August 1803 he writes to Southey, at once asserting himself, albeit in the weakened form of an awkward double negative (he is braced by 'the knowledge that I am not of no significance'), and confessing his weakness and egoism:

> All this added together might possibly have been a somewhat far worse than *Vanity* – . . . far worse if it had not existed in a nature where better Things were indigenous – A sense of weakness – a haunting sense, that I was an herbaceous Plant, as large as a large Tree, with a Trunk of the same Girth, & Branches as large & shadowing – but with *pith within* the Trunk, not heart of Wood / – that I had *power* not *strength* – an involuntary Imposter – that I had no real Genius, no real Depth / This on my honor is as fair a statement of my habitual Haunting, as I could give before the Tribunal of Heaven / How it arose in me, I have but lately discovered / – Still it works within me / but only as a Disease . . . (*Letters* II, 959)

It is a self-assessment that Carlyle would have been only too happy to endorse. Coleridge possessed genius ('better things were indigenous') but he has been hollowed out by disease, and become an 'involuntary Imposter', while 'haunting' suggests spectral materialism, the modern state of phantasmagorical being. Coleridge hints that he has recently discovered the nature of his disease. Medical disquisitions pepper his notebooks and letters around this time. In a notebook entry from January 1804, Coleridge writes:

> Images in sickly profusion by & in which I talk in certain diseased States of my Stomach / Great & innocent minds *devalesce*, as Plants & Trees, into beautiful Diseases / Genius itself, many of the most brilliant sorts of English Beauty, & even extraordinary Dispositions to Virtue, Restlessness in good – are they not themselves, as I have often said, but beautiful Diseases – species of the Genera, Hypochondriasis, Scrofula, & Consumption! (*Notebooks* I, 1822)

An object 'devalesces' when it rots from its own excess: as such, this is a recuperative entry, in which Coleridge reads his affliction as a 'beautiful disease', of genius in fatal superabundance. The passage reveals how much Coleridge was reading his medical textbooks, and interpreting himself in their light. The dominant model of medicine was still humoural, supported by a vascular system of ever finer capillaries pervading the physical frame: fevers and diseases accrue as a result of inflammations of, or sedimentations within, the capillary system. Plants are also vascular: thus trees, and human genii, may find that through their own excess of sap the wood within has become 'pith', as the sap has gone to feed the gorgeous explosion of flora.

Earlier, Coleridge cites gout as the culprit in a letter to Southey, dated 14 August 1803:

> I have been very ill, & in serious dread of a paralytic Stroke in my whole left Side. Of my disease there now remains no Shade of Doubt: it is a compleat & almost heartless Case of Atonic Gout. If you would look into the Article Medicine, in the Encyc. Britt. Vol. XI. Part 1– No 213. p. 181. – & the first 5 paragraphs of the second Column / you will read almost the very words, in which, before I had seen this article I had described my case to Wordsworth. (*Letters* II, 974)

Gout in fact links up with the hypochondria mentioned in the Notebook entry. They are both vascular disorders with common origins in excess studiousness. Atonic, or irregular, gout proceeds from inflammations of the extremities, from a build-up of sedimentary material (hence the threat of the stroke Coleridge mentions in his letter). Hypochondria derives from digestive disorders. Their symptoms, however, are similar: under 'Hypochondriasis' one encounters

> certain sorts of Epileptic winds & breezes, gusts from the bowels of the Volcano upward to the Crater of the Brain, rushings & brain-horrors, seeming for their immediate proximate Cause to have the pressure of Gasses on the stomach, acting possibly by their specified noxious chemical &tc.

In the letter to Southey in which Coleridge interprets his disease as a heartless case of atonic gout, Coleridge goes on to amend the unphilosophically expressed language:

> there is a state of mind, wholly unnoticed, as far as I know, by any Physical or Metaphysical Writer hitherto, & which yet is necessary to the explanation of some of the most important phaenomena of Sleep & Disease / it is a transmutation of the *succession of Time* into the *juxtaposition* of *Space*, by which the smallest Impulses, *if* quickly & regularly recurrent, *aggregate* themselves – & attain a kind *of* visual magnitude with a correspondent

> Intensity *of* general Feeling. – The simplest Illustration would be the *circle* of Fire made by whirling round a live Coal – only here the mind is passive. Suppose the same effect produced ab intra – & you have a clue to the whole mystery of frightful Dreams, & Hypochondriacal Delusions. – I merely *hint* this; but I could detail the whole process, complex as it is. Instead of 'an imaginary aggravation &c' it would be better to say – an *aggregation of* slight Feelings by the force *of* a diseasedly retentive Imagination. (*Letters* II, 974)

Rather than the unified, and unifying, transcendental imagination Coleridge intellectually forges at this time (en route to its finished expression in the *Biographia*), he experiences streamy gusts of association, 'epileptic winds and breezes', and a 'diseasedly retentive Imagination', in which words and things have broken apart, and into, a visual, punning, phantasmagoria. Or rather, that is how Coleridge medicalizes his poetic talents. After distinguishing between fancy and imagination in Chapter XIII of *Biographia Literaria*, Coleridge makes a promise, never fulfilled, to elaborate on the 'powers and privileges of the imagination' in an essay he will append to a new edition of 'The Ancient Mariner'. The intention strongly suggests that Coleridge felt that his own poetic genius, or imaginative capacity, was best expressed in his poems of the supernatural, in 'The Ancient Mariner', 'Christabel' and 'Kubla Khan', the poems which teem most in crowded, sweating, half-verbal, half-visual metaphors. They were also all written before Coleridge's break with materialism, which is to say, before his transcendental construct of genius assumed its mature shape. What once was creative facility in Coleridge was now stigmatized as disease or (much worse) 'fancy'. Unable to fit with his own transcendental paradigm, Coleridge fell back into poetic introversion, in which his creative genius dwelt, in the most marvellous prose, on his own inadequacy or poetic misfitting. This to Godwin, 10 March 1801:

> You would not know me –! all sounds of similitude keep at such a distance from each other in my mind, that I have *forgotten* how to make a rhyme – I look at the Mountains (that visible God Almighty that looks in at all my windows) I look at the Mountains only for the Curves of their outlines; the Stars, as I behold them, form themselves into Triangles ... The Poet is dead in me – my imagination (or rather the Somewhat that had been imaginative) lies, like a Cold Snuff on the circular Rim of a Brass Candle-stick, without even a stink of Tallow to remind you that it was once cloathed & mitred with Flame. That is past by ! – I was once a Volume of Gold Leaf, rising & riding on every breath of Fancy – but I have beaten myself back into weight & density, & now I sink in quicksilver, yea, remain squat and square on the earth amid the hurricane, that makes Oaks and Straws join in one Dance, fifty yards high in the Element. (*Letters* II, 714)

Even as Coleridge transforms his experience into something of great literary value, in his own mind he casts himself down into the materialism – the 'weight and density' – he is in the process of rendering abject. The date of the passage is crucial for understanding the process whereby Coleridge renders himself his own misfit, as it is on the cusp of his transition from a corporeal poetic practice of crowded, sweating metaphors to the lofty strains of the secondary imagination and the 'one life', a perilous moment expressed in 'every breath of fancy', the very creative faculty shortly to be stigmatized and rendered abject as mere mechanical creation. As Coleridge poeticizes depth, inserting it into the discipline to be practised by a future clerisy, he loses his creative faculty, now deemed – by the new, transcendental Criticism he himself had helped to import – shallow, dense and abject.

4
The Romantic-era Novel

1. The generic misfit

The Romantic-era Novel is a generic misfit. For the greater part of the duration in which English has been an institutionalized discipline with recognizable fields – the Medieval, Early Modern, Victorian and so on – Romanticism was uniquely pared down to a singularity of gender and genre, to a corpus of six male poets. Two simple facts accentuate the strangeness of this singularity. First, much of the disciplinary energy driving the preceding period – the eighteenth century – centred on the rise of the novel, where it was understood, in large part, as the genre that was produced by, and which registered, the making of the modern world.[1] Second, as bibliographers now unequivocally confirm, the period in which the novel takes off, deflecting upwards, as regards production and readership, was the Romantic one.[2] The novel was most ignored just as it consolidated itself in the mainstream of our literary culture. Of course the novel resumes its central role in the story of 'English' once we break through to the safe territory of Victorian fiction, where prose once again resumes its stately voyage towards its present generic supremacy.

As even the genre's defenders admit, critics fell silent before the Romantic novel, because embarrassed by its mediocrity.[3] The view seems plausible enough given the sudden flood of popular novels. To use the favourite cliché of the time, the press at Leadenhall groaned under the burden of supplying the maw of the circulating libraries. If we think of the modern novel as the sole literary genre regularly distinguished by a mass sale, then the Minerva Press is the clear point of origin. But in other respects Minerva differed radically from the modern paperback with its celebrity authors. Minerva sold books, not by authors, but by genre (just as DVD stores divide their wares into 'adventure', 'comedy' or 'horror', rather than by 'auteur'). Most Minerva authors were anonymous, usually producing just one book according to the latest formula.[4] Many of them were young. However talented they may have been, it was difficult for talent to flower under such conditions. Much of Minerva's production was, indeed, as the slang phrase went, 'trash'.

As the old bias has begun to right itself, a truer view of the Romantic novel's career has become possible. For a start, it needs to be emphatically said that the Romantic-era novel does not represent a sudden, embarrassing, diminution of quality. As far as the novel is concerned the Romantic period is brief: the thirty or so years that extend from 1789, and the appearance of *The Castles of Athlin and Dunbayne*, Ann Radcliffe's first Romance, to that indefinite point in the 1820s where the Victorian novel begins its conventional rise. For such a short period the Romantic novel is distinguished by remarkable brilliance, not mediocrity. The Romantic novel certainly has its fair share of 'trash'. But a genre must be judged, not on its failures, but its successes. Radcliffe, Burney, Smith, Godwin, Edgeworth and Hogg all produced works which, if not of the first rank, are powerful enough to make one query what 'first rank' actually means. This is to set aside the many others who produced work that was very good indeed, such as Hays, Inchbald, Bage, the Lee sisters, Opie, Potter or Lewis. But the really salient fact is that the Romantic period produced two British novelists who have rightfully assumed their places among the rank of World-historical writers: Austen and Scott. The novel produced not only the single most canonical work of the Romantic period, in Mary Shelley's *Frankenstein*, but the Romantic-era writer with the greatest current readership, and the most formidable cultural power: Jane Austen.

I argue that the Romantic novel was disparaged, and pushed to the margins, because it was a continuation of an eighteenth-century form. Many of its chief practitioners subscribed to the late Enlightenment belief in a rational, political, public sphere. Its principle modality is symbolism, the propensity to rise above the literal in an attempt to form what we would now call ideological perspectives. The Romantic novel's political tendencies and its symbolic reach – often verging on allegory – were assailed as aesthetically incorrect, an attack that was, at bottom, a continuation of the process that elevated the private Wordsworth as the religious poet of nature over the public Wordsworth of discomfiting others. The same fragmentation of the public sphere that was a pre-condition for the institutionalization of the 'Wordsworthian reader' also undermined the aesthetic ground on which the Romantic novel might sustain itself. The century and a half of critical abuse that extends from the first critics of Godwin and the Anti-Jacobin novelists[5] to the aesthetic rigours of the New Critics[6] has its beginnings in the 1790s decay of the public sphere.

However, if Austen and Scott helped make the Romantic novel great, they also left the field confused. Or rather, their reception did. Paradoxically, their success – one immediate, the other eventual – contributed to the obscurity, and miscomprehension, of the Romantic-era novel. I will return to this, but for now I want to dwell on a salient fact that needs to be borne in mind when considering the Romantic novel: Austen revolutionized the genre, changing it forever. We are all Austenians now and, if we are to understand the institutional eclipse of the form in the Romantic period, we need to identify the ways Austen's success distorts a retrospective view.

Modern readers of Jane Austen are often surprised to discover that her genius was not instantly recognized. Compared to Scott, her fame burned slowly until finally catching fire – in a blaze of Janeite enthusiasm – with the publication of her nephew's biography, in 1870.[7] Nevertheless it is not quite true to say that although she revolutionized the novel, no one noticed. Scott himself was perturbed by one of her revolutionary qualities, although he couldn't quite put his finger on it. He himself was the master of the big 'bow wow'; yet there was something about her finely realized scenes of country life among the middling sorts that strangely drew him.[8] It was left to Richard Whateley, his successor in the pages of the *Quarterly Review*, to identify the mysterious quality that set her work apart. Whateley argues that there has been a revolution in the fortunes of the novel. No longer despised as a childish diversion full of exploded wonders the novel had now risen to a position of respectability, buoyed up by its superior philosophical qualities. To develop his case Whateley wheels out Aristotle's venerable distinction between history and poetry, in which poetry is judged to be the more philosophical genre, because founded on probability – and therefore on principles – rather than on the random unfolding of events. For Whateley, Jane Austen is the novelist who incorporates philosophical probability most fully into her fictional practice, hence her place at the vanguard of the aesthetic revolution.[9]

'Probability' was Austen's own most cherished term for her distinctive difference, the watchword of her fiction. It is clear that Austen meant numerous things by this slippery term, as when she advises her niece against cliché, cautioning against ready-made phrases or outlandish events, such as 'whirlpool of dissipation' or having one's heroine shoot Niagara Falls in a canoe; and it seems reasonable to infer that the term was lurking in the back of her mind, when she said that one ought to write about what one knew, such as the four or five country families by which one was, for better or worse, surrounded, or when she characterized her own art as a matter of particular and exact minutiae, such as implicitly follows from the metaphor of two inches of ivory covered with a fine, detailed, and therefore accurate brush.

One of the great surprises produced by a rereading of Austen is just how much intrusive third-person commentary there is, often mocking, self-conscious and venomous. We are surprised because Austen's novels live in the memory as worlds sustained by an effortless suspension of disbelief, as illusions undisturbed by authorial intrusion. As a narrator Austen has an almost faultless pitch whereas the works of her contemporaries seem full of discordant notes. Scott's narrative voice is ponderous and clunking by comparison, his third person marred by an odd monotony of diction, or full of laboured litotes, ironic allusions and undercut hyperboles. Godwin's affected phrasing was the butt of contemporary satire, and while we might take a different view, it nevertheless imparts an artificial flavour to his work.[10] Radcliffe's tone often crashes, bathetically, from poetic sublimity to tiresome prolixity as she veers from mountains to servants. Maturin is simply eccentric, in the root meaning of the phrase, flying off at tangents. Even the sophisticated Edgeworth wobbles by comparison, as she lurches from the dignified pathos of Lady Delacour to her friends' comic freaks. For their contemporaries these discordances were not, necessarily, a problem. If they seem so to us – not so much as problems, perhaps, but as embarrassing lapses in taste, craft or sophistication – it is because we view them through the prism of Austen.

The discipline imposed by her dedication to probability was one aspect of her even tone. Yet another was her pioneering use of free indirect speech. After Austen one can trace its growing use from George Eliot to Henry James and Joseph Conrad, before reaching an apogee of sophistication with Joyce's *Dubliners*. It is a pervasive device in high Modernist irony, from Kafka to Woolf, and is ubiquitous in modern literary writing. However, it was not always so. There were certainly writers who used free indirect speech before Austen, such as Edgeworth, Burney, possibly Radcliffe and even Walpole, but no novelist until Austen used it so proficiently, and with such sophistication. Her predecessors tended to employ the device intermittently, whereas Austen's use of it was so extensive, and pointed, that it became a meaningful aspect of her form.[11] As a result modern readers find it easier to enter her fictional worlds than those of her contemporaries because we are used to her form of realism, of probable events filtered through the consciousness of characters further realized through the subtle use of (linguistic) manners.

2. The moment of *Waverley*

Sir Walter's Scott's decision to enter the market, in 1814, with *Waverley*, was a decisive moment in the history of the Romantic-era novel.[12] As William Godwin later ruefully remarked, who knew, until Scott, that it was possible to write more than three novels, and still sell?[13] The success of the Scott 'brand' was owing, in part, to the canniness of Scott, the operator. The half-open secret of his anonymity was a brilliant marketing ploy, but it also registered the trickiness of his position. Before 1814, the prestige of the novel had been steadily rising, with Frances Burney, Maria Edgeworth and Ann Radcliffe, especially, earning kudos, but it was still generally regarded as a step down from the commanding heights of poetry. Scott's anonymity helped him hedge his bets, until he had successfully transformed the novel, which he did, literally, by publishing in the expensive, prestigious quarto format, previously reserved for serious genres, like history and poetry. As Peter Garside has argued, Scott 'remasculinised' the novel form, by infusing it with prestige as the revealed 'Wizard of the North', thus making it safe for male novelists to 'out' themselves: by the 1820s, when the Scott effect was being felt, the number of anonymous novelists sharply fell, with a corresponding rise in self-declared male authors.[14] Scott knew the novel market so well, because he himself was a tremendous consumer of novels, and as the prospective editor of Ballantyne's Novelist's Library, one of the form's ablest critics. The introductory chapter to *Waverley*, with its shrewd glance aside at the competition, thus provides us with an astute assessment of the state of the novel, from the very middle of the Romantic period. Together with Scott's other writings on the subject it provides an accurate picture of the Romantic novel as it was prior to Austen, and as it came under pressure from her. The story of this moment is not uncomplicated. As Homer O. Brown notes, Scott's intervention was instrumental in the institutionalization of the 'novel', a rising that came with the suppression of lowly 'romance'.[15] For Scott, the difference between romance and novel was epitomized in the example of Austen, as the exemplar of a new kind of more probable fiction.[16] In retrospect it may seem as if Scott took up Austen as a handy club to beat the opposition, on the grounds that she wrote like him, or as he wished to write, and that in doing so he cemented the rise of the 'probable' novel. But, of course, Scott did not write like Austen. Rather than his natural ally, she constituted his principal competition. In the complex history of their entangled reception, the fate of the Romantic novel, or philosophical romance, has largely been obscured. In order to untangle it I begin by looking closely at the way in which Scott registered the challenge posed by Austen. The challenge was registered largely through a series of self-serving revisions to literary history. Such revisions are the stock-in-trade of all respectable artists seeking to create space for themselves; but while understandable, they also had consequences. At the centre of Scott's revisions lay his desire for priority, for having come first in his own school of fiction. As Scott makes clear in his criticism, he attributes the highest aesthetic value to generic priority.[17]

Scott's acute sense of priority and generic subdivision is comically, self-consciously present in his anonymous review of his own *Tales of My Landlord* published in the 1817 *Quarterly Review*. He begins by speculating, disingenuously, that the unknown author of *Waverley* would sink in the public's estimation if the reader knew that his scenes were not invented at all, but copied from 'existing nature' (239). He observes that 'every spectator at once recognizes in those scenes and faces which are copied from nature an air of distinct reality' missing from the purely fanciful (238), the clear implication being that the works of the author of *Waverley* possess this unmistakable air. The observation about sinking is disingenuous, because the mark of the real is the value Scott esteems above all others, a quality he later refers to as 'the authenticity of ... historical representations' (252). Scott continues in the same vein of mock criticism by referring to the Great Unknown's 'slovenly indifference' to 'probability and perspicuity of narrative', which he sacrifices to his desire to produce 'effect', to 'surprise and elevate' (239). Once in the know the ironic drift is perfectly clear: we are to esteem what the reviewer deprecates, and vice versa. Even so, the slighting reference to 'probability' should give us pause, placing a question mark over the quick assumption that probability was a transparent aesthetic good for Scott, rather than something he learned from Austen. To an extent the contradiction eases once one realizes the sly manner in which Scott advances his theory of the historical novel. Probability of narrative is sacrificed, because, like the history painter, the historical novelist must be free to subordinate the arrangement of his materials to the requirements of sublime effect. 'Perspicuity' also undergoes a process of ironic inversion. Lack of perspicuity is actually good, because instrumental to the mode of historical fiction. It is not the narrator's job to explain events, rendering them clear. The reviewer concedes there is 'system' in the historical novelist's apparent eccentricity. The author of *Waverley* has

> avoided the common language of narrative, and thrown his story . . . into a dramatic shape. In many cases this has greatly added to the effect, by keeping both the actors and action continually before the reader, and placing him, in some measure, in the situation of the audience at a theatre, who are compelled to gather the meaning of the scene from what the dramatic personae say to each other, and not from any explanation addressed immediately to themselves. (239)

One might characterize the author's withdrawal here as a matter of paring one's fingernails while the world unfolds beneath the author's detached gaze. But then Joyce's version of the Modernist author is just an apotheosis of the quality identified by Frank Kermode as decisive in the emergence of modern literature, the breaking of the unspoken 'contract' between author and reader, that the former will supply the latter with a meaning.[18] *Waverley*'s dramatic indeterminacy places it at the cutting edge.

Scott's trick is to adopt the persona of a Tory fogy too old fashioned to realize he's describing avant garde work, characterizing as 'carelessness' the very features which impart value. The reviewer thus worries over another advanced feature of Scott's fiction, the fact that his heroes, like Waverley, are 'insipid' (240). 'His chief characters are never actors, but always acted upon by the spur of circumstances, and have their fates uniformly determined by the agency of subordinate persons' (240). In his review of Jane Austen's *Emma*, two years earlier, also in the *Quarterly*, Scott identifies two features common to the post-Romance novel prior to Austen. One is the representation of ideal sentiments, the other, the improbable portrayal of heroes who effortlessly rise above the tide of events that sweep along lesser mortals (228–9). Scott's heroes are 'insipid', because realistically caught up in the flow of history, which they are unable either to resist or to rise above. As Michael Gamer has recently noted, Scott's protagonists – tossed about by events – bear a closer resemblance to the subjects of 'object narratives', such as the *Tale of a Guinea*, than they do the heroes of conventional novels, and that is because, for Scott, history possesses agency and not individuals.[19]

Scott's double masquerade (of anonymously reviewing and critiquing his anonymous self) may seem bizarre, but it helped him establish his claims to priority, which he could not achieve, so efficaciously, as himself. About two-thirds of the way through the review Scott pulls together his various threads. He argues that if 'Historical Romances' have had objections raised against them it is owing to 'the universal failure of that species of composition' rather than to 'any inherent and constitutional defect' (256). In the guise of the crusty *Quarterly* reviewer – whose objectivity is apparently vouchsafed by his earlier severity – Scott delivers his trump: while others may have pioneered the Historical Romance before the author of *Waverley*, their failures were so utter *Waverley* was effectively the first of its kind, the start of a new school or class of fiction. The feature that sets the *Waverley* novels apart is the copying from nature, introduced near the start of the review. Previous historical romances failed completely, because they injudiciously blended together the manners of different ages. The Great Unknown has revolutionized the historical romance by keeping them distinct. At this stage in the review Scott has ceased to speak ironically. We hear his own voice, liberated by his mask. 'Looking not merely to the litter of the novels that peep out for a single day from the mud where they were spawned', but even to those with pretensions, it is clear that the Great Unknown's stand out because he looks to 'the great book of Nature' (258) for his plots and characters, whereas his muddled predecessors copy slavishly from each other. As he warms to his theme, Scott pulls out all the stops, comparing himself to the Bard: 'The characters of Shakespeare are not more exclusively human ... than those of this mysterious author', because, like the dramatist's, they are 'sketched from real life. He must have mixed much and variously in the society of his native country', and while his historical personages are 'the creatures of his own imagination' they convey the impression of having been conjured from their graves 'in all their original freshness, entire in their lineaments, and perfect in all the minute peculiarities of dress and demeanour'. The mysterious author, it seems, is a 'man of the very highest genius' (258).

The concern with priority is equally evident in the introduction to *Waverley*, published three years earlier. As in his self-review, Scott's main tactic is to make space for himself by acknowledging, and thus dismissing, his predecessors. As in the review of himself, Scott speaks through a complex series of masks and personae. He is an anonymous author assuming the persona of a worldly-wise novelist introducing the work of a fictional self. Again, this layering of imposture frees Scott to play fast and lose in the interests of the actual writer. We are told that although *Waverley* was published in 1814 it was begun in 1805, hence the 'Sixty Years Since' of the subtitle, which takes us back to 1745, the year of the events described by Scott. Peter Garside makes a compelling case that the earliest sections of the novel (the first seven chapters) date from the 1808–10 period.[20] Building on Garside's work, Michael Gamer argues that the purpose of Scott's legerdemain was, in part, to claim priority.[21] True to the precept he was later to adduce in his review of himself, Scott makes it clear, in the Preface, that works that imitate and challenge each other are doomed to mediocrity. Scott also makes the point in his review of *Emma*: 'The first writer of a new class is ... placed on a pinnacle of excellence, to which, at the earliest glance of the surprised admirer, his ascent seems little less than miraculous' (230). The burden of *Waverley*'s first chapter is to assist readers in straining their necks as they stare upward in surprised admiration at the anonymous author's miraculous novelty.

Scott's persona boasts that he has a bookseller's eye to the marketing cues embedded in paratextual materials, and that title pages are an open book to him.[22] But rather than a demonstration of encyclopedic marketing knowledge he settles for just a few examples of the subtitles he eschews. 'A Tale of Other Days' will signify Radcliffean Gothic to all but the dullest reader. 'A Romance from the German', will conjure images of 'a profligate abbot, an oppressive duke, a secret and mysterious association of Rosycrucians and Illuminati' (3), while the adjective 'Sentimental' will bring to mind the national tale with an 'auburn' haired, naturally poetic, peasant heroine (4). Scott's final example of a subtitle to avoid, is 'A Tale of the Times', which would lead the reader to expect 'a dashing sketch of the fashionable world', with thinly veiled gossip of high life, 'a heroine from Grosvenor Square, and a hero from the Barouche club of the Four-in-Hand ...' The last two subtitles are particularly interesting for, as Gamer argues, they at once

> invoke and anticipate Sydney Owenson's *Wild Irish Girl*, published in 1806, and *The Mask of Fashion* and *The Barouche Driver and his Wife*, both published in 1807. Clearly 1805 provides *Waverley*, among other things, an illusion of being first among its contemporaries – of coming not just before *The Wild Irish Girl* but also before Charles Maturin's *The Wild Irish Boy* (1807) – before Maria Edgeworth's *Ennui* (1809) and Jane Porter's *Scottish Chiefs* (1808), and before Elizabeth Hamilton's *Cottagers of Glenburnie* (1808), to name just a few contemporary influences.[23]

The game with subtitles does more than give a false impression of the Northern Wizard's precocity, of having anticipated and rejected – or superseded – works that were yet to be written. It forms the foundation for a binary that enables Scott to locate his fictional, authorial self in an unoccupied middle. 'By fixing then the date of my story Sixty Years before this present 1st November, 1805, I would have my readers understand that they will meet in the following pages neither a romance of chivalry, nor a tale of modern manners ...' (4). *Waverley* is neither romance nor novel, but a hybrid, the model for a new class of fiction we have since come to call the historical novel. From Scott's choice of subtitle, and 'aera', the 'discerning critic' will presage 'that the object of my tale is more a description of men than manners' (4). For a tale of manners to be interesting it must either draw upon the glamour of 'venerable antiquity' or 'it must bear a vivid reflection of those scenes which are passing daily before our eyes, and are interesting from their novelty' (4). As the recent past of two generations ago affords neither it follows that Scott will focus on 'the characters and passions of the actors; – those passions common to men in all stages of society, and which have alike agitated the human heart', whether it throbbed in the distant past or yesterday. Although manners are important for 'colouring' it is 'from the great Book of nature' that Scott 'reads' his tale (5).

Between 1814 and 1817 Scott's views (mediated through, and liberated by, his masks) undergo a complete revolution. In the introduction to *Waverley* Scott deprecates manners as mere colouring; three years later, in his review of himself, their faithful reproduction is the hallmark of Shakespearean genius. The reason for this shift is to be found in his intervening reading – and review – of Austen. As we saw earlier, Scott sketches a genealogy of the modern novel in his essay on *Emma*. 'In its first appearance, the novel was the legitimate child of the romance'. Although it forswore the magic and enchantment of its parent, the novel retained two kinds of improbability: of plot (the hero's unfeasible adventures) and of sentiment (too ideal). However, a new 'style of novel has arisen' in the last 'fifteen or twenty years' (230) which has refined these two forms of improbability out of existence, replacing the interest generated by them with 'the art of copying from nature as she really exists in the common walks of life, and presenting to the reader, instead of the splendid scenes of an imaginary world, a correct and striking representation of that which is daily taking place around him' (230). The positive wording may be compared with the negative inflection the same phrase receives in *Waverley*, where 'it must bear a vivid reflection of those scenes which are passing daily before our eyes' is attached to the novelty generated by the inferior novel of modern manners typified by the subtitle 'A Tale of the Times'.

Scott is clearly wrestling with one of the enduring conundrums of art: does one achieve the universal through the general or the particular? In *Waverley* Scott opts for the former, arguing that his authorial persona copies from the great book of Nature, from its enduring patterns over which flow the accidentals of time and tide. Under pressure from Austen, Scott changes tack. Whereas in *Waverley* a vivid depiction of modern manners only generates novelty (and is therefore dispensable), in the Austen review it is more positively inflected. 'Correct and striking' is part of this revaluation, as is Scott's praise for Austen's 'spirit and originality' in 'keeping close to common incidents' (231). As yet Scott lacks words for describing what is new about Austen, apart from saying that she keeps to the 'middling classes of society' and that like those of a Flemish painting her subjects 'are finished up to nature, and with a precision which delights the reader' (235).

The anonymous review of himself of the following year allows Scott to amend the record while finding language for Austen's elusive difference.

Scott does not altogether abandon his position. He repeats the phrase, from the *Waverley* introduction, regarding the copying from the great book of Nature, but whereas, previously, the accurate portrayal of manners was mere colouring, in the review of himself it becomes one side of an even balance:

> At once a master of the great events and minuter incidents of history, and of the manners of the times he celebrates, as distinguished from those that now prevail, – the intimate thus of the living and of the dead, his judgment enables him to separate those traits which are characteristic from those that are generic; and his imagination, not less accurate and discriminating than vigorous and vivid, present to the mind of the reader the manners of the times, and introduces to his familiar acquaintance the individuals of his drama as they thought and spoke and acted. (256–7)

Scott now arrives at the truth of history not by reading from the great book of Nature, alone, but by being able to discriminate between the characteristic and the generic, the particular and the universal, manners and a transhistorical human nature, reaching the one, through the other.

Scott, of course, has not changed his style of novel writing over this period. The review of himself is, rather, an exercise in rebranding, a means of strengthening his claim to belong among the 'favoured few' who have begot their own school of fiction, one bearing the unmistakable and unique mark of the 'real'. What has changed, is the prospect from the unoccupied middle between romance and novel, which had seemed unclouded from the vantage point of 1808, when he apparently wrote it. Scott's list of subtitles is indeed very telling, as they reveal that Scott understood his chief competition to be coming from various versions of 'romance'. While such versions may indeed offer numerous examples of 'novels that peep out for a single day from the mud where they were spawned', their progenitors were, themselves, members of the 'favoured few', and praised as such by Scott (the review of Radcliffe being a prime example). 'A Romance from the German' might very well include the wretched *Horrid Mysteries*, or the unintelligible *Victim of Magical Delusion*, with their convoluted narratives of illuminati, secret brotherhoods and revolutionary intent, as popularized by the Abbé Barruel in his paranoid *Proofs of A Conspiracy*, but such aesthetic lowlife was engendered by the great Schiller, whose *Ghostseer* Scott evidently has in mind, to judge from the properties he associates with the genre – 'black cowls, caverns, daggers, electrical machines, trapdoors and dark lanterns' (*Waverley*, 3–4) – all of which figure in Schiller's powerful, hugely influential novella. Similarly, the national tale has Lady Morgan as its eminent progenitor. The antithetical novel of modern manners, in contrast, according to the cues given us by Scott, can boast no better origin than the anonymous author of *The Barouche Driver and his Wife*. In effect, for Scott, the middle is no middle at all, but a place from which he was to supplant all other aspirants to the modern, realistic novel, effortlessly overstepping its current pretenders. And then came the author of *Emma*, who deeply upset Scott's calculations, forcing a hasty, anonymous repositioning.

Even more pertinent is the fact that *Waverley* shamelessly plunders, or recycles, the very romances it ostensibly supplants. As Ina Ferris has argued, the ur-plot of the national tale, as developed by Lady Morgan, is for a male traveller from the dominant culture to experience a revaluation of his prejudices and opinions through his romance with a young woman who embodies the virtues of the marginal nation he visits – a fairly precise description of Waverley and Flora McIvor. One is not being entirely unfair in saying that Scott's major deviation from the Lady Morgan formula is to transform Flora's hair from auburn to brunette.[24] And so it is with the other genres Scott claims not to be writing. As Scott himself notes, spending a night in a hidden cave with feasting banditti under flickering torchlight is de rigeur for the German tale. The episode of Donald Bean Lean and his brigands in their Lochside cave is a bravura example of the genre. Similarly the picturesque and sublime scenery experienced by the unknowingly 'kidnapped' Waverley as he is led by the nose into the Jacobite Ich Van Vor's mountain fastness is simply Radcliffe transplanted. Indeed, as Gamer notes, Scott's central device is to render events probable by first alluding to the original he imitates before creating difference through comic deflation. Bean's cave is both a copy from the German, and its comic Highland antithesis, significant for not being, as Carlyle phrases it, full of 'bewhiskered cat o' mountain brigands'.[25] Just as Waverley appears on the verge of consummating the national tale, through his love interest in Flora McIvor, events intervene, and Waverley reverts to the placid, un-exotic and implicitly Anglo 'Rose'.

Imitation and deviation are the ruling principles of genre. In staking out his claims to generic priority Scott stresses his deviance: he does not copy from his rivals, but from the great book of Nature. As we have seen, such a claim is, at the very least, problematic. A better way of putting it would be to say that Scott turns litotes into a narratological principle. He moves forward to a more probable narrative texture by negating the antonym he does not wish to reproduce, the net effect of which is to produce both imitation and deviation, the original he does not want to imitate, and then his distinct version of it. Of course, many – perhaps all – writers do this, but generally they leave the original as an unstated ghostly presence. In *Waverley*, from his prefatory remarks on, Scott explicitly cites the original from which he deviates. In both theory and practice he makes it clear that his Highland world is no simple National Tale; that his hero's comic abduction is no straightforward version of the Radcliffean travel narrative towards a mysterious mountain castle; that his banditti are no ordinary bewhiskered cat o' mountain brigands. The rhetorical purpose of litotes is to create a more effective claim through understatement. The purpose of Scott's narratological litotes is to create a probable effect – the illusion that we read from the great book of Nature – by ironically undercutting the literary originals he refashions.

3. A new technology

The paradoxical effect of Scott's mode of proceeding was that it locked him firmly within the very generic conventions from which he sought to break free. A double negative may produce a positive, but it is dependent upon the antonym it negates. Scott's strategy may have seemed viable from the perspective of 1808, but by 1817 Jane Austen had materially changed the prospect by providing an example of a technique that incorporated probability without depending on narrative 'litotes'. Austen's novels are no less literary than Scott's, and no less dependent upon copied originals. As Marilyn Butler has observed, Austen's scenes are never original, are always at least twice-told. But, unlike, Scott Austen does not explicitly cite the original she refashions.

Scott's real affinity, then, was not with the new novel, embodied, above all, by Austen, but with the various forms of romance he sought to supplant. Much of Scott's struggles become clear, once filtered through Ian Watt's useful schema of emergent Modernity. For Watt, the novel was part of the Modernist project because it embodied the numerous shifts involved in the transformation from a Medieval outlook, in which enduring ideas or concepts were 'real' and real life ephemeral and essentially meaningless, to our contemporary sense that 'realism' is constituted by the gritty feel of the quotidian. Modernism – meaning the Western world post Bacon and Descartes – favours the experiential over the received, the empirical over the abstract, the inductive method over the deductive, the particular over the general, the individual over the species, and time-bound experience over eternal prospects. In Watt's schema, the novel was fostered by prose romance; but it also decisively broke with it by internalizing modern concerns with the timebound experience of individuals realized through closely observed particulars. Although Watt argues that the decisive break came with Defoe, it was not until the end of the eighteenth century that the matter of nomenclature was finally settled, with 'novel' emerging as the unambiguous term for realist fiction in contradistinction to symbolic 'romance'. Austen may have clarified the debate – and the narrative practices implicated by the contending terms – with crushing finality, but the lessons of her victory took time to digest. Scott, meanwhile, operated in a liminal zone between romance and novel. Watt refers to four specific characteristics that mark the latter form: plots derived from the texture of experience rather than from other plots or romances; characters who are individuals rather than types, a difference signaled by proper names; a concern with identity as it is conditioned by time; and attention to concrete particulars.[26] In both his introduction to *Waverley*, and the novel itself, Scott wavers between the two. He identifies second-hand plots as the essential mark of the unoriginal (creatures spawned from mud), and then recycles the plots of others, playing a weird self-inculpating game in his introductory remarks. He initially relegates concrete particulars, or manners, to a subsidiary position in his Preface, before elevating them again in his review of himself, three years later. While Waverley is, one might say, the child of time – an insipid character taking form from active forces around him – he is also strangely impervious to time, in the sense that he retains an enduring, even allegorical, quality, one summed up by his name. Indeed, it is in the name of his hero that Scott most thoroughly confuses Watt's schema. In his Preface Scott insists that he has chosen the name 'Waverley' precisely because it is a proper name uncontaminated by previous fictional practice. But as Michael Gamer points out, 'Waverley' was, in fact, a not uncommon name in contemporary fiction.[27] More to the point it appears to have been chosen precisely because of its symbolic overtones, one pointing to Waverley as a vacillating type, a 'wavering' sort.

One might conclude that Scott was a bit slow in catching up with the new, Austen, novel. Alternatively, we can say that Watt's thesis is overly teleological and that it grossly exaggerates the preponderance of the 'novel', from Defoe onwards. The romance did not just disappear. On the contrary, forms of romance coexist alongside – and, indeed, within – the novel from the eighteenth century to the present.[28] So when I say that the Romantic novel was itself a generic misfit, a number of diverse things are encompassed by the phrase. At its simplest, during the Romantic period the novel was consolidated into two broad streams of romance and novel (even if each was characterized by innumerable tributaries). As regards canon formation and the institutionalization of literature, the novel was found acceptable, but with its concentration on the messy quotidian was excluded by the dominant definitions of Romanticism, which privileged the transcendental. As a master of the quotidian Austen was canonized, but in another field (the 'novel').[29] Romance did concern itself with transcendental matters, but on the grounds that it did so badly (quixotically blending the supernal with realism) it found itself excluded from its natural home of 'Romanticism'.[30]

The branch of the novel that was excluded is best referred to as the 'philosophical romance'. I borrow the phrase from Hugh Murray, a contemporaneous critic who used it to designate the dangerous tendency of the Jacobin novel, in general, and the work of William Godwin, in particular.[31] Murray employs the phrase in a restricted sense, meaning a 'reasoning fiction' that supports a 'philosophical opinion'. 'Philosophical romances are a very late invention ... Some of the first ... were written with the view of supporting some very ill-founded and dangerous principles.' That the Jacobins had hijacked the philosophical romance was an 'accidental circumstance', for the form 'might have been employed in support of useful, as well as of pernicious doctrines'. However, even here the form runs into trouble. Murray's concern is to trace the moral effects of fiction; he therefore considers the consequence for readers of being exposed to philosophical opinions. Such opinions will only be efficacious if applied to 'the conduct of life'. Realism is therefore an inescapable criterion: 'everything unnatural and improbable is to be excluded'. If so, philosophical romances might work. However, a consideration arises that undermines the philosophical romance as an effective genre. It 'tends to form a very pernicious habit ... of resting philosophical opinion' on a foundation other than that of 'well ascertained facts'. The building upon facts 'by what is termed the method of induction, is now universally allowed to be the only road which can lead to the discovery of important truth'.[32]

Although an undoubtedly slight work of literary theory, Murray's book is significant as a bell weather sign for the dramatic rise in the novel's prestige in the early years of the nineteenth century. As such it deserves to be set beside John Colin Dunlop's *The History of Fiction* (1814), which set out to do for prose what Thomas Warton and others had done for poetry, by narrating the novel's origins from the Greeks and Romans to the present day, in three stuffed volumes. Previous to Dunlop the history of fiction had confined itself to the modest 'progress' genre, pioneered, principally, by James Beattie and Anna Letitia Barbauld, which were largely extended essays.[33] Dunlop's three-volume treatment, destined to become a staple of Victorian libraries, implicitly announced that the novel had come of age. To judge from Murray's work, it was indeed the novel, and not romance, that had risen, for the feature he cites as the sine qua non of the genre was the 'inductive method' of building on concrete particulars, later identified by Ian Watt as the novel's abiding principle.

As it stands, this is a misleading picture. Murray may sound like a proponent of the modern, probable, naturalistic novel, but in fact his outlook was strongly shaped by his eighteenth-century education, especially by the works of Lord Kames, which permeated the curriculum of Edinburgh products, such as Murray. The evidence is there, from the first sentences of the introduction:

> In all stages of human society, from the time at least of its emerging from absolute barbarism, no disposition seems more general than the delight which is taken in works of fiction. These form part, and generally a favourite part, of the literature of every nation. Considering the consummate wisdom which is displayed in every other part of the human constitution, it appears improbable that so universal an inclination should be altogether of a vicious or hurtful nature, or that there should not be some useful purposes which it is destined to serve.[34]

The assertion that the appetite for improving fictions is a providential aspect of the human constitution is pure Kames. Murray's thesis is that fiction has the capacity for improving the morality of readers through the power of example. To buttress his argument he cites the authority of the 'three most distinguished critics of the last age': Hugh Blair, Samuel Johnson, and – at the head of the list – Kames. Murray extracts a long section from the *Elements of Criticism* in which Kames argues that we possess a '*sympathetic emotion of virtue*' which Kames categorizes as an instinctual 'appetite' alongside 'hunger, thirst, and animal love'.[35] Murray quotes Kames's theory of how the sympathetic emotion of virtue works: 'A single act of gratitude produceth in the spectator or reader, not only love or esteem for the author, but also a separate feeling of gratitude without an object; a feeling, however, that disposes the spectator or reader to acts of gratitude ...'[36] Depictions of any one of the several virtues will incite sympathetic feelings in search of an object. But while we have an instinct for virtue, 'no man hath a propensity to vice as such: on the contrary, a wicked deed disgusts him, and makes him abhor the author ...'[37] Fiction is a providential contrivance for it serves to exercise the sympathetic emotion of virtue, transforming the expression of warmth towards virtuous deeds, and disgust towards vicious ones, into habit.

Murray may argue that the inductive method of building on facts is essential for morally efficacious fictions, but he otherwise subscribes to an exemplary model of narrative in which readers – or spectators, as Kames tellingly puts it – are moved by the scenes unfolding before them. The Austenian novel may have perfected the inductive method of creating scenes of striking verisimilitude through the close notation of social particulars (manners), but that is only one aspect of its novelty. The other was the great leap forward it represented as regards 'psycho-narration', the expression of shifting, complex, internal states of mind through free indirect speech. For Kames 'reader' and 'spectator' are equivalent terms, because he is wedded to his model of ideal presence, in which the act of reading recreates spectatorship (as if the acts depicted were running through the reader's mind on an internal screen, or camera obscura). Kames and Murray are not interested in the interiority of the characters depicted but in the interiority of the reader or spectator, whereas, for Austen, the interiority of her heroines is everything.

In her self-reflexive *Northanger Abbey* Austen playfully alludes to her vastly different understanding of the morality of fiction. Catherine's response to some equivocal wording of her friend, Eleanor Tilney, as to the circumstances of her mother's death, is represented to us as free indirect speech. 'Catherine's blood ran cold with the horrid suggestions which naturally sprang from these words. Could it be possible? – Could Henry's father? And yet how many were the examples to justify even the blackest suspicions!'[38] His 'air and attitude' clinch her suspicion that General Tilney is, indeed, 'a Montoni'. The 'examples' Catherine judges from are those provided by what we now refer to as the Gothic novel. Hugh Murray would heartily agree that the 'horrids' provide exact specimens of the unnatural examples he deplores. But Austen's point is that fictional examples are, morally speaking, useless, even if built on foundations set in place by the inductive method. Through the free indirect speech of a callow teenager, the theory of fictional example is satirically, and completely, under cut. Catherine Morland does not learn by being exposed to superior examples – not even those delivered by the excellent Henry – but through the moral suasion exercised upon her by the complex interaction of desire, society, fiction (good and bad), a broadly diffused Christian culture, the vanity of wishing to be thought well of, admirable friends, deplorable acquaintances and many people somewhere in-between. As with Wordsworth's depiction of complex interactions with others, Austen has moved decisively away from an older model of moral effect predicated on the efficacy of moving spectacles in favour of an involved interiority that imagines itself as having effect only insofar as the reader displays a willingness to accompany the character, vicariously, through her own, modern, pilgrim's progress towards moral improvement. In Austen, if the reader's interiority is at stake, it is because it is a shadow of the heroine's.

In contradistinction the philosophical romance directly continues the stimulus-response mechanism implicit in the associationist model advanced by Kames, and embraced by Murray. Murray was not, conspicuously, behind the times: it would be many decades before critics caught up with the aesthetic revolutions set in train by Wordsworth and Austen. Although one might call the model 'Kamesian', it had many authors – principally Locke, Hartley, Hume, Hutcheson and Longinus.[39] As mentioned earlier, Locke was the chief architect of the associationist model, Hume and Hartley (aided by Priestley) its chief popularizers. Hutcheson supplied the instinctual moral sense. Longinus was the conventional Classical source for the belief that poets excelled by virtue of their ability to convey images – through rhetorical means – with an intensity capable of sustaining the 'reality effect'. The reader would seem to behold the image conveyed in the act of reading, so that reading, and spectatorship, were virtually synonymous. As we earlier saw, Kames brought all this together under the convenient and memorable rubric of 'ideal presence'. 'Ideal presence' was such a pervasive and influential model of readerly experience because it was founded on Lockean assumptions that were deeply engrained in the culture, and because Kames with his fellow Scots were staples of the school curriculum in both Britain and America.[40] 'Paradigm' is a much-abused word, but if there are indeed cultural formations worthy of the term (in something like Thomas Kuhn's sense), the structure of moral-aesthetic assumptions denoted by 'ideal presence' is surely among them.

In his preface to *Political Justice* William Godwin declares that 'Few engines can be more powerful, and at the same time more salutary in their tendency, than literature.'[41] Conservative critics, such as the hectoring T. J. Mathias, took a similar view: 'LITERATURE, *well or ill conducted*, IS THE GREAT ENGINE *by which*, I am fully persuaded, ALL CIVILIZED STATES *must ultimately be supported or overthrown*.'[42] Godwin intended 'literature' in its most expansive sense, as did Mathias, but for both the novel was the form that possessed the greatest practical efficacy (but also threat), a point Godwin underscored by making his next project a novel, and Mathias, by ending his polemic with an attack on Matthew Lewis's *The Monk*. It was a view widely shared. Thus Anna Laetitia Barbauld, who quipped: 'It was said by Fletcher of Saltoun, "Let me make the ballads of a nation, and I care not who makes the laws." Might it not be said with as much propriety, Let me make the novels of a country, and let who will make the system?'[43] For all three writers, novels were a form of cultural technology, instrumental in altering the system, or engineering change.

During the 1790s the production of novels rose sharply. As the next century progressed new technologies and lowered costs brought novels to an ever-widening readership just as political reaction against the French Revolution deepened. The natural consequence was a spike in attacks against the novel. The typical complaint was that novels turned readers' heads, inducing them to daydream of a life above their station, from which they would awake, ready for revolution. Prior to 1790 the ideal presence 'paradigm' was sustained by the belief that our Hutchesonian 'sympathetic emotion of virtue' would rise above our other appetites, such as 'hunger, thirst, and animal love'. Such a belief was largely confined to the more progressive, or Whiggish, sections of the intelligentsia. By 1800, the optimistic assessment of the novel as a cultural technology powered by ideal presence became difficult to sustain, even among radicals. In this context Matthew Lewis's *The Monk* is particularly eloquent.[44] The demonic Matilda seduces Ambrosio by presenting him with a magic mirror in which the viewer may see the object of his thoughts. As the lecherous monk dwells on Antonia her image swims into view in the act of bathing, a Venus de Medici who veils herself in an instinctive act of modesty. According to the sentimental values that inflect Kames's theory, Ambrosio should avert his gaze in an instinctive act of sensibility.[45] Instead, his lust is fatally ignited. If Kames's theory conceives of novels as a technology, the technology it mimics is the camera obscura, with both projecting images as if sense data cast in the waking moments of real life. This is exactly how Matilda's mirror works: Antonia appears in its glassy surface in the self-same manner as an image cast by a camera obscura. The mirror and Kames's theory share the same trigger: the images that appear are those of the person on whom one's thoughts are bent. The main difference is that, in Lewis's figure, ethical desire ('a separate feeling of gratitude without an object') is entirely supplanted by 'animal love'. In effect Lewis represents the novel form as if it really were a camera obscura furnished with Coleridge's feared magic power of projecting one man's reveries into the mind of another. The magic mirror may thus be regarded as an allegory of the contemporary critical anxiety directed towards illicit reading, a fear Lewis further satirized through his scandalous suggestion that mothers should stop their daughters conning the Bible and so prevent the projection of its lubricious scenes onto the mind's inner tablet, where they might flicker into corrupting life.

As a form of cultural technology the philosophical romance drew its power from the Kamesian paradigm of ideal presence. Eventually ideal presence gave way to a new model of ethical affect, based on Austen's practice, and first articulated by Scott and Whateley. This new model saw fiction drawing its power from probability and the inductive method. The assertion may sound like Watt, but in many respects it is an inversion of his argument. For Watt, Austen may have perfected, but she was also the beneficiary of the innovations of Defoe, Richardson and Fielding. My argument, rather, is that these earlier writers, and Fielding in particular, were still working within the Kamesian model of aesthetic and ethical affect. To put matters slightly differently, I entirely agree with Scott and Whateley, who registered that Austen was indeed doing something new.

4. Foundlings

To grasp Austen's novelty we have to probe deeper into the generic anatomy of the Philosophical Romance. As we saw earlier, Scott identifies two features common to the post-Romance novel prior to Austen. One is the Kamesian representation of ideal sentiments, the other, the improbable portrayal of heroes who effortlessly rise above the tide of events that sweep along lesser mortals. More often than not, such heroes were foundlings.

The foundling is a central figure in Western Literature, including, as it does, Oedipus, Moses and, in a sense, Jesus Christ. From the perspective of the philosophical romance the key figure is probably Shakespeare, as his late Romances dusted down, burnished and restored the figure as a viable motif for modern literature. Perhaps his most significant innovation was to marry the foundling story to comedy. The discovery of the foundling's true identity was tied to the marriage plot, which in turn figured the restoration of social order and the proper hierarchy. As these were royal marriages (*Cymbeline* and *A Winter's Tale* being the obvious models) the moment of discovery also implicated the legitimacy of the state, as the true heir comes to supplant the false, or renew the old. The foundling motif was a popular one in eighteenth-century fiction, the most distinguished example being *Tom Jones*. In Fielding's novel Tom's restoration to his natural-born rights does not directly signify the nation's return to legitimacy. The matter is instead figured indirectly, in proportion to the intensity of its ideological interest. If the hero has been found in modest circumstances, it is also because he has been usurped. The question of bloodlines, inheritance and legitimacy is thus echoed, confusingly, by the noises off, of the Jacobite uprising (in other words, by the historical commotion created by the efforts of a usurped anti-hero who was, by the lights of the old dispensation, the true heir). As an ideological fiction – as a romance with what Frederick Jameson would call a political unconscious – *Tom Jones* represents the countervailing claims of English, Whig legitimacy through the displaced action of a foundling who embodies the right stuff eventually coming into his own through providential triumphs over enemies who are self-evidently the wrong stuff.[46]

As nearly all historians of nationalism agree, the eighteenth century was the period in European history when nationalist ideologies arose or intensified.[47] In England and Scotland the pressure was especially acute, partly owing to the weight exerted by the colossal project of forging Britain as a new, collective identity, and partly owing to the circumstance of being governed by a royal regime that twice had to resist the claims to legitimacy of a better placed rival. For Whig apologists the matter was especially acute, or would have been, had they not, over time, constructed a robust mythology that explained and justified their possession of the spoils. The essential point of this mythology was that the true origin of state legitimacy was not a sacred blood line but an ancient constitution, one going back beyond the Normans, and their conquest, to the deep woods of Germany, which is where the Ancient, or Gothic, constitution was understood to have had its source, before it was brought to England by the Saxons.[48] According to Whig political mythology, the Saxon Witan was the germ of the English Parliament, which engendered the spirit of English liberty, which begat Magna Carta, which begat the English Reformation, which begat the Glorious Revolution, which in turn codified the Bill of Rights while delivering England forever from Popery, Divine Rule and the Stuarts.

The Whig mythology may have been a rickety fabrication but there is scant evidence that Whig politicians ever gave its validity a second thought. However, such unresolved contradictions have a way of resurfacing in the cultural imaginary. Thus, while Sir Robert Walpole sailed serenely on, laden down with the spoils of office, unperturbed by his enemies' salvos, of being a Craftsman, a Merlin, or blood-sucking Vampyre, his son, Horace, thought otherwise.[49] Or rather, he did so in fiction's indeterminate spaces. In our retrospective view *The Castle of Otranto* seems the clear source for the Gothic novels that were eventually to proliferate, dominating the fiction market of the 1790s. Walpole's faux-Medievalism and fictional experiment of marrying old romance with the modern novel certainly had novelty value, but in other respects he was simply dabbling in the wider, Romance tradition. Walpole's most significant innovation was to weave the foundling motif into the Whig political unconscious. The story ostensibly concerns the efforts of a twelfth-century Italian usurper, named Manfred, to maintain possession of a kingdom originally secured when his grandfather murdered Alfonso, the true prince, while serving as Alfonso's groom on a crusade to the Holy Land. Supernatural or providential forces govern the action. Manfred believes the prophecy that Otranto will return to its rightful heirs when his own line peters out. Naturally enough he is anxious that his only son, the sickly Conrad, should marry, but before the ceremony can be completed, tying him to the Princess Isabella, a giant helmet falls from the ceiling, crushing the heir apparent. Manfred instantly resolves on divorcing his now barren wife,

Hippolyta, so that he can wed Isabella himself and beget new heirs, a prospect that understandably sends the young woman scurrying through the castle's crypts and secret passageways. To make matters worse, Alfonso's true heir turns up, as the peasant foundling, Theodore. As the story progresses, so do Manfred's catastrophes. It seems that the unquiet spirit of the murdered Alfonso inhabits the fabric of the Castle. At key moments the spirit intervenes, often by sending yet another gigantic, armoured relic crashing down on his enemies. But as father Jerome makes clear, the real string puller is the Deity himself, who ensures that the sins of the fathers are punished to the third and fourth generation, even if this means orchestrating the murder of the innocent Matilda, who dies, stabbed by her furious, jealous father, who mistakes her for Isabella in the gloom of the church, conversing criminally with the hated Theodore.

However, as Freud would put it, that is merely the work's manifest content. Walpole hides the latent, through his cunning use of frames. It seems the story's composition was not coeval with its action, but was the imposture of a counter-Reformational monk, who has used the technology of the 'innovators' to confound their purposes, by turning their 'own arms' against them. By 'innovators' Walpole means the Reformers, or Protestants, and by 'arms', the art of clear writing (in Godwin's terms, the 'engine of literature'). It seems that the game of the crafty priest who forged the work was to defeat the Reformation by using its principle invention – the press – to renew the grip of superstition among the unlearned by disseminating a tale of providential vengeance in strong, nervous language, thus striking a blow for the true church. However, that is merely the first of Walpole's frames. The next is provided by Walpole's adoption of the pseudonym, William Marshall, Gentleman, who allegedly found the book in the library of an ancient Catholic family from the North of England. Although he does not say so, Marshall, himself, is presumably Catholic and possibly a member of the family in question, themselves likely Jacobites. In the surface story the foundling is called the 'gift of God' (that is, Theodore) because that is what he was according to the doctrine of the Divine Right of Kings. And so, indeed, was Bonnie Prince Charlie. As the author of the preface, and, indeed, as possible author of the entire work, William Marshall fights a rearguard, Jacobite action by insinuating the claims of his rightful king through his 'found' medieval romance. The story dwells on the theme of 'usurpation' and by extension, on the Reformation – the foundational events of Whig political mythology. Walpole's double game, it seems, is to undermine the Jacobite cause by arguing badly for it in the guise of the crafty, forging Marshall, linking Jacobitism with the worst excesses of Catholic obscurantism.

The final frame occurs in the preface to the second edition, when Walpole, standing exposed as the true author, essays a defence of his imposture by claiming to have married the modern novel with the ancient romance. Walpole situates his innovation in the Shakespeare/Voltaire debate, claiming a nationalist cachet by arguing that his experiment amounts to no more than upholding the example of the divine Shakespeare, England's Homer, against arid, foreign, French Neo-Classicism. In this context the 'arms of the innovators' reaches out to include the techniques of the modern, probable novel. In turning the novel against itself (which he did, effectively, including a pioneering use of free indirect discourse),[50] Walpole means to convey his aristocratic prerogative to do both, to dabble in the era of 'fine fabling', as Richard Hurd put it,[51] while also showing his mastery of the techniques developed by the bourgeois producers of the modern novel. As a private sport produced on a press outside the commercial economy of the novel Walpole wishes to display all sides of his aristocratic identity, part of which is the ability to take a playful approach to sensitive, Whig, ideological material, with which he thought himself as having a special, proprietary relationship.

Much to his own surprise, Walpole had let a genie out of a bottle. Slowly at first, but eventually through a startling acceleration, his version of the foundling story took the novel by storm. Clara Reeve's *The Old English Baron* (1777), Sophia Lee's *The Recess* (1783–85) and Ann Radcliffe's *The Castles of Athlin and Dunbayne* (1789), all revolve around the foundling motif. Together they form the conventional genealogy of the 'tale of terror', as it was then called. Their principal innovation was to represent history as 'history'. Walpole's aim was to mimic the manners of a past age, convincingly enough, at least, to palm his forgery off on the undiscerning (thus affording a good laugh for his aristocratic cronies).[52] Reeve, and those that followed her, were more concerned with historical process, and the emergence of the modern. Their principal device was to contrast a version of an ancien regime (usually feudal in character) with emergent, modern, 'sensibility'. In *The Old English Baron* the hero, a foundling, and usurped heir, is really a figure for the contemporary 'man of feeling', and is distinguished from his medieval foil by being far more flexible in his attitudes towards class and gender. Indeed, his affective capacities for love, as well as for otherness, are directly, yet firmly, tied to his fitness to govern his 'household' (that is, both the domestic and public realms), so that moral fitness and lineal descent fall into line, thus joining the twin senses of 'legitimacy'. *The Recess* contrasts the harsh world of Elizabethan real politic – the first growth of the future commercial state – with the romantic sensibility of Mary Queen of Scot's two, secret, daughters. They are, as it were, foundlings born outside of history, which is another way of saying that they cannot be found and restored. Their secret dooms them to peripheral status, no matter how often the plot threatens – through the love interest – to move them to the historical centre stage. As Gillian Beer points out, paradoxically, their peripheral status locks them within history, by history.[53] They represent another path 'legitimacy' may have taken, one informed by the softening values of sensibility, unlike history's actual course, which moves smoothly towards what Scottish stadialists would have termed the commercial age: unsentimental, harsh and indifferent towards value beyond the 'cash nexus'. As the next in line, *The Castles of Athlin and Dunbayne* has the opportunity of making the implicit explicit, which it duly does. Once again the foundling, and true heir, merits the aristocratic marriage his intrinsic sensibility demands, in contrast to the principal villain, Malcolm, who serves as a cartoon feudal lord, the sort giving 'medieval' its bad name (among other evil things he threatens to murder the heroine's brother, held up in chains on the castle parapet, unless she submits to his vile desires). To ensure the reader understands that the sensibility evinced by her heroes is thoroughly modern, Radcliffe furnishes them with contemporary allusions to, for example, Beattie's *The Minstrel,* the precursor of the *Prelude*'s archetypal modern Romantic subject. However, it was in Radcliffe's next novel, *A Sicilian Romance,* that she joined up the dots, and represented the contrast as historical process, as a conflict between generations spanning the gap between 'feudal' and 'modern', with the modern naturally predominating through the marriage plot. Another of her innovations was to change the gender of her foundlings, from the customary male, in *The Romance of the Forest* (1791) and *The Italian* (1797). The focus on heroines striving to attain their natural rights helped sharpen the gender politics implicit in the ideology of sensibility, even if the plot equivocates between the two senses of 'natural': Paine's or Burke's. In McKeon's terms, the female Gothic represents the next dialectical turn in the development of romance, a turn made possible by Walpole who clarified the political unconscious of aristocratic romance by alluding to the ideological context that imparted meaning to the form. Women writers built on this contested ground, in the process transforming romance into a bourgeois form narrating, not the restoration of ancient rights, but the transition from feudal to modern with its 'normative ideals'.

5. C. R. Maturin and the national romance

Ireland was especially fertile ground for the foundling story, because so many of its ancient houses had been 'usurped' by the English. To visit Ireland was to encounter houses in a state of dilapidation, as in Maria Edgeworth's *Castle Rackrent,* or exchanged for a hovel, as in Lady Morgan's *The Wild Irish Girl,* while the English visitor gazed on, often from the windows of the big house, the former homes of the usurped. As earlier discussed, the motif of the visitor from the dominant culture falling in love with a displaced native is the fundamental strand of the National Tale's generic DNA.[54] The motif provides the foundation for the international theme (later embroidered, and given a twist, by Nathaniel Hawthorne and Henry James), in which the male visitor, representing modernity, falls in love with an exotic who also represents a past his own culture has been instrumental in rendering 'past'. The encounter naturally prompts some soul searching and an implicit contrast of cultures, plus an opportunity for a collective nostalgia as the cosmopolitan reader simultaneously regrets, and rejoices, their escape from what Herman Melville would call the 'povertiesque'. In *Corinne* (1807), De Stael codified the role of the heroine in the national tale, rendering her both glamorous and abstract. Corinne is the soul of her fragmented nation, the anthropomorphized correlative of that which does not yet exist, and as such bears its qualities: beautiful, captivating, and filled with the Southern spirit of a people not yet a people. But because she represents that which is fragmented she is only truly herself – she only comes together, as a whole – as the improvisatrice. It is only as the medium of a homeless spirit, a spirit taking up temporary residence in her, that she is ever, really, herself: the rest of the time she merely acts.

'Eccentric' was the word that came most readily to the pen of English reviewers taking notice of the Irish writer, Robert Charles Maturin.[55] Maturin was, in many ways, a perfect misfit, in that he flamboyantly lived out the myth of Romantic genius. But in other respects 'eccentric' is deeply misleading, for as a writer he did not fly off at a tangent from the emerging generic conventions of his day, so much as he piled them up. Like his mentor, Sir Walter Scott, Maturin was an acute student of the passing fictional scene. His play, *Bertram* (1816), was a distillation of the Byronic diabolisms – the 'Satanic school' – then taking London by storm. His novels are equally attuned to passing fashion. His two national tales – *The Wild Irish Boy* (1808) and *The Milesian Chief* (1812) – eloquently rework Lady Morgan, Edgeworth, De Stael, Radcliffe and Walpole. Both texts are allegories, with the marriage plots acting as a dark conceit for the coming together of the Irish and English in a mutual process of national self-definition. Another dominant feature of both texts is their theatricality. Maturin's central characters suffer an authenticity deficit, owing to their enforced deracination and usurpation. As with De Stael's Corinne, for those lacking strong national roots, all the world's a stage. The protagonists of both tales search for the home (or nation) they have lost, and with it the grounds of a stable rather than theatrical identity.

The wild Irish boy is Ormsby Bethel, who is neither very Irish nor very wild. Ormsby's father was one of four penniless Milesian brothers named Delacy, who, in the manner of down-at-heel aristocracy, have become professional soldiers freebooting across Europe. A maternal uncle unexpectedly leaves the Delacys a fortune, under the condition that they take his name of Bethel. The others, beginning with the eldest, proudly refuse to sell their Milesian heritage in this way, except for Ormsby's father, a luxury-loving libertine, who lives abroad with his mistress, Ormsby's mother, Miss Percival, a promiscuous Godwinian bluestocking. Ormsby's parents are an odd couple: he loves claret and a good dinner, she's infatuated with radical Enlightenment philosophy; he's a ruined dandy, while she dresses in the austere fashion of a Voltairean freethinker. However, they are not characters but representations of the two main branches of libertinism, the moral and philosophical. As committed libertines, they naturally do not marry, leaving Ormsby to cope with his illegitimacy as best he can. With his health and fortune broken, Bethel retires to Ireland, to be near the Milesian Chief, his older brother, whose fortunes have now been repaired, in the hopes of making Ormsby the heir. While in Ireland Ormsby falls in love with Lady Montrevor, who has followed her English husband to his Irish estates following the shameful revelation of his having usurped his English title and property for some thirty years. The brilliant socialite Lady Montrevor is closely modelled on Maria Edgeworth's Lady Delacour, from *Belinda* (1801), an example of Irish literary success much admired and envied by Maturin. Lady Montrevor has several daughters, married to the great and good of English society, including the British Prime Minister. Although a matron, she becomes Ormsby's passionate, and secret, love object. She naturally has her own secret sorrow, which is that in her youth she quarrelled with her true love, marrying (out of spite) Lord Montrevor, a cold, vain, punctilious English fop.

Ormsby is brought up abroad, first in France, and then England. He has a favourite daydream born out of his deracinated existence:

> I have imagined some fortunate spot, some abode peopled by fair forms, human in their affections, their habits, in everything but vice and weakness; to these I have imagined myself giving laws, and becoming their sovereign. I therefore imagined them possessed of the most shining qualities that can enter into the human character, glowing with untaught affections, and luxuriant with uncultivated virtue; but proud, irritable, impetuous, insolent, and superstitious ... (Maturin 1808: I, 102)

As Ireland is the 'fortunate spot' the dream is a fantasy of national self-becoming. The longed-for event is implicitly linked to the advent of a Washington, a father/Moses figure. Although it is not stated, this is what, implicitly, Ormsby is, or hopes to be.

As the putative, future father of the Irish nation, Ormsby draws his authority from his genealogical links with the past, here embodied by the Milesian chief: 'They who speak of a Milesian Chief describe him as a being, obsolete as Brien Born, or Fingal; as a being, who talks the language of Ossian, and wears the robes of a bard ...' (Maturin 1808: I, 181). But the myth is real, for this is exactly the character of the elder Delacy: 'His demeanour was marked with dignity, but it was a wild and original dignity; that of a chief of a warlike country, lofty with unborrowed grandeur and habitual command; amid the polished forms of modern life, he looked the oak, amid the poplar and the willow' (Maturin 1808: I, 182). The Milesian chief himself makes the case for the antiquity of the Irish. Here he explains why there are no physical remnants of past Irish greatness: 'Because the monuments of recent greatness are more easily preserved than those of the remote; the structures of Irish greatness, were perhaps falling into ruins before those of Rome were erected.

The great enemy to the existence of our ancient monuments was Christianity' (Maturin 1808: I, 194). Maturin's strategy is to adopt a timeframe that renders the Reformation insignificant. Maturin's Irish nationalism is not an internecine question of Protestant versus Catholic vying for supremacy; for Maturin, such a division is itself a product of Ireland's modern history of fragmented statehood.[56] Thus there is no contradiction, or tension, in the mysteriously Protestant Ormsby Bethel becoming the adamantly Catholic Delacy's heir.

Ormsby marries Lady Montrevor's daughter by mistake, after Delacy privately arranges the marriage assuming that the daughter, not the mother, is Ormsby's secret love. In many respects the rest of the complicated story is about how Ormsby learns to prefer his wife to his mother-in-law. Ormsby's progress is counterpointed by the Gothic subplot. A spectral figure haunts a ruined tower next to the property of the Milesian chief. He is, above all else, a figure of Irish dispossession. He is also, it turns out, in true Shakespearean fashion, Lady Montrevor's first lover, Delacy's brother, Ormsby's father, and an Irish aristocrat. It seems that the promiscuous Miss Percival had, as a Godwinian proponent of free love, taken both brothers as lovers in quick succession; having been impregnated by the elder brother, she blames it on the younger. A series of providential deaths clears the way for the marriage of Ormsby's father and Lady Montrevor, the new Milesian chief and the brilliant Anglo-Irish woman. The marriage symbolizes the unification of Ireland, and the restoration of the ancient line of Irish self-rule. Ormsby's infatuation with Lady Montrevor was in fact a symptom of his national alienation, his un-rootedness; with order restored, his love naturally refocusses on his wife, child and Irish futurity.

The indirectness of the text as an expression of Irish national aspirations is owing to the allegorical nature of the tale and to the obfuscations of the property plot, which deals with usurpation obliquely by displacing the act onto Lord Montrevor. Although he holds his Irish lands by just title, he comes to Ireland tainted with the scandal of his English usurpation. Although Montrevor is an English usurper living in Ireland, he is not, legally, a usurper of Ireland.

Maturin's next romance, *The Milesian Chief* (1812), tackles the property issue head on. Thirty years previous to the time of the story, the English Lord Montclare had bought an estate from a ruined Milesian family, the O'Morvens. Scandalously to both sides of the family, Montclare's sister married 'the son of the ancient proprietor' (Maturin 1812: I, 48), bearing him two children, Connal and Desmond. The elder child is raised by his grandfather in an ancient tower, the last remnant of the O'Morven property. As far as the grandfather is concerned, Montclare's possession of the O'Morven estate is a simple case of usurpation, brought on by English policies since the time of Elizabeth, when the last expression of Gaelic nationhood, the uprising of Hugh O'Neill, the 'Irish Prince', was crushed in 1601.[57] Interestingly, the heroine of the tale, Armida, Montclare's daughter, a woman of extraordinary talents and learning, employs the plot of *Otranto* to imagine the plight of the young O'Morvens: she thinks of the state of mind 'that comforts itself in being compelled to inhabit ruins by tracing among them the remains of ancient palaces; that like the spirit in Otranto stalks amid its ancient seat till it swells beyond it, and stands forth amid the fragments dilated and revealed, terrifying the intrusion of modern usurpers' (Maturin 1808: I, 52). Armida is also an improvisatorice, or Irish Corinne. Or rather, while not Irish herself, as an improvisatorice (a stateless person raised in Italy with all the arts at her fingertips) she has an especial affinity for the state of Irish usurpation.

The Montclares are, indeed, the legal usurpers of Irish territory. A clause in the contract stipulates that the estate shall revert to the O'Morvens in the event of there being no male heir. Nor is there one, for the apparent son, Endymion, is really a girl in disguise. In order to retain a hold over Lord Montclare, and then the property itself, Lady Montclare raises her daughter, Inez, as a boy. Somewhat improbably, Inez is unaware of her true gender until her love for Desmond brings about a crisis of disclosure. Although both Desmond and Connal discover the imposture, their extreme pride prevents them from profiting from the knowledge, until too late. Connal O'Morven is the very image of a Celtic chief, by way of Ossian: of gigantic stature, proud, warlike, chivalrous, with an exquisite sensibility. Hence his squeamishness in pursuing his own self-interests, in complete contrast to Armida's betrothed, the wicked Colonel Wandesford. Once again a vivacious Anglo-Irish heroine is inappropriately linked to a shallow, vain, ill-educated Englishman. He is also the apparent villain of the piece. Despite herself, Armida falls in love with Connal, who is driven into a rebellion through Wandesford's double dealing. It is, it appears, 1798 all over again, or, perhaps more topically, a reference to Robert Emmet's uprising of 1803.[58] Armida elopes with Connal to his rebel camp, where they marry. When we first encounter Armida, in Naples, she, too, suffers the paradox of national inauthenticity. Caught up in the luxury of artistic refinements, she is only able to be herself when placed on show. In marrying Connal she becomes rooted in a national soil and identity, and as a result recovers her authenticity and, with it, a womanly simplicity.

The rebellion fails. Armida commits self-slaughter after Connal has been executed through Wandesford's connivance. But Wandesford is not the ultimate antagonist. The person pulling the strings, including Wandesford's, is Lady Montclare, an Italian Catholic who selfishly manipulates her family through her agent, the priest Morosoni. Generically, Maturin appears to be writing a tragic national tale in which Ireland's historical misfortunes are laid at the door of the Anglo-Irish ascendancy (a class about which Maturin, as a poor Huguenot, had mixed feelings). But at the last he switches to the Gothic, and a convenient Catholic foil, in order to stymie the nationalist logic of his own text.

Another way of putting Maturin's eccentricity is that he is unable to keep to generic decorum: instead his invention proliferates, his narrative strands weaving themselves into a dense mass. Compared to Austen's crystalline plots, Maturin's are a turbid mess. But his practice also sharply brings home the differences between them. For Maturin, probability is a dead letter. His plots are driven, not by the inductive method, but by ideas. Like Walpole's, Maturin's marriage plots figure the fate of the nation.

The Wild Irish Boy joins the family with the national romance, with Ormsby exchanging his apparent family (the embarrassing libertine odd couple) with an idealized union of old Milesian blood and Anglo-Irish sensibility, who, between them, and in their union, represent a usurped and fractured nation made whole again, thus restoring legitimacy to the erstwhile bastard, Ormsby, whose wild state is resolved, not by his taming, but by his return to native ground. As such Maturin's plot imagines what legitimacy might look like in the fraught aftermath of a Revolutionary decade that had brought nationalist, and with it ideological, matters to the fore in Ireland. *The Milesian Chief* makes *Otranto* even more central in its cultural and ideological imagining, in part through direct reference, and as a consequence Maturin is unable to find a satisfactory conclusion to the sharp questions posed by the usurpation of the Milesians, which is to say, of the native Irish. If Connal is Otranto (that is, Alfonso), haunting the ruins of his former domains, no one in the romance corresponds to Theodore. Connal and Armida die without issue, as does the restoration plot.

6. The philosophical romance

I have dwelt on Maturin's two novels, because they sum up what the philosophical romance had become at end of the first decade of the nineteenth century, when Scott was poised to make his entrance even as Austen quietly revolutionized the form. Maturin's novels promiscuously mix genres, in that they combine the foundling-romance plot, the Gothic and the National Tale. Insofar as Maturin's romances narrate history, and the fate of the nation, they are allegorical, with the foundling-marriage plots serving as a device for exfoliating the themes of usurpation and restoration. As such they mount a critique against the legitimacy of the Anglo-Irish ascendancy, or at least those segments supporting the Union of 1801, an event strongly opposed by Maturin. And as a stylist Maturin is strongly drawn to tableaux, to a theatrical style with a strong emphasis on moving spectacles.

Of course, most Romantic-era novels are not like Maturin's. As we saw with Scott's expert examination, the divisions of the novel were many. Nor was Austen quite so alone. Scott for his own purposes might characterize the novel of manners as a 'tale of the times', and advance the anonymous author of the *Barouche Driver and his Wife* as its chief exponent, but against this we must put Burney, Edgeworth and Smith, as other novelists with a significant ability to create narratives that were contemporary and probable. Given the proliferation of fictional subgenres and the rapid rise of the realist novel, we may even argue that the philosophical romance was a distinct, minority form. Even then, many philosophical romances eschewed the 'romance' element in favour of a dialogical exploration of ideas, often set in the present (the novels of Mary Hays, in particular, fall into this category). But if we ask, in what ways does the novel during this period recapitulate the same process we have seen at work in poetry, where critique surrenders to Counter-Enlightenment; or, differently, in what ways is the novel itself, generically, a Romantic misfit; the answer we get pushes us to works like Maturin's. It pushes this way, because it is in the philosophical romance that we find the radical Enlightenment at work. The foundling plot provided a narrative language for exploring the vexed issue of legitimacy, thus mounting a 'critique' (Kant's definition of 'doing Enlightenment') in which we discover the ways in which we are not bound by traditional authority. The home/house/nation trope, encountered in philosophical romances from Walpole to Maturin, and beyond, is foundational to the grammar of philosophical romance, a grammar generating numerous examples of national exploration. Given the overdetermined nature of the foundling and the fall-of-the-house-of plots, the form naturally tends towards metaphor, in contradistinction to the stubbornly metonymic (and quotidian) particulars favoured by Watt as the sine qua non of the emerging realist novel. The commitment to Kames's ideal presence meant the practitioners of the philosophical romance also embraced his Enlightenment values, where readers become ethically shaped subjects; by the same token, they subscribed, implicitly, to a version of the public sphere. As we have seen, for Kames 'reader' and 'spectator' are exchangeable terms. When reading – in the moment of ideal presence – we become spectators of the scenes we imagine with an intensity that challenges the real. For Kames, such spectatorship is normative: given his Hutchesonian assumptions, the uncorrupted self will always respond warmly to depictions of virtue, and with disgust to images of vice. For Kames, readers were not isolated individuals consuming fictions in their closets, but spectators of a common scene. They were also members of a virtual public rationally shaped through a normative technology. Given its allegorical character the philosophical romance was a vehicle for the rational exploration of ideas central to the public interest.

Hugh Murray was thus entirely correct in identifying William Godwin as the chief practitioner of the philosophical romance. Godwin's two novels of the 1790s – *Caleb Williams* and *St Leon* – are both studies in the cultural work of ideology. Like another novel published in 1794, Radcliffe's *Mysteries of Udolpho, Caleb Williams* turns on the moment in which a child transgresses an interdiction to respect parental secrets. In *Udolpho,* Emily St. Aubert breaks the sanction her deceased father placed on reading his private papers through an accidental glimpse that harrows her soul. Emily misreads, what, we never quite learn, although the text hints that it portends her illegitimacy in a threatened reversal of the foundling story. Caleb burns with curiosity to sound the mystery of the trunk jealously guarded by Falkland, with the tragic plot set in train by Caleb's overhearing Falkland's tortured communion with his secret. As Radcliffe's romance makes clear, the figure of the father is at the apex of the ideological structure that links sensibility (properly disciplined), property and legitimacy. Emily's glimpse into the ambiguous language of her father's secret papers threatens the very architecture of her identity, so that any recurrence of the memory triggers a fugue state. Godwin plays with the narrative grammar of the philosophical romance, making explicit what is implicit in Radcliffe. Caleb tells us that Falkland adopted him after Caleb became orphaned, having observed (through his steward, Collins) that he was a boy of parts. In romances boys who appear able above their station pose questions as to who they really are. There is no evidence that Caleb is Falkland's illegitimate child, while Caleb himself makes a point of noting their physical dissimilarity. Evidence is unnecessary. In the narrative grammar of romances, gifted orphans attached to childless aristocratic patrons are linked to them in a simple binary of being, or not being, the lost heir. Godwin alludes to the possibility in order to scotch it, and that is because he wishes the reader to focus, not on the biological possibility, but on what it is that drives Caleb's fascination with Falkland and his secret. As Godwin writes in his *Enquiry into Political Justice*, the ruling passion of the present day is the 'love of distinction'.[59] In post-Marxist terms one would say this amounts to class-consciousness, to artificial markers of superiority derived from the inversions of ideology's 'camera obscura', or simply leave the phrase as it is in the recognition that it comes full circle in the work of Bourdieu. In any event, the love of distinction is very much a form of false consciousness for Godwin, as it involves a distortion of what a rational apprehension of the good might be. Falkland's own love of distinction is the root of the evil that besets him, and is made manifest in his passion for 'chivalry', Burke's outdated Gothic code institutionalized, oppressively, in the system of laws that governed the kingdom (so that the book turns on the standard Jacobin critique whereby Blackstone's renovated mansion of Gothic laws becomes Thelwall's detested Gothic customary).[60] With this connection in mind we can see that Godwin was being brutally direct in the suppressed first preface: 'It is but of late that the inestimable importance of political principles has been adequately apprehended. It is now known to philosophers that the spirit and character of the Government intrudes itself into every rank of society'.[61] By 'of late' he doubtlessly means his own *Political Justice*. Falkland's love of chivalry is itself an expression of the 'spirit and character of the Government' which 'extols in the warmest terms the existing constitution of society'.[62] That the chivalric Falkland comes to use a corrupt system of laws to persecute his secretary follows directly, not from the accidentals of the plot, but from Godwin's philosophical logic. The same love of distinction that motivates Falkland drives Caleb, who is in a 'pre-critique' stage of development, bound, fast, within 'things as they are'. Falkland and Caleb share, not a secret blood line, but a system of values they have unconsciously internalized and which keeps them tied in an abusive relationship of mutual recognition, loathing, and sentimentality, evident, above all, in their self-dramatizing acts of public forgiveness. In the end, Caleb is not a foundling or Falkland's heir; instead the romance reveals connections that are deeper, and more binding, than simple biology.

Even a quick dip into Hansard's records of the state trials of the 1790s will reveal the radical sophistication of the Jacobins.[63] Honed by a verbal culture in pitched battle over the most deeply held values, their discussion of rights, power and chicanery is several degrees sharper than our own political discourse: they shred and dice their opponents' rhetoric, until the bones are flayed. However, there is one gap in their political vocabulary, the want of which often transports their arguments back to the eighteenth century, rather than forward to the nineteenth. That gap is the one filled by the word 'ideology' itself, the sense, that is, that sets of values have a systematic relationship to vested interests. This 'want' influences Godwin's discussion of 'distinction' in *Political Justice*. Godwin is very clear that 'distinction' belongs to the logic of what will later be called 'commodity fetishism'; that it is the stimulus for, and product of, artificial desires set in train by the rise of commerce (a connection that will become the given of *St Leon*, his next romance). Godwin also understands that the love of distinction and the artificial desires it sustains, and which, in turn, sustain it, are systemic. It is in his cure that Godwin suddenly leaps backward. All one need do, he argues, is come to a rational apprehension of what one's real needs are, and what the greater good really is, and one will defeat 'luxury' at a stroke. This may be too bald a statement, but I think it generally true that in his prescriptions Godwin sounds like almost any other civic humanist worrying about the spread of luxury sped on by the irrational stoking of artificial desire endemic in a commercial state. In Isaac Kramnick's phrase, Godwin's radicalism is bourgeois in that it lacks connection to a material base, with the result that Godwin appears blithely unaware that his own leisure for contemplating a rational world where both the population and the economy would be smaller and in balance depends upon the continued mindless labour of countless wealth-producers currently alienated from the value of their work.[64] From a Marxist perspective, *Caleb Williams* is doubtless no more satisfactory than Godwin's *Enquiry*. But in terms of exemplifying how power is systemic – how the 'spirit and character of government' is a constitutive determinant of 'things as they are' – the novel marks a great leap forward, not least in realizing the aim, retrospectively articulated by Godwin, of composing an affective engine for bringing home the power of the system to his reader's very nerve ends. As a philosophical romancer Godwin understands that debates over legitimacy have advanced beyond Jacobite arguments over blood lines to questions over abstractions: accordingly he holds out a superficial connection only to replace it with another of a deeper, more philosophical kind.

In *Frankenstein* Mary Shelley adapts the foundling story and in the process produced the most famous philosophical romance of the age. The monster is, literally, a foundling, being composed of 'found' body parts. The brilliance of the conceit is that it shifted the question of origin from the register of 'lineage', consolidated by Walpole, to a 'scientific' one in which natural science, philosophy, myth and religion may all be read against each other, with no explanation ostensibly privileged over another. It is the overdetermined nature of origin, informed by Mary Shelley's prodigious reading in the months leading up to the book's composition, that has sustained the novel's rich corpus of interpretation. One does not have to scratch too far beneath the book's surface – especially of the 1818 edition – to begin to discover Shelley's radical politics. One finds it, for example, in the monster's allusions to Rousseau and Volney; in the daring references to materialism; in the logic of the creature/creator relationships; or in the treatment of gender. From her father Shelley learned the importance of keeping point of view strictly limited to the consciousness of each of her benighted narrators. Combined with the overdetermined themes, the ironic poise of the Chinese-doll mode of narration ensured that the ideas set free by the romance were allowed to rub against each other in the attentive reader's mind.

The philosophical romance went on to have a distinguished career in the nineteenth century, nowhere more so than in America, where it arguably reached its purest form in the work of Nathaniel Hawthorne and Herman Melville. Most of both writers' long prose works fit the rubric – especially Hawthorne's *Marble Faun* and Melville's *Mardi* and *Moby Dick* – but the two works that best exemplify the cultural work performed by the philosophical romance are *The House of the Seven Gables* and *Pierre, or the Ambiguities*, both explicit reworkings of Walpole's *Castle of Otranto*. Hawthorne's novel is built on an act of usurpation, of the Maules by the Pyncheons, a sin visited on the third and fourth generations. Situating the act in a moment foundational to New England history – the Salem Witch trials – allows Hawthorne to draw out the national implications of the family 'house'. Like *Otranto*, there is a curse which finally works itself out when the foundling figure – Holgrave, the lineal descendent of the Maules – repossesses the house through his marriage to the last of the Pyncheons, the exiguous Phoebe. However, this is merely the surface story; the buried one links the narrative to the unfinished business that most perturbs the national project, slavery, and the theft of Indian lands. Melville finished his version of *Otranto*, *Pierre*, shortly after Hawthorne published his (during a period in which the relationship between the two writers was at its most intense), and as might be expected his version makes the link even more explicit, as it, too, uses the philosophical romance form to worry away at the challenge to American legitimacy posed by the unresolved acts of theft that marked the nation's beginnings. Apart from the generic markers of aristocratic houses, usurpation, curses, foundlings, and final catastrophes both works recall the heyday of the philosophical romance through their extensive use of ideal presence, striking tableaux, and framing devices that help create depth, and distance, through irony. This is especially true in the case of Hawthorne, whose education at Bowdoin College versed him thoroughly in the aesthetic theories of Kames and Alison.[65]

7. Conclusion

The 'philosophical romance', then, is my answer to the question, 'What is the Romantic novel?' It is Romantic, because it is the subgenre of the novel that most explicitly explores, and questions, the underpinnings of the nationalist ideologies that did so much to shape the literature of the Romantic period. The fact that it was not recognized as such during the course of the canonization that was eventually to produce the academic field of Romanticism is possibly the single greatest oddity of the process.

In part it was misrecognized because mislabelled as 'Gothic', mislabelled, at least, in this regard: by 'Gothic' critics largely meant a formulaic, senseless genre, in which motifs were endlessly recycled to meet the undiscriminating reading appetites of the low end of the market, whereas the philosophical romance was distinguished by especially articulate utterances generated by a sophisticated narrative grammar. Emily Brontë's *Wuthering Heights* (1847) is another complex yet perfectly intelligible experiment in the genre. We encounter the usual elements: a usurped house, a foundling, multi-generational suffering, and a love interest broken on the difference between two irreconcilable houses. Wuthering Heights, moreover, is cthonically linked with the nation (in this case, the provincial, anti-cosmopolitan, anti-Home Counties outlook of ancient Yorkshire). The mix of these elements signified, not writing to recipe, but evidence of a particularly agile mind exploring the roots of her provincial experience. Readers have long recognized *Wuthering Heights* as a deeply Romantic work – mainly because of the strangely asexual love of Heathcliff and Cathy that seems to betoken a quasi-incestuous identity pre-existing socialization, thus drawing on desires somehow deeper than sex – but this ambiguous celebration of the inner child only emerges because of Brontë's cleverness in literalizing the implicit comparison found in the philosophical romances from *Otranto* to *Pierre*, between the ancient house that dominates the work and the modern one the reader metaphorically inhabits. If Wuthering Heights signifies ancient Yorkshire, with its roots twisted deep in the thin, peaty soil, Thrushcross Grange represents comfortable, bourgeois modernity. It is the tortuous difference between them that creates the unquiet space for Heathcliff and Cathy.

Pierre and *Wuthering Heights* were both badly received when published, and while critics eventually recognized that these works could not be accommodated within the usual category of Gothic or formula fiction, they did not know where to put them, even though the obvious category of 'Romantic literature' beckoned. F. R. Leavis pronounced *Wuthering Heights* a 'sport', outside the main traditions of the novel,[66] while critics of American literature went to great lengths to account for the sheer oddity – eccentricity, as Marius Bewley termed it – of American romance.[67] Lionel Trilling was in the vanguard of an entire school of criticism that exercised immense ingenuity in explaining why the novelists of the 'American Renaissance' did not write like Jane Austen, with the consensus following Henry James in attributing the Romance habit to the lack of social density that only comes with several hundred years of history.[68] The simple answer was that Hawthorne and Melville did not write like Jane Austen because they did not want to. Writing like Austen meant adopting the inductive method of resonant particulars, or manners; but to do so was to accept that the self was what society made us whereas the philosophical romancers were more concerned with possibility.[69]

In his unfinished essay, 'On History and Romance', Godwin critiques the modern prejudice that associates 'ancient history' with 'exaggeration and fable':

> It is not necessary here to enter into a detail of the evidence upon which our belief of ancient history is founded. Let us take it for granted that it is a fable. Are all fables unworthy of regard? Ancient history, says Rousseau, is a tissue of such fables, as have a moral perfectly adapted to the human heart. I ask not, as a principal point, whether it be true or false? My first enquiry is, 'Can I derive instruction from it? Is it a genuine praxis upon the nature of man? Is it pregnant with the most generous motives and examples? If so, I had rather be profoundly versed in this fable, than in all the genuine histories that ever existed.'[70]

As Godwin's phrasing makes clear, he is still wedded to the novel as an exemplary technology, one founded, not on 'facts', or historical 'truth', or, indeed, 'probability', but on a 'genuine praxis upon the nature of man', which must include, not simply what history, or society, has made us, but also our potential for 'generous motives and examples'. D. H. Lawrence's excitement on reading nineteenth-century American literature flowed from his recognition that their fictional practice, as philosophical romancers, anticipated his own concerns, especially his desire to escape the suffocating pressure of the English novel of manners. As he explains in a letter to Edward Garnett, he is not interested in the 'diamond' of character, but in the carbon; not in subjectivity, or what Lawrence calls the 'old stable ego of the character', as it has been formed by the immense weight of history, but in its plastic potentiality.[71] What Lawrence is recording is the fact that in the nineteenth century – beginning before Austen, but consolidated by her practice – the novel had come to be associated with manners, with selfhood as it was already informed and inflected by social pressures.[72]

This view of the 'realist novel' has recently been challenged, but also rearticulated and reinforced, by William Galperin in his *The Historical Austen*. Drawing on Michel de Certeau, Galperin posits the radical heterogeneity of history, of 'what really happened', and how, in contradistinction to this, history, memory, and narrative instantiate a particular, normative version of the past, a version that becomes normative, simply by being narrative and 'history'. The fulcrum of Galperin's argument is the rise of the realist novel, the genre that more than any other served to instantiate an ideologically overdetermined 'probable'. Galperin argues that Austen has been fundamentally, and systematically, misunderstood as a writer of the 'probable', and therefore as a dismal proponent of an ever-straitening courtship plot, in which bright, spirited heroines, like Catherine Morland in *Northanger Abbey*, are simultaneously broken of their romantic habits of unconstrained imagination and socialized in the grim realities of a newly rising, soon-to-be hegemonic, domestic ideology. While Galperin leaves this narrative of the realist novel intact, he radically revises Austen by arguing that the pigeonholing of her as a writer of the 'probable' was largely the work of her two early influential reviewers, Walter Scott and Bishop Whateley in the *Quarterly Review*, and that she is, on the contrary, a writer of 'possibility', of someone who always keeps uncannily in view, through the radical alterity of her superabundant textual details, the prospect of how things might be – might have been – radically otherwise.[73] Galperin does not understand himself to be reading against the grain; rather his 'historical Austen' encompasses such possibilities, as minute acts of intention, even as she finds herself equipped with an almost preternatural sense of where the 'probable', historically speaking, will lead.[74]

Galperin's study has caused a commotion in Austen studies, but in at least one respect it is a dangerously misleading argument.[75] Galperin's 'possibility' is manifestly not the possibility of philosophical romance, and certainly not the possibility routinely opposed to the 'probable and ordinary' in the nearly two hundred years of debate on the differences between romance and novel. The possibility of Radcliffe and Mary Shelley, Hawthorne and Melville, belongs rather to the logic of the fantastic, of the 'marvellous' as a means of psychic exploration. However much Austen's novels might open up prospects in the gaps of narration, her narrative procedure of inductive particulars clearly differentiates her novels from the praxis of romance. But in other respects Galperin's study represents yet another iteration of the longstanding take on Austen – nearly as old as the discipline itself – that her works constitute an epitome of the realist novel, and that the cultural work her novels perform is 'regulative'.[76] Galperin posits this reading in order to undermine it; and in advancing it he takes it as read that Austen's status as the epitome of realism is so well established it requires little, or no, argument. For Galperin such an orthodoxy represents a two-hundred-year history of misreading, beginning with Scott and Whatley, who set the terms of this systematic misprision. But as we saw, Scott did not impose 'probability' on Austen, as a blanket smothering Austen's radical prospects; rather Austen's practice schooled Scott in the art of the probable, who in turn set up the terms for Whateley's article.

In other words, nothing is to be gained from denying the radical difference of Austen's fictional practice, or its power in shaping, not just the future direction of the 'English novel', but debates about what the novel is, and was. The period of Austen's reception, and appreciation, as a radical innovator – roughly 1850 to 1870 – coincides with the final eclipse of the philosophical romance. Where Hawthorne, or other provincials, such as the Brontës, thought of nothing else, a generation later Henry James viewed it with guarded embarrassment.[77] One can certainly argue that Austen's 'realism' has been misunderstood, along with her Toryism, and that her works are more sharply, and critically, engaged with the political realities of her present; but that is a separate matter from dislodging her from her position as the most significant Romantic innovator in the techniques of what we have come to call 'realism'. And it is as a result of the critical prestige gained by realism that the philosophical romance struggled. In particular, it struggled because its narrative address differed fundamentally from Austen's. As a result of Austen's use of free indirect discourse the reader enjoys the heroine's *Bildungsroman* vicariously. We share her misunderstandings, errors and slow illumination. Drawn in by her glamour, the irresistible appeal of her depth, or interiority, we share her values as they are ironically communicated to us through the heroine's own language; so when her pride leads to a fall – of which there is no better example than the consequence of Emma's humiliation of Miss Bates – we fall with her, and share her shame. In Galperin's account of the mainstream criticism of Austen, such as, for instance, Clara Tuite's *Romantic Austen*, the reader is being schooled in the imprisoning 'probable' of a hegemonic domestic ideology. As such, Tuite and Galperin both agree, the conventionally consumed Austen novel is 'regulative'. It labours towards a heteronormativity.[78]

Be that as it may, the key point is that compared to the philosophical romance, the Austen novel encourages isolated interiority: the responsive reader turns inward to interrogate her compromised enjoyment of the 'sins' the heroine is surprised to discover lurking in her own, ill-understood motives and behaviour. As such the Austen novel departs radically from the philosophical romance, which, insofar as it is predicated on ideal presence also invites identification, but of a substantially different kind: that is, not identification with the heroine, but the kind of identification that is implicit in the 'reading trance' that is ideal presence. But from Walpole onwards, the philosophical romance engages various techniques to distance the reader – such as the device of found narratives, embedded narratives, unreliable narrators and allegory – in order to unloose the dialectical play of ideas. Another way of regarding the difference is that in the high tradition of the philosophical romance irony serves to alienate the reader in a manner analogous to Brecht's epic theatre, whereas Austen's irony (especially the play between a self-identified sardonic narrator and the free indirect discourse constituting the consciousness of the characters in and through whom it plays) serves to deepen the reader's moral embarrassment. For Jürgen Habermas, the private and public are two sides of a single dyad, as the purpose of the bourgeois public sphere is to ensure an unchallenged space for the cultivation of interiority. One might say that the philosophical romance and the Austen novel are similarly connected as the two narrative sides of the bourgeois public sphere dyad; the point is that in Austen's reception such a connection was severed, with the result that the philosophical romance appeared ungainly, schizophrenic, or downright confused, nowhere more so – its opponents argue – than in the style, crimes committed by its desire to engage rationally with ideas fundamental to the praxis of human nature.

The Austenian eclipse of the philosophical romance happened much later in the century, during a crucial phase in the institutionalization of (English) literature as a discipline. As such the philosophical romance was a victim of a long-developing pincer movement, the opposite claw being the romances of Sir Walter Scott. One need not go so far as Mark Twain, and claim that Walter Scott was responsible for the American Civil War owing to his prowess in spreading a sham Medievalism with its cult of chivalry and political feudalism. Instead one may turn to Scott's own, mid-century defenders, such as the arch-Tory, Archibald Alison, the aesthetic philosopher's son:

> It is not going too far to say, that the romances of Sir Walter Scott have gone far to neutralise the dangers of the Reform Bill. Certain it is that they have materially assisted in extinguishing, at least in the educated classes of society, that prejudice against the feudal manners, and those devout aspirations on the blessings of democratic institutions, which were universal among the learned over Europe in the close of the eighteenth century. Like all other great and original minds, so far from being swept away by the errors of his age, he rose up in direct opposition to them. Singly he set himself to breast the flood which was overflowing the world. Thence the reaction in favour of the institutions of olden time in church and state, which became general in the next generation, and is now so strongly manifesting itself, as well in the religious contests as in the lighter literature of the present day.[79]

Scott was by far and away the most effective philosophical romancer of the Romantic period. In all respects except one, Scott's novels – but especially the hugely influential *Waverley* and *Ivanhoe* – were philosophical romances: they are predicated on modernity as a deflection point into the unknown; they are suffused with a nostalgia for an irrecoverable past; they narrate historical process itself; they verge on allegory, especially as they engage with the national theme; and they both invite and stymie readerly indentification, typically through the device I called narrative litotes, in the interests of the ironic play of ideas largely inhering within the register of a public sphere. The one exception relates to the stance Scott's novels adopt towards 'critique'. Whereas the mainstream of the philosophical romance probes the ideological mise en abyme of origin and legitimacy – the stream conventionally lumped together as 'Gothic' – Scott's novels worked hard to turn Burke's counter-Enlightenment, post-revolutionary fashioning of Whig organicism into a cultural fact, through the cultural work of his romances. Just as modern critics of Austen will find complexities beyond the ken of a general reading public hooked on Austen's romantic plots, so they naturally find a darker side to Scott's apparent endorsement of a Burkean formula of national progress through limited miscegenation: the English Edward Waverley and the Lowland Rose (but not the Jacobite Flora) equals modern Scotland, just as Saxon Ivanhoe and Norman Rowena (but not Jewish Rebecca) equals modern England. But as Archibald Alison, for one, shows, Scott's readers took little notice of the complexities that give pause to modern criticism. Balkanized into Gothic, the historical romance (Scott) and the novel (Austen), Romantic-era fiction was fundamentally severed from the historic moment that gave it meaning, as a Romantic genre.

5
Dissent: Anna Letitia Barbauld

1. Dissent

On 9 January 1796, Samuel Taylor Coleridge left Bristol for the major Midland cities intent on securing subscribers for *The Watchman*, his anti-ministerial journal. As his trumpet of sedition was still squeaking he went armed with 'a flaming prospectus, "Knowledge is Power," etc. to cry the state of the political atmosphere, and so forth' (*BL*: I, 179). Coleridge's itinerary was nicely judged. His tour of Birmingham, Manchester, Nottingham, Derby and Sheffield included towns stirred by the Revolutionary tumult. As Richard Holmes comments, it was here that Coleridge 'reckoned his natural readership lay ... among the reading groups of skilled workers in the manufacturies; among book clubs; and among all those who had felt the direct impact of Pitt's war measures and taxes'.[1] As a 'watchman' Coleridge was a political radical, but he was also a 'zealous Unitarian in religion' (*BL*: I, 180).

The phrase sounds the leitmotif of Coleridge's retrospective narrative, which he starts with a comic tale of a grotesque 'Brummagen', a 'rigid Calvinist, a tallow-chandler by trade':

> He was a tall dingy man, in whom length was so predominant over breadth, that he might almost have been borrowed for a foundry poker ... The lank, black, twine-like hair, *pingui-nitescent*, cut in a straight line along the black stubble of his thin gunpowder eyebrows, that looked like the scorched *after-math* from a last week's shaving ... But he was one of the *thorough-bred*, a true lover of liberty, and (I was informed) had proved to the satisfaction of many, that Mr Pitt was one of the horns of the second beast of Revelations, *that spoke like a dragon*. (*BL*: I 180–1)

Sensing a sale, Coleridge prophesies the 'near approach of the millennium, finishing the whole with some of my own verses describing that glorious state out of the *Religious Musings*' (*BL*: I, 181). Coleridge believes he has his man – it was 'a melting day with him' – but his scheme founders on another trait of the stock Calvinist: meanness. Finding four-pence per number too steep, the canny Brummagen begs off.

The vignette serves complex ends. The first thing it tells us is that *The Watchman* was a hare-brained scheme. The Calvinist (as a token of the Midland type) is mean where he wants generosity, intellectually limited where he requires imagination to grasp the complexity of the fight for liberty, and where imagination should be, there is the enthusiasm of the crazed sectarian leveller. Coleridge enters the comedy by representing himself as if another Richard Brothers, prophesying uplifting millennial doom, before making his excuses in the next paragraph: 'O! never can I remember those days with either shame or regret. For I was most sincere, most disinterested! My opinions were indeed in many and most important points erroneous; but my heart was single' (*BL*: I, 97). Coleridge's offence was not that he was Unitarian, but 'zealous', or enthusiastical. Coleridge represents himself entering into the tallow-chandler's dangerous enthusiasm but he supplements the picture with another view of himself, as someone who was at least sincere, carried away by fellow-feeling and political hope. The Brummagen Calvinist, by contrast, is an ill assortment of contradictory qualities, and, for that reason, dangerously unregulated.[2]

Coleridge makes no bones about *Biographia Literaria* being a self-serving document; even so, his account is disingenuous. The Midland towns were the strongholds of the 'Dissenting communities', of the 'rational' or 'free' Dissenters.[3] These communities included Presbyterians, Congregationalists, Quakers, disaffected Anglicans, and, latterly, Unitarians. However diverse, they were united in their steady movement away from the sectarian enthusiasms of the English Civil War period and in their equal dislike of evangelical theatrics and Calvinistical rigidity. Coleridge's colourful tallow-chandler, a Calvinist and an enthusiast, is thus a misrepresentation of the Dissenting networks he was attempting to contact, as subtle as it is profound. Coleridge may have been a flighty Jacobin ready to sing the apocalypse with Richard Brothers, but the sober 'free reasoners'[4] he set out to meet were not, nor were they diehard Calvinists. The misrepresentation, and the subtlety, permeates his second vignette, which begins with Coleridge overindulging in ale and tobacco. Naturally it was the fault of his tradesman acquaintance – he only had one glass – nor was he a hardened smoker. The fresh air on the way to the unnamed but presumably Dissenting Minister's house intensified the narcotic effects, and Coleridge fell into a swoon while the Jacobinical worthies gathered, 'to the number of from fifteen to twenty'. A guest politely engaged the stupefied Watchman by offering him the day's paper, which Coleridge, addled, refused, on the grounds that newspapers or matters of political interest were unsuitable reading for a Christian. The ludicrous sally broke the ice and a famous evening ensued:

> Never, perhaps, in so mixed and numerous a party have I since heard conversation sustained with such animation, enriched with such variety of information and enlivened with such a flow of anecdote. Both then and afterwards they all joined in dissuading me from proceeding with my scheme; assured me in the most friendly and yet most flattering expressions, that the employment was neither fit for me, nor I fit for the employment. Yet if I had determined on preserving in it, they promised to exert themselves to the utmost to procure subscribers, and insisted that I should make no more applications in person, but carry on the canvass by proxy. (*BL*: I, 183–4)

Coleridge concludes by saying that he received the same kind offers wherever he went on his tour, adding that some of his new acquaintances became lifelong friends and all could swear that even then he wasn't a Jacobin. He ends the episode with the finish of *The Watchman*, six months later, which he attributes to the alienation of his audience and subscribers, owing to his incorrigible habit of objecting to Jacobin policy.

As Lucy Aikin was later to comment, while no sect differed so substantially from the Established Church as the Dissenters, as regards doctrine, no group was so similar as regards manners.[5] Culturally the Dissenters were not just free reasoners, but free livers. In the vignette Coleridge takes more than he gives. He praises the Dissenting communities for their easy, polished and advanced sociability, but only after clouding the issue with a tale of narcotic excess (where he plays the wandering innocent); and while he flatters their politics by citing them as witnesses for his anti-Jacobinism, he implicitly blames the collapse of the enterprise on their stubborn radical attachments. Read from the viewpoint of a Lucy Aikin, a different picture emerges. The Dissenters do indeed represent an advanced sociable culture based on the practised exchange of information, from whose perspective Coleridge would appear a young, print-culture Luddite, quixotically tramping the country drumming up subscribers in person rather than using more advanced means. They politely suggest it would be better to 'carry the canvass on by proxy'. Employing their networks, they quickly produce a thousand subscribers.

Coleridge's 'zealous Unitarian' may be regarded as another version of what I earlier called 'his own misfit'. The young Coleridge is the 'other' of the *Biographia Literaria*, an object of intense fascination to the mature writer, but still someone he is anxious to distance. While it was the wayward enthusiast who produced the poetry, *Biographia Literaria* narrates the growth of the critic's mind. The mature critic comes to recognize the supreme place held by Wordsworth in the development of modern poetry, an elevation he defends through a theory of the imagination that would lay the intellectual foundations for the disciplined activities of a new 'clerisy'. As Jon Mee argues, Coleridge's theory of the imagination is deeply imbricated in the discursive project of 'regulating enthusiasm', of bringing a new 'affective' subjectivity under control.[6] Confusingly, 'enthusiasm' had no set value: context was everything. One's own enthusiasm was good, and others' bad or dangerous; one's own was inspiration, while others' were crazed visions, especially if the 'other' in question crossed a class or denominational line. In Coleridge's version 'fancy' assumes the abject position of uncontrolled enthusiasm, because uncoupled from the esemplastic power of the deep self, in its turn regulated by its internalization ('echo', Coleridge calls it) of the Divine I AM (*BL*: I, 304). As one of the chief architects of the disciplinary field we now call Romanticism, Coleridge distances, marginalizes and finally discards the 'enthusiasm' of the young poet's 'zealous Unitarianism'. Where Coleridge appears double (playing a deep game of counterfeiting the enthusiasm of visionary Jacobins while keeping his irony under wraps) he restores singularity by insisting on the purity of his motives (his 'heart was single'); and where the Dissenters were historically singular, in their polished sociability and measured distance from enthusiasm, Coleridge conjures doubleness through hints of excess and a comic Calvinist doppelganger.[7]

As a group the Dissenters fare no better in the standard literary histories of the period than they do in Coleridge's self-serving narrative. Burke's taunt from the *Reflections* – that Dissenting intellectual culture was a 'hortus siccus', a dry garden full of dead flowers – stuck.[8] Worse, the Anti-Jacobin press represented them as dangerous visionaries intent on blowing up the foundations of the state. They either evinced too little sensibility, in their dessicated philosophy, or too much, in their wild political plans. For Burkeans this was not a contradiction.[9] From the Burkean perspective the free use of reason, however arid, was itself dangerous enthusiasm. For conservatives the independent intellect was self-evidently unsafe, especially in religious matters. The wiser course was to rely upon the accumulated wisdom of the ages as expressed in the organic evolutions of the Established Church. To strike out on one's own guided by nothing more than one's independent intellect, as urged by Dissenting culture, was itself a rash, visionary act, even if conducted according to the rational tenets of one of Priestley's or Godwin's dull, dispiriting tomes.

In effect the Dissenters found their place in conventional literary history among other exemplars of the Enlightenment, as intellectual fathers the rising generation of poets needed to slay, in order to live. They generally appear as dry-as-dust theologians, natural and revealed, with a threadbare Lockean philosophy, or as shallow political utopians put to flight by the powerful bass notes of Burke's prescient reading of historical complexity. In Abrams's terms, the Dissenters were stuck in the mirror stage of Romantic development. Needless to say, such caricatures are no more accurate than Coleridge's Calvinist Brummies and inebriated socialites. A literary history based on authors and opinions will naturally confirm the drift of such partial representations. In later life both Coleridge and Wordsworth sniped at, traduced or distanced their Dissenting peers;[10] Blake's epigrammatic attacks on natural theology provide ample ammunition for those arguing for the un-Romantic nature of Deistical thought; while for the later generation of Romantics the philosophical outlook of Richard Price or Joseph Priestley would have faded into irrelevance. But if we think of literary history in terms of cultural affiliations, a very different picture emerges. Throughout his productive poetic career Coleridge was a zealous Unitarian. During the same period Wordsworth's views and poetry were revolutionized by his conversion to the Dissenting culture of Nonconformist London, with its resurrected, Old Commonwealth traditions, where he was an enthusiastic participant in the Dissenting public sphere.[11] Blake was himself a dangerous enthusiast, a Nonconformist in religion influenced by his mother's Moravian faith.[12] William Godwin, a product of the strong Dissenting communities of Norwich and London, was the son of a Dissenting minister, and the grandchild of Philip Doddridge (as were the Aikins), whose Northampton academy schooled both his father and uncle.[13] While Mary Wollstonecraft had a conventional Anglican upbringing, early on in her professional career she was absorbed into the London Dissenting community.[14] Amelia Opie, Mary Hays, Ann Radcliffe, Harriet Martineau and, of course, Barbauld, all had Dissenting backgrounds. However, among the younger Romantics only the Hunts[15] and Hazlitt[16] emerged from a Dissenting culture. But this is only to recapitulate the general thesis, that if early Romanticism was a Dissenting project, the late was built on their exclusion.

The picture sharpens if we think of culture as a form of information technology. Non-Conformists generally were about eight per cent of the population.[17] Rational or free Dissenters were, in turn, a minority of Nonconformists. However, they were exceptionally well organized. At the centre of this organization were their academies, at Northamption, Daventry, Norwich, Hackney, but above all, Warrington.[18] Unlike the senescent ancient universities the Dissenting academies directly addressed the needs of their clientele, commercial as well as scientific. In the words of the academy's first historian, the 'most profound and far-reaching influence of the Academy ... was in its effect on the educational curriculum. Founded upon a more liberal basis than previous dissenting academies, the Warrington academy attempted to give a liberal education to students from all walks of life and its courses of study were both varied and secular.'[19] The college's original remit refers to 'theology, moral philosophy, including logic and metaphysics, natural philosophy, including the mathematics, and in the languages and polite literature'.[20] Through both ideological outlook and economic necessity the Dissenting academies had an open admissions policy, drawing students from the Dissenting community itself, but also from the aristocracy, the rising merchant class, or West Indian planters. The diversity of their clientele ensured they were connected, politically, while also serving as an aid to recruitment, as many students converted to Non-Conformity once exposed to the Academy's discipline of free thought. As the young Anna Letitia Aikin boasted in *The Invitation*, Warrington was

> The nursery of men for future years!
> Here callow chiefs and embryo statesmen lie,
> And unfledg'd poets short excursions try. (ll. 82–4)

Warrington had its own 'University Press', run by the excellent William Eyres, who published virtually all of the teaching materials produced by and for the Academy, while the Dissenters, generally, were well served by the London press of Joseph Johnson, who was both a member of the Dissenting community and its most effective conduit to the wider world.[21] Eyres and Johnson did not publish Dissenters, exclusively, but they did ensure that Dissenting views were disseminated, from the works of leading members of the Warrington circle, such as Joseph Priestley, Gilbert Wakefield, William Enfield and the Aikins, to the Dissenting London intelligentsia of William Godwin, Mary Wollstonecraft, William Blake and William Wordsworth. As the period progressed several journals came to supplement the work of Johnson's press, such as the *Monthly Magazine, Analytical Review, Annual Register* and the *Eclectic*.[22]

But perhaps the most important aspect of Dissenting 'connectivity' was the strength of the community's social networks. Information circulated through them, but so did individuals. Joseph Priestley's career typifies the progress of the Dissenting intellectual. He started at Daventry ('This vortex of unsanctified speculation and debate'),[23] which was, itself, the successor to Doddridge's Northampton academy. He started his own academy at Nantwich, moving next to Warrington where he took the chair of languages and belles letters before turning to the natural sciences when that chair fell vacant. From Warrington he moved to Leeds after receiving an invitation to serve as the minister of the Dissenting congregation at Mill Hill. From there he went to Calne, Warwickshire, after Richard Price used his influence to secure Priestley the post of 'companion' to Lord Shelburne, where he was able to serve the Dissenting interest on behalf of the Chathamite faction. He moved from there to Birmingham, where he was close to the Dissenting community and advanced scientific research of the Lunar Men. After his books were burnt and his laboratory sacked by a King and Church mob he relocated to Hackney, taking up a post at its Dissenting academy, before finally moving to America, towards which the centre of Unitarianism was shifting. The Barbaulds circulated from Warrington to Palgrave to Stoke Newington, each a Dissenting stronghold. John Aikin moved from Warrington to Norwich to Great Yarmouth, before rejoining his sister at Stoke Newington, whose circle included the Presbyterian dramatist, Joanna Baillie. At Norwich, John Aikin socialized with both sets of the unrelated Taylors, with all attending the Octagon Chapel, presided over by Dr William Enfield, the quondam Chair of Belles Lettres at Warrington. John, the hymn writer, was the grandson of John Taylor, another of the Warrington academy's founding fathers. William Taylor, a former pupil of Mrs Barbauld's, at Palgrave, was also a prominent Dissenter, as well as a translator and reviewer, especially of German works ('Hazlitt later credited Taylor with pioneering "philosophical criticism" '),[24] while his translation of Bürger's *Lenore* inspired Walter Scott, who claimed that hearing it prompted his career in poetry.[25] Both sets of Taylors were connected to the Martineaus and Opies, to Harriet and Amelia.[26] Gilbert Wakefield circulated from Warrington to Hackney, where his pamphlet, *Reply to the Bishop of Landaff's Address*, landed himself and his publisher, Joseph Johnson, in gaol for sedition.

Johnson himself first made contact with Warrington through his Liverpool friend Matthew Turner, chemist, surgeon and radical theologian. When Josiah Wedgwood came to Liverpool in 1762, to be treated by Turner for an injured knee, he was introduced to his future partner, Thomas Bentley (1730–80), a leading supporter of the Liverpool Academy, as well as to the most prominent tutors at Warrington. Favourably impressed, Wedgwood sent his son John to the academy. Through his frequent visits to Bentley's Liverpool home Wedgwood also met Priestley; it may have been here that Priestley was in turn introduced to Joseph Johnson,[27] who published *A view of the Advantages of Inland Navigation*, written by Bentley at Wedgwood's request.[28] Bentley was Ann Radcliffe's uncle (and, for a period, stood *in loco parentis*). Through Bentley the young Ann Ward was exposed to the leading women intellectuals of the day, including Mrs Barbauld and Mrs Carter, before marrying William Radcliffe, an Oxford lawyer and London newspaperman noted for his 'democratic' and Dissenting views. Mrs Radcliffe was also related to Joseph Jebb, the famous Cambridge theologian who was one of the Dissenting intellectuals under whose influence Gilbert Wakefield switched from Anglican to non-juror. The Wedgwood loop also includes Coleridge, sponsored by Josiah Wedgwood during the poet's 'zealous Unitarian' phase.

Although England was approaching eight million the percentage of the population educated to an advanced level (either through the ancient universities or the Dissenting academies) was minute, especially by present standards. Given the restricted numbers one might expect everyone (who was anyone) to know everyone else. The class of gentry to which Jane Austen belonged was also small, as regards numbers, and here, too, there was a level of connection similar to the one found among the Dissenters. Generally speaking the two communities did not overlap. Thus, within each community, one might easily go on to show that any individual was within one or two removes of anyone else. However, the point is not simply that the Dissenting communities were close knit, mobile, with a ready flow of advanced information; they were also culturally and philosophically harmonious. One of the pupils at Warrington later recalled that

> Without the least tincture of superstition or enthusiasm, both Dr Aikin and Dr Priestley endeavored to instill into the minds of the students an habitual regard to good morals, and a veneration for the Supreme Being, and for the Christian Scriptures of the Old and New Testament, the great purpose and design of which, to instruct and improve mankind in piety and virtue, they judged to be best promoted by the most thorough, liberal and unbiased inquiry into the evidence of their divine authority, and the true meaning of their contents.[29]

The Dissenters were unusual in the intensity of their twin commitments to revealed religion and to 'liberal and unbiased inquiry'. They were also remarkable in believing that the two impulses (towards religious feeling and free inquiry) were complementary. To the Unitarian mind, the universe was unfolding exactly as it should. A contemporary of Mrs Barbauld comments that for her 'the republic of letters was real, and she was a firm believer in the equality of man and state of freedom. All her writings prove her reasonable hope and belief in human progress, and manifest a great degree of modesty.'[30] A deep belief in the providential reasonableness of the world meant that the Dissenters were, as a group, the perfect embodiment of the public sphere. For them the 'republic of letters was real' because belief activated the phrase's performative meaning. They believed in the reality of the figurative space of the republic, in its essential equality as well as in the instrumental power of the rational exchange of political ideas. As a group the Dissenters would have found no lurking ambiguities in Habermas's characterization of its rationalist assumptions as a 'normative ideal'.

Between one Dissenter and another there was plenty of scope for principled, philosophical difference, as between, for example, Priestley and Barbauld on the question of devotion, or Gilbert Wakefield and everyone else on public worship. But beneath these differences there was a foundation of shared views expressed through a common, Unitarian 'radical style' (to borrow Tom Paulin's phrase). There were two main aspects of this style, one of which is summed up in Joseph Priestley's reference to the joint project as 'Necessarian',[31] the other epitomized in Hazlitt's 'gusto'. The same two aspects were, rather more prosaically, in the associationist language bequeathed by Locke, 'habit' and 'novelty'. As Paulin argues, John Locke, John Milton and Isaac Newton jointly and severally embodied the political, religious and scientific principles of free enquiry, thus forming the holy trinity of Unitarian thought. For the Unitarian outlook, providential design was latent in nature, but also in the mind. Disclosing nature's secrets through the exercise of the reason was in itself a religious or devotional act, of which there was no better example than the brilliant, devout Newton. Milton summed up the old, independent, 'commonwealth' spirit, while also exemplifying the turning of exceptional personal gifts to the appropriate devotional and political ends. But the prime architect of the Unitarian radical style was John Locke. His attack on innate ideas laid the philosophical groundwork for theories of political equality; his writing on government enshrined the principle of a contract between free and equal subjects; while his theory of mind stressed the value of both free inquiry and education. His theory of the association of ideas was equally influential, in part because of what later commentators built onto it, such as David Hume, but especially Frances Hutcheson and David Hartley. For Locke the mind was a blank slate on which sense data left their residues. As we recollect or retrieve data our ideas are ordered in accordance with the basic principles of association, codified by David Hartley as similarity, contrariety and contiguity, in his hugely influential *Observations on Man*, a work largely known in the version edited by Joseph Priestley. Hartley's theory of vibrations was meant to provide association with a physiological, and therefore predictive, basis for understanding mental development. This aspect of Hartley's theory was, perhaps, the least effective – Priestley jettisoned it – but the normative consequences of the theory were influential, especially as it promised a progressive pedagogy. Hutcheson, for his part, added a belief in the essentially benevolent nature of the self, together with an innate sense of the moral and the beautiful. Hutcheson's arguments might seem to contradict Locke, as regards innate ideas, but Hutcheson's point, rather, was that an appetite for goodness (as well as the beautiful) was an integral aspect of the mind, part of its providential character, or constitution. Our ideas were not innate, but design characteristics were. The difference might not get past the philosophically pernickety, but whatever awkwardness it posed was swept aside by general enthusiasm for Hutcheson's picture of the self as inherently good, with an instinctive sense for what was right or pleasing. Together Hartley and Hutcheson help explain why 'habit' was such a key term in Dissenting culture. Given that associations follow normative pathways, and given, too, that the self was inherently benevolent, it followed that if the child was only exposed to the best examples, or to visual and aural stimuli most suited to elicit the child's instinctive moral and aesthetic sense (such as scenes from nature), good would most certainly follow, especially if repeated and reinforced, thus strengthening the associative pathways. Simply put, habit would bind positive association. The Unitarian philosophy was thus, as Priestley expressed it, 'Necessarian', meaning, not that we live in a deterministic universe, but that, given the appropriate stimuli, certain consequences would, of necessity, follow, an outlook Godwin took to its logical, rational extreme in his *Enquiry into the Principles of Political Justice*.

Despite appearances, the Lockean, associationist model of the mind was neither mechanistic nor passive. That is to say it was regulated, and driven, by another providential aspect of the mind, our love of novelty, although it might be more accurate to say that we love the new because the mind is inherently energetic, active and curious. As Tom Paulin stresses, the Unitarian outlook was materialistic. The divine was immanent in the material world, hence the tendency of the Unitarian mind to press its nose up against nature's surface, reaching out towards its distant anima through inductive, scientific reasoning. A late product of the culture, Hazlitt referred to the Unitarians' this-worldly, energetic savouring of the material world and its beauties, natural and artificial, as 'gusto'. 'Happiness, active energy, free rational enquiry, communication, liberty – these terms reverberate through Unitarian discourse', as Dissenting preachers asserted 'the need to change both society and the way people think'.[32] Hazlitt's 'gusto' is Unitarian shorthand for the progressive spirit of free rational enquiry.

Paulin draws a telling contrast between Burke's *Reflections on the Revolution in France,* which embraces 'sluggishness' as 'part of the national preference for the unwritten, the intuitive, the ancient and the concrete, as against the abstract and theoretical' and the effervescence of the soda water invented by Joseph Priestley. Hazlitt's 'poetics of bubbling motion follows Priestley's energized materialism, while Burke rejects such a view of matter, because he is opposed to the release of energy in both social and material terms. In a sense, soda-water is the physical presence of Priestley's dynamic concept of matter.'[33] Compared to Burke it is also perky, optimistic and un-Romantic: 'Burke is the wild gas on the loose, a barbarian romantic battering down the enlightened, rational, Hellenic structure of Dissent.'[34] The same contrast is found in the stylistic differences between Richard Price's *On the Love of our Country* and Burke's *Reflections,* which it prompted. Price's work bears the marks of its origins, an address delivered to the Dissenters gathered at their customary London meeting-house, the Old Jewry, to celebrate the French Revolution as an event following the model of the Glorious Revolution of 1688, proving, in the process, that the upward gyres of providence were in motion. Price's rhetoric bears the mark of the collective, the celebration of a joint project in language that seeks out a common ground of understanding and use, where the speaker is the mere medium of a larger message. Burke's rhetoric, by comparison, bears the marks of the famous performer from the people's lower house, the star turn used to holding a chamber in his rapt spell as his periods rise, fall, and rise again, in giddy, irresistible perorations the writer knows the audience will recognize as a style already marked, publicly, as 'Burkean'. As a Hackney graduate, Hazlitt is steeped in the optimistic, political effervescence of Priestley's soda-water, even as he is enraptured (against his best instincts) by Burke's poetic celebration of English 'sluggishness' that praises the nameless many in the accented voice of noted celebrity. Paulin nicely captures Hazlitt's ambivalence: 'He knows that the classicism of Rational Dissent and of high Whig politics is *passé,* as well as tame or insipid. Burke is associated with the dark murderous power of the gothic: bloody castles, churches, organized religion, murderous statecraft, a kind of heritage modernity.'[35]

It is unquestionably the case that for the post-1800 generation, Dissenting culture was *passé*. For a generation growing up steeped in war, privation and panic, Priestley's soda water was not just effervescent, but light. Paulin's characterization of the matter is one way of putting the overall frame of my argument, that the Romanticism into which Dissent did not fit was a form of 'heritage modernity', anti-theoretical, nostalgic and politically regressive, to be sure, but also 'modern', an aspect of a fragmenting growth economy.[36]

Of course there are other ways one might conceive Romantic energy. For instance one might think of it as the empowerment of the self. However, there is a difference between the rise of the individual and the rise of individualism. The first may be taken to refer to the historic empowerment of the middle class during the period, the second (and naturally not unconnected with it) to ideological matters. Thus even as he was committed, politically, to the first, Hazlitt was beguiled by the second, especially as it was embodied by the glamorous figure of the stylish Burke. Insofar as we conceive of Romanticism as the self and nature aglow with the nimbus of transcendental presence, Dissenting culture certainly will not fit. And yet, as regards the first, the engineering of the rise of the individual, no sector of the generation we think of as early Romantic did more than the 'free Dissenters'. Coleridge toured the Dissenting strongholds of the Midlands because that was the best place to seek subscribers for an anti-ministerial journal, like *The Watchman*; but this is only another way of saying that the centres of the transformative energy of the country, both industrial and cultural, were the Northern and Midland towns.

Thus while it may be true to say that the Dissenters (always a beleaguered minority) did not fit into the Romantic mainstream, it is equally true to say that Romanticism is unthinkable without the culture of Dissent. This is true whether one thinks of Romanticism narrowly, as an institutionalized field, or widely, as cultural expression. According to George Sainsbury, 'the first systematic lecturer in English Literature was Dr. John Aikin'.[37] William Enfield's *The Speaker*, an anthology of the best examples of English writing, including modern poets, designed for Warrington students, became the dominant anthology of the age, passing through numerous editions – a sort of early Norton. It also inspired imitations by Mrs Barbauld (the *Female Speaker*) and Mary Wollstonecraft (the *Female Reader*). Together these anthologies did much to create the taste for poetry – and writing – that so transformed the following, Romantic generation. And if in the early 1790s it was bliss to be alive it was only because of the overwhelming presence of a Dissenting discourse that construed events across the channel as a providential dawning.

Coleridge's break with Hartley over the 'necessarian' implications of his theory ('All that nonsense of vibrations', *Letters*: I, 625–6) has often been taken as a moment emblematic of the Romantic mind coming into self-consciousness, a snapping of the spell exerted by the mirror stage of Lockean passivity.[38] The creative self was not, after all, a kind of Aeolian harp, a passive object played upon by the passing breezes, but a self-generating lamp, lit by the internal fires of genius.[39] By the early nineteenth century, Hartley, Hutcheson and the associationist language inherited from Locke were, indeed, things of the past, as Hazlitt discovered when he tried to revive such language in his early, Hartleyian, *Essay on the Principles of Human Action*. But there is more to be said of the philosophical and cultural project of the Dissenting Enlightenment than that it was left behind by intellectual fashion. For a start, pedagogically, it was empowering, for it was premised on a universal model of the mind. Given the same set of stimuli, all minds would end up in a similar condition, driven by the love of novelty, and consolidated through habit. The fundamental faith in the transformative power of education, for all, led Dissenting culture to another pioneering area: the writing of books for children. Mrs Barbauld was universally recognized for her contribution in this area, through her *Lessons for Children* (1787, 1788) and *Hymns in Prose for Children* (1781), both published by Joseph Johnson. The books broke new ground as physical objects, employing good paper, large clear type, and a child-sized format. Their content was innovative, in that the books were pitched at the level of the intended audience; were written in accessible language; depended on iteration to consolidate learning; and trusted to the child's sense of wonder to keep her alert and interested. Children's literature – meaning bespoke books for children – was largely a Dissenting project in the late eighteenth century. Besides Barbauld's works (including her contributions to her brother John Aikin's *Evenings at Home*), there was Wollstonecraft's *Original Stories from Real Life*, illustrated by Blake, who made his own idiosyncratic contribution to the genre with his Barbauld-inspired *Songs of Innocence*, together with works by Thomas Holcroft, William Godwin and the Edgeworths, and, while Sarah Trimmer was a stout Anglican, she was first published and encouraged by Joseph Johnson.

In various ways, then, Dissenting culture was a project that sought to empower the individual: through its academies, presses and networks, and through its philosophical and ideological commitments, from the republic of letters to children's education. In 1797, *The Spirit of the Public Journals* complained that, in the Revolution controversy, 'the balance of intellect is entirely on the side of the Jacobins'.[40] In 1798 the *Anti-Jacobin* came into being, with the express purpose of turning the intellectual tide, and in its opening editorial its prime target was the Dissenters, which we can take as a tacit acknowledgement of their dominance of 1790s' cultural technologies.[41] It is because of this dominance that I think it reasonable to say that 1790s' Romanticism was largely a Dissenting project. As Romanticism (meaning, in this instance, the disciplinary field) developed, post-1800, the key contribution of the Dissenters not only faded from view but also lived on, in historical memory, as (and here Coleridge's *Watchman* anecdote is typical) the thesis against which the Romantic antithesis defined itself – the career of Anna Letitia Barbauld being a case in point.

2. Anna Letitia Barbauld: the stranger within

In the history of Romantic misfitting nowhere is the process more painful to consider than in the case of Anna Letitia Barbauld. As her most recent editors observe, 'As a poet, Barbauld can claim to be considered a founder of British Romanticism.'[42] In the 1790s Mrs Barbauld was assiduously courted by the first generation Romantics, owing to her stature as, possibly, 'the most eminent living poet, male or female, in Britain'.[43] Lisa Vargo has documented, not just her influence, but the jibes and scurrilities exchanged by Coleridge and Charles Lamb, especially, as they privately sought to diminish her stature and consequence, as her star waned.[44] Her reputation was, indeed, notoriously reduced by John Wilson Croker's vicious review of *Eighteen Hundred and Eleven*, in which Barbauld was cast as a know-nothing old busybody wittering over the clack of her knitting needles. While the claim of an early biographer that the review ended her career is, possibly, exaggerated, there is no question that it depressed her expectations, so that she began to think, not of a present, but a posthumous audience.[45] So successful was the assault on her that her reputation, and place, in 'Romanticism' dwindled to the point of two small cameos in which she featured as the stiff, uncomprehending, Enlightenment other – as the dim-witted old woman who wanted more of a moral for the *Ancient Mariner*, and as Charles Lamb's bête noir, the unimaginative moralist who banished mystery from the tales of the nursery. To suggest that Coleridge's poem wanted a moral was to produce clear evidence that she lacked the first notion of Romantic irony, where the imposture of 'naive' unreadability was axiomatic, while to be opposed to ghosts and other mysteries in children's stories was to be lumped in with the dessicated crew who had tried to strangle the Romantic imagination, at birth. In both stories she was the starchy Dissenting schoolmistress who just didn't get it.

Recently Anna Letitia Barbauld has been brought back from obscurity and restored to her proper place as a foundational figure in the rise of British Romantic culture, initially by feminist critics reassessing the bizarre erasure of women poets from the Romantic canon and more latterly by scholars interested in the similar fate suffered by the Dissenters.[46] As Jonathan Wordsworth comments in his introduction to the facsimile of Joseph Johnson's seminal 1792 edition of her poems, 'Unitarianism gave a new role to the imagination, as the faculty that apprehended the presence of the divine',[47] and the writer who engineered this new role, more than any other, was Barbauld. As Wordsworth also notes (drawing upon recent scholarship), it was Barbauld's 'A Summer Evening's Meditation' that especially influenced Wordsworth and Coleridge.[48] In her poem she reaches back through Dissenting culture towards the Earl of Shaftesbury and Neoplatonism, for which he was a major conduit. 'Her reading has taken her to pre-Christian philosophers, Stoics and early Platonists, who saw God as mind or an impersonal life force.' Coleridge's 'Great Universal teacher' who 'from eternity doth teach / Himself in all, and all things in himself', from 'Frost at Midnight', and Wordsworth's deeply interfused 'presence' ('Tintern Abbey'), both draw upon the same source: Barbauld.[49]

As we saw in Chapter 2, the reception of Wordsworth's poetry was initially handicapped by the tendency of reviewers to associate its pantheistical overtones with the Unitarian theology and politics of Barbauld's circle; but as time passed, and the debates faded from memory, the narrow sectarian associations fell away from the poetry, so that the very same expressions of non-specific devotion to an interfusing eternal presence that were previously deprecated were now taken as the acme of a sanative Christian spirituality. As the contemporary resonances fell away, so, too, did Barbauld's contribution to a poetic we now think of as distinctly Romantic, or, at rate, as typical of the young Wordsworth and Coleridge. Her contribution radiates from a term and concept – 'devotion' – she made her own. Her essay 'Thoughts on the Devotional Taste, on Sects, and on Establishments' was written early (1775), and, while she changed over the course of her career, her thoughts on devotion remained a relative constant.[50] The term is a highly charged one for her, interconnected as it is with issues that preoccupied and defined her intellectual community, generating much friction. Her essay begins by noting that 'a late most amiable and elegant writer' observes 'that Religion may be considered in three different views'.[51] Barbauld simplifies them in line with Dissenting priorities, beginning with the essential and ending with the nugatory.

> As a system of opinions, its sole object is truth, and the only faculty that has any thing to do with it is Reason, exerted in the freest and most dispassionate inquiry. As a principle regulating our conduct, Religion is a habit, and like all other habits, of slow growth, and gaining strength only by repeated exertions. But it may likewise be considered as a taste, an affair of sentiment and feeling, and in this sense it is properly called Devotion. Its seat is in the imagination and the passions, and it has its source in that relish for the sublime, the vast, and the beautiful, by which we taste the charms of poetry and other compositions that address our finer feelings; rendered more lively and interesting by a sense of gratitude for personal benefits. It is in a great degree constitutional, and is by no means found in exact proportion to the virtue of a character.[52]

Reason, habit and taste: each term is carefully weighed and measured against Dissenting values. The first appears a Dissenting bromide. For 'free reasoning' Presbyterians, religion is indeed a matter of Reason and truth, for it was an article of faith that the world was providentially ordered, from which it followed that free reason would naturally unfold theological truth. But the opening 'system of opinions' invites the unwelcome association of opinions with prejudices, a piece of semantic brinkmanship designed to discomfit

Joseph Priestley, her friend, colleague and chief interlocutor.[53] If Dissenters relied upon the free exercise of reason as the chief means of ensuring their children's proper religious education, 'habit' was its principal auxiliary. From Priestley's perspective it was so far so unexceptional. The shock is delivered through the suave 'But it may likewise be considered as a taste'. As Jon Mee points out, for Priestley, 'taste' was a matter of mere received opinion, or prejudice, or worse, fashionable affectation. As such it signalled a worldly form of popery, or superstition, and was the antithesis of 'free enquiry'.[54] It was for this reason that he reacted so strongly against his friend's essay, going so far as to claim to detect something papist in her romancing of taste.[55] As if sensing the direction from which objections will come, Barbauld quickly shores up her position in the remainder of her paragraph by locating religious devotion in the same 'constitutional' moral and aesthetic sense advocated by the impeccably Whiggish Shaftesbury and Hutcheson.

Barbauld is not testing the Warrington project; rather she is renovating some of its key concerns in order to advance its purchase and power in the wider, Anglican world.[56] The paragraph's key phrase is the odd one left dangling in the middle of it, where our 'finer feelings', responding to a 'relish for the sublime, the vast, and the beautiful', are 'rendered more lively and interesting by a sense of gratitude for personal benefits'. Pierre Bourdieu would doubtless read this gratitude as an expression of satisfaction at finding one's status rising through shrewd investment in the symbolic capital of newly dynamic areas of cultural expression. Regardless, the phrase echoes, creatively, against Shaftesbury's well-known hostility to the dominant tradition of Christian ethics, which he saw as a system of egoism (we are good because of the bribes, or 'personal benefits', promised, up to and including the soul's immortality). What then, is the nature of the benefits accrued by the devoted subject, if not the narrow ones of religious virtue? The answer appears to lie in some form of self-aggrandizement, but at this early stage of the essay its character is left an open, teasing, question.

As Mee notes, it was impossible to broach religious warmth, or devotion, without invoking the vexed issue of enthusiasm.[57] In dealing with this difficult material Barbauld follows David Hume, who argues that despite appearances the fanaticism of Catholics and Puritans, French peasants and English levellers are distinct phenomena separable into the antithetical categories of 'superstition' and 'enthusiasm'.[58] Protestant enthusiasm is a function of egotism, as in the transported individual who believes himself exalted as a particular favourite of the Deity, whereas Catholic superstition is a form of 'abjection' in which the individual defers authority to others, abasing himself through a blind belief in magic or the intercessionary powers of mysterious superiors.[59] Protestant enthusiasts also differ in being primarily motivated by a love of liberty. Anti-authoritarian, inquisitive and self-reliant, they are open to persuasion, and ultimately to reason. For Hume, Puritan extremists are redeemable, whereas Catholic abjection is intractable; thus he ends by praising the Non-Conformist community for progressing beyond the enthusiastical extremes of the Civil War period, becoming 'Deists' and 'free reasoners' in the process.[60]

Barbauld intervenes by giving Hume's scheme another turn. She sees herself flanked by egotistical enthusiasm and abject superstition, only inverted. Enthusiasts are to be found, not among the Nonconformist community but the Anglican, where 'florid declaimer(s)', that is to say, Wesleyan Methodists, 'work upon the passions of the lower class'. Superstitious abjection, meanwhile, is associated with a very surprising source: philosophy. Barbauld asserts her originality by tilting at the fathers of her intellectual community. Thus she spends some time attacking ridicule as an activity that corrodes healthy devotion, whereas it was Shaftesbury's chief cure for the enthusiastical passion.[61] Elsewhere she critiques the disputatious spirit of 'free enquiry': 'there is nothing more prejudicial to the feelings of a devout heart, than a habit of disputing on religious subjects' (Barbauld 2002: 213). This 'prejudicial' habit was fixed within the Warrington curriculum and associated with its leading theological warriors, such as Priestley. But her most audacious move was to attack the abject tendencies of modern 'philosophy', by which she means, primarily, the natural sciences so firmly entrenched at Warrington:

> Philosophy does indeed enlarge our conceptions of the Deity, and gives us the sublimest ideas of his power and extent of dominion; but it raises him too high for our imaginations to take hold of, and in a great measure destroys that affectionate regard which is felt by the common class of pious Christians. When, after contemplating the numerous productions of this earth, the various forms of being, the laws, the mode of their existence, we rise yet higher, and turn our eyes to the magnificent profusion of suns and systems which astronomy pours upon the mind – When we grow acquainted with the majestic order of nature, and those eternal laws which bind the material and intellectual worlds – When we trace the footsteps of creative energy through regions of unmeasured space, and still find new wonders disclosed and pressing upon the view – we grow giddy with the prospect; the mind is astonished, confounded at its own insignificance; we think it almost impiety for a worm to lift its head from the dust, and address the Lord of so stupendous a universe; the idea of communion with our Maker seems shocking, and the only feeling the soul is capable of in such a moment is a deep and painful sense of its own abasement. (Barbauld 2002: 215–16)

Stunned by the astronomical sublime the abject soul collapses into wormlike 'abasement'. As her editors note, this is an extraordinary peroration given that she had, scant years before, in 'A Summer Evening's Meditation', praised just such a sublime survey of interstellar space.[62]

The contradiction is explicable in terms of the 'personal benefits' left dangling in the opening paragraph. Unlike Priestley, Barbauld did not believe in the triumphant powers of the free enquiring mind. For her knowledge was not pursued in an abstract or disconnected world, where the possession of the truth might indeed be sufficient. Knowledge, and its value, was, rather, 'situational'.[63] The point is strongly expressed in her late essay on prejudice. For Priestley, prejudice had no value, whatever. In the largely Lockean model in which he was working, prejudice was what you got rid of after successfully interrogating one's cumulative sense data, disentangling what one knew through experience and effort from what one had inadvertently taken in, at second hand.[64] Barbauld points out that prejudice is inevitable, even for those enjoying an ideal Warrington education, as learning necessarily meant relying on intellectual hand-me-downs, on what one had imbibed from the community. The pertinent point was the value a prejudice might have. In her essay she travels some distance towards Burke, for whom prejudice was the very means by which the community's accumulated wisdom survived and circulated, before breaking off to insist upon each prejudice being weighed and measured. And for her, the issue that counts most is the advancement of each self and, through cumulative selves, the community.

To put matters another way, Barbauld is less interested in a Priestleyan search for truth, and more in a socially conceived will to power. Thus in her essay on public worship (1792), she writes that

> The metaphysical reasoner, entangled in the nets of sophistry, may involve himself in the intricacies of contradictory syllogisms till reason grows giddy, and scarcely able to hold the balance; but when he acts in the presence of his fellow creatures, his mind resumes its tone and vigour, and social devotion gives a colour and body to the deductions of his reason.[65]

For Barbauld, devotion is inherently social. The conceit of the 'metaphysical reasoner, entangled in nets of sophistry' hangs suspended between her earlier tilt with Priestley and her later, now famous, admonitory poem 'To Mr. S. T. Coleridge' (1799), where it is recast as the 'maze of metaphysical lore'. While the 'Gossamer' threads entangling Coleridge refer more to 'generous enterprise' than to squabbling syllogisms, the conclusion is the same: 'Active scenes / Shall soon with healthful spirit brace thy mind' (ll. 38–9), as it exerts itself 'For friends, for country . . .' The inner directed pursuit of metaphysical truth may be a glamorous enchantment, but it threatens transformation into bestial egotism. Coleridge appears to have brooded on the accusation:

> What is it, that I employ my Metaphysics on? To perplex our clearest notions, & living moral Instincts? To extinguish the Light of Love & of Conscience, to put out the Life of Arbitrement – to make myself & others *Worthless*, *Soul*-less, *God*less – No! To expose the Folly & the Legerdemain

> of those, who have thus abused the blessed Organ of Language, to support all old & venerable Truths, to support, to kindle, to project, to make the Reason spread Light over our Feelings, to make our Feelings diffuse vital Warmth thro' our Reason – these are my Objects – & these my Subjects. Is this the metaphysics that bad Spirits in Hell delight in? (*Notebooks*: I, 1623)

This *Notebook* entry, from 1803, fours years after the publication of Barbauld's poem in the Dissenting *Monthly Magazine*, reveals a Coleridge wrestling with Kant, to be sure ('Arbitrement' being his riposte to the categorical imperative), but the dominating presence is Barbauld's, the reciprocity of reason and feeling being, effectively, the polemical gist of her essay on devotion. Coleridge insists, to himself, that he fights the good fight, that he is not abusing his intellect to pleasure himself (a bad spirit capering in Hell); and yet, in the middle of it, an ambiguity in the phrasing reveals that, from Barbauld's perspective, he still doesn't get it. 'To expose the Folly & the Legerdemain of those, who have thus abused the blessed Organ of Language' was the task of all oppositional figures set against the Anti-Jacobinical lie-machine, especially when it did so (and it always did so) under the guise of supporting 'all old & venerable Truths'. And yet Coleridge's syntax preserves the comma after 'language', so that he is the one 'supporting all old & venerable Truths'. Coleridge's position is far more Burkean than anything envisaged by Barbauld in her tilt with Priestley. Its surrender of 'critique' would also jeopardize reason's social mission.

Barbauld naturally thinks of the will to power in terms of the individual self of her own class (the 'middle station'). Even so her ethical vision is inclusive, spreading down, as well as out. In her essay on public worship she writes: 'Here the poor man learns that, in spite of the distinctions of rank, and the apparent inferiority of his condition, all the true goods of life ...' that every one wants – 'a sound mind, a healthful body, and daily bread' – lie within his scope too. 'He rises from his knees, and feels himself a man ... Every time Social Worship is celebrated, it includes a virtual declaration of the rights of man.'[66] Barbauld guards her particular form of 'devotion' against accusations of 'enthusiasm' ('He learns philosophy without its pride, and a spirit of liberty without its turbulence'),[67] but it is also clear that she conceives of social devotion as an empowering exercise, one that guards against the abject state. Her thoughts on the social, empowering nature of devotion thus lead seamlessly to the political activism of her *Civic Sermons to the People* (1792). Again, there is a sharp contrast with Coleridge, who was, at this time, anxious that he should be understood to be speaking for, rather than to, the people.[68] In contrast to this timorousness, Barbauld, emboldened by her belief in the reality of the public sphere, addressed her civic sermons to no one else but the 'people'. Using the same techniques pioneered in her *Lessons for Children* and *Hymns in Prose for Children*, Barbauld employs clear language carefully tailored to fit the capacities of her audience as she takes them from foundational precepts to more complex ideas. She begins with the customary swipe at Burke's 'swinish multitude', insisting that to discourse is human, and therefore any one who would disbar 'poor people, or those who work to maintain themselves' from rational discourse on government, that is, from the public sphere, not only sinks 'you from your station' but degrades 'you from your species'.[69] '*Judgment* depends upon good sense and information' and Barbauld aims to inculcate and supply both, by taking her readers through the 'abc's of the social contract, explaining why government is a matter for them. She ends the second sermon with a vision of the nation as an imagined community, driving the point home by conceiving her readers explaining the point to their own children, in the manner of one of her 'lessons':

> Now, my child, if you travel on, you come to other towns, and field and villages, and others still beyond them far, and further than you can see, East and West, and North and South, reaching on every side to the great Ocean, and all these together make up that large society called a *State*; so large is it, that you must stretch your imagination to conceive properly of its extent; it contains thousands and thousands of families whom you never have seen, nor probably ever will see; yet of all this you are a part, and joined to it in a most intimate and binding connection, like a limb to the body, or a single shoot to a large tree. These are all governed by the same rules; they speak the same language; they make war or peace together. *My child, love your Country*.[70]

The echo of Richard Price is calculated, as is the strategic employment of the organic metaphor. A state requires security of persons and property; laws and a police; a judicature; a revenue for public works; and to put all this in place, ruling powers and an executive force, which cumulatively constitute a government. 'There is nothing of mystery in this, nothing that requires to be wrapt up in strange and unintelligible terms; the steps are plain and easy; the benefits felt by all, and therefore it may be comprehended by all.'[71] She ends, though, not with an appeal to knowledge as power, but with an image of the collective ('Citizens, expand your minds to take in these ideas! Let your Country occupy a large space in your minds!').[72] One should love one's country, not because of Burke's famous, tautological chiasmus ('To make us love our country, our country ought to be lovely')[73] but because

> it includes every other object of love, because it unites all separate energies into one energy, all separate wills into one will; and having united and declared them, calls it Law ... In yourselves you are weak, but in your Country you are strong; in yourselves you are obscure, but in your Country

> you are celebrated; in yourselves you are unlearned, but in your Country you possess all sciences and all art; in your own selves you are defenceless, but in your Country you're invincible ... (II, 20–1)

To a modern ear *Civic Sermons* may sound patronizing; but in the context of the times, when any attempt to speak directly to the people on political topics was considered sinister, to reach down, in such clear, inclusive terms, in order to embrace all of society in a national republic of letters, took special daring.

The social, political and personally empowering aspects of devotion come together in Barbauld's poetic, as expressed in this key passage from 'Thoughts on the Devotional Taste':

> Yet there is a devotion generous, liberal, and humane, the child of more exalted feelings than base minds can enter into, which assimilates man to higher natures, and lifts him 'above this visible diurnal sphere.' Its pleasures are ultimate, and when early cultivated continue vivid even in that uncomfortable season of life when some of the passions are extinct, when imagination is dead, and the heart begins to contract within itself. Those who want this taste, want a sense, a part of their nature, and should not presume to judge of feelings to which they must ever be strangers. No one pretends to be a judge in poetry or the fine arts, who has not both a natural and *a cultivated relish* for them; and shall the narrow-minded children of earth absorbed in low pursuits, dare to treat as visionary, objects which they have never made themselves acquainted with? Silence on such subjects will better become them [my italics].[74]

The political charge is delivered in the quotation from Milton ('above this visible diurnal sphere' [*Paradise Lost*, VII, 22]).

The point becomes clearer when we set the passage beside its principal influence, Isaac Watt's 'The Adventurous Muse'. Watts was the dominant English hymn writer before the Wesleys, who were in any event distrusted by Barbauld, in sharp contrast to Watts, who was himself not only a distinguished Dissenter but a friend and colleague of her revered Grandfather, Dr Doddridge, a co-editor of Watts's collected works. The internal evidence suggests that Barbauld not only knew Watts's poem but also knew it well. The adventurous muse is Urania, the muse of astronomy. According to J. R. Watson, the poem sets out Watts's 'boldest statement of poetic belief'.[75] It turns on the contrast between the adventurous muse, who

> Springs, unerring, upward to eternal day,
> Spreads her white sails aloft, and steers,
> With bold and safe attempt, to the celestial land

and duller sorts:

> Whilst little Skiffs along the mortal Shores
> With humble Toil in Order creep,
> Coasting in sight of one another's Oars,
> Nor venture thro' the boundless Deep.

In other words, the trope of star gazing (astronomy) breaks down into the vehicle of inter-stellar travel carrying the tenor of poetic inspiration:

> Give me the Muse whose generous Force,
> Impatient of the Reins,
> Pursues an unattempted Course,
> Breaks all the Critics Iron Chains,
> And bears to Paradise the raptur'd Mind.[76]

'There *Milton* dwells': for Watts, poetically speaking, Milton is the fit emblem of the 'raptur'd mind', a point Barbauld echoes by quoting Milton's 'above this visible diurnal sphere' to describe the state of the transported soul. Barbauld reworks the contrast between the dull earthly and the inspired heavenly, incorporating Milton's Old Commonwealth values through the clever quotation that simultaneously takes us back to Watts.

All Romantics have adventurous muses; but Wordsworth's appears to have internalized Barbauld's poetic, wholesale. The clue is in the single word 'relish'. Barbauld uses the word twice in the essay on devotion, first, to refer to a taste for 'the sublime, the vast, and the beautiful', and second, quoted above, to qualify 'taste' as a natural or constitutional sense, yet one that also has to be 'cultivated'. It is in exactly this qualified sense that Wordsworth uses the word, when he asks, in 'Essay, Supplementary to the Preface' (1815), 'And where lies the real difficulty of creating that taste by which a truly original poet is to be relished?' (*SP*: 408), a sense that connotes work and energy ('gusto', as Hazlitt would put it), the antithesis of passive aristocratic connosieurship or popular, stupefied, wonder. Relish is what distinguishes 'devotion' ('generous, liberal, and humane, the child of more exalted feelings' [Barbauld 2002: 212]) from mere taste. As regards the appreciation of poetry – assessing the virtues of a truly adventurous muse – the difference has two aspects. First, 'devotional taste', or 'relish', is active. As Wordsworth puts it, it involves 'intellectual *acts* and *operations*' (*SP*: 409) And second, devotion makes us better: galvanized by the original poet (says Wordsworth) the reader is 'humbled and humanized' as a preliminary step to being 'purified and exalted'. Barbauld returns to the word in the pamphlet, *On Being Born Again*: 'Do you relish the word of God? I ask not do you *read*, though that were perhaps a question to be asked, but do you *relish* it?'[77] Barbauld employs 'relish' in her precise, devotional sense. Elsewhere in the essay Barbauld refers to the 'immortal part within you' and 'to your inward man', meaning the inner self that is to be born again:[78] and, as her essay on devotion has it, the fire is lit and the embers kept warm by an early 'relish for the sublime, the vast, and the beautiful' (Barbauld 2002: 211), which exists as a combustible resource in the adult self, a belief that was to became a desideratum for the epigonic Wordsworth.

'A Summer Evening's Meditation' is Barbauld's version of Watts's 'The Adventurous Muse' translated into a Romantic idiom. Watts's muse is externalized through the conventional, Classical figure of Urania. Barbauld's is internalized as an inward creative force – the 'inward man' – she refers to as a 'stranger'. Whereas Watts's allegorical figure gallops across the universe, in Barbauld's poem it is the 'I' itself who is simultaneously the 'soul' and the mysterious inner self:

> At this still hour the self-collected soul
> Turns inward, and beholds a stranger there
> Of high descent, and more than mortal rank;
> An embryo God; a spark of fire divine ... (2002: 53–6)

It is easy to pass over these lines as a conventional expression of a Romantic cliché. As Mee argues, the discourse of genius is a form of regulated enthusiasm. As an enthusiastical experience it follows that the creative act will be marked by a fanning of one's inner 'spark of fire divine', the self as 'embryo God'. This inner spark both is, and is not, the soul. It is, insofar as genius is the flaring up of the creative part of one's inner self that communes with the 'Divine mind', a 'presence' in nature; but it is not, insofar as the emerging language of genius connects an older, aesthetic language, in which genius figures as a talent, or special ability, quite distinct from religious notions of the soul, with a newer, evangelical discourse, which conflates them. In the older language, one 'has', in the newer, one 'is', a genius. But the genius that one is is not necessarily known to oneself. On the contrary it is elusive, and only made manifest in moments of inspiration, or creative ecstasy, when the divine furor is upon one. In this respect one's genius is a stranger to oneself, as elusive as the soul, whose nature it partially, perhaps wholly, but certainly mysteriously, shares. This stranger is, axiomatically, hard to know, otherwise we would all be geniuses.

We are, then, in the semantic territory of the Aeolian harp, of inscrutable, vagrant winds and open, responsive, creative souls; of inner selves quickening with correspondent breezes, as elusive presence calls to elusive presence; or of an inner creative self whose identity echoes the divine 'I am'. For post-Romantics, the stranger within was the myth they had to debunk. Thus, if the self is an onion, the 'stranger' would be the 'absent presence' at the centre of it, once the layers had been peeled; or, to use Herman Melville's version, the empty sarcophagus once one had successfully mined the pyramid of the self.[79] Barbauld's version of the creative self ('the stranger there') thus seems to draw on the stock tropes of Romantic genius, which, by the 1770s, were already well on their way to being formed. While this may be true of the overall gist of 'A Summer Evening's Meditation', her phrasing is, in fact, highly unusual. The nearest echo is to be found in Edward Young's *Conjectures on Original Composition*, published nearly twenty years earlier (1759). Young's essay enjoyed considerable celebrity, and was a landmark in the formation of Romantic genius. 'Since it is plain that men may be strangers to their own abilities; and by thinking meanly of them without just cause, may possibly lose a name, perhaps, a name immortal; I would find some means to prevent these Evils.'[80] In order to prevent them, Young recommends 'two golden rules from Ethics ... 1. Know thyself; 2dly, Reverence thyself'.

> 1st. Know thyself. Of ourselves it may be said, as Martial says of a bad neighbour, Nil tam prope, proculque nobis.
>
> Therefore dive deep into thy bosom; learn the depth, extent, biass, and full fort of thy mind; contract full intimacy with the Stranger within thee; excite, and cherish every spark of Intellectual light and heat, however smothered under former negligence, or scattered through the dull, dark mass of common thoughts; and collecting them into a body, let thy Genius rise (if a Genius thou hast) as the sun from Chaos; and if I should then say, like an Indian, worship it, (though too bold) yet should I say little more than my second rule enjoins, (viz.) Reverence thyself.[81]

Know and reverence thyself were two Greek maxims with a long history in Classical thought as well as the Christian tradition, into which they were quickly absorbed. From Young's Calvinist perspective the seminal fact was that 'the theme of self-knowledge' was 'developed at some length in the religious writing of Luther and Calvin, where the focus is primarily on the knowledge of the human soul, its sinful state, and its need for redemption'.[82] In referring to the self as the 'stranger within', Young reaches back to Neoplatonic traditions of the sixteenth century where it was common to speak of knowing one's soul, in the sense of an elusive inner essence released in the ecstatic state, as opposed to the Calvinist insistence on a generic soul in a perilous condition, knowledge of which enjoined immediate attention be paid to one's maker.

Young's formulation of a deep, creative, elusive self – a stranger – was to prove foundational for Romantic poetics, one clearly anticipating its ultimate expression as the unconscious. The very slipperiness of its phrasing encodes the historic transformation of 'soul' to 'self'.[83] For Young, as for those that came after, if authenticity was the highest creative virtue, the 'Stranger within' was the self one was true to, when one was being true (that is, sincere and, as a result, authentic). Similarly, creativity – the stamp of true genius – derived from the imprimatur of the authentic self (for Wordsworth and Coleridge, the hallmark that distinguished true poetry from mechanically produced verse). There is every reason to believe that Barbauld was familiar with Young's novel phrasing. 'A Summer Evening's Meditation' begins with a quotation from Young's *Night Thoughts*: 'One sun by day, by night ten thousand shine'. The section in which Young's line is embedded provides the setting and theme of Barbauld's poem: a meditative soul transported by a night reverie where the stars 'light us deep into the Deity', with the self suspended between humility and exaltation. The conclusion Young draws anticipates Barbauld's key theme, if not her register: 'Devotion, Daughter of Astronomy! / An *undevout* astronomer is *mad*' ('The complaint. Or, night-thoughts on life, death, and immortality', *Night IX*). The statement loops us back to Watts, whose *First Principles of Astronomy and Geography* begins by asserting the essential connection between astronomy and a proper understanding of the scriptures.[84]

Watts is also significant in that he supplies two of the rare analogues to Young's and Barbauld's conceit of the inner stranger. Both occur in poems from *Horae Lyricae*. In 'Happy Frailty' the poet is found overhearing his soul's soliloquy. First she complains 'How meanly dwells th' immortal mind! / How vile these bodies are' (stanza i, line 1). The I of the poem, impressed, mourns 'our frail state' (stanza iv, line 13), till 'sudden from the cleaving sky / A gleam of glory shone' (stanza iv, lines 15–16). Inspired, the soul 'changes her key', and ecstatically calls for the shuffling off:

> Now let the Tempest blow all round,
> Now swell the Surges high,
> And beat this house of Bondage down,
> To let the Stranger fly. (stanza ix, lines 33–6)

The poem ends with the soul harking to her Saviour's call:

> 'I come, my Lord, my Love':
> Devotion breaks the Prison-Walls,
> And speeds my last Remove. (stanza xii, lines 46–8)

The *Horae Lyricae* reveal a strong, unobtrusive, metaphysical influence in the use of colloquial voice and a strong speaking line, but especially in the Neoplatonic habit of conversing with the soul, or of representing out-of-body experiences in which the soul acquaints itself with the works of the 'Divine mind'. The lines appear to echo Donne's *Holy Sonnets*, but the influence may simply be one of strong, cultural continuity. Regardless, 'Happy Frailty' anticipates the ontological ambiguity that distinguishes Young's 'stranger' trope, in which the soul, stranger and self are, like the Trinity, at once distinct and identical aspects of inner being. Thus the soul refers to letting the 'stranger fly' while in the final quatrain within three lines 'my' segues from speaking soul to self. In 'True Riches' the self-divided theme continues, with the speaker referring to an inner self that is an immense, inner Eden, a Neoplatonic zone where 'on all the shining boughs / Knowledge fair and useless grows' (lines 25–6). The zone, or soul, 'is a region half unknown' (line 47). However, the 'silly wandering mind' (line 59) explores the more constrained, limited, external world of sense so that she becomes to 'herself a stranger living' (line 68).

The poem adjacent to 'Happy Frailty', in all eighteenth-century editions of *Horae Lyricae*, is 'The Adventurous Muse' (which provides the link between the stranger motif and interstellar reverie). The presiding influence on 'A Summer Evening's Meditation', however, is not so much Young or Watts, as Shaftesbury. As her modern editors comment, 'Barbauld probably knew the Earl of Shaftesbury's paen to the planets in *The Moralists*' (1709) by the time she wrote her poem, as she later published it in *The Female Speaker*.[85] Through Theocles Shaftesbury addresses the deity as 'O Mighty Genius! Sole-animating and inspiring power! Author and subject of these thoughts! Thy influence is universal, and in all things, thou are inmost.' Theocles moves from the wonders of the micro- to the macro-scopic world, praising the Divine maker, or mind, in a Neoplatonic panegyric in which he contemplates metempsychosis, the indestructibility of the soul, eternity, the perfection of creation, before the final wonder of the planets.

If Shaftesbury lies behind Barbauld, Young and Watts, there is also a significant difference, evident, especially, in Shaftesbury's conception of the self. For Shaftesbury the Classical, ethical injunction 'Recognize your-self' (as he translates it) should really be 'divide your-self'.[86] He refers to the ancient authors' habit of alluding to an inner daemon or genius – a kind of guardian spirit – which, he concludes, is merely figurative. What they meant, he says (in a passage strangely reminiscent of late Foucault), is that 'we had each of us a patient in *our-self*; that we were properly our own subjects of practice; and that we then became due practitioners, when by virtue of an intimate *recess* we could discover a certain *duplicity* of soul, and divide ourselves into two partys'.[87] One party would exert its superiority over the other, as regards sagacity. The gaining of wisdom thus became a matter of revolving inwards, to the inner recess, and through soliloquy to hold oneself in talk, with the wiser self predominating, as no man, in such converse, would willingly appear a knave to himself. Such self-division and soliloquy were the peculiar achievements of philosophers; for Shaftebury, such an elevating discipline was equally rare among moderns. Mee argues that Shaftesbury's self-division was a means of regulating enthusiasm, ensuring that otherworlding was restricted to the disciplined, generally learned, few.[88] If so, then Young's revisiting of the theme is equally regulatory, in that he tautologically defines the work of the 'stranger' as that of uplifting Christian genius (whatever deviates from this, such as Swift's scatological humour, is, for Young, by definition, self-betrayal).[89] But in other respects Young could not be more different: his 'stranger within' is, implicitly, socially ubiquitous. It is also inward in the modern evangelical sense of a better self smothered with sin – a buried, dispersed other we can release, and enjoy, if we only open our hearts ('dive deep into thy bosom'). For Shaftesbury self-division is a serene, closeted, aristocratic experience, whereas in Young's *Conjectures* intimacy with the inner stranger is hectic and feverish, with jumpy, declamatory rhythms, as if calling out to a crowd, seeking conversion.

By contrast Barbauld's inner stranger, released by the self-collected soul, is calm, cool and yet, implicitly, common. It represents the transgressive self in an optative, devotional mood. As Jonathan Wordsworth comments, though 'little known, Barbauld's *Meditation* is surely the most adventurous poetry written by a woman before the later nineteenth century' (Barbauld 1993: n.p.). There are several aspects to its spirit of adventure, but the most obvious is the accomplished use of Miltonic free verse to transport an avowedly female 'I' across interstellar vastness, as if an unfallen Lucifer. As we saw with Watts, it was conventional to represent the soul as feminine. Barbauld's *Poems* were not anonymous, appearing, with éclat, under her own name. As the collected soul revolves inward to greet 'the stranger there / of high descent' ('A Summer Evening's Meditation'), what emerges is not the representation of a conventional, disembodied, feminine soul, in a state of ecstatic transportation, ventriloquized by a male, and certainly not an allegorical Urania, but the poet's confident, brazen, female 'I'. The introversion towards an inner recess is not a matter of self-division, with the better self predominating, or a matter of conforming to an evangelical self: what emerges, rather, is an empowering 'embryo God', unperturbed by shadows cast by a circling superego.

Barbauld's thought is, daringly, both Unitarian and Platonic. In her essay on the *Pleasures of the Imagination* Barbauld sketches Akenside's Platonism:

> [T]he Author begins by unfolding the Platonic idea that the universe with all its forms of material beauty was called into being from its prototype, existing from all eternity in the divine mind. The different propensities that human beings are born with to various pursuits, are enumerated in some very beautiful lines, and those are declared to be the most noble which lead a chosen few to the love and contemplation of the Supreme Beauty, by the love and contemplation of his works. The Poet thus immediately, and at the very outset, dignifies his theme, by connecting it with the sublimest feelings the human mind is capable of entertaining, feelings without which the various scenes of this beautiful universe degenerate into *gaudy* shows, fit to catch the eye of children, but uninteresting to the heart and affections; and those laws and properties about which Philosophy busies herself, into a bewildering mass of unconnected experiments and independent facts. [my italics][90]

The passage serves as a gloss of her earlier poem. Thus, when she writes 'Contemplation ... wrapt in solitude ... mused away the gaudy hours of noon' ('A Summer Evening's Meditation', ll. 18–21) we understand that noonday thoughts are 'gaudy' because unillumined by the 'sublimest feelings the human mind is capable of entertaining', which is to say, 'by devotion', or, as she styles it here, 'the heart and affections'. But unlike Akenside, Barbauld does not suggest that contemplation of the 'mighty mind' is restricted to the chosen few. Rather, Barbauld shifts from the generic to the particular, from a universal 'self-collected soul' to 'I', as if the transition were open to any contemplative individual. In her essay on devotion the astronomical sublime sinks into superstitious abjection because unillumined by our 'sublimest feelings'; for the narrow, scientific mind, the 'desarts of creation, wide and wild' risk becoming a 'bewildering mass of unconnected ... facts'. But in 'A Summer Evening's Meditation' the devout, contemplative 'I' rises above the abject state, steering a course between superstitious abasement and vain-glorious enthusiasm. With this in mind the apparent contradiction between the essay on devotion and the poem – the latter celebrating the astronomical sublime, the former deprecating it – disappears, for the issue is less about aesthetics and more of what empowers the self. The soaring mind's encounter with the 'solitudes of vast unpeopled space' (l. 94) brings the poem to its crisis: 'fancy droops, / And thought astonish'd stops her bold career' (ll. 97–8). In the essay the next step is the undevout self's abasement, her grovelling sense of inferiority. In the poem, the speaker addresses the 'mighty mind' of creation, asking 'Where shall I seek thy presence?' The question is left unanswered; instead, the speaker shifts tack, and speaks for the 'mighty mind', assuring 'guilty man' that the deity does not favour 'dread' and 'terror', but 'hast a gentler voice, / That whispers comfort to the swelling heart, / Abash'd, yet longing to behold her Maker' (ll. 109–11). In effect, Barbauld terminates the Burkean sublime before it arrives at the next conventional step: a consideration of man's puniness and the emptiness of his vaunted ambition. Barbauld repudiates the aesthetic instrumentality of terror, favouring, instead, a poetic of devout equilibrium, as in, for instance, the balance struck between the simultaneous 'swelling' and 'Abash'd'. The speaker embodies just such a powerful equilibrium in the act of breaking with Burke, assuring man of the Maker's benign nature – that is, as a woman, speaking confidently of the Platonic nature of creation – something she could not do, if not empowered. In the last movement of the poem the speaker rises above abjection, to wait in the soul's Watts-like 'mansion' (a place of Platonic 'inner riches', 'Drest up with sun, and shade, and lawns, and streams ... full replete with wonders' [ll. 114–16]), ripening for the 'sky'.

In my earlier discussion of the essay on devotion I referred to the mysterious 'personal benefits' that accrue from having our finer feelings activated by 'the sublime, the vast and the beautiful'. The benefits are mysterious because Barbauld refers to them, not in the context of Christian belief but of devotional 'taste'. At the time I suggested that such benefits could certainly be regarded as rising cultural capital. But in the wider context of Barbauld's thought, perhaps a better way of putting it would be to say that the benefits reflect the rewards of a steadfast 'will to power'. The phrase comes from Friedrich Nietzsche, for whom the will to power was a fragile resource. That is, as Nietzsche saw it, we could never access our will to power if entrenched in conventional values or the inauthentic personae society furnishes us with. To access the self's primitive vigour we needed to tear off masks, stripping away the distracting layers of adventitious identity. And yet not all of them; for the very process of stripping away might wound the self, leading to a powerless nullity. In the end, some level of socially constructed identity was necessary, if the self was to will itself effectively. Barbauld's thoughts on taste and devotion have this kind of nuanced balance. Thus Barbauld's poem follows the contours, not of, say, the fashionable Burkean sublime, or a vainglorious natural science, but the psychological needs of a self seeking a grounded, balanced power. The 'benefits' Barbauld refers to are part of her ideological drive to promote the individual, primarily of the middle station, as regards her practice, although more generally so, in theory. Owing to her strong sense of the collective she instinctively pulls back from that which promotes the glamour of the individual 'I', as a distracting snare.

3. Conclusion: 'Frost at Midnight'

Coleridge's divergence from Barbauld may be traced to his conversation poems, insofar as they record the moment in which he retires from politics and the public sphere, having broken his squeaking trumpet. As Judith Thompson puts it, 'the conversation poems have long been taken as typical of that broad transition in voice and vision that defines romanticism: from public genres to private, lyric modes, from the world of radical political activism to the solitary, transcendent realm of imagination'.[91] Of the conversation poems 'Frost at Midnight' is generally seen as the most successful, and influential, not least in providing the inspiration for 'Tintern Abbey'. Recent criticism of the poem has split into two main camps. One coalesces around work done by Kelvin Everest, but especially Paul Magnuson, in situating the poem in its original publishing context. Magnuson notes that 'Frost at Midnight' was issued together with 'Fears in Solitude' and 'France: an Ode' by Joseph Johnson a few short months after the radical publisher's conviction for seditious libel in the Gilbert Wakefield case, and argues that Johnson and Coleridge were both seeking to ingratiate themselves with the authorities; 'Frost at Midnight' thus 'presents a patriotic poet, whose patriotism rested on the love of his country and his domestic affections'.[92] Magnuson's work fits neatly into Jerome McGann's influential polemic on the Romantic ideology; the retreat into domestic harmony and inward contemplation thus becomes a 'displacement or occlusion of historical reality'.[93] For critics in the other camp 'Frost at Midnight' is chiefly notable for the way the poem articulates an aesthetic freed from Hartley, Priestley and their 'necessarian' fellow-travellers, having caught the wind of a Kantian revolution Coleridge will do much to consolidate.[94] For the second camp, Coleridge is a pioneer of modern subjectivity:

> Coleridge implicitly posits the autonomous self as the favored basis for metaphysical truth and as the normative source for such discoveries. In terms familiar to us from Michel Foucault, Coleridge establishes himself as at once the transcendental subject and empirical object of knowledge that marks the founding moment of modernity and the introduction of Man.[95]

Both camps agree that 'Frost at Midnight' is a foundational text for Romanticism, and, indeed, for modernity itself; but they sharply disagree about the character and significance of Coleridge's inward turn, with one side seeing escape and evasion, and the other, evidence of the mature Coleridge's Kantian project.

In either case, Barbauld would serve as a convenient straw man. As McGann tartly remarks in relation to Jane Austen, 'the greatest artists in any period often depart from their age's dominant ideological commitments . . . '[96] Bearing in mind the short shrift Barbauld gives to Coleridge's retirement and abstruse musing one can safely say that Barbauld does not share the 'grand illusion of every Romantic poet': the 'idea that poetry, or even consciousness, can set one free of the ruins of history and culture . . . '[97] Clearly, if she had, she would not have written *Eighteen Hundred and Eleven*, which locates transcendence not in poetry or consciousness but a place: America. While for those who see Kant as the first figure to diagnose the consequences of the Enlightenment – the radical freedom, or autonomy, of the subject – Barbauld's assessment of his importance will not impress:

> [I]n [Madame De Stael's] account of Kant and other German philosophers she has got, I fancy, a little out of her depth. She herself is, or affects to be, very devotional; but her religion seems to be almost wholly a matter of imagination, – the *beau ideal* impressed upon us at birth, along with a taste for beauty, for music, &c. As far as I understand her account of the German schools, there seems to be in many of them a design to reinstate the doctrine of innate ideas, which the cold philosophy, as they would call it, of Locke discarded. They would like Beattie and Hutcheson better than Paley and Priestley.[98]

One cannot hold a writer to account for the intellectual content of a gossipy letter; even so, her characterization of space and time as 'innate ideas' rather than constitutive mental categories does not bode well, while the reference to devotion and the imagination reminds us that she could never have found sympathy with Kant's argument that the aesthetic is a product of reflection, not feeling.[99]

What I've called the two main camps in recent criticism of 'Frost at Midnight', one New Historicist, the other Kantian, have more in common than their sense of Barbauld's lack of fit, for they share the same reading of history, with only the emphasis differing. Thus, for McGann, the

> field of history, politics, and social relations is everywhere marked in the Romantic period by complex divisions and conflicts previously unprecedented in Europe. Romantic poetry develops an argument that such dislocations can only be resolved beyond the realm of immediate experience, at the level of the mind's idea or the heart's desire.[100]

McGann contrasts the particular historical situation of the Romantics, waking up to the absence of a 'stable conceptual frame of reference in which [a poem's] problems can be taken up and explored', with writers of the Renaissance, where there was 'unquestioning acceptance' of a 'stable conceptual frame of reference'.[101] The Romantic belief in the power of the autonomous self to fabricate a simulacrum of the old theological wholeness, now in secular ruins, through an exertion of the imagination – a reaching out through a projective self in concert with a receptive nature, a 'theoretical consubstantiality of thought and thing',[102] with eye and ear corresponding with an indwelling thing-in-itselfness – is something both Kantians and New Historicists can agree on. The latter may consider the solutions arrived at by Kant, and seized on by Coleridge, only temporary and peculiar to the ideological situation of some writers of the Romantic period, whereas the former may see a more durable significance; but both sides would concur with the analysis, and therefore with Barbauld's marginal status as a Romantic poet. I want to conclude the chapter, and the book, by testing this exclusion against 'Frost at Midnight', in part because it is a cornerstone of institutional Romanticism, but also because it is peculiarly fitting that we should do so, for Coleridge's poem is one of the few to pick up, and rework, Barbauld's trope of the inner stranger. As Coleridge famously explained in a note to the 1798 version of the poem, the 'stranger' on the grate – the idling 'film' – was believed to presage a visit from a friend. On the face of it the allusion differs radically from the register that imparts meaning to Barbauld's trope, but things change as we look closer.

Since the work of Jack Stillinger it has become customary to begin a discussion of 'Frost at Midnight' by acknowledging that the poem exists in at least ten different versions, with three main variants: the first edition of 1798; the version printed in the *Poetical Register* of 1812; and the final version of 1829. Between the first and last there are two substantive changes that have exercised critics: the amputation of the final six lines, depicting Hartley with his soul suspended by the icicles produced by the frost's secret ministry, an experience that will 'make thee shout, / And stretch and flutter from thy mother's arms / As though would'st fly for very eagreness' (Stillinger 1994: 157); and a reworking of the 'stranger' passage, with the final version achieving a compression lacking in the two earlier ones, the meaning drawn in by the concise – and more pejorative – 'and makes a toy of Thought' (Stillinger 1994: 155). Unsurprisingly, New Historicists tend to see the revisions underlining the thesis that the poem enacts a retreat from the public sphere and history, while Kantians detect a process of clarification.[103]

'In moments of crisis the Romantic will turn to Nature or the creative Imagination as his place of last resort.'[104] If McGann's generalization holds true, it is because 'Frost at Midnight' succeeded as the archetype of the Romantic poem by doing both at the same time:

> In "Frost at Midnight" ... there is an acknowledgement of the isolation of the imagining consciousness and a similarly problematic attempt to achieve an experience of communion which will make nature thought and thought nature. The frost, secret and inaccessible, embodies the spontaneous, productive energy of nature as it both creates and reflects, hanging its icicles up to the gaze of the moon.[105]

As Tilottama Rajan hints, the secret ministry of frost tropes what Coleridge will eventually term 'the primary imagination', a hint seemingly confirmed by the final version of the poem, which makes it clear that the isolated speaker is in a purely fanciful mood:

> Methinks, its motion in this hush of nature
> Gives it dim sympathies with me who live,
> Making it a companionable form,
> Whose puny flaps and freaks the idling Spirit
> By its own moods interprets, every where
> Echo or mirror seeking of itself,
> And makes a toy of Thought.

Rajan's commentary makes the point:

> The film on the grate, a residue of desire rather than evidence of the genius that joins the subjective to the objective world, seems to image the emptiness of the imagining consciousness. It dreams but does not produce anything, imagines and heralds a life beyond itself, but does not make it present except as an echo.[106]

The poet begins the poem in a state of idle fancy, his imagination deadened. Most commentaries agree that the poem carves an arc – at least on the surface – towards some kind of resolution. Reeve Parker's characterization of it has been much quoted: the poem moves from the 'superstitious solipsism of a depressed sensibility, toying with a companionable form, to the apprehension of a regenerate companionship, based not on superstition but on substantial belief'.[107] Read retrospectively through *Biographia Literaria*, the apostrophe to Hartley figures the missing third element, the secondary imagination, projected into futurity through the embodiment of his son who, raised in the country rather than the city, will 'wander like a breeze / By lakes and sandy shores, beneath the crags/ Of ancient mountains . . . ' so that 'thou shall see and hear / The lovely shapes and sounds intelligible / Of that eternal language' (Stillinger 1994: 157) uttered by the divine, 'universal Teacher'.

Unsurprisingly, critical variation turns on the textual details that vex and trouble this optative arc. Rajan argues that the regeneration or movement from adult to child, winter to spring, father to son, city to country, inside to outside, fancy to imagination, is simply an 'hypothesis' advanced by the poem, for 'experience puts in doubt the theoretical consubstantiality of thought and thing. The marriage between the spirit of desire and the body of the world often taken for granted in post-Kantian idealism, proves precarious and inevitably brings human creativity up against a radical self-doubt.'[108] Criticism has tended to fasten on the poem's numerous hints of Kantian misgiving. A very broad hint lies on the very surface of the poem: the name 'Hartley'. As Kathleen Wheeler has demonstrated, Coleridge's final break with Hartley's associationist philosophy occurred in 1801; however, it was a long, reluctant process, with hints of Coleridge's uneasiness with the mechanical, deterministic elements of Hartley's theory appearing as early as 1794.[109] As the *Biographia Literaria* makes clear, Coleridge organized his dissatisfaction with Hartley's theory through the metaphor of the wind playing on the Aeolian harp, which turns the self into a 'blind mechanism' (*BL*: I, 116) and an 'infinite spirit' into 'mere articulated motions of the air' (*BL*: I, 120). As we saw in Chapter 3, by 1798 Coleridge was already struggling towards a conception of the one-life and the mystery of the deep-willing, autonomous self, capable of making 'nature thought and thought nature'. So when Coleridge opens the poem with 'The frost performs its secret ministry, / Unhelped by any wind', we should be alert to the possibility that Coleridge is hinting at a creative process based on a metaphor in explicit opposition to the Aeolian harp, with its unfortunate, materialist undertones.

As many critics have observed, 'Frost at Midnight' is based on repetition. The question is whether the repetition is progressive, and therefore dialectical, or regressive, and therefore neurotic. Some of the repetitions are trivial (the hooting owl; the refrain 'Sea, hill, and Wood'), and some portentous (the parallel between the 'stern preceptor' who rules Coleridge's urban school and the 'Great universal Teacher' who will instruct the rural Hartley). Others are mysterious, such as the difference between the absences that are 'absence' (the extreme quiet that vexes meditation) and the absence that is 'presence' (the frost's 'secret ministry'). It is this context that makes the treatment of the 'stranger' so significant. As the poem moves forward the stranger trope introduces what seems to be a dialectical repetition. As both the note and the poem explain, believing a film of carbon prophesies the arrival of a loved one is a superstition; we are thus readied for the contrast between an absence or a lack that will not produce a transitive action (mere superstition) and one that will (the creative imagination, where the projective mind and receptive nature meet halfway). If the childish Coleridge straining for sight of the prophesied friend is an unconscious John the Baptist, the Christ figure is Hartley, who will move beyond idle superstition to the status of a true visionary. This dialectical movement is expressed in the poem by the difference between the lack announced by the stranger, which cannot be satisfied – a lack governing the imagination of Coleridge, the child, in his urban privation – and the very different kind of lack instilled in Coleridge's child through his education in a transcendental nature: God, as the Great universal Teacher 'shall mould / Thy spirit, and by giving make it ask' (Stillinger 1994: 157). Such asking – and wanting – is preparatory to the creative reception that ends in writing.[110]

The term for repetition without progression is 'doubling'. 'Frost at Midnight' plays with doubles and doubling. The childish Coleridge strains his eyes at his school desk hoping for the appearance of the beloved friend augured by the 'stranger', such as his sister, 'My play-mate when we both were clothed alike' (Stillinger 1994: 157). In the 1798 version, Hartley will 'stretch and flutter' from his mother's arms, words and actions that double the film on the grate. Just as the 'stranger' fluttering on the grate prophesies the immanent presence of the absent beloved, so the speaker prophesies a future fluttering presence, his inspired son (now, in a manner of speaking, Barbauld's 'stranger' within, or inner creative self, only displaced across a generation). The dialectical movement of the poem requires the appearance of a different kind of agency; the nugatory power of superstition for bringing about presence must be replaced by the effective agency of a deep willing self or spirit which nature will 'mould', or the father foretell. Either the father is an inspired 'echo' of the Great universal Teacher who may truly prophesy (because a true poet) or the Great universal Teacher is a mere echo of the father who creates his son in his own image (in part through the agency of 'prophecy'), in the manner of a coercive shaping of a passive subject (a 'blind mechanism' [*BL*: I, 116]). The philosophical shorthand for these alternatives is Kant and (David) Hartley. The first alternative carries forward the poem's dialectical movement while the second collapses it into the Gothic nightmare of 'necessitarianism',[111] the 'phantasmal chaos of association' [*BL*: I, 116], where the horror of Hartley, the son, is that he is, indeed, creatively speaking, an instance of the philosophy of his namesake, David, the product of blind mechanism, as if his name were a perverse destiny.

As the poem develops, 'stranger' becomes an ever more slippery word, as Thomas Greene notes:

> The very word "stranger" applied hopefully to the film focusses a paradox emerging from the poem. In a sense it's the wrong word, since the film portends a visit from a friend – one who is a stranger only in the sense of living at a distance and unlikely to put in an appearance. The word "stranger" really means its opposite, by a metamorphosis akin to the shift from the alien film to a loved one, one's second self.[112]

The 'stranger' initially appears the obverse of Barbauld's or Young's; not the stranger within, but the 'silly wandering mind' estranged from its deeper self or soul. The film can only signify the 'stranger', in Barbauld's or Young's sense, in the completion of prophecy (where the 'stranger' calls to mind a non-solipsistic communion with the true, creative, inner self, in a manner analogous to the superstitious augury; that is, through a promised presence invoked by what it is not). Coleridge's final revision seals off the double sense of 'stranger', locking in the forward movement of the poem through its terse characterization of his meditation as an instance of the baffled mind ('and makes a Toy of Thought'), a depression preparatory to the spring forward through his promised second-self, the regenerate Hartley. It locks it in, because the 1798 version loosely allows another construction. It presents projection as an innocent habit of the 'self-watching subtilizing mind' (Stillinger 1994: 155); and what it apparently projects is its own self onto the film:

> But still the living spirit in our frame,
> That loves not to behold a lifeless thing,
> Transfuses into all it's own delights
> It's own volition ... (Stillinger 1994: 155)

The 1798 version toys with the thought that the 'stranger', the 'sooty revenant',[113] is an image of the 'stranger within', the inner creative self. If the poet's meditative (and creative) self projects itself onto the film, because of a fanciful similarity, then the thought naturally arises that just as the self is like the film, the film is like the self – that is, just so much dancing carbon, a mysterious materiality. The point is underlined by yet another doubling, the repetition of the frost's secret ministry, of process without external motion, with the stranger on the grate (the film dances, even though the flame 'quivers not'). In other words, even as the poem works towards a transcendental version of the creative imagination, emancipated from materiality (with the poet's hopes concentrated in the figure of Hartley, the son), the complex patterning of the poem permits a contrary reading of doubling rather than dialectic, where Hartley, the materialist philosopher, predominates, rather than Hartley the idealized son and creative second self.

The footnote informing us that 'In all parts of the kingdom these films are called *strangers*' was dropped by Coleridge after 1812, a move that seems logical enough, given the alleged ubiquity of the practice. However, it is also consistent with the general drift of Coleridge's revisions, which is to remove the textual features linking the poem to the Gothic. As the footnote tell us, the belief is a superstition about a supernatural power, the germ of many a Gothic tale. If we come at the poem from the direction of the Gothic, the poem's meaning is plain enough. Leonard Tennenhouse has argued that the cultural work performed by the Gothic is to ask of that culture, what is the worst? the 'whatever else, but not that'? And having asked the question, the Gothic supplies an answer, secreted in the text. For Coleridge, in 1798, but increasingly so afterwards, the 'whatever else, but not that' was that the soul, or self, was, indeed, a material residue, a 'film' wafted by a mysterious and chaotic breeze. To put it in Barbauld's terms, it's as if, in the moment of sublime exaltation (awed, say, by the prepotent ministry of nature), one turned inward to find a stranger there, and encountered a mere 'sooty revanant'. For anyone schooled in the Gothic, 'Frost at Midnight' leaps out as a poem about doubling, doubles, and dopplegangers, with the dancing film a kind of imp of the perverse egging the meditative speaker on to think what must not be thought. As is often the case in Gothic, the horror turns on the literalization of an erstwhile metaphor, so that the 'stranger' (within) becomes a wafted material film. The terse, final revision of lines 20–3 may initially sound as if it is concentrating the image of the film as a kind of Gothic mirror – a mirror in which one might glimpse the worst – but in fact it works hard to do the reverse: the speaker's 'idling spirit', far from projecting itself onto the film (thus risking double entailment), finds its thought everywhere turned back and baffled by the 'stranger', which rejects 'projection'. To put matters at their simplest, in the 1798 version it's as if the meditative self were saying to the film 'I can see myself in you', whereas in the last, the speaker is saying, 'I can get no purchase on you; I only see myself reflected back to me; my thought is simply turned back on itself.' Of course, one can argue the cat is out of the bag, and without too much syntactic violence read the final version's 'idling spirit' as also referring to the anthropomorphized film, in which case Coleridge finds that his imp of the perverse has foiled him again. Similarly, one can interpret the elision of the final six lines (in which the idling 'stranger' is repeated in and by the fluttering babe) as another attempt to stifle the intellectual ghost of Hartley, the philosopher, appearing, disconcertingly, in the place of the idealized son.

As a mass literary phenomenon I think it possible to view the Gothic as following on, historically, from the kind of ideological work G. J. Barker-Benfield has influentially attributed to sensibility. For Barker-Benfield, sensibility is the natural consequence of social pressures created by an accelerating commercial culture that seeks to cultivate a fashion for the appetitive, consuming self, while ensuring that the desire that was constantly being elicited was simultaneously disciplined to express itself in socially responsible ways.[114] The Gothic belongs to a later stage of capitalist growth, distinguished, in part, by an explosion in print and print media. In this context, 'genius' follows the same cultural logic as sensibility. On the one hand, the Romantic cult of personality, the unprecedented interest in the writer's psychology, the mysterious depths of his genius, and the 'originality' that flows from it, helped brand a writer's work as something distinctive from the flood of other literary products; individualism was, in this context, a desirable commodity. On the other hand, 'genius' was regulative, insofar as it embedded 'depth' within a semi-religious discourse. Writing in the Dissenting *Eclectic Review*, John Foster compliments Coleridge on his ability to negotiate the fine line between a liberal yet Christian belief in a supreme being and pantheism (or worse).

> His mind lives almost habitually in a state of profound sympathy with nature, maintained through the medium of a refined illusion of genius, which informs all nature with a kind of soul and sentiment, that brings all its forms and entities, animate and inanimate, visible and invisible, into a mystical communion with his feelings.[115]

Coleridge's tactful 'devotion' (as Barbauld would term it) 'turns all things into their ghosts'; and as a consequence listening to Coleridge was like hearing the echoing voice of someone speaking from a deep shaft.[116] In Foster's discourse, genius, depth and religion are all of a piece.

In the Gothic, tropes of ghosts and depths and eerie voices become the genre's stock features, part of its selling formula. The Gothic in this respect is not separate from the cultural logic that produced Romanticism, but is part-and-parcel of it, the difference being that in the Gothic the glamorous aspect of a literary celebrity culture, with its cult of genius, depth and deep selves – the stranger within – becomes endlessly reworked, as haunting, the spectral and the phantasmal.[117] In 'Frost at Midnight' Coleridge skirts the Gothic, eliciting a dark counter-narrative of doubling and suppressing it at the same time, perhaps most profoundly in insisting on the originality of the experience, and the poem that expresses it, while flirting with the 'original' from William Cowper's *The Task*, knowledge of which threatens to turn Coleridge's poem into a copy of an original, and therefore, in Coleridge's terms, into an empty eggshell, or counterfeit.[118] I earlier quoted the following from Tilottama Rajan, as an example of the Kantian camp of Romantic criticism: 'The marriage between the spirit of desire and the body of the world often taken for granted in post-Kantian idealism proves precarious and inevitably brings human creativity up against a radical self-doubt'. Institutionalized Romanticism has invested a great deal in reading Romantic poetry as a precarious balance between the reaching and overreaching of the autonomous subject (and to an extent this also goes for much New Historicist criticism). We (that is to say, those of us raised in Romanticism's institutionalized critical practices) are schooled in, and are adept at, locating within the Romantic poem the moment in which the poet projects and overprojects onto nature; when the poet mistakes rhetoric for presence; or when, overreaching, the poet suspects the rhetorical structure is unravelling. As a consequence we are at home in poetry, in which, like 'Frost at Midnight', the Romantic ideology is put in play, with the success, failure or meaning of the exertions of the autonomous self to effect a marriage between 'the spirit of desire and the body of the world' being largely a matter of theoretical preference. As a consequence those poets, such as Barbauld, who read the world in resolutely social and political terms simply do not sound, or feel, 'Romantic', as they lack the Romantic 'depth' that comes from a hermeneutic of a presence that is radically indeterminate.

But if we judge from Barbauld's perspective, poets such as Coleridge are caught up in the factitious glamour of personality, of 'depth', of 'individualism', where there is scant difference between the abstruse musing of 'Frost at Midnight' – with its 'maze of metaphysical lore' – and the Gothic nonsense of spectral presences. For Barbauld, both Coleridge's inward turn and the commercial chaos of Minerva represent a turning away from, or fracturing through sheer noise, of the republic of letters, a rational public sphere in which the actual interests of the individual might be advanced. From Barbauld's perspective 'Frost at Midnight' does not represent the empowering meditation of an individual but a self-indulgent playing in the ideology of individualism, where spectres of depth, doubles and transcendent originals are mere fractal expressions of a false consciousness generated by a newly accelerating print culture, from which she, herself, was deeply alienated.

Late in life Barbauld returned to her extended conversation with Coleridge by essaying a version of Coleridge's foundational conversation poem. *The First Fire*, produced in 1815, was written at a time when Barbauld's initial hopes, and subsequent fears, for Coleridge were already amply confirmed. Her poem resolutely sticks to an Enlightenment mode of social utility.[119] Reading it one hears none of the Romantic music of a projective self and receptive nature meeting and disjoining. In the usual sense of the phrase, it is not a Romantic poem. But to concur in this judgment is simply to repeat the aesthetic values of a Counter-Enlightenment that was already in process at the time Barbauld elected not to publish her poem. Jerrold E. Hogle has analysed how 'Frost at Midnight' plays with what he calls the 'ghost of the counterfeit'.[120] As Hogle explains, the Gothic revival, or 'neo-Gothic', amounted to the 'refaking of a fake', in that it recalls the Renaissance, the period in which 'Gothic' was first used to signal a nostalgic breach with an even earlier period – the Medieval – allegedly distinguished by signs anchored in an unchanging social reality. The Gothic recalls, not a moment of signifying stability, but an earlier historical moment in which signs were first 'counterfeited' as a stay against the radical mobility of signifieds in the modern, commercial world. In Hogle's reading, the 'stranger' veers between the uncanny (in that it betokens an identity that was once familiar, possibly in a deep, primitive sense, but which is now shrouded in superstitious fear) and a more prosaic sense that is arguably worse, where 'stranger' is mobile and attachable to anyone or anything. In his aesthetics Coleridge sought to reground the modern mobility of signs, above all in what we have come to call the Romantic symbol, a transcendent image capable of defeating the purely arbitrary. For Hogle, the ghost of the counterfeit haunts Romantic poetry because it signifies the linguistic condition of modernity abjected by Romantic poets, such as Coleridge, as they endeavoured to erect the transcendental structure of Romantic symbolism. Building on boggy ground, the repressed was bound to seep back in. Never tempted by the maze, it is easy to dismiss Barbauld as singularly un-Romantic, a writer who did not fit her time; but then we would miss the ways she did, indeed, fit, together with the challenges posed by her writing.

Notes

Introduction

1. See St. Clair 2004: table 12.1, 217.
2. *SP*: 395.
3. Montgomery 1833: 378–9.
4. Curran 1986: 15.
5. St. Clair 2004: 87.
6. Smail 2003.
7. Wrigley 1983.
8. St. Clair 2004: table 3.1, 54, 120.
9. Bourdieu 1999: 5.
10. Bourdieu 1999: 6.
11. Bourdieu 1999: 31.
12. Butler 1979: 4; see also Briggs 1991.
13. Siskin 1988: 12.
14. The classic study in this change is Poovey 1984.
15. For recent explorations of this view, see Galperin 2003; Tuite 2002.
16. Jeffrey 1802.
17. McGann 1983: 19.
18. Kermode 1961.
19. Cronin 2000: 3.
20. Cronin 2000: 3–4, 9.
21. Schmidt 2006: 651, 655.
22. For instance, see Schmidt 2000b.
23. Sheehan 2003.
24. Sheehan 2003: para. 31.
25. O'Brien 2005: 243–4.
26. O'Brien 2005: 245.
27. Berlin 1979: 1–24. For sample critiques, see *Encyclopedia of the Enlightenment* 2000; Schmidt 2000a.
28. Sheehan 2003: para. 18.
29. For example, see Leighton 1999; McMahon 1998 and 2001; Wolin 2004.
30. McMahon 1998: 86; and 2001: 43–6.
31. Berlin, 'The Counter-Enlightenment' and 'Joseph de Maistre and the Origins of Fascism' (1990): 91–174; and 1999.
32. McMahon 2001: 95–106.
33. Maxwell 2001. Maxwell argues that Scott's 'synthesis between simultaneity and synchronicity' was a key feature of Scott's originality. 'Simultaneity' invokes historical change on a global scale, while 'synchronicity' suggests that the meaning of such a crisis-ridden past is universally available; however, the past that is available is one that narrates irrevocable change.
34. Hobsbawm 1990: 84.
35. Russell and Tuite, 'Introducing Romantic Sociability' (2002: 1–21).
36. Cronin 8–9; and Christensen 1994: 457–60.
37. Schwarzmantel 1998: 63.

38. Mackintosh 1813: 206.
39. For a discussion on how psychoanalytical abjection and Romantic misfitting relate, see Miles 2001a; and cf. Nancy Armstrong, 'How the Misfit Became a Moral Protagonist' (2005: 27–52).
40. For the public sphere and literary correspondence see Goodman 1994: 15–21; for Freemasonry, see Jacobs 1991; for coffee houses, see Clery 2004: 13–25; for the dissenting academies, see White 2007; Paulin 1999; and Roe 1997.
41. For an account of this tension, see Calhoun 1992a: 40; for Habermas's response to his critics, see Habermas 1992a: 463–4.
42. Austin 1962.
43. 'A portion of the public sphere comes into being in every conversation in which private individuals assemble to form a public body' (Jürgen Habermas, quoted by Theresa M. Kelley n.d.).
44. Fraser 1992; Mellor 1994; and, in answer to it, Wang 1994.
45. Habermas 1992b: 427–9.
46. This is the broad tenor of the articles assembled by John Klancher in a special issue on Romanticism and the public sphere, in *Studies in Romanticism* 33 (1994).
47. Eley 1992: 280.
48. Quoted Gilmartin 1994: 550.
49. Eley 1992: 290.
50. Quoted Bruce Robbins, quoted in Gilmartin 1994: 549.
51. I describe the 'radical underground' that developed amid the ruins of the public sphere: see McCalman 1988.
52. For an extended discussion of these codes, see Miles 2005b.

1. The Original Misfit

1. See Baines 1994 and 1999; Bate 1993; Grebanier 1966; Groom 2002; Haywood 1986; Kahan 1998; McGowen 1993/94; Mair 1938; Martin 1995; Schoenbaum 1991.
2. William Henry Ireland 1805 (1969): Preface, n.p.
3. William Henry Ireland 1805 (1969): 6.
4. Grebanier 1966: 50–3.
5. Greig 1922: I, 1133.
6. Croft 1780: 92–3.
7. See W. H. Ireland, Letter to Samuel Ireland (undated), London: British Library manuscripts, Additional 30, 346: 307.
8. Brewer 2004; Novak 1997: 190.
9. Armstrong 1987: 4; Moretti 1987: 4–5; Siskin 1988: 12.
10. See McDayter 1999: 43–62. McDayter argues that Byron's dangerous charisma was troped as vampirism.
11. Habermas 1990: 50.
12. Habermas 1990: 50.
13. Brewer 1997: 56–124.
14. *London Review* 1.14 (1860): 321. Samuel Ireland's background was in fact more mysterious. According to Grebanier, Samuel studied architecture, was awarded a medal by the Society of Arts in 1760, becoming an honorary member of the Royal Academy in 1768, when he quit architecture to start a silk weaving business in Spitalfields (Grebanier 1966: 42).

15. 'The Progress of Engraving in England', *Gentleman's Magazine* 59 (1789): 404.
16. According to W. H. Ireland, Sandby was Samuel Ireland's art teacher, whose instruction rendered Ireland's style 'more free' (YI Folio Ireland, W. 287917, Huntington Library).
17. Grebanier 1966: 50–3.
18. See Schoenbaum 1991: 132.
19. Malone 1796: 15.
20. Samuel Ireland 1796a.
21. British Library Manuscripts, Additional 30, 346: 264.
22. William Henry Ireland, rev. of *An Authentic Account of the Shakespearian Forgeries*, *Gentleman's Magazine* 66 (1796): 1101. See also *True Briton* (22 December 1796); *Herald* (23 December 1796); and *Oracle* (26 December 1796), collected in British Library Manuscripts, Additional 30, 349: 107, 110.
23. William Henry Ireland 1796; 1832. Ireland made numerous short defences of his fabrications, first in the preface to *The Abbess* (1799), and then anonymously in later works such as *Chalcographimania* (1814) and *Scribbleomania* (1815).
24. By 'Sir Bertram' Ireland presumably means Sir Bertrand, the eponymous hero of 'Sir Bertrand, a Fragment', by Anna Laetitia and John Aikin (1773).
25. Ireland 1832: iii–iv.
26. Martelli 1962: 40.
27. Brewer 2004: 20.
28. *Gentleman's Magazine* 49 (1779): 210.
29. Burgess 1995: xiv. See also Brewer 2004: 47.
30. Dawes 1779b: 15–16.
31. Croft 1780: 275.
32. Novak 1997: 193.
33. Briggs 1991: 255.
34. *St. James's Chronicle*, or *British Evening Post* (Thursday 15 April to Saturday 17 April); *General Advertiser, and Morning Intelligencer* (Monday 19 April).
35. Novak 1997: 193.
36. The statement occurs in the advertisement for the fifth edition, which is pasted into the British Library's copy of Dawes, *The Case and Memoirs of the Late Rev. Mr. James Hackman* (1779).
37. *Gentleman's Magazine* 50 (1780): 288.
38. *Gentleman's Magazine* 49 (1779): 210.
39. *Gentleman's Magazine* 50 (1780): 287.
40. See Duff 1767 (1964); 1973; and Gerard 1774.
41. Young 1759: 53.
42. See Lynch 1998.
43. Moretti 1987: 4–5.
44. British Library Manuscripts, Additional 30, 346: 288.
45. British Library Manuscripts, Additional 30, 346: 52.
46. British Library Manuscripts, Additional 30, 346: 229.
47. British Library Manuscripts, Additional 30, 346.
48. Schoenbaum 1991: 154–5.
49. British Library Manuscripts, Additional 30, 346: 202–3. Samuel Ireland confides his 'thoughts on the subject of the ms. Papers'. Although he fears that the papers might be forgeries he thinks his son is only a pawn used 'to exculpate the grand mover in the business'. Even then he appears to believe that the accusation of forgery is being used as a smokescreen for a deeper game.

50. See Huntingdon Library (YI Folio Ireland, W. 287917), and the Robert H. Taylor Collection, Ireland's Confession, Firestone Library, Princeton.
51. If Farington is correct about Mrs. Freeman's background, unlike the indigent Martha Ray, she did not compromise herself with Sandwich through the desire for wealth. As a woman of respectable family and fortune, she had everything to lose, and very little to gain.
52. W. H. Ireland 1832: xiii.
53. The article is W. H. Ireland's obituary from Cobbet's *Register*, but is pasted, without date or page numbers, in British Library Manuscripts, Additional 37, 831.
54. Letter to W. H. Ireland (15 June 1796), British Library Manuscripts, Additional 30, 346: 244–6 (244).
55. British Library Manuscripts, Additional 30, 347: 25.
56. As Benjamin Fisher comments, Ireland was an infallible 'barometer of the early nineteenth-century literary climate' (Ireland 1799: x), and thus an astute guide to the changing scene of Romantic-era literary culture.
57. H.-P. Coll. 321.
58. H.-P. Coll. 321.
59. For a recent treatment of the vexed facts of Savage's biography, see Holmes 1994.
60. Holmes 1994: 119.
61. Holmes 1994: 136.
62. Quoted Holmes 1994: 135–6.
63. Holmes 1994: 52.
64. Boaden 1831: I, 297.
65. The affair is detailed in H.-P. Coll. 323.
66. W. H. Ireland 1832: vi. In his preface to the 1799 edition of the play, Samuel Ireland makes the same point. See <http://www.lib.rochester.edu/camelot/ireland.htm> (accessed 12 April 2008).
67. The reviews are collected in Samuel Ireland, British Library Manuscripts, Additional 30, 349.
68. Boaden 1: 297
69. On 4 February 1801, Ireland wrote to Kemble asking his assistance in having his play read for production at Drury Lane, supposing him a gentleman above 'private pique'. Kemble reassured Ireland that such 'prejudice' was groundless and 'stupid' and that he 'heartily' hoped Ireland would succeed. See H.-P. Coll. 321.
70. As discussed in the Introduction, revisionist attacks on Habermas frequently concentrate on the threats posed to his theory by the multiplicity of publics in the 1790s. For Kevin Gilmartin (1994), recognizing this diversity (and its fluctuations) is to provide Habermas's theory with historical nuance; for Geoff Eley (1992: 306), such proliferation severely tests it; while for John Klancher (1987: 98), it threatens to undermine it altogether. I argue that the fragmenting of the bourgeois public sphere is less crucial than the dissolving of the belief in the public sphere as a normative ideal, as the dissolution robbed 'public sphering' of its performative meaning. For further discussion, see the Introduction and Miles 2005b.
71. Habermas 1990: 53.
72. Miles 2005b.
73. See Miles 2005b: 335–6.
74. Scrivener 2007: 3.
75. Mathias (as Antenor) 1800: 9–10.
76. Malone 1796: 5.
77. Miles 2005b: 329–30.
78. Huntington Library HM 31427: 3.

79. Pronouncing on the Chatterton case, Malone stated that only those with a taste for, and a critical knowledge of, English poetry from the time of Chaucer to Pope are competent to judge the spuriousness of the Rowley poems (1781). Malone's comments made him notorious among more liberal members of the republic of letters.

2. Gothic Wordsworth

1. Simpson 1987: 161.
2. Chard 1972.
3. Jacobus 1976: 7.
4. Gamer 2000: 90–126; Trott 2000.
5. See Clery 1995; Gamer 2000; James Watt 1999.
6. For fast moving, see Miles 2002b; for ubiquitous, see Garside 2000: II, 56.
7. The works of Abbé Barruel and John Robison, from late in the decade, are conventionally credited with introducing into Britain the belief that a conspiracy of Illuminati were seeking European-wide revolution after their successes in France. However, as Seamus Deane points out, Burke had long-established links with Barruel, and was a significant co-author of the conspiracy theory of recent history (Deane 1988: 11). The editors of the *Edinburgh Review* thought this theory deplorable enough to devote the lead article of the first issue to the matter, through a review of Joseph Mournier's myth-puncturing attack on Barruel.
8. Burke 1987: 66.
9. Christie 2000.
10. Wordsworth 1988: 275. Subsequent references are cited parenthetically in the text, abbreviated as *SP*.
11. Chard notes that Wordsworth and Christie were both in Paris at the time the latter wrote his reply to Burke and that they shared the same publisher, Joseph Johnson (Chard 1972: 126–7). For the similarities between Christie's reply and Wordsworth's *Letter to the Bishop of Llandaff,* see Chard 1972: 137–8.
12. Castle 1992.
13. Coleridge 1971: 30.
14. Chandler 1984: 17.
15. Duggett 2007. Also see Miles 2002b.
16. Paulin 1999: 148.
17. Wordsworth 1982: 38.
18. Rieder 1997: 32.
19. Review of *The Poetical Works of William Wordsworth* and *Selections from the Poems of William Wordsworth*, *Quarterly Review* LII (1834): 317–57 (338).
20. Bromwich 1998: 23–43.
21. Eliot 1981: 243.
22. Hayden 1971: 34.
23. Charles Burney (Review of *Lyrical Ballads*, *Monthly Review*, XXIX [June 1799]: 203), quoted Jacobus (1976: 160). Of course Wordsworth was not alone in importing the novel's concern with 'unmerited distress' into poetry: one could also point to Anna Letitia Barbauld, Charlotte Smith, Helen Maria Williams and Thomas Cowper, among others. Even so, this migration of the novel's concerns into poetry struck contemporary reviewers as distinctly odd, a feeling compounded by the particular intensity, and lack of ritualized presentation, in Wordsworth's writing.

24. Bromwich 1998: 40.
25. Wordsworth 1979. See Preface, x–xi, for the textual history of the poem.
26. Wordsworth 1979: 57, *Ruined Cottage* (ll. 208–13).
27. Wordsworth 1979: 59, *Ruined Cottage* (ll. 221–36).
28. Gamer 2000: 13.
29. Wordsworth, *Prelude*, XI, 171–6. All references from *The Prelude*, unless indicated, are taken from Wordsworth 1972.
30. Porter 2000.
31. See Jay 1993: 69. Jay argues that an antiocularcentric bias has crept into Western culture since the beginning of the Romantic period, which Jay sees as 'imbued with a profound suspicion of vision and its hegemonic role in the modern era' (14).
32. Wood 2001: 7.
33. See Altick 1978.
34. Wordsworth, 'Preface to *Lyrical Ballads*', *SP*: 284.
35. As Gamer shows, this pressure led Wordsworth to equate the Gothic and the picturesque as similar expressions of 'false taste', from 1800 onwards (Gamer 2000: 21).
36. Kames 1774.
37. For the pervasiveness of ideal presence in eighteenth-century aesthetics, see Miles 1999.
38. Jonathan Crary provides a helpful take on Wordsworth's dilemma. Wordsworth's anti-visual animus, or anti-commercial instincts, had this self-defeating consequence: by stressing the importance of the individual to revolve back within himself in order to glimpse presence (idealizing the ideal) he was helping to disseminate the discursive construction of the isolated observer (a pure eye, detached from touch) that was to become the discursive construction of the modern consumer of the 'spectacle' (Crary 1990).
39. Wordsworth 1984b: 72, ll. 359–60.
40. Wordsworth 1984b: 74, ll. 385–8.
41. Wordsworth 1975; 127, ll. 136–44.
42. Sedgwick 1986.
43. Hartley 1794: 14.
44. Miles 2002c.
45. Wordsworth 1975a: 127, ll. 154–62.
46. Wordsworth 1940–49: IV, 463.
47. Wordsworth 1982.
48. Wordsworth 1975a: 138, ll. 406–14.
49. For Wordsworth's extension of Radcliffe's explained supernatural, see Trott 2000: 47.
50. Wordsworth 1975a: 126, ll. 118–26.
51. Wordsworth 1975a: 127, l. 131.
52. Stafford and Terpak 2001: 86.
53. Castle 1995: 141.
54. Wordsworth 1975a: 154, ll. 820–8; 1975c: 236.
55. Gatrell 1994: 8–9.
56. Wordsworth 1975b: 281–2, ll. 658–66.
57. Gill 1989: 99.
58. 'The drop' was a euphemism for hanging. For a discussion of the purpose of the pun, see Hamilton 1986: 35.
59. Bialostosky 1992: 12.

60. As reported by Coleridge (*BL*: II: 49).
61. Simpson 1987: 161.
62. Wordsworth, 'The Thorn' (1992): 80, l. 115. Wordsworth's later revision of the line ('Full twenty years are past and gone') makes the time reference exact.
63. Wordsworth, 'The Thorn' (1992): 77, ll. 1–22.
64. For Martha Ray's trials before the press, see Brewer 2004.
65. Mighall 2000.
66. Wordsworth 1982: 62.
67. Wordsworth 1982: 67.
68. Wordsworth 1982: 66.
69. Hume 1758.
70. Wordsworth 1982: IV, ii, 133–9.
71. For the equation of rational dissent with 'enthusiasm' see Mee 2003; and McMahon 2001.
72. For the turn to Burke, see Deane (1988: 41) and Chandler (1984: xviii). Chandler argues that Wordsworth's turn to Burke preceded *The Prelude* – in fact, began with the completion of *The Borderers*. It is a position I follow.
73. For example, Thomas Christie called the phrase a contradiction in terms, like 'square circle', while for Joseph Priestley the phrase signalled humiliating self-abasement (see Clery 1995: 245–6).
74. Liu 1989: 484.
75. The phrase 'love of distinction' is a Godwinism, for whom it signifies class consciousness and a corrupting, material acquisitiveness: Godwin 1796: I, 332. Wordsworth recurs to the phrase in *Reply to Mathetes* (1809) where it also represents the desire for the wrong kind of fame (*SP*: 114).
76. Simpson 1987: 161.
77. Gill 1998: 23.
78. Williams 2002: 89.
79. In his review of the *Poems in Two Volumes* (1807) James Montgomery found Wordsworth's claim that 'A poet . . . is no ordinary man' but one with 'more than usual organic sensibility', that is, biologically different, strange enough to make a point of it (Hayden 1971: 29). Wordsworth makes the claim in the 'Preface to the *Lyrical Ballads*' (*SP*: 283).
80. Gill 1998: 20.
81. Rieder 1997: 20.
82. Siskin 1990.
83. *Quarterly Review* 29 (1816): 187–201.
84. Hobsbawm 1990.
85. Wordsworth 1852.
86. Goldberg 1996: 681–706.
87. For example, see Alison 1790.
88. Alison 1790: 9–13.
89. From 'Lines (Left upon a Seat in a Yew-Tree)'. Fittingly the poem opposes the 'pure of heart', not to, say, a man of business (the usual suspect) but to a neglected genius who has turned his isolation into a source of pride, perverting the very love of nature that otherwise distinguishes him. The *Quarterly Review* wants to promote socially responsible geniuses, like Wordsworth, who respond to neglect by remaining 'pure of heart', and devoted to nature, rather than turning inward and cultivating socially irresponsible 'supernatural intellects'.
90. Lowell 1904: 125.

3. The Romantic Abject: Cagliostro, Carlyle, Coleridge

1. Thomas Carlyle on Count Cagliostro: Carlyle 1869: V, 64–126. The essay was first published in 1833 in *Fraser's Magazine*. All future references cited parenthetically in the text.
2. I am indebted to Paul Hamilton for first putting me onto this line of enquiry.
3. Kristeva 1983.
4. On historicizing abjection, see Miles 2001a; and Armstrong 2005.
5. Goethe's *The Great Cophta*, and Schiller's *The Ghost-Seer*, both adopt critical positions towards Cagliostro. Mozart's treatment of the Masonic sect in *The Magic Flute* takes a more positive view, but it is unclear whether Cagliostro is explicitly intended, as he is in the works by Goethe and Schiller.
6. McCalman 2003; Gervaso 1974; Dumas 1966.
7. Jacobs 1991.
8. For the death of Cagliostro, see McCalman 2003.
9. For instance, Henry Ridgely Evans, author of *Cagliostro and His Egyptian Rite of Freemasonry* (1930), was himself, as the title page declares, 'Inspector General Honorary of the Supreme Council, 33° , Ancient and Accepted Scottish Rite of Freemasonry for the Southern Jurisdiction of the United States'.
10. Carlyle, *Frederick the Great*, quoted in Schmidt 2006: 648.
11. Carlyle 1869: V, 131–200; Castle 1995: 11.
12. For Clifford Siskin, such a formation is simultaneously a function of disciplinarity – of the new discipline called 'Literature' – and the expression of discursive power. 'Romanticism deepened' the 'mystery' of professionalism 'by producing the deep self'. Thus, far from being 'the culmination of English Romanticism, as the anthologies insist, the 1830s marked the moment in which the constructs and strategies of Romantic texts became "normal" within and for the very culture that had produced them' (1990: 305). Written precisely at this historical moment Carlyle's essay suggests that such 'constructs and strategies' had become 'normal' at the level of identity formation, through the psychological and cultural process of abjection.
13. Carlyle 1971: 15.
14. Carlyle 1971: 316–17.
15. Carlyle 1971: 317.
16. Sanders 1977: 53.
17. Sanders 1977: 42–53 (53).
18. Carlyle 1972: 251.
19. Sanders 1977: 40.
20. Sanders 1977: 40.
21. Sanders 1977: 42.
22. Sanders 1977: 42.
23. Sanders 1977: 43.
24. Sanders 1977: 48.
25. Sanders 1977: 60.
26. For example, see Preston 1801: 46.
27. Crawford 1998: 22–36.
28. Hamilton 1983: 4–6.
29. As James Engell and Walter Jackson Bate point out in their notes, Coleridge is here closely following Schelling (*BL*: I, 152, n. 2).
30. See Wheeler 1981.

31. Coleridge 1956: I, 112.
32. Castle 1995: 140–67.
33. See *BL*: I, 169, n. 2, for examples.
34. See McKusick 1985.
35. Roe 1988. Coleridge is in fact quoting himself from *The Watchman* (see *BL*: I, 190, n. 1).
36. Cronin 2000. Cronin shows how during his Unitarian phase Coleridge appealed to both an 'Elect' of 'Philosophers and Bards' and the 'common Reader', an ambivalence he later covered up as his allegiance shifted from the materialism of Priestley and Hartley to Berkeleyan Neoplatonism.
37. Coleridge 1957: 1623.
38. *The Anti-Jacobin Review and Magazine; or, Monthly Political and Literary Censor* 1 (1798): iii.
39. S. T. Coleridge, 'Dejection: An Ode', in Coleridge 1969: 366, ll. 85–6.
40. According to Griggs, Coleridge's opium addiction only began in May 1801 as a result of self-medication for a swollen knee, the complaint Coleridge mentions to Poole in his letter of 17 May. If so, Coleridge's creative crisis predates his addiction.
41. To Thomas Poole (23 March 1801), 'Newton was a mere materialist – Mind in his system is always passive – a lazy Looker-on on an external World. If the mind be not passive, if it be indeed made in God's Image, & that too in the sublimest sense – the Image of the Creator – there is ground for suspicion, that any system built on the Passiveness of the mind must be false, as a system' (Coleridge 1956: II, 709 [letter 388]).

4. The Romantic-era Novel

1. Watt 1957; McKeon 1987; and, more recently, Armstrong 2005.
2. Garside, Raven and Schöwerling 2000. See in particular Raven 2000: I, 72; and Garside 2000: II, 38.
3. Kiely 1972; Johnson 1995. For a discussion, see Miles 2001b.
4. Garside 2000: II, 63–76.
5. Grenby 2001.
6. For an idiosyncratic but not untypical example of New Critical contempt for allegory in the Romantic novel, see Winters, 'Maule's Curse: Hawthorne and the Problem of Allegory' (1947).
7. Southam 1968: 1–34.
8. Scott 1950: 135, 400.
9. Whateley 1821.
10. For a discussion, and examples, of Godwin's 'foppery of style', see Miles 2005a: xli.
11. See Miles 2003: 61–109.
12. Homer Obed Brown 1997: 180–3. As Brown notes, a key aspect of this moment was the publication of a series of editions of the British novels that effectively created the modern canon, that is, Barbauld's *British Novelists* (1810) and Scott's Ballantyne's Novelist's Library (1821–24). See also Armstrong 2005: 21; and Johnson 2001: 163–79.
13. Godwin 1831: v–vi.
14. Garside 2000: II, 44–5 and 74–5.
15. Homer Obed Brown 1997, cited Armstrong 2005: 7.

16. Armstrong 2005: 7.
17. For example, he says of Radcliffe that she 'has the most decided claim to take her place among the favoured few, who have been distinguished as the founders of a class, or school': Sir Walter Scott 1968: 110; see also 103. Further references are cited parenthetically in the text. Scott makes the same approving claim with regards to Walpole's *Castle of Otranto* (85) and Shelley's *Frankenstein* (260).
18. Kermode 1975: 108.
19. Gamer 2005.
20. P. D. Garside 1986; 1991. Cf. The Walter Scott Digital Archive, Edinburgh University Library, <http://www.walterscott.lib.ed.ac.uk/works/novels/waverley.html> (accessed 14 April 2008).
21. Gamer 2005.
22. Scott 1986: 4. Further references are cited parenthetically in the text.
23. Gamer 2005.
24. Ferris 1991: 123–5; and 1996.
25. Carlyle 1869: I, 32.
26. Watt 1957: 9–34.
27. Gamer 2005.
28. In Michael McKeon's terms, 'novel' and 'romance' accrue differential meanings only because of the recursive, dialectical relationships between varieties of narrative form: see McKeon 1987. For Armstrong, realism and the Gothic exist in a 'mutually defining relationship' (2005: 3).
29. For a relatively recent example of Austen's expulsion from Romanticism, see McGann 1983: 19.
30. For example, Kiely influentially dubbed the Romantic novel 'schizoid' (1972: 26).
31. Murray 1805: 8.
32. Murray 1805: 8–10.
33. See Beattie 1783; Barbauld 1810.
34. Murray 1805: 1.
35. Murray 1805: 154.
36. Murray 1805: 152.
37. Murray 1805: 154.
38. Austen 1995: 176.
39. For an extended defence of this assertion, see Miles 1999a.
40. Terence John Martin 1961.
41. Godwin 1793: I, 20.
42. Mathias 2004: 7.
43. Quoted Grenby 2001: 13.
44. Gamer 1999.
45. See Miles 2002: 56–7.
46. See McKeon who reads the story of Tom Jones, the foundling, 'wandering in search of his patrimony', as a parody of Bonnie Prince Charlie searching for his (1987: 418).
47. See Gellner 1983; and 1998; Hobsbawm 1990; Anderson 1991.
48. Smith 1987; Kliger 1952.
49. 'Political Vampyres', in Clery and Miles 2000: 24–5.
50. Marshall Brown 2005: 34–41.
51. Hurd 1762: 120.
52. Watt 1999: 32–3.
53. Beer 1982.

54. See Ferris 1996.
55. For examples, see 'Rev. R. C. Maturin', *GM*, 1st ser., 95/1 (1825), 84–5; Review of *Melmoth the Wanderer, Edinburgh Magazine and Literary Miscellany* 87 (January 1821): 412; Review of *The Albigenses, Blackwoods Magazine* (February 1824): 192–3.
56. Maturin's nationalism bears some affinity with that of the United Irishmen; see Thuente 1992.
57. Foster 1989.
58. Henderson 1980: 86.
59. See Godwin 1796: I, 332.
60. Thelwall 1796a: 15; Duggett 2007.
61. Godwin 1982: 1.
62. Godwin 1982: 1.
63. For example, see the trial of Henry 'Redhead' Yorke, in Howell 1818: 1003–1154 (Entry 609).
64. Kramnick 1990.
65. Terence John Martin 1961.
66. Leavis 1972: 39.
67. Bewley 1959.
68. Trilling 1976: see in particular 'Manners, Morals and the Novel' and 'Art and Fortune'. Besides Bewley and Trilling, also see Chase 1958.
69. Poirier 1966: 106, 145–6.
70. Godwin 2000.
71. Quoted Leavis 1972: 24.
72. Poirier 1966: 5.
73. Galperin 2003.
74. Cronin 2003: 192.
75. Siskin 2006.
76. Galperin 2003: 2.
77. See James 1880.
78. Tuite 2002: 17.
79. Alison 1845: 347.

5. Dissent: Anna Letitia Barbauld

1. Holmes 1989: 107.
2. Mee 2003.
3. Holmes 1989: 107.
4. Hume 1758: 50.
5. Rodgers 1958: 53.
6. Mee 2003: 11–12.
7. The best measure of Coleridge's disingenuousness in seeming to link the Calvinist Brummagen with his sociable hosts in a single Dissenting culture is Coleridge's use of language. Rational Dissent scorned the apocalyptic, millenarian style of Religious Musings as the irrational, mystic language of the chapel. The real kinship was between the rhapsodic Calvinist and the enthusiastical Coleridge. See Kitson 1993.
8. Burke 1790: 15. For Hazlitt's lifelong struggle with the taunt, see Paulin 1999: 163.
9. Mee 2003: 81.

10. For Wordsworth's break with Dissenting culture, see Chard 1972: 188–228; for Coleridge's attacks on Dissenters, generally, but Mrs Barbauld in particular, see Vargo 1998.
11. Chard 1972: 188–228; Paulin 1999: 71–2.
12. For Blake's radical Antinomianism, see Mee 1992; for Blake's Moravian connections, see Schuchard 2006.
13. Philip 2006.
14. Taylor 2004.
15. Leigh Hunt's parents had a mixed Nonconformist (Quaker) and Anglican background but became 'Unitarians, universalists, and republicans' who 'supported the "new opinions" and "new tendency" of the French Revolution' (Roe 2004).
16. Paulin 1999: 2–4.
17. Braithwaite 2003: 44.
18. O'Brien 1989; Davie 1993: 29–30.
19. Turner 1957: i.
20. Turner 1957: 4.
21. O'Brien 1993; Braithwaite 2003.
22. For the importance of the Dissenting reviews, see Butler 1993: 120–47.
23. The words of Robert Hall, a renowned Baptist minister. See O'Brien 1989: 30.
24. Chandler 2004.
25. Jewson 1975: 144.
26. Jewson 1975: 7, 42.
27. Tyson 1979: 20–1.
28. Tyson 1979: 20–1.
29. Turner 1957: 26.
30. Ellis 1874: I, 250.
31. Ellis 1874: I, 25.
32. Paulin 1999: 8.
33. Paulin 1999: 122.
34. Paulin 1999: 124.
35. Paulin 1999: 148.
36. For Burke's – and Romanticism's – hostility to theory, see Simpson 1993; and Deane 1988.
37. Quoted Rodgers 1958: 44.
38. For an example of reading that takes Coleridge's break with Hartley as itself a constitutive moment in the history of English Romanticism, see Wheeler, 'The Struggle with Associationism' (1981: 1–16).
39. See Abrams 1953: 58.
40. *The Spirit of the Public Journals* (1797): iv.
41. *Anti-Jacobin Review and Magazine* (1798): 626.
42. Barbauld 2002: 11.
43. Barbauld 1994: xxxiii.
44. Vargo 1998: 55–63.
45. Ellis 1874: I, 279. The argument that Croker's review brought Barbauld's career to a premature end is made by Keach (1994). In *Mothers of the Nation* (2002), Anne Mellor makes the case that Barbauld kept writing and collecting her earlier work for publication.
46. Janovitz 2004; White 2007; Mee 2003.
47. Jonathan Wordsworth, Introduction (Barbauld 1993).
48. Barbauld 2002: 100, n. 1.
49. Barbauld 1993.

50. For instance, see Janowitz 2002. Janowitz portrays Barbauld's career as carving an increasingly radical arc.
51. Barbauld summarizes John Gregory, *A Comparative View of the State and Faculties of Man with the Animal World*. See Barbauld 2002: 211, n. 1.
52. Barbauld 2002: 211.
53. Mee 2003: 174–5.
54. Mee 2003: 175.
55. Coleman 2002.
56. McCarthy and Kraft argue that Barbauld may be characterized 'in the phrase coined by Antonio Gramsci, as an "organic intellectual," an intellectual who articulates the issues of her own social class at a time when that class is asserting its claims to power and respect' (Barbauld 2002: 13).
57. Mee argues that 'devotion' was Barbauld's word for negotiating 'the treacherous ground between enthusiasm and cold formalism' (2003: 174).
58. See Hume 1758; Barbauld 2002: 220, n. 1.
59. Superstition renders men 'tame and abject, and fits them for slavery': Hume 1758: 50.
60. Hume 1758: 50.
61. Shaftesbury 1727: I, 15–17.
62. Barbauld 2002: 216, n. 1.
63. Barbauld 2002: 334.
64. Barbauld 2002: 333.
65. Barbauld 1792c.
66. Barbauld 1792c: 46.
67. Barbauld 1792c: 46.
68. *BL*: I, 185. Coleridge first uses the phrase 'pleading to the poor and ignorant, instead of pleading for them' in *The Friend* (see *BL*: I, 185, n. 2). In the first number of *The Watchman* Coleridge's phrasing is equivocal in that he pleads for a 'diffusion of Knowledge', the most effective current agents of which are the Dissenters. Whether such a diffusion is possible, speaking over the heads of the 'poor and ignorant', is not addressed (Coleridge 1970: 11–12).
69. Barbauld 1792a: I, 4–5.
70. Barbauld 1792b: 7–8.
71. Barbauld 1792b: 13–14.
72. Barbauld 1792b: 20.
73. Burke 1790: 116.
74. Barbauld 2002: 212–13.
75. Watson 1997: 147.
76. Watts 1737: 185–8.
77. Barbauld, *A Discourse on Being Born Again* (1830): 7, 9, 10. The *Discourse* is not generally included in a list of Barbauld's works. However, it is catalogued as such by the British Library, an attribution strengthened by stylistic and thematic similarities with her other work.
78. Barbauld 1830: 7, 10.
79. Melville 1996: 285.
80. Young 1759: 51–2.
81. Young 1759: 53.
82. Sanderson 1975: 118.
83. For instance Ashton Nichols argues that *The Prelude* 'seeks to authorize and account for a new view of the "self", or more precisely, to chart one version of the emergence of the concept of "self" out of the earlier concept of "soul"...

By 1770, at the latest, a modernized version of the "soul" – called the "self" – came to require just such forms of self-definition' (1998: 10).

84. Watts 1752: vi.
85. Barbauld 2002: 98.
86. Shaftesbury 1727: I, 170.
87. Shaftesbury 1727: I, 169.
88. Mee 2003: 39–40.
89. Young 1759: 62.
90. Barbauld 1794: 10–11.
91. Judith Thompson 1997: 427.
92. Quoted in Stillinger 1994: 56.
93. Jackson 2003: 118.
94. Rajan 1980: 224; Jackson 2003: 120.
95. Jackson 2003: 122.
96. McGann 1983: 19.
97. McGann 1983: 91.
98. Ellis 1874: I, 288.
99. Jackson 2003: 123.
100. McGann 1983: 69.
101. McGann 1983: 73.
102. Rajan 1980: 225.
103. For a recent history of New Historicist criticism of Coleridge's revisions of 'Frost at Midnight', see Van Winkle 2004: 583–98.
104. McGann 1983: 66.
105. Rajan 1980: 224.
106. Rajan 1980: 225.
107. Quoted by Rajan 1980: 227.
108. Rajan 1980: 225.
109. Wheeler 1981: 2, 12.
110. Thomas Greene argues that this line hints at Coleridge's belief that 'all imaginative writing derives from a certain experience of privation' (1995: 908).
111. As Wheeler points out, the trope that nature is an infallible scene of instruction for the innocent or benevolent soul is pure Hartley (1981: 4).
112. Greene 1995: 920.
113. Van Winkle 2004: 587.
114. Barker-Benfield 1992.
115. Hayden 1971: 124.
116. Hayden 1971: 127–8.
117. Wang 2007.
118. For 'Frost at Midnight' as a 'double' of Cowper's *The Task*, see Hogle 1998: 287.
119. Anderson 1994.
120. Hogle 1998: 283–92.

Bibliography

Manuscripts

Additional 30, 346. Ireland Manuscripts (London: British Library).
Additional 30, 349. Ireland Manuscripts (London: British Library).
Additional 37, 831. Ireland Manuscripts (London: British Library).
H.-P. Coll. 321, Ireland Manuscripts (Edinburgh: Edinburgh University Library).
H.-P. Coll. 322, Ireland Manuscripts (Edinburgh: Edinburgh University Library).
H.-P. Coll. 323, Ireland Manuscripts (Edinburgh: Edinburgh University Library).
Robert H. Taylor Collection. Ireland's Confession. Firestone Library at Princeton.
YI Folio Ireland, W. 287917. Ireland Manuscripts. Huntington Library.

Books and articles

Abrams, M. H. (1953), *The Mirror and the Lamp: Romantic Theory and Critical Tradition* (Oxford: Oxford University Press).

Aikin, Anna Laetitia, and John Aikin (1773), 'Sir Bertrand, a Fragment', *Miscellaneous Pieces in Prose* (London: Joseph Johnson): 119–37.

Albertan-Coppola, Sylviane, 'Counter-Enlightenment', in *Encyclopedia of the Enlightenment* (2003): I: 307–11.

Alison, Archibald (1790), *Essays on the Nature and Principles of Taste* (Dublin).

Alison, Sir Archibald (1845), 'The Historical Romance', *Blackwoods Magazine* LVIII: 341–56.

Altick, Richard D. (1978), *The Shows of London* (Cambridge, Mass.: Harvard University Press).

Anderson, Benedict (1991), *Imagined Communities: Reflections on the Origin and Spread of Nationalism* (London: Verso).

Anderson, John M. (1994), 'The First Fire: Barbauld Rewrites the Greater Romantic Lyric', *SEL* 34.4 (Autumn): 719–38.

Armstrong, Nancy (1987), *Desire and Domestic Fiction: A Political History of the Novel* (New York and Oxford: Oxford University Press).

— (2005), *How Novels Think: The Limits of Individualism from 1719–1900* (New York: Columbia University Press): 27–52.

Austen, Jane (1995), *Northanger Abbey*, ed. Marilyn Butler (Harmondsworth: Penguin).

Austin, J. L. (1962), *How to Do Things with Words* (Oxford: Oxford University Press).

Baines, Paul (1994), '"All of the House of Forgery": Walpole, Chatterton, and Antiquarian Commerce', *Poetica: An International Journal of Linguistic-Literacy Studies* 39–40: 45–72.

— (1999), *The House of Forgery in 18th-Century Britain* (Brookefield, USA; Singapore; Sydney: Ashgate).

Barbauld, Anna Letitia (1792a), *Civic Sermons to the People*, Vol. I (London: J. Johnson).

— (1792b), *Civic Sermons to the People*, Vol. II (London: J. Johnson).

— (1792c), *Remarks on Mr. Gilbert Wakefield's Enquiry into the Expediency and Propriety of Public or Social Worship*, 2nd edn (London: J. Johnson).

— (1794), 'A Critical Essay on the Poem', in Mark Akenside, *The Pleasures of Imagination* (London: T. Cadell and W. Davies): 1–36.

— (1810), *The British Novelists; With an Essay, and Prefaces Biographical and Critical* (London: F. C. & J. Rivington).
— (1830), *A Discourse on Being Born Again*, 2nd edn (Boston: Gray and Bowen).
— (1993), *Poems 1792*, ed. Jonathan Wordsworth (Oxford: Woodstock).
— (1994), *The Poems of Anna Letitia Barbauld*, ed. Elizabeth Kraft and William McCarthy (Athens and London: University of Georgia Press).
— (2002), *Anna Letitia Barbauld: Selected Poetry and Prose*, ed. Elizabeth Kraft and William McCarthy (Peterborough, Ontario: Broadview).
Barker-Benfield, G. J. (1992), *The Culture of Sensibility: Sex and Society in Eighteenth-Century Britain* (Chicago: University of Chicago Press).
Barrell, John (2000), *Imagining the King's Death: Figurative Treason, Fantasies of Regicide, 1793–1796* (Oxford: Oxford University Press).
Barruel, Abbé (1798), *Memoirs, Illustrating the History of Jacobinism*,trans. Robert Clifford (London).
Bate, Jonathon (1993), 'Faking It: Shakespeare and the 1790s', *Essays and Studies* 46: 63–80.
Beattie, James (1783), 'On Fable and Romance', *Dissertations Critical and Moral* (London).
Beer, Gillian (1982), "'Our unnatural No-voice": The Heroic Epistle, Pope, and Women's Gothic', *The Yearbook of English Studies* 12: 125–51.
Berlin, Isaiah (1979), *Against the Current: Essays in the History of Ideas*, ed. Henry Hardy (London: Hogarth Press).
— (1990), *The Crooked Timber of Humanity: Chapters in the History of Ideas* (London: John Murray).
— (1999), *The Roots of Romanticism: The A. W. Mellon Lectures in the Fine Arts 1965, the National Gallery of Art, Washington, DC* (London: Chatto & Windus).
Bewley, Marius (1959), *The Eccentric Design : Form in the Classic American Novel* (London: Chatto & Windus).
Bialostosky, Don H. (1992), *Wordsworth, Dialogics and the Practice of Criticism* (Cambridge: Cambridge University Press).
Boaden, James (1831), *The Life of Mrs. Jordan; Including Original Private Correspondence, and Numerous Anecdotes of Her Contemporaries* 2nd ed. 2 vols. London.
Bonaparte, Louis (1829), *Answer to Sir Walter Scott's History of Napoleon*, trans. W. H. Ireland (London: Thomas Burton, J. Ridgway and H. Phillips).
Botting, Fred (ed.) (2001), *The Gothic*, Essays and Studies (Cambridge: D. S. Brewer).
Bourdieu, Pierre (1993), *The Field of Cultural Production: Essays on Art and Literature* (Cambridge: Polity Press).
— (1999), *Distinction: A Social Critique of the Judgement of Taste*, trans. Richard Nice (London: Routledge).
Braithwaite, Helen (2003), *Romanticism, Publishing, and Dissent: Joseph Johnson and the Cause of Liberty* (Basingstoke: Palgrave, now Palgrave Macmillan).
Brewer, John (1997), *The Pleasures of the Imagination: English Culture in the Eighteenth Century* (London: HarperCollins).
— (2004), *A Sentimental Murder: Love and Madness in the Eighteenth Century* (London: HarperCollins).
Briggs, Peter (1991), 'Laurence Sterne and Literary Celebrity in 1760', *The Age of Johnson: A Scholarly Annual* 4: 251–80.
Bromwich, David (1998), *Disowned by Memory: Wordsworth's Poetry of the 1790s* (Chicago and London: University of Chicago Press).

Brown, Homer Obed (1997), *Institutions of the English Novel from Defoe to Scott* (Philadelphia: University of Pennsylvania Press).
Brown, Marshall (2005), *The Gothic Text* (Stanford: Stanford University Press).
Burgess, Gilbert (ed.)(1995), *The Love Letters of Mr. H. [i.e. J. Hackman] & Miss R. [i.e. Martha Reay], 1775–1779. [With an appendix on Thomas Chatterton. Attributed to Sir Herbert Croft.]* (London: William Heinemann).
Burke, Edmund (1790), *Reflections on the Revolution in France*, 2nd edn (London: J. Dodsley).
— (1796), *Thoughts on the Proposal of a Regicide Peace, in a Series of Letters* (London: J. Owen).
— (1969), *The Correspondence of Edmund Burke, Vol VIII, September 1794–April 1796*, ed. R. B. McDowell (Chicago: Chicago University Press).
— (1987), *Reflections on the Revolution in France*, ed. J. G. A. Pocock (Indianapolis and Cambridge: Hackett Publishing Company).
Butler, Marilyn (1975), *Jane Austen and the War of Ideas* (Oxford: Clarendon Press).
— (1979), *Peacock Displayed: A Satirist in His Context* (London, Boston and Henley: Routledge & Kegan Paul).
— (1981), *Romantics, Rebels & Reactionaries: English Literature and Its Background 1760–1830* (Oxford: Oxford University Press).
— (1993), 'Culture's Medium: The Role of the Review', in Curran 1993: 120–47.
Calhoun, C. (1992a), 'Introduction: Habermas and the Public Sphere', in Calhoun 1992b: 1–48.
— (ed.) (1992b), *Habermas and the Public Sphere* (Cambridge, Mass., and London: MIT Press).
Carlyle, Thomas (1869), *Critical and Miscellaneous Essays*, 7 vols (London: Chapman and Hall).
— (1971), *Thomas Carlyle: Selected Writings*, ed. Alan Shelston (Harmondsworth: Penguin).
— (1972), *Reminiscences*, ed. Charles Eliot Norton (London: J. M. Dent & Sons).
The Case and Memoirs of Miss Martha Reay, to Which Are Added Remarks, by Way of Refutation, on the Case and Memoirs of the Rev. Mr. Hackman (London: Fourdinier, 1779).
Castle, Terry (1992), 'Marie Antoinette Obsession', *Representations* 38: 1–38.
— (1995), *The Female Thermometer: Eighteenth-Century Culture and the Invention of the Uncanny* (New York and Oxford: Oxford University Press).
Chalmers, George (1797), *An Apology for the Believers in the Shakespeare-Papers, Which Were Exhibited in Norfolk-Street* (London: Thomas Egerton).
— (1799), *A Supplemental Anthology for the Believers in the Shakespeare-Papers: Being a Reply to Mr. Malone's Answer, Which Was Very Early Announced, but Never Published. With a Dedication to George Steevens, F.R.S. S.A., and a Postscript to T. J. Mathias, F.R.S. S.A., the Author of the Pursuits of Literature* (London: Thomas Egerton).
Chandler, David (2004), 'Taylor, William (1765–1836)', in Matthew and Harrison 2004: <http:// www.oxforddnb.com/view/article/27092> (accessed 30 January 2007).
Chandler, James K. (1984), *Wordsworth's Second Nature: A Study of the Poetry and Politics* (Chicago and London: University of Chicago Press).
Chard, Leslie F. (1972), *Dissenting Republican: Wordsworth's Early Life and Thought in Their Political Context* (The Hague and Paris: Mouton).
Chase, Richard (1958), *The American Novel and Its Tradition* (London: G. Bell).
Christensen, Jerome (1994), 'The Romantic Movement at the End of History', *Critical Inquiry* 20.3: 452–76.

Christie, Thomas (2000), 'Letters on the Revolution in France', in Clery and Miles 2000: 244–5.

Clery, E. J. (1995), *The Rise of Supernatural Fiction, 1762–1800* (Cambridge: Cambridge University Press).

— (2004), *The Feminization Debate in Eighteenth-Century England: Literature, Commerce and Luxury* (Basingstoke: Palgrave Macmillan).

Clery, E. J., and Robert Miles (eds) (2000), *Gothic Documents: A Sourcebook, 1700–1820* (Manchester: Manchester University Press).

Coleman, Deidre (2002), 'Firebrands, Letters and Flowers: Mrs Barbauld and the Priestleys', in Russell and Tuite 2002: 82–103.

Coleridge, S. T. (1956) *Collected Letters of Samuel Taylor Coleridge*, ed. Earl Leslie Griggs, Vols I and II (Oxford: Clarendon Press).

— (1957), *The Notebooks of S. T. Coleridge*, ed. Kathleen Coburn, Vol. I (London: Routledge and Kegan Paul).

— (1969), *Coleridge: Poetical Works*, ed. Ernest Hartley Coleridge (Oxford: Oxford University Press).

— (1970), *The Watchman, The Collected Works of Samuel Taylor Coleridge*, Vol. II, ed. Lewis Patten (London and New Jersey: Routledge and Kegan Paul, and Princeton University Press).

— (1971), *Lectures 1795, on Politics and Religion*, The Collected Works of Samuel Taylor Coleridge I, ed. Lewis Patten and Peter Mann (London and New Jersey: Routledge and Kegan Paul and Princeton University Press).

— (1983), *Biographia Literaria, or Biographical Sketches of My Literary Life and Opinions*, ed. James Engell and W. Jackson Bate, 2 vols, *The Collected Works of Samuel Taylor Coleridge* (London and New Jersey: Routledge and Kegan Paul, and Princeton University Press): Vol. VII.

Craciun, Adriana (2005), *British Women Writers and the French Revolution: Citizens of the World*. Basingstoke, Hants and New York: Palgrave.

Crary, Jonathon (1990), *Techniques of the Observer: On Vision and Modernity in the Nineteenth Century* (Cambridge, Mass., and London: MIT Press).

Crawford, Robert (1988), *The Scottish Invention of English Literature* (Cambridge: Cambridge University Press).

Croft, Herbert (1780), *Love and Madness: A Story Too True, in a Series of Letters, between Parties Whose Names Would Perhaps Be Mentioned, Were They Less Known, or Less Famous* (London: G. Kearsly).

Cronin, Richard (2000), *The Politics of Romantic Poetry: In Search of the Pure Commonwealth* (Basingstoke: Macmillan, now Palgrave Macmillan).

— (2003), Review of *The Historical Austen* by William Galperin, *Wordsworth Circle* 34: 192–3.

Curran, Stuart (1986), *Poetic Form and British Poetry* (New York: Oxford University Press).

— (ed.) (1993), *The Cambridge Companion to British Romanticism* (Cambridge: Cambridge University Press).

Davie, Donald (1993), *The Eighteenth-Century Hymn in England* (Cambridge: Cambridge University Press).

Dawes, Mannaseh (1779a), *The Case and Memoirs of the Late Rev. Mr. James Hackman, and His Acquaintance with the Late Miss Martha Ray*, 7th edn (London: G. Kearsly).

— (1779b), *The Case and Memoirs of the Late Rev. Mr. James Hackman, and His Acquaintance with the Late Miss Martha Ray: with a commentary on his Conviction, distinguishing between his crime in particular, and that of others who have been condemned for murder*, 2nd edn (London: G. Kearsly).

de Burgh Coppinger, Anna Maria (1771), *The Doctor Dissected: Or, Willy Cadogan in the Kitchen. Addresses to All Invalids, and Readers of a Late Dissertation on the Gout, &C. &C. &C.* (London: T. Davies, Covent Garden; and S. Learcroft, Charing Cross).

Deane, Seamus (1988), *The French Revolution and Enlightenment England, 1789–1832* (Cambridge, Mass.: Harvard University Press).

Duff, William (1767 [1964]), *An Essay on Original Genius and Its Various Modes of Exertion in Philosophy and the Fine Arts, Particularly in Poetry* (Gainesville, Florida: Scholars' Facsimiles and Reprints).

— (1973), *Critical Observations on the Writings of the Most Celebrated Geniuses in Poetry, Being a Sequel to the Essay on Original Genius* (London, Delmar, New York: Scholars' Facsimiles and Reprints).

Duggett, Tom (2007), 'Wordsworth's Gothic Politics and *The Convention of Cintra*', *Review of English Studies* 58.234 (February): 186–211.

Dumas, François Ribadeau (1966), *Cagliostro*, trans. Elisabeth Abbot (London: George Allen and Unwin).

Dunlop, John Colin (1814), *The History of Fiction; being a critical account of the most celebrated works of Prose Fiction* (Edinburgh: J. Ballantyne).

Eley, Geoff (1992), 'Nations, Publics, and Political Cultures: Placing Habermas in the Nineteenth Century', in Calhoun 1992b: 289–339.

Eliot, George (1981), *Middlemarch*, ed. W. J. Harvey (Harmondsworth: Penguin).

Ellis, Grace A. (1874), *A Memoir of Mrs. Anna Laetitia Barbauld with Many of Her Letters*, 2 vols (Boston: James R. Osgood and Company).

Encyclopedia of the Enlightenment, ed. Alan Charles Kors, 4 Vols (Oxford: Oxford University Press, 2003).

Evans, Henry Ridgely (1930), *Cagliostro and His Egyptian Rite of Freemasonry* (New York: Masonic Bibliophiles).

Fergus, Jan (1991), *Jane Austen: A Life* (Basingstoke: Macmillan, now Palgrave Macmillan).

Ferris, Ina (1991), *The Achievement of Literary Authority: Gender, History, and the Waverley Novels* (Ithaca, NY: Cornell University Press).

— (1996), 'Narrating Cultural Encounter: Lady Morgan and the Irish National Tale', *Nineteenth Century Literature* 51: 287–303.

Foster, R. F. (1989), *Modern Ireland 1600–1972* (London: Penguin).

Fraser, Nancy (1992), 'Rethinking the Public Sphere: A Contribution to the Critique of Actually Existing Democracy', in Calhoun 1992b: 109–42.

Fulford, Tim, and Morton D. Paley (eds) (1993), *Coleridge's Visionary Languages: Essays in Honour of J. B. Beer* (Cambridge: D. S. Brewer).

Galperin, William H. (2003), *The Historical Austen* (Philadelphia: University of Pennsylvania Press).

Gamer, Michael (1999), 'Genres for the Prosecution: Pornography and the Gothic', *PMLA*: 1043–54.

— (2000), *Romanticism and the Gothic: Genre, Reception, and Canon Formation* (Cambridge: Cambridge University Press).

— (2005), '*Waverley* and the Object of (Literary) History', plenary address, 'Deviance and Defiance' (Montreal: North American Society for the Study of Romanticism).

Garside, Peter (1986), 'Dating *Waverley*'s Early Chapters', *Bibliotheck* 13: 61–81.

— (1991), 'Popular Fiction and National Tale: Hidden Origins of Scott's *Waverley*', *Nineteenth-Century Literature* 46: 30–53.

— (2000), 'The English Novel in the Romantic Era: Consolidation and Dispersal', in Garside, Raven and Schöwerling 2000: II, 15–103.

Garside, Peter, James Raven and Rainer Schöwerling (2000), *The English Novel, 1770–1829: A Bibliographical Survey of Prose Fiction Published in the British Isles*, 2 vols (Oxford: Oxford University Press).
Gary, Taylor (1989), *Reinventing Shakespeare: A Cultural History from the Restoration to the Present* (London: Hogarth).
Gatrell, V. A. C. (1994), *The Hanging Tree: Execution and the English People 1770–1868* (Oxford: Oxford University Press).
Gellner, Ernest (1983), *Nations and Nationalism* (Oxford: Blackwell).
— (1998), *Nationalism* (London: Phoenix).
Gerard, Alexander (1774), *An Essay on Genius* (London and Edinburgh: W. Strachan, T. Cadell & W. Creech).
Gervaso, Roberto (1974), *Cagliostro: A Biography*, trans. Cormac O'Cuilleanain (London: Victor Gollancz).
Gill, Stephen (1989), *William Wordsworth: A Life* (Oxford: Clarendon Press).
— (1998), *Wordsworth and the Victorians* (Oxford: Clarendon Press).
Gilmartin, Kevin (1994), 'Popular Radicalism and the Public Sphere', *Studies in Romanticism*: 549–57.
— (1996), *Print Politics: The Press and Radical Oppostion in Early Nineteenth-Century England* (Cambridge: Cambridge University Press).
Godwin, William (1793), *An Enquiry Concerning Political Justice and Its Influences on General Virtue and Happiness*, 2 vols (London: G. G. J. & J. Robinson).
— (1796), *Enquiry Concerning Political Justice, and Its Influence on Morals and Happiness*, 2 vols, 2nd edn (London).
— (1831), *St. Leon : A Tale of the Sixteenth Century*, Standard Novels (London: H. Colburn and R. Bentley).
— (1982), *Caleb Williams*, ed. David McCracken, The World's Classics (Oxford: Oxford University Press)
— (2000), 'On History and Romance', in Clery and Miles 2000: 260–5.
Goldberg, Brian (1996), 'Romantic Professionalism in 1800: Robert Southey, Herbert Croft, and the Letters and Legacy of Thomas Chatterton', *ELH*: 681–706.
Goldman, Lawrence *see* Matthew, H. C. G., and Brian Harrison (eds) (2004).
Goodman, Dena (1994), *The Republic of Letters: A Cultural History of the French Enlightenment* (Ithaca and London: Cornell University Press).
Grebanier, Bernard D. N. (1966), *The Great Shakespeare Forgery: A New Look at the Career of William Henry Ireland* (London: Heinemann).
Greene, Thomas (1995), 'Coleridge and the Energy of Asking', *ELH* 62.4: 907–31.
Greig, James (1922), *The Farington Diary*, 6 vols (London: Hutchinson).
Grenby, M. O. (2001), *The Anti-Jacobin Novel: British Conservatism and the French Revolution* (Cambridge: Cambridge University Press).
Groom, Nick (2002), *The Forger's Shadow: How Forgery Changed the Course of Literature* (London: Picador).
Habermas, Jürgen (1990), *The Structural Transformation of the Public Sphere: An Inquiry into a Category of Bourgeois Society*, trans. Thomas Burger with the assistance of Frederick Lawrence (Cambridge, Mass.: MIT Press).
— (1992a), 'Concluding Remarks', in Calhoun 1992b: 462–79.
— (1992b), 'Further Reflections on the Public Sphere', in Calhoun 1992b: 427–9.
Hamilton, Paul (1983), *Coleridge's Poetics* (Oxford: Basil Blackwell).
— (1986), *Wordsworth* (Brighton, Sussex: Harvester Press).
Hartley, David (1794), *Argument on the French Revolution and the Means of Peace* (London).

Hayden, John O. (1971), *Romantic Bards and British Reviewers: A Selected Edition of the Contemporary Reviews of Wordsworth, Coleridge, Byron, Keats and Shelley* (Lincoln: University of Nebraska Press).

Haywood, Ian (1986), *The Making of History: A Study of the Literary Forgeries of James Macpherson and Thomas Chatterton in Relation to Eighteenth-Century Ideas of History and Fiction* (London and Toronto: Associated University Press).

Henderson, Peter Mills (1980), *A Nut between Two Blades: The Novels of Charles Robert Maturin* (New York: Arno Press).

Hobsbawm, E. J. (1990), *Nations and Nationalism since 1780: Programme, Myth, Reality* (Cambridge: Cambridge University Press).

Hogle, Jerrold E. (1998), 'The Gothic Ghost as Counterfeit and Its Haunting of Romanticism: The Case of "Frost at Midnight"', *European Romantic Review* 9.2: 283–92.

Holmes, Richard (1989), *Coleridge: Early Visions* (London: Hodder & Stoughton).

— (1994), *Dr. Johnson & Mr. Savage* (London: HarperCollins).

Home, Henry, *see* Kames, Henry Home, Lord

Howell, T. B. (1818), *A Complete Collection of State Trails from the Year 1783 to the Present Time*, Vol. XXV (London: Hansard).

Hume, David (1758), 'Of Superstition and Enthusiasm', *Essays and Treatises on Several Subjects* (London and Edinburgh: Millar, Kincaid and Donaldson).

Hurd, Richard (1762), *Letters on Chivalry and Romance* (London).

Ireland, Samuel (1790), *A Picturesque Tour through Holland, Brabant, and Part of France: Made in the Autumn of 1789. Illustrated with Copper Plates in Aqua Tinta. From Drawings Made on the Spot by Samuel Ireland*, 2 vols (London).

— (1791), *Picturesque Views on the River Thames, with Observations on the Works of Art in Its Vicinity, by S. Ireland* (London).

— (1794), *Graphic Illustrations of Hogarth, from Pictures, Drawings, And ... Prints in the Possession of S. Ireland, Author of This Work, Etc.* 2 vols (London: R. Faulder and J. Egerton).

— (1796a), *Miscellaneous Papers and Legal Instruments under the Hand and Seal of William Shakespeare. Including the Tragedy of King Lear and a Small Fragment of Hamlet, from the Original Mss. In the Possession of Samuel Ireland, of Norfolk Street* (London).

— (1796b), *Mr. Ireland's Vindication of His Conduct Respecting the Publication of the Supposed Shakespeare Mss. Being a Preface or Introduction to a Reply to the Critical Labours of Mr. Malone* (London).

— (1796c), *A Picturesque Tour through Holland, Brabant, and Part of France; Made in the Autumn of 1789. Illustrated with Copper Plates, Etc.* Second edition, with additions, 2 vols (London).

— (1798), *An Investigation of Malone's Claim to the Character of Scholar, or Critic, Being an Examination of His Inquiry into the Authenticity of the Shakespeare Manuscripts, & C.* (London).

Ireland, William Henry (1796), *An Authentic Account of the Shakespearian Manuscripts* (London: J. Debrett).

— (1799), *The Abbess: A Romance*, Forward by D. P. Varma; Introduction by Benjamin Franklin Fisher IV; 4 vols (rpt; New York: Arno Press, 1974).

— (1801), *Ballads in Imitation of the Antient* (London: T. N. Longman and O. Rees).

— (1804a), *The Angler, a Didactic Poem, by Charles Clifford* (London: J. Willis).

— (1804b), *Rhapsodies* (London: Longman and Rees).

— (1805a), *Effusions of Love, from Chatelar to Mary Queen of Scotland, Trans. From a Gallic Manuscript in the Scotch College at Paris. Interspersed with Songs, Sonnets, and Notes Explanatory, by the Translator* (London: C. Chapple).
— (1805b), *Gondez, the Monk. A Romance of the Thirteenth Century* (London: W. Earle and J. W. Hacklebridge).
— (1805 [1969]), *Confessions of William-Henry Ireland Containing the Particulars of His Fabrication of the Shakespeare Manuscripts*, ed. Richard Grant White (rpt; New York: Burt Franklin).
— (1807), *Stultifera Navis; or, the Modern Ship of Fools* (London: William Miller).
— (1808), *The Fisher Boy: A Poem. Comprising His Several Avocations, During the Seasons of the Year*, Ed. H. C. Esq. (London: Vernor, Hood & Sharpe).
— (1809), *The Sailor Boy. A Poem in Four Cantos. Illustrative of the Navy of Great Britain. By H.C. Esq. Author of the Fisher Boy* (London: Vernor, Hood & Sharpe).
— (1810), *The Cottage-Girl. A Poem. Comprising Her Several Avocations During the Four Seasons of the Year. By H.C. Esq. Author of the Fisher-Boy and the Sailor-Boy* (London and Bristol: Longman, Hurst, Rees, Orme and W. J. Sheppard).
— (1812a), *Monody Upon the Death of the Most Noble William Cavendish, Late Duke of Devonshire. Inscribed (by Permission) to Elizabeth, Duchess of Devonshire*, Vol. b (London: Wilson).
— (1812b), *Neglected Genius: A Poem, Ilustrating the Untimely and Unfortunate Fate of Many British Poets; from the Period of Henry the Eighth to the Aera of the Unfortunate Chatterton. Containing Imitations of Their Different Styles, &C, &C*. Vol. a (London: George Cowie).
— (1814), *Chalcographimania; or, the Portrait-Collector and Printseller's Chronicle, with Infatuations of Every Description. A Humorous Poem. In Four Books. With Copious Notes Explanatory. By Satiricus Sculptor, Esq.* (London: R. S. Kirkby).
— (1815), *Scribbleomania: Or, the Printer's Devil's Polichronicon. A Sublime Poem. Ed. By Anser Pen-Drag-on, Esq.* (London: Sherwood, Neely and Jones).
— (1828), *The Life of Napoleon Bonaparte*, 4 vols (London: John Fairburn).
— (1828–30), *A New and Complete History of the County of Kent; Embellished with a Series of Views, from Original Drawings, by G Shepherd, H. Gatineau, &C. With Historical, Topographical, Critical, and Biographical Delineations* (London: G. Virtue).
— (1832), *Vortigern; an historical play; with an original preface* (London: Joseph Thomas).
— (1849), *Rizzio; or, Scenes in Europe During the 16th Century, by the Late Mr. Ireland*, ed. G. P. R. James, 3 vols (London: T. C. Newby).
— (2002), *Ireland's History of Chislehurst, Compiled by John W. Brown* (London: Local History Reprints).
Jackson, Noel B. (2003), 'Critical Conditions: Coleridge, "Common Sense," and the Literature of Self-Experiment', *ELH* 70: 117–49.
Jacobs, Margaret (1991), *Living the Enlightenment: Freemasonry and Politics in Eighteenth-Century Europe* (Oxford: Oxford University Press).
Jacobus, Mary (1976), *Tradition and Experiment in Wordsworth's Lyrical Ballads* (Oxford: Clarendon Press).
— (1989), *Romanticism, Writing and Sexual Difference: Essays on the Prelude*. Oxford: Clarendon Press).
James, Henry (1880), *Nathaniel Hawthorne*, English Men of Letters Series (London: Macmillan).
Janowitz, Anne (2002), 'Amiable and Radical Sociability: Anna Barbauld's "Free Familiar Conversation"', in Russell and Tuite (2002): 62–81.

— (2004), *Women Romantic Poets : Anna Barbauld and Mary Robinson*, Writers and Their Work (Tavistock : Northcote House in association with The British Council).

Jay, Martin (1993), *Downcast Eyes : The Denigration of Vision in Twentieth-Century French Thought* (Berkeley: University of California Press).

Jeffrey, Francis (1802), 'Southey's Thalaba: A Metrical Romance', *Edinburgh Review* 1: 63–82.

Jewson, C. B. (1975), *The Jacobin City: A Portrait of Norwich in Its Reaction to the French Revolution, 1788–1802* (Glasgow: Blackie).

Johnson, Claudia L. (1995), *Equivocal Beings: Politics, Gender, and Sentimentality in the 1790s: Wollstonecraft, Radcliffe, Burney, and Austen* (Chicago: University of Chicago Press).

— (2001), "'Let Me Make the Novels of a Country": Barbauld's "the British Novelists" (1810/1820)', *NOVEL: A Forum on Fiction* 34.2: 163–79.

Johnston, Kenneth R. (1998), *The Hidden Wordsworth: Poet, Lover, Rebel, Spy* (New York and London: W.W. Norton & Co.).

Kahan, Jeffrey (1998), *Reforging Shakespeare: The Story of a Theatrical Scandal* (Cranbury, NJ: Lehigh University Press; London: Associated University Presses).

— (2004), 'Introduction: A Romantic by Any Other Name: The Poetry of William-Henry Ireland', in *The Poetry of W. H. Ireland (1801–1815), Including the Poet's Imitations, Satires, Romantic Verses, and Commentaries on Coleridge, Wordsworth, Satires & Others*, Studies in British Literature 85 (Lampeter: Edwin Mellen Press): xiii–xlv.

Kames, Henry Home, Lord (1774), *Elements of Criticism*, 2 vols, 5th edn (Edinburgh and London: Kincaid, Creech, Bell, Johnston & Cadell).

Keach, William (1994), 'A Regency Prophecy and the End of Barbauld's Career', *Studies in Romanticism*: 569–77.

Keen, Paul (1999), *The Crisis of Literature in the 1790's: Print Culture and the Public Sphere* (Cambridge: Cambridge University Press).

— (ed.) (2004), *Revolutions in Romantic Literature: An Anthology of Print Culture, 1780–1832* (Peterborough, ON: Broadview Press).

Kelley, Theresa M. (n.d.), 'Romanticism and Philosophy in an Historical Age: Romantic Interiority and Cultural Objects', *Romantic Circles Praxis Series* 5 <http://www/re.umd.edu/praxis/philosophy/kelley1/tk1.html> (accessed 15 April 2008).

Kenneally, Michael (ed.) (1992), *Irish Literature and Culture*, Irish Literary Studies 35 (Gerrards Cross: Colin Smythe): 35–54.

Kermode, Frank (1961), *Romantic Image* (London: Routledge and Kegan Paul).

— (1975), *The Classic* (London: Faber).

Kiely, Robert (1972), *The Romantic Novel in England* (Cambridge: Harvard University Press).

Kitson, Peter (1993), 'The Whore of Babylon and the Woman in White: Coleridge's Radical Unitarian Language', in Fulford and Paley 1993: 27–39.

Klancher, John P. (1987), *The Making of English Reading Audiences, 1790–1832* (Madison, Wis.: University of Wisconsin Press).

Kliger, Samuel (1952), *Goths in England: A Study in Seventeenth and Eighteenth Century Thought* (Cambridge, Mass.: Harvard University Press).

Kramnick, Isaac (1990), *Republicanism and Bourgeois Radicalism: Political Ideology in Late Eighteenth-Century England and America* (Ithaca, NY: Cornell University Press).

Kristeva, Julia (1983), *Powers of Horror: An Essay on Abjection* (New York: Columbia University Press).

Le Breton, Anna Letitia (1874), *Memoir of Mrs. Barbauld Including Letters and Notices of Her Family and Friends. By Her Great Neice* (London: George Bell and Sons).

Le Breton, Philip Hemery (1864), *Memoirs, Miscellanies and Letters of the Late Lucy Aikin* (London: Longmans).

Leavis, F. R. (1972), *The Great Tradition: George Eliot, Henry James, Joseph Conrad* (Harmondsworth: Penguin).

Leighton, C. D. A. (1999), 'Hutchinsonianism: A Counter-Enlightenment Reform Movement', *Journal of Religious History* 23.2 (June): 168–84.

Levinson, Marjorie (1986), *Wordsworth's Great Period Poems: Four Essays* (Cambridge: Cambridge University Press).

Lewis, Matthew G. (1800), *Tales of Wonder* (London: J. Bell).

— (1998), *The Monk*, The World's Classics (Oxford: Oxford University Press).

Life of Joseph Balsamo, Commonly Called Count Gagliostro: Containing the Singular Adventures of That Extraordinary Personage, from His Birth, Till His Imprisonment in the Castle of St. Angelo. To Which Are Added, the Particulars of His Trile before the Inquisition, the History of His Confessions Concerning Common and Egyptian Masonry and a Variety of Other Interesting Particulars. Trans. from the Original Proceedings published at Rome by Order of the Apostolic Chamber (Dublin: P. Byrne, 1792).

Liu, Alan (1989), *Wordsworth: The Sense of History* (Stanford, Calif.: Stanford University Press).

Lowell, James Russell (1904), *Literary and Political Addresses* (Boston: Houghton Mifflin).

Lynch, Deidre (1998), *The Economy of Character: Novels, Market Culture, and the Business of Inner Meaning* (Chicago: University of Chicago Press).

McCalman, Iain (1988), *Radical Underworld: Prophets, Revolutionaries and Pornographers in London, 1795–1840* (Cambridge: Cambridge University Press; Oxford: Oxford University Press, 1993).

— (2003), *The Last Alchemist: Count Cagliostro, Master of Magic in the Age of Reason* (New York: HarperCollins).

McDayter, Ghislaine (1999), 'Conjuring Byron: Byromania, Literary Commodification and the Birth of the Celebrity', in Frances Wilson (ed.), *Byromania: Portraits of the Artist in Nineteenth- and Twentieth-Century Culture* (Basingstoke: Macmillan, now Palgrave Macmillan): 43–62.

McGann, Jerome (1983), *Romantic Ideology: A Critical Investigation* (Chicago: University of Chicago Press).

— (1996), *The Poetics of Sensibility: A Revolution in Literary Style* (Oxford: Clarendon Press).

McGowen, Randall (1993/94), 'Forgery Discovered; or the Perils of Circulation in Eighteenth-Century England', *Angelaki* 1: 113–29.

Mackay, Charles (1860), *The London Review*.

McKeon, Michael (1987), *The Origins of the English Novel, 1600–1740* (Baltimore: Johns Hopkins University Press).

Mackintosh, James (1813), review of *D'Allemagne*, by Madame de Stael, *Edinburgh Review* xxii: 198–239.

McKusick, James C. (1985), 'Coleridge and Horne Tooke', *Studies in Romanticism* (Spring): 85–111.

McLachlan, Herbert (1943), *Warrington Academy: Its History and Influence* (Manchester).

McMahon, Darrin (1998), 'The Counter-Enlightenment and the Low-Life of Literature in Pre-Revolutionary France', *Past and Present* 159 (May): 77–112.

— (2001), *Enemies of the Enlightenment: The French Counter-Enlightenment and the Making of Modernity* (Oxford and New York: Oxford University Press).

Mair, John (1938), *The Fourth Forger: William Ireland and the Shakespeare Papers* (London: Cobden-Sanderson).

Malone, Edmond (1781), 'Remarks on the New Publication of Rowley's Poems', *Gentleman's Magazine* 51: 555.

— (1796), *An Inquiry into the Authenticity of Certain Miscellaneous Papers and Legal Instruments . . . In a Letter Addressed to the Right Hon. James, Earl of Charlemont* (London: T. Cadell & W. Davies).

Martelli, George (1962), *Jemmy Twitcher: A Life of the Fourth Earl of Sandwich, 1718–1792* (London: Jonathan Cape).

Martin, Peter (1995), *Edmond Malone, Shakespeare Scholar: A Literary Biography* (Cambridge: Cambridge University Press).

Martin, Terence John (1961), *The Instructed Vision: Scottish Common Sense Philosophy and the Origins of American Fiction* (Bloomington: Indiana University Press).

Mathias, T. J. (1798), *The Pursuits of Literature*, 8th edn (Dublin: J. Milliken).

— (2004), 'The Pursuits of Literature', in Paul Keen (ed.), *Revolutions in Romantic Literature: An Anthology of Print Culture, 1780–1832* (Peterborough, Ontario: Broadview): 7–8.

Mathias, T. J. (as Antenor) (1800), *Antenor's Letter to George Chalmers, Esq.* (London).

Matthew, H. C. G., and Brian Harrison (eds) (2004), *Oxford Dictionary of National Biography* (Oxford: Oxford University Press); online ed. Lawrence Goldman <http://www.oxforddnb.com.ezproxy.library.uvic.ca/view/> (accessed 15 April 2008).

Maturin, Charles Robert (1808), *The Wild Irish Boy* (London: Longman).

Maxwell, Richard (2001), 'Inundations of Time: A Definition of Scott's Originality', *ELH* 68.2: 419–68.

Mee, Jon (1992), *Dangerous Enthusiasm: William Blake and the Culture of Radicalism in the 1790s* (Oxford: Clarendon Press).

— (2003), *Romanticism, Enthusiasm, and Regulation: Poetics and the Policing of Culture in the Romantic Period* (Oxford: Oxford University Press).

Mellor, Anne K. (1988), *Romanticism and Feminism* (Bloomington: Indiana University Press).

— (1993), *Romanticism and Gender* (London: Routledge).

— (1994), 'Joanna Baillie and the Counter-Public Sphere', *Studies in Romanticism* 33: 559–67.

— (2002), *Mothers of the Nation: Women's Political Writing in England 1780–1830* (Bloomington: Indiana University Press).

Melville, Herman (1996), *Pierre or The Ambiguities*, ed. William C. Spengemann (Harmondsworth: Penguin).

Mighall, Robert (2000), *A Geography of Victorian Gothic Fiction: Mapping History's Nightmares* (Oxford: Oxford University Press).

Miles, Robert (1999a), '"The Eye of Power": Ideal Presence and Gothic Romance', *Gothic Studies* 1.1: 10–30.

— (1999b), '"Tranced Griefs": Melville's Pierre and the Origins of the Gothic', *ELH* (1999): 157–77.

— (2001a), 'Abjection, Nationalism and the Gothic', in Botting 2001: 47–70.

— (2001b), 'What Is a Romantic Novel?', *NOVEL: A Forum on Fiction* 34.2: 180–201.

— (2002a), *Gothic Writing, 1750–1820: A Genealogy*, 2nd edn (Manchester: Manchester University Press).

— (2002b), '1790s: The Effulgence of Gothic', in Jerrold E. Hogle (ed.), *The Cambridge Companion to Gothic Fiction* (Cambridge: Cambridge University Press): 41–62.

— (2003), *Jane Austen*, Writers and Their Work (Tavistock: Northcote House in association with the British Council).

— (ed.) (2005a), *St. Godwin*, Anti-Jacobin Novels, Vol. IX, gen. ed. W. M. Verhoeven (London: Pickering and Chatto).

— (2005b), 'Trouble in the Republic of Letters: Reception of the Shakespeare Forgeries', *Studies in Romanticism* 44.3: 317–40.

Montgomery, James (1833), *Lectures on Poetry and General Literature Delivered at the Royal Institution in 1830 and 1831* (London: Longmans).

Moretti, Franco (1987), *The Way of the World: The Bildungsroman in European Culture*, trans. Albert Stragia (London and New York: Verso).

Murray, Hugh (1805), *Morality of Fiction; or, an Inquiry into the Tendency of Fictitious Narratives, with Observations on Some of the Most Eminent* (Edinburgh: Mundell & Son).

Nichols, Ashton (1998), *The Revolutionary 'I': Wordsworth and the Politics of Self-Presentation* (Basingstoke: Macmillan, now Palgrave Macmillan).

Novak, Maximillian (1997), 'The Sensibility of Sir Herbert Croft in Love and Madness and the "Life of Edward Young" ', *Age of Johnson: A Scholarly Annal* 8: 189–207.

O'Brien, Karen (2005), 'World Changing Ideas', review of Alan Charles Kors (ed.), *Encyclopedia of the Enlightenment*, *History Workshop Journal* 59: 243–5.

O'Brien, Padraig (1989), *Warrington Academy 1757–86: Its Predecessors and Successors* (Wigan: Owl Books).

— (1993), *Eyre's Press, Warrington (1756–1803): An Embryo University Press* (Wigan: Owl Books).

Paulin, Tom (1999), *The Day-Star of Liberty: William Hazlitt's Radical Style* (London: Faber & Faber).

Philip, Mark (2004), 'Godwin, William (1756–1836)', in Matthew and Harrison 2004: Vol. III online <http://www.oxforddnb.com.ezproxy.library.uvic.ca/view/article/10898> (accessed 15 April 2008).

Photiades, Constantin (1932), *Count Cagliostro: An Authentic Story of a Mysterious Life* (London: Rider).

Poirier, Richard (1966), *A World Elsewhere: The Place of Style in American Literature* (Oxford: Oxford University Press).

Poovey, Mary (1984), *The Proper Lady and the Woman Writer : Ideology as Style in the Works of Mary Wollstonecraft, Mary Shelley and Jane Austen* (Chicago: University of Chicago Press).

Porter, Roy (2000), *Enlightenment: Britain and the Creation of the Modern World* (London: Allen Lane).

Preston, William (1801), *Reflections on the Peculiarities of Style and Manner in the Late German Writers Whose Works Have Appeared in English, and on the Tendency of Their Productions* (Dublin).

Rajan, Tilottama (1980), *Dark Interpreter: The Discourse of Romanticism* (Ithaca and London: Cornell University Press).

Ratchford, Fannie E., and William H. McCarthy Jr. (eds) (1980), *The Correspondence of Sir Walter Scott and Charles Robert Maturin* (New York and London: Garland Publishing).

Raven, James (2000), 'Historical Introduction: The Novel Comes of Age', in Garside, Raven and Schöwerling 2000: I, 15–121.

Reed, Henry (ed.) (1852), *Wordsworth's Life* (Philadelphia: Troutman and Hayes).

Riede, David G. (1991), *Oracles and Heirophants: Constructions of Romantic Authority* (Ithaca and London: Cornell University Press).

Rieder, John (1997), *Wordsworth's Counterrevolutionary Turn: Community, Virtue, and Vision in the 1790s* (London: Associated University Press).

Robison, John (1798), *Proofs of a Conspiracy against All of the Governments of Europe, Carried on in Secret Meetings of Freemasons, Illuminati, and Reading Societies*, 5th edn (Dublin).

Rodgers, Betsy (1958), *A Georgian Chronicle: Mrs. Barbauld & Her Family* (London: Methuen).

Roe, Nicholas (1988), *Wordsworth and Coleridge: The Radical Years* (Oxford: Clarendon Press).

— (1997), *John Keats and the Culture of Dissent* (Oxford: Clarendon Press).

— (2004), 'Hunt, (James Henry) Leigh (1784–1859)', in Matthew and Harrison 2004: <http://www.oxforddnb.com.ezproxy.library.uvic.ca/view/article/14195> (accessed 15 April 2008).

Russell, Gillian, and Clara Tuite (eds) (2002), *Romantic Sociability: Social Networks and Literary Culture in Britain 1770–1840* (Cambridge: Cambridge University Press).

St. Clair, William (2004), *The Reading Nation in the Romantic Period* (Cambridge: Cambridge University Press).

Sanders, Charles Richard (1977), *Carlyle's Friendships and Other Studies* (Durham, NC: Duke University Press).

Sanderson, L. (1975), *Sir John Davies* (Boston: Twayne Publishers).

Schmidt, James (2000a), Review of Berlin (1999), in *Journal of the History of Philosophy* 38.3 (July): 451–2.

— (2000b), 'What Enlightenment Project?', *American Historical Review* 28.6 (December): 734–57.

— (2006), 'What Enlightenment Was, What It Still Might Be, and Why Kant May Have Been Right after All', *American Behavioral Scientist* 49.5: 647–63.

Schoenbaum, Samuel (1991), *Shakespeare's* Lives, new edn (Oxford and New York: Oxford University Press).

Schuchard, Marsha Keith (2006), *Why Mrs Blake Cried: William Blake and the Sexual Basis of Spiritual Vision* (London and New York: Century).

Schwarzmantel, John (1998), *The Age of Ideology: Political Ideologies from the American Revolution to Postmodern Times* (New York: New York University Press).

Scott, Sir Walter (1950), *The Journal of Sir Walter Scott* (Edinburgh and London: Oliver and Boyd).

— (1968), *Sir Walter Scott on Novelists and Fiction*, ed. Ioan M. Williams (London: Routledge & Kegan Paul).

— (1986), *Waverley; or, 'Tis Sixty Years Since*, ed. Claire Lamont (Oxford: Oxford University Press).

Scrivener, Michael (2007), 'Romanticism and the Law: The Discourse of Treason, Sedition, and Blasphemy in British Political Trials, 1794–1820', Romantic Circles Praxis Series <http://www.re.umd.edu/praxis/law/lawcov.htm> (accessed 12 April 2008).

Sedgwick, Eve Kosofsky (1986), *The Coherence of Gothic Conventions* (New York and London: Methuen).

Shaftesbury, Anthony Ashley Cooper, 3rd Earl of (1727), *Characteristicks of Men, Manners, Opinions, Times*, 4th edn, 3 vols (London).

Sheehan, Jonathan (2003), 'Enlightenment, Religion, and the Enigma of Secularization: A Review Essay', *American Historical Review* <http://www.historycooperative.org/cgi-bin/cite.cgi?f=ahr/108.4/sheehan.html> (accessed 25 April 2008).

Simpson, David (1987), *Wordsworth's Historical Imagination: The Poetry of Displacement* (New York and London: Methuen).

— (1993), *Romanticism, Nationalism, and the Revolt against Theory* (Chicago: University of Chicago Press).
Siskin, Clifford (1988), *The Historicity of Romantic Discourse* (New York and Oxford: Oxford University Press).
— (1990), 'Wordsworth's Prescriptions: Romanticism and Professional Power', in Gene W. Ruoff (ed.), *The Romantics and Us: Essays on Literature and Culture* (New Brunswick and London: Rutgers University Press): 303–22.
— (1999), *The Work of Writing: Literature and Social Change in Britain, 1700—1830* (Baltimore and London: Johns Hopkins University Press).
— (2006), Review of *The Historical Austen* by William Galperin, *Modern Language Quarterly* 67.4: 536–43.
Smail, John (2003), 'The Culture of Credit in Eighteenth-Century Commerce: The English Textile Industry', *Enterprise & Society* 4.2 (June): 299–325.
Smith, R. J. (1987), *The Gothic Bequest: Medieval Institutions in British Thought, 1688–1863* (Cambridge: Cambridge University Press).
Southam, Brian (ed.) (1968), *Jane Austen: The Critical Heritage*, Vol. I (London: Routledge & Kegan Paul).
— (1987), *Jane Austen: The Critical Heritage*, Vol. II (London: Routledge & Kegan Paul).
Stafford, Barbara Maria, and Frances Terpak (2001), *Devices of Wonder: From the World in a Box to Images on a Screen* (Los Angeles: Getty Research Institute).
Stillinger, Jack (1994), *Coleridge and Textual Instability: The Multiple Versions of the Major Poems* (New York: Oxford University Press).
Taylor, Barbara (2004), 'Wollstonecraft, Mary (1759–1797)', in Matthew and Harrison 2004: online <http://www.oxforddnb.com.ezproxy.library.uvic.ca/view/article/10983> (accessed 15 April 2008).
Thelwall, John (1796a), *The Rights of Nature, against the Usurpations of Establishments. A Series of Letters to the People of Great Britain, on the State of Public Affairs and the Recent Effusions of the Right Honourable Edmund Burke*, 3rd edn (London: H. D. Symonds; Norwich: J. March).
— (1796b), *The Rights of Nature against the Usurpations of Establishments: Part the Second* (London).
Thompson, E. P. (1970), *The Making of the English Working Class* (Harmondsworth: Penguin).
— (1993), *Witness against the Beast* (Cambridge: Cambridge University Press).
— (1997), *The Romantics: England in a Revolutionary Age* (Woodbridge: Merlin Press).
Thompson, Judith (1997), 'An Autumnal Blast, a Killing Frost: Coleridge's Poetic Conversation with John Thelwall', *Studies in Romanticism* 36.3 (Fall): 427–56.
Thuente, Mary Helen (1992), 'The Literary Significance of the United Irishmen', in Kenneally 1992: 35–54.
Trilling, Lionel (1976), *The Liberal Imagination: Essays on Literature and Society* (New York: Charles Scribner's Sons).
Trott, Nicola (2000), 'Wordsworth's Gothic Quandary', *The Charles Lamb Bulletin* New Series No. 110: 45–59.
Trumpener, Kate (1998), *Bardic Nationalism: Romantic Novel and the British Empire* (Princeton, NJ: Princeton University Press).
Tuite, Clara (2002), *Romantic Austen: Sexual Politics and the Literary Canon* (Cambridge: Cambridge University Press).
Turner, William (1957), *The Warrington Academy*, rpt from articles originally published in the *Monthly Repository*, Introduction by G. A. Carter (Warrington: Library and Museum Committee).

Tyson, Gerald P. (1979), *Joseph Johnson: A Liberal Publisher* (Iowa City: University of Iowa Press).
Van Winkle, Matthew (2004), 'Fluttering on the Grate: Revision in Frost at Midnight', *Studies in Romanticism* 43.4: 583–98.
Vargo, Lisa (1998), 'The Case of Anna Laetitia Barbauld's "to Mr C[olerid]ge"', *The Charles Lamb Bulletin* New Series No. 102 (April): 55–63; rpt <http://www.usask.ca/english/barbauld/> (accessed 15 April 2008).
Wang, Orrin N. C. (1994), 'Romancing the Counter-Public Sphere: A Response to Romanticism and Its Publics', *Studies in Romanticism* 33: 579–88.
— (2007), 'Ghost Theory', *Studies in Romanticism* 46:2 (Summer): 203–25.
Watson, J. R. (1997), *The English Hymn: A Critical and Historical Study* (Oxford: Clarendon Press).
Watt, Ian P. (1957), *The Rise of the Novel: Studies in Defoe, Richardson, and Fielding* (Berkeley and Los Angeles: University of California Press).
Watt, James (1999), *Contesting the Gothic: Fiction, Genre, and Cultural Conflict, 1764–1832* (Cambridge: Cambridge University Press).
Watts, Isaac (1737), *Horæ Lyricæ. Poems Chiefly of the Lyric Kind, in Three Books*, Seventh Edition corrected (London: Richard Hett).
— (1752), *The Knowledge of the Heavens and the Earth Made Easy; or, the First Principles of Astronomy and Geography*, 5th edn (London: T. Longman).
Watts, Michael R. (1978), *The Dissenters*, Vol. I (Oxford: Clarendon Press).
Whateley, Richard (1821), unsigned review of *Northanger Abbey and Persuasion*, *Quarterly Review* 24 (January): 352–76, repr. in Southam 1968: 87–105.
Wheeler, Kathleen M. (1981), *The Creative Mind in Coleridge's Poetry* (London: Heinemann).
White, Daniel E. (2007), *Early Romanticism and Religious Dissent* (Cambridge: Cambridge University Press).
Williams, John (2002), *William Wordsworth*, Critical Issues (Basingstoke and New York: Palgrave, now Palgrave Macmillan).
Winters, Yvor (1947), *In Defense of Reason: Primitivism and Decadence: A Study of American Experimental Poetry; Maule's Curse: Seven Studies in the History of American Obscurantism; the Anatomy of Nonsense; the Significance of the Bridge by Hart-Crane, or What Are We to Think of Professor X?* (New York: Swallow Press and W. Morrow).
Wolin, Richard (2004), *The Seduction of Unreason: The Intellectual Romance with Fascism: From Nietzsche to Postmodernism* (Princeton, NJ, and [Great Britain]: Princeton University Press).
Wood, Gillen D'Arcy (2001), *The Shock of the Real: Romanticism and Visual Culture, 1760–1860* (Basingstoke: Palgrave, now Palgrave Macmillan).
Wordsworth, William (1852), *The Complete Poetical Works of William Wordsworth*, ed. Henry Reed (Philadelphia: Troutman and Hayes).
— (1940–49), *The Poetical Works of William Wordsworth*, ed. E. de Selincourt and H. Darbishire, 5 vols (Oxford: Oxford University Press).
— (1972), *The Prelude: A Parallel Text*, ed. J. C. Maxwell (Harmondsworth: Penguin).
— (1975a), *Adventures on Salisbury Plain*, in Wordsworth 1975c.
— (1975b), *Guilt and Sorrow*, in Wordsworth 1975c.
— (1975c), *The Salisbury Plain Poems of William Wordsworth*, ed. Stephen Gill (Ithaca, NY: Cornell University Press).
— (1979), *The Ruined Cottage and the Pedlar*, ed. James Butler (Ithaca: Cornell University Press; Hassocks: Harvester).

— (1982), *The Borderers*, ed. Robert Osborn (Ithaca and London: Cornell University Press).
— (1984a), *Descriptive Sketches*, ed. Eric Birdsall, and Paul M. Zall (Ithaca and London: Cornell University Press).
— (1984b), *An Evening Walk*, ed. James Averill (Ithaca: Cornell University Press).
— (1988), *Selected Prose*, ed. John O. Haydon (Harmondsworth: Penguin).
— (1992), *Lyrical Ballads, and Other Poems, 1797–1800*, ed. James Butler and Karen Green (Ithaca, NY: Cornell University Press).
Worrall, David (1992), *Radical Culture: Discourse, Resistance and Surveillance, 1790–1820* (Detroit: Wayne State University Press).
Wrigley, E. A. (1983), 'The Growth of Population in Eighteenth-Century England: A Conundrum Resolved', *Past and Present* 98: 121–50.
Young, Edward (1759), *Conjectures on Original Composition. In a Letter to the Author of Sir Charles Grandison* (London: A. Millar and R. and J. Dodsley).

Index